KU-649-721

THE HUNTER

TANA FRENCH

VIKING

an imprint of

PENGUIN BOOKS

VIKING

UK | USA | Canada | Ireland | Australia
India | New Zealand | South Africa

Viking is part of the Penguin Random House group of companies
whose addresses can be found at global.penguinrandomhouse.com.

First published 2024

001

Copyright © Tana French, 2023

The moral right of the author has been asserted

Set in 12/14.75pt Dante MT Std
Typeset by Jouve (UK), Milton Keynes
Printed and bound in Great Britain by Clays Ltd, Elcograf S.p.A.

The authorized representative in the EEA is Penguin Random House Ireland,
Morrison Chambers, 32 Nassau Street, Dublin D02 YH68

A CIP catalogue record for this book is available from the British Library

HARDBACK ISBN: 978–0–241–68426–9
TRADE PAPERBACK ISBN: 978–0–241–68430–6

www.greenpenguin.co.uk

MIX
Paper | Supporting
responsible forestry
FSC® C018179

Penguin Random House is committed to a
sustainable future for our business, our readers
and our planet. This book is made from Forest
Stewardship Council® certified paper.

For David, who now has to be nice to me forever

I

Trey comes over the mountain carrying a broken chair. She carries it on her back, with the legs sticking out round her waist and held over her shoulders. The sky is a blue so hot it looks glazed, and the sun is burning the back of Trey's neck. Even the faint pin-sharp calls of birds, too high up to be seen, vibrate with heat. The woman who owns the chair offered Trey a lift back with it, but Trey has no inclination to let the woman into her business, and neither the inclination nor the ability to make conversation for the length of a car journey over the potholed mountain roads.

Her dog Banjo lollops in wide circles off the path, snuffing and burrowing among the thick heather, which is too brown-edged and heavily scented for July. It makes crisp rattling sounds as he pushes through it. Every few minutes he comes bounding back to tell Trey, with small happy puffs and moans, what he's found. Banjo is a mutt, black and tan, with a beagle's head and body set on the legs of something stubbier, and he's a lot more talkative than Trey is. He got his name from a banjo-shaped patch of white on his belly. Trey wanted something better for him, but her mind doesn't run easily to fancy things, and everything she came up with sounded like what some tosser out of a schoolbook would call a dog. In the end she left it at Banjo. Cal Hooper, the American who lives down near the village, has Banjo's litter-mate and named him Rip, and if a plain name is good enough for Cal's dog, it's good enough for Trey's. Besides, she spends much of her waking time at Cal's place, meaning the two dogs spend much of their time together, and it would sound stupid if they didn't match.

Cal's place is where Trey is taking the chair, later on. Cal and Trey mend furniture for people, or make it, and they buy old wrecked furniture and fix it up to sell at the Saturday market in Kilcarrow town. One time they picked up a side table that to Trey looked useless, too little and spindly to hold anything worthwhile, but when Cal went on the internet it turned out to be almost two hundred years old. When they got through with it, they sold it for a hundred and eighty quid. The chair Trey is carrying has two stretchers and one leg in splinters, like someone gave it the kind of kicking that takes time and dedication, but once she and Cal get done with it, no one will be able to tell it was ever broken.

She's going home first, for lunch, because she wants to eat dinner at Cal's – Trey is growing fast enough, this summer, that she marks out her days mainly in terms of food – and her pride shies from turning up on his doorstep looking for two meals in the one day. She watches her boundaries extra hard because, if she had her wish, she'd live there. Cal's place has peace. As far up the mountain as Trey's house is, and as far from any other, it ought to be peaceful enough, but it crowds her. Her oldest brother and sister are gone, but Liam and Alanna are six and five and are mostly yelling for one reason or another, and Maeve is eleven and is mostly complaining and slamming the door of the room she shares with Trey. Even when they accidentally go a few minutes without making a racket, the buzz of them is always there. Their mam is silent, but it's not a silence with peace in it. It takes up space, like some heavy thing made of rusted iron built around her. Lena Dunne, who lives down below the mountains and who gave Trey the dog, says her mam used to be a talker, and a laugher too. Trey doesn't disbelieve her, exactly, but she finds the image inaccessible.

Banjo explodes out of the heather, delighted with himself, carrying something that Trey can smell coming a mile off. 'Drop it,' she orders. Banjo gives her a reproachful look, but he's well trained; he drops the thing, which hits the path with a sodden flop. It's narrow and dark, a young stoat maybe. 'Good dog,' Trey says, taking a hand off the chair to rub his head, but Banjo isn't mollified. Instead of galloping off again, he trudges along beside her, drooping at both ends, to show her his feelings are hurt. Cal calls Banjo a big old baby. Rip is the kind of scrapper who could get a leg chopped off and keep on coming, but Banjo likes people to appreciate his suffering.

The downward slope gets steep in places, but Trey's legs are accustomed to this mountain, and she keeps her stride. Her runners raise small spurts of dust. She lifts her elbows to let the air dry her armpits, but there's not enough breeze to make a difference. Below her, the fields sprawl out, a mosaic of varying greens in odd-angled shapes that Trey knows as well as the cracks on her bedroom ceiling. The haymaking is underway: tiny baling machines trundle back and forth, deftly tracking the unexplained curves of the stone walls and leaving yellow cylinders in their wake like droppings. The lambs are white scraps skittering across the grass.

She cuts off the path, over a drystone wall tumbledown enough that she doesn't have to help Banjo clamber it, across an expanse of thigh-high gnarled weeds that used to be a field once, and into a thick band of spruce trees. The branches sift and scramble the sunlight into a confusing dazzle, and their shade cools her neck. Above her small birds are drunk on summer, zipping back and forth, all trying to be the loudest. Trey whistles a trill up at them and grins when they freeze into silence, trying to figure her out.

She comes out of the trees to the cleared ground behind her house. The house got a fresh coat of butter-coloured paint and some patches to the roof a couple of years back, but nothing can paper over its air of exhaustion. Its spine sags, and the lines of the window frames splay off-kilter. The yard is weeds and dust, blurring into the mountainside at the edges, scattered with things Liam and Alanna were using for toys. Trey has brought each of her school friends here once, to show she's not ashamed of it, and hasn't asked them again. Her default position is to keep things separate. It's made easy by the fact that none of her friends come from this townland anyway. Trey doesn't hang around with people from Ardnakelty.

As soon as she steps inside the kitchen door, she knows the house is different. The air is taut and focused, with no scattering of movement and noise. Before she has time to do more than register that fact and the smell of cigarette smoke, she hears, from the sitting room, her father's laugh.

Banjo lets out a preliminary huff of a bark. 'No,' Trey says, low and fast. He shakes off heather and dirt, his ears flapping, and lunges for his water bowl.

Trey stands still for a minute, in the wide band of sunlight falling through the door onto the worn linoleum. Then she goes into the hall, moving quietly, and stops outside the sitting room. Her father's voice runs clear and merry, tossing out questions that get back an excited babble from Maeve or a mumble from Liam.

Trey thinks about leaving, but she wants to see him, to know for sure. She pushes open the door.

Her dad is sitting smack in the middle of the sofa, leaning back and grinning, with his arms spread wide around Alanna and Maeve. They're grinning too, but uncertainly, like they just got a great big Christmas present that they might not want. Liam is squashed into a corner of the sofa, staring at their dad with his mouth open. Their mam is sitting on the edge of an armchair, with her back straight and her hands flat on her thighs. Even though she's been there all along and their dad hasn't been there in four years, Sheila is the one who looks like she can't feel at home in the room.

'Well, God almighty,' Johnny Reddy says, his eyes twinkling at Trey. 'Would you look at that. Little Theresa's after growing up. What age are you now? Sixteen? Seventeen?'

Trey says, 'Fifteen.' She knows that, if anything, she looks younger.

Johnny shakes his head, marvelling. 'I'll be beating the young lads away from the door with a stick before I know it. Or am I too late? Have you got yourself a fella already? Or two or three?' Maeve giggles sharply, and looks up at his face to check if that's right.

'Nah,' Trey says flatly, when it becomes clear he's waiting for an answer.

Johnny lets out a sigh of relief. 'I've time to find myself a good stick, so.' He tilts his chin at the chair, which Trey has forgotten to put down. 'What's that? Didja bring me a present?'

'Gonna mend it,' Trey says.

'She makes money at it,' Sheila says. Her voice is clearer than usual, and there are high spots of colour on her cheekbones. Trey can't tell whether she's glad or angry about him being back. 'That's what bought the new microwave.'

4

Johnny laughs. 'A chip off the old block, hah? Always got a bitta something on the go. That's my girl.' He winks at Trey. Maeve wriggles under his arm, to remind him she's there.

Trey remembered him big, but he's only a middling-sized man, and slight with it. His hair, which is the exact same mousy brown as hers, flops across his forehead like a teenager's. His jeans and his white T-shirt and his black leather jacket are the newest things in the house. The sitting room looks even messier around him.

She says, to her mam, 'Taking this to Cal's.' She turns around and goes out to the kitchen.

Behind her she hears Johnny say, with a laugh in his voice, 'Cal, is it? Is that one of Senan Maguire's young lads?'

Banjo is still at his water bowl, lapping noisily, but when Trey comes in he bounces up, wagging his whole rear end and looking hopefully at his food bowl. 'Nah,' Trey tells him. She puts her face under the tap and rubs at it, stripping off sweat and dust. She rinses her mouth and spits hard into the sink. Then she cups her hand again and drinks for a long time.

She turns quick when she hears a sound behind her, but it's Alanna, holding her limp stuffed rabbit under one armpit and swinging the door back and forth with the other hand. 'Daddy came home,' she says, like it's a question.

Trey says, 'Yeah.'

'He says to come on back inside.'

'Going out,' Trey says. She rummages in the fridge, finds ham slices, and shoves a thick wad of them between two slices of bread. She wraps the sandwich in kitchen roll and crams it into the back pocket of her jeans. Alanna, still swinging the door, watches her as she hoists the chair onto her back, snaps her fingers for Banjo, and heads into the expanse of sunlight.

———

Cal is ironing his shirts on the kitchen table and considering shaving his beard off. When he grew it, back in Chicago, his idea of Irish weather was based on tourist websites, which were heavy on lush green fields and happy people in knit sweaters. For his first two years here, the climate lived up to the advertising, more or less. This summer appears to have snuck in from an entirely different website, maybe one about Spain. The heat has a brazen, unbudging quality that Cal, who has become accustomed to any given day containing a few scraps of sunshine, numerous degrees of cloud and several varieties of rain, finds slightly unsettling. It's at odds with the landscape, whose beauty is founded on subtlety and flux, and it's pissing off the farmers: it's messed up their schedule for silage and hay, it's making the sheep irritable, and it's threatening the grazing. Among the guys in the pub, it's become the main topic of conversation, pushing aside the upcoming National Sheep Dog Trials, the woman Itchy O'Connor's eldest brought in from Dublin to marry, and the probable bribery involved in the construction of the new leisure centre up in town. One of its minor inconveniences is that Cal's beard has turned into a heat trap. Whenever he goes outside, the lower half of his face feels like it has its own tropical climate.

Cal is fond of the beard, though. It was originally connected, in a hazy way, with his early retirement: he had had enough of being a cop, and of looking like a cop. In terms of the people round Ardnakelty, the beard turned out to be pointless – they had him pegged before he even got unpacked. To him, though, it means something.

Even in the heat, his house is cool. It's an undersized 1930s cottage with nothing noteworthy about it, but the walls are thick and solid, built to do their job. When Cal bought it, it was on the verge of falling apart, but he's brought it back, taking his time, since he doesn't have much else that needs doing. The room he's in, which is mainly living room and a little bit kitchen, has reached the point where it no longer feels like a project; it's turned into simply a good place to be. He's painted it white, with the east wall pale yellow-gold – Trey's idea – to match the sunset light that hits it. Along the way he's acquired furniture, to expand on the previous owners' leftovers: he now has three chairs around the kitchen table, an old desk where Trey does her homework, an armchair, a faded blue sofa that could use reupholstering, and even a standing lamp. He's also acquired a dog. In his corner beside the fireplace,

Rip is being thorough with a rawhide bone. Rip is small, floppy-eared, and built like a brick shithouse. He's half beagle, with a beagle's sweet face and a beagle's haphazard patches of black and tan and white, but Cal hasn't worked out the other half. He suspects wolverine.

Through the open window comes the exuberant riot of birds, who, unlike the sheep, are glorying in the heat and the abundance of bugs it's brought them. The breeze flows in soft and sweet as cream. A bumblebee blunders in with it and bumps itself against cupboards. Cal gives it a little time to think, and eventually it figures out the window and swerves off into the sunlight.

Outside the back door, there's a scuffle and a burst of happy barking. Rip shoots out of his corner and hurls himself down the hall to plaster his nose against the door firmly enough that Cal won't be able to open it. This happens every time Trey and Banjo arrive, but Rip, who is a sociable creature, gets too overexcited to remember.

'Back,' Cal orders, nudging Rip out of the way with his toe. Rip manages to restrain himself, quivering, long enough that Cal can get the door open. Two young rooks rocket up off the step and head for their oak tree at the bottom of the garden, laughing so hard they tumble in the air.

Rip streaks after them, vowing to tear them apart. 'Well, son-ofabitch,' Cal says, amused. He's been trying to build up a relationship with his colony of rooks ever since he arrived. It's working, but the relationship isn't exactly what he had in mind. He had some Disney idea of them bringing him presents and eating out of his hand. The rooks definitely feel he's an asset to the neighbourhood, but mainly because he leaves them leftovers and because they like fucking with him. When they get bored, they yell down his chimney, drop rocks into his fireplace, or bang on his windows. The barking is new.

Almost at the tree, Rip does a 180 and tears off around the house towards the road. Cal knows what that means. He heads back into the house, to unplug the iron.

Trey comes in the door alone: Rip and Banjo are playing tag

around the yard, or hassling the rooks, or rooting out whatever they can find in the hedges. The dogs know the boundaries of Cal's land, which is ten acres, more than enough to keep them occupied. They're not going to go chasing sheep and getting themselves shot.

'Went and got this,' Trey says, swinging the chair off her back. 'Your woman over the mountain.'

'Good job,' Cal says. 'You need lunch?'

'Nah. Had it.'

Having grown up dirt-poor himself, Cal understands Trey's prickly relationship with offers. 'Cookies in the jar, if you need to top up,' he says. Trey heads for the cupboard.

Cal puts his last shirt on a hanger and leaves the iron on the kitchen counter to cool off. 'Thinking of getting rid of this,' he says, giving his beard a tug. 'What do you figure?'

Trey stops with a cookie in her hand and gives him a stare like he suggested walking naked down what passes for the main street in Ardnakelty. 'Nah,' she says, with finality.

The look on her face makes Cal grin. 'Nah? Why not?'

'You'd look stupid.'

'Thanks, kid.'

Trey shrugs. Cal is well versed in the full range of Trey's shrugs. This one means that, having said her piece, she no longer considers this her problem. She shoves the rest of her cookie in her mouth and takes the chair into the smaller bedroom, which has turned into their workshop.

The kid's conversational skills being what they are, Cal relies on the timing and quality of her silences to communicate anything he ought to know. Normally she wouldn't have dropped the subject that fast, not without giving him more shit about what he would look like clean-shaven. Something is on her mind.

He puts his shirts in his bedroom and joins Trey in the workshop. It's small and sunny, painted with the leftovers from the rest of the house, and it smells of sawdust, varnish, and beeswax. Clutter is everywhere, but it's ordered. When Cal realised they were getting serious about carpentry, he and Trey built a sturdy shelving unit for boxes of nails, dowels, screws, rags, pencils, clamps, waxes, wood stains, wood oils, drawer knobs, and everything else. Pegboards on the walls hold rows of tools, each one with its shape traced in its proper place. Cal started off with his granddaddy's toolbox and has since accumulated just about every carpentry tool in existence, and a few that don't officially exist but that he and Trey have improvised to suit their needs. There's a worktable, a lathe bench, and a stack of mixed scrap wood in a corner for repairs. In another corner is a dilapidated cartwheel that Trey found somewhere, which they're keeping on the grounds that you never know.

Trey is kicking a drop cloth into place on the floor, to stand the chair on. The chair has good bones. It was handmade, long enough ago to have a dip worn into the seat by many rear ends, and another worn into the front stretcher by many feet. The back and the legs are delicate turned spindles, ringed and beaded here and there for decoration. It's spent much of its life near cooking or burning, though: smoke, grease and layers of polish have left it covered in a dark, tacky film.

'Nice chair,' Cal says. 'Gonna have to clean it up before we do anything else.'

'I told her that. She said good. Her granddad made it.'

Cal tilts the chair to inspect the damage. 'On the phone she said the cat knocked it over.'

Trey makes a sceptical *pfft* noise. 'Yeah,' Cal says.

'Her Jayden's in my school,' Trey tells him. 'He's a prick. Hits little kids.'

'Who knows,' Cal says. 'All these are gonna need replacing. What wood do you figure?'

Trey examines the seat, which all those rear ends have kept clean enough to show the grain, and the insides of the breaks. 'Oak. White.'

'Yeah, me too. See if we've got a piece thick enough to turn. Don't worry about matching the colour; we're gonna have to stain it anyway. Just get the grain as close as you can.'

Trey squats by the assortment of scrap wood and starts poking around. Cal goes out to the kitchen and mixes white vinegar and warm water in an old jug. Then he dusts off the chair with a soft cloth, leaving space for the kid to talk into if she feels like it, and watches her.

She's grown. Two years ago, when she first showed up in his back yard, she was a scrawny, silent kid with a self-inflicted buzz cut and a half-grown bobcat's urge towards both flight and fight. Now she's up past his shoulder, the buzz cut has relaxed into a rough crop, her features are getting a new clarity, and she rummages and sprawls around his house like she lives there. She even has entire conversations, or at least most days she does. She's got none of the polish and artifice that some teenagers start developing, but she's a teenager all the same, both her mind and her life getting more intricate every day. The things she says, just about school and her friends and whatever, have new layers underneath them. Cal is having more trouble with it than she seems to be. These days, every time he picks up a whiff of something on her mind, the bloom of terror inside him spreads wider and darker. Too many things can happen, at fifteen, and do too much damage. Trey seems solid as hardwood, in her own way, but she's taken too many knocks in her life not to have cracks in there somewhere.

Cal finds a clean rag and starts rubbing down the chair with the vinegar mix. The sticky coating comes away well, leaving long brown streaks on the rag. Outside the window, blackbirds' rambling songs carry from far across the fields, and bees revel in the clover that's commandeered Cal's back yard. The dogs have found a stick to play tug-of-war with.

Trey, holding two pieces of wood side by side to compare them, says, 'My dad came home.'

Everything in Cal comes to a dead stop. Of all the fears that were milling inside him, this wasn't one.

He says, after what seems to be a long time, 'When?' The question is a dumb one, but it's all that comes into his head.

'This morning. While I was getting the chair.'

'Right,' Cal says. 'Well. He here for good? Or just for a while?'

Trey shrugs extravagantly: no idea.

Cal wishes he could see her face. He says, 'How're you feeling about it?'

Trey says flatly, 'He can fuck off.'

'OK,' Cal says. 'That's fair.' Maybe he ought to be giving the kid some bullshit speech that includes the words 'but he's your daddy', but Cal makes it his practice never to bullshit Trey, and his feelings on Johnny Reddy happen to coincide with hers.

Trey says, 'Can I stay here tonight?'

Cal's mind stops again. He goes back to rubbing down the chair, keeping his rhythm even. After a moment he says, 'You worried about something your dad might do?'

Trey snorts. 'Nah.'

She sounds like she's telling the truth. Cal relaxes a little bit. 'Then what?'

Trey says, 'He can't just walk back in.'

She has her back to Cal, rummaging among the wood, but her whole spine has a taut, angry hunch. 'Right,' Cal says. 'I'd probably feel the same way.'

'Can I stay, so?'

'No,' Cal says. 'Not a good idea.'

'Why not?'

'Well,' Cal says. 'Your dad might not be happy about you taking off the minute he's back in town. And I figure I'd best not start out by pissing him off. If he's gonna stick around, I'd rather he didn't have a problem with you hanging out over here.' He leaves it at that. She's old enough to understand some, at least, of the other reasons why not. 'I'll call Miss Lena, see if you can spend the night there.'

The kid starts to argue, but she changes her mind and rolls her eyes instead. Cal finds, to his surprise, that he feels shaken, like he just fell off something high and he needs to sit down. He props his ass on the worktable and pulls out his phone.

On reflection, he texts Lena rather than calling her. *Could Trey stay at your place tonight? Don't know if you heard but her dad just came home. She doesn't feel like hanging out with him.*

He sits still, watching the sunlight shift across Trey's thin shoulders as she pulls out lengths of wood and discards them, until Lena texts back. *Fuck's sake. I don't blame her. Yeah she can stay no problem.*

Thanks, Cal texts. *I'll send her over after dinner.* 'She says you're welcome to stay,' he tells Trey, pocketing his phone. 'You gotta tell your mama where you are, though. Or ask Miss Lena to.'

Trey rolls her eyes harder. 'Here,' she says, thrusting an old oak sleeper at him. 'This?'

'Yeah,' Cal says. He goes back to the chair. 'That's good.'

Trey marks the end of the sleeper with a swipe of black Sharpie and puts it back in the corner. 'That stuff coming off?' she asks.

'Yeah,' Cal says. 'It's fine. Easy as pie.'

Trey finds a clean rag, dips it in the vinegar mix and wrings it out hard. She says, 'What if he's not OK with me coming here?'

'You reckon he'll have a problem?'

Trey considers this. 'He never gave a shite where we went before.'

'Well then,' Cal says. 'Most likely he won't give a shit about this, either. If he does, we'll deal with it then.'

Trey throws a quick glance up at him. Cal says, 'We'll deal with it.'

Trey nods, one decisive jerk, and starts in on the chair. The fact that his word can reassure her makes Cal want to sit down all over again.

Reassured or not, she's still not feeling talkative, even by her own standards. After a while, Rip and Banjo get thirsty and come in the open front door, take a long noisy drink from their bowls, and bounce into the workshop for some attention. Trey squats to make a fuss over them, even laughing when Rip nudges her under the chin hard enough that she falls on her backside. Then the dogs flop down for a rest in their corner, and Trey picks up her rag again and gets back to work.

Cal doesn't feel much like talking either. He never for a minute expected Trey's father to come home. Even made up entirely of anecdotes, Johnny Reddy has always struck Cal as a type he's encountered before: the guy who operates by sauntering into a new place, announcing himself as whatever seems likely to come in handy, and seeing how much he can get out of that costume before it wears too thin to cover him up any longer. Cal can't think of a good reason why he might want to come back here, the one place where he can't announce himself as anything other than what he is.

————

Lena is hanging her washing on the line. She takes an unreasonable amount of private pleasure in this job. It makes her keenly aware of the air around her, warm and sweet with cut hay, of the generous sunlight covering her, and of the fact that she stands where generations of women have stood, doing the same task against the greens of the fields and the faraway outline of the mountains. When her husband died, five years back, she learned the skill of taking every scrap of happiness where she could find it. A fresh bed or a perfectly buttered piece of toast could lighten the weight enough to let her catch a breath or two. A small breeze swells the sheets on the line, and Lena sings to herself, low fragments of songs she picked up off the radio.

'Well, would you ever look at that,' a voice says behind her. 'Lena Dunne. Large as life and twice as gorgeous.'

When Lena turns around, it's Johnny Reddy, leaning on her back gate and looking her up and down. Johnny always did have a way of inspecting you like he was remembering, with approval, what you were like in bed. Since he was never in Lena's bed and isn't going to be, she has no time for this.

'Johnny,' she says, looking him up and down right back. 'I heard you were home, all right.'

Johnny laughs. 'God almighty, word still travels fast around here. The place hasn't changed a bit.' He gives her an affectionate smile. 'Neither have you.'

'I have,' Lena says. 'Thank God. You haven't.' It's true. Apart from the first smattering of grey, Johnny looks the same as he did when he used to throw pebbles against her window and bring her and half a dozen others to the disco in town, all of them piled on top of each other in his dad's rickety Ford Cortina, speeding through the dark and shrieking at every pothole. He even stands

the same, easy and light as a young lad. He confirms Lena's obser-
vation that the men who age best are the feckless ones.

He grins, running a hand over his head. 'I've still got the hair,
anyway. That's the main thing. How've you been getting on?'

'Grand,' Lena says. 'How's yourself?'

'Never better. It's great to be home.'

'Lovely,' Lena says. 'That's nice for you.'

'I was in London,' Johnny tells her.

'I know, yeah. Off making your fortune. Did you?'

She's expecting a flourish-laden story about how he was within
touching distance of millions when some villain swooped in and
robbed the chance from under his nose, which would at least make
his visit interesting enough to be halfway worthwhile. Instead,
Johnny gives the side of his nose a mischievous tap. 'Ah, now, that'd
be telling. It's under construction. Authorised personnel only.'

'Ah, shite,' Lena says. 'I forgot my hard hat.' She goes back to
her washing, feeling that Johnny could at least have waited until
she was done enjoying it.

'Will I give you a hand with that?' he asks.

'No need,' Lena says. 'It's done.'

'Brilliant.' Johnny opens her gate wide and sweeps a hand
towards it. 'You can come for a walk with me, so.'

'This isn't the only thing I've to do today.'

'The rest'll keep. You deserve a bit of a break. When was the last
time you skived off for the day? You used to be great at that.'

Lena looks at him. He still has that smile, the wide impish crin-
kle that woke your reckless side and lured you into thinking the
stakes were low. Lena kept them that way, except for that speeding
Cortina. She had a laugh with Johnny, but even though he was the
finest thing and the biggest charmer within miles of Ardnakelty, he
never stirred enough in her to get him beyond the outside of her
bra. He had no substance; there was nothing in him to hold her. But
Sheila Brady, who was Lena's friend back then, kept believing the
stakes were low and the substance was in there somewhere, till she
came up pregnant. From there the momentum just kept on rolling
her downhill.

Sheila was big enough and smart enough to make her own decisions, but Johnny's momentum took their kids along too. Lena has got fonder of Trey Reddy than she is of just about any other human being.

'You know who'd only love to skive off for the day?' she says. 'Sheila. She used to be great at it, too.'

'She's at home with the kiddies, sure. Theresa went off somewhere – she's a chip off the old block, that one, got itchy feet. The rest are too small to mind each other.'

'Then away you go and mind them, and Sheila can go for a walk.'

Johnny laughs. He's not putting it on; he's genuinely not shamed, or even annoyed. This was one of the things that stopped Lena from ever getting drawn in by Johnny: you could see right through him, and let him know you had, and he wouldn't be one bit bothered. If you didn't fall for his shite, there were plenty of others who would.

'Sheila must be sick of the sight of these fields. I'm the one that's been missing them for years. Come on and help me enjoy them.' He waggles the gate invitingly. 'You can tell me what you've been at all this time, and I'll tell you how I got on in London. The aul' lad upstairs from me was from the Philippines, and he had a parrot that could swear in their lingo. You wouldn't get that in Ardnakelty. I'll teach you how to call anyone that annoys you a son of a grasshopper.'

'I've sold that land you're standing on to Ciaran Maloney,' Lena says, 'is what I've been at. If he sees you there, he'll run you off it. You can call him a son of a grasshopper.' She picks up her wash basket and goes inside.

She watches from her kitchen window, staying well back, as Johnny moseys off across the field to find someone else to smile at. His accent hasn't changed, anyway; she has to give him that. She'd have bet on him coming back talking like Guy Ritchie, but he still sounds like a mountain lad.

Something that was nudging at her mind has made it to the surface, now that her anger is fading and leaving room. Johnny always liked to make a fine entrance. When he turned up outside her window, he came smelling of expensive aftershave – robbed, probably – with his jeans ironed, every hair in place, and the Cortina waxed to a sparkle. He was the only fella Lena knew who never had broken fingernails. Today, his clothes are shiny-new right down to the shoes, and not cheap shite either, but his hair is straggling over his ears and flopping in his eyes. He's tried to slick it into place, but it's too overgrown to behave. If Johnny Reddy has come home in too much of a hurry to get a haircut, it's because he's got trouble following close behind.

———

By the time Trey and Banjo head to Lena's, it's gone ten o'clock, and the long summer evening has run itself out. In the vast stretch of darkness, moths and bats are whirling; as Trey passes between fields, she can hear the slow shifting of cows settling themselves to sleep. The air still has the day's heat left in it, coming up off the earth. The sky is clear, packed with stars: tomorrow is going to be another hot one.

Trey is going over the things she remembers about her dad. She hasn't used up a lot of thought on him since he left, so it takes her a while to find things to go over. He liked to distract their mam, grab her when she was scrubbing the cooker and dance her around the kitchen floor. Occasionally, when he had drink taken and something had gone wrong, he hit them. Other times he would play with them like another kid. He and Trey's big brother, Brendan, would take the little ones on their backs to be cowboys and chase Trey and Maeve around the yard, trying to capture them. He liked to promise them things; he loved to see their faces light up when he said he'd bring them to the circus in Galway, or buy them a toy car that climbed up walls. He didn't seem to feel any need to follow through on his promises; in fact, he always seemed a little bit surprised and aggrieved when they asked. After a while Trey stopped playing the cowboy games.

Lena's house is lit, three small clean rectangles of yellow against the great black fields. Her dogs, Nellie and Daisy, let her know

Trey and Banjo are coming; before they're in the gate, she opens the door and stands waiting in the light. The sight of her loosens Trey's muscles a little. Lena is tall and built strong, with deep curves, wide cheekbones and a wide mouth, heavy fair hair and very blue eyes. Everything about her has a heft to it; nothing is half there. Cal is the same: he's the tallest man Trey knows and one of the broadest, with thick brown hair and a thick brown beard, and hands the size of shovels. Trey herself is constructed for agility and inconspicuousness, and has no issue with this, but she takes a deep pleasure in Cal's and Lena's solidity.

'Thanks for having me,' she says on the doorstep, handing Lena a Ziploc bag full of meat. 'Rabbit.'

'Thanks very much,' Lena says. Her dogs swivel between Trey, Banjo, and the bag. Lena palms their noses away from it. 'Did you get it yourself?'

'Yeah,' Trey says, following Lena inside. Cal has a hunting rifle, and a warren on his land. The rabbit was his idea: according to him, it's mannerly to bring your hostess a gift. Trey approves of this. She dislikes the thought of being indebted, even to Lena. 'Fresh tonight. Hasta go in the fridge for a day, or else it'll be tough. Then you can put it in the freezer.'

'I might eat it tomorrow. It's been a while since I had rabbit. What's that way you and Cal fry it up?'

'Garlic and stuff. And then tomatoes and peppers in with it.'

'Ah,' Lena says. 'I've no tomatoes. I'd have to get them off Noreen, and then she'd want to know what I was cooking, and where I got the rabbit, and what you were doing over here. Even if I told her nothing, she'd smell it off me.' Lena's sister Noreen runs the village shop, and the rest of the village while she's at it.

'Probably she knows already,' Trey says. 'About my dad.'

'I wouldn't put it past her,' Lena says. 'No need to give her a leg up, though. Let her work for it.' She puts the rabbit away in the fridge.

They make up a bed for Trey in the spare room, which is big and airy, painted white. The bed is a broad solid thing with knobbed bedposts, seventy or eighty years old by Trey's guess, made of battered oak. Lena pulls off the patchwork quilt and folds it up. 'You won't be wanting that in this heat,' she says.

'Who else stays here?' Trey asks.

'No one, these days. Sean and I used to have friends down from Dublin for weekends. After he died, there was a while when I'd no wish to see anyone. I never got back into the habit.' Lena dumps the quilt into a chest at the foot of the bed. 'Your dad called round this afternoon,' she says.

'Didja tell him I'd be coming here?' Trey demands.

'I did not. I texted your mam, though.'

'What'd she say?'

' "Grand." ' Lena takes a sheet from a pile on a chair and shakes it out. 'I had these out on the line for a while; they should be aired enough. What do you reckon about your dad coming home?'

Trey shrugs. She catches two corners of the sheet when Lena flips them to her, and starts stretching it over the mattress.

'My mam coulda told him to fuck off,' she says.

'She'd have had every right to,' Lena agrees. 'I wouldn't say he gave her a chance, but. I'd say he showed up on the doorstep with a big smile and a big kiss, and waltzed inside before she could get her bearings. By the time she'd her head together, it was too late.'

Trey considers this. It seems likely. 'She could do it tomorrow,' she says.

'She might,' Lena says, 'or she might not. Marriage is an odd thing.'

'I'm never gonna get married,' Trey says. Trey has a bone-deep mistrust of marriage or anything resembling it. She knows that Lena sometimes stays the night at Cal's place, but Lena also has a place of her own, which she can go back to whenever she wants, and where no one else has any say or any right of entry. To Trey, this seems like the only possible arrangement with any sense to it.

Lena shrugs, tucking a corner in more tightly. 'Some people would tell you you'll change your mind. Who knows. Marriage suits some people, for some of their lives, anyway. It's not for everyone.'

Trey asks abruptly, 'Are you gonna marry Cal?'

'No,' Lena says. 'I loved being married, mostly, but I'm done with it. I'm happy as I am.'

Trey nods. This comes as a relief. The question has been on her mind for a while. She approves of Cal and Lena being together – if one of them went out with someone else, it would complicate matters – but she likes things the way they are, with them in two separate places.

'I've had offers, mind you,' Lena adds, snapping the top sheet out across the bed. 'Bobby Feeney came down here a coupla years back, all spruced up in his Sunday best and carrying a bunch of carnations, to explain why he'd make a fine second husband.'

Trey lets out a crack of laughter before she knows it's coming. 'Ah, now,' Lena says reprovingly, 'he was dead serious. He'd it all thought out. He said I'd be handy with the sheep, since I know my way around livestock, and he's great at mending things, so I'd never have to worry if a fuse went or a handle came off the door. Since I was getting too old for babies, I wouldn't be expecting him to be a daddy; and he's no spring chicken himself, so he wouldn't be always at me. And most evenings he's down the pub or else up the mountains looking for UFOs, so he wouldn't be under my feet. His only worry was that his mam didn't approve, but he was certain we'd get round her in the end, specially if I could make a good rice pudding. Mrs Feeney's a martyr to the aul' rice pudding, apparently.'

Trey can't stop grinning. 'What'd you say?'

'Bobby's all right,' Lena says. 'He's an awful eejit, but I can't hold that against him; he's been that way since we were in nappies. I said he'd made a lot of good points, but I'd got too settled in my ways to go making changes. Then I gave him a jar of my blackberry jam, for his mam to put on her rice pudding, and sent him on his way. I'd say the jam made him a lot happier than I would've.' She tosses Trey a pillowcase. 'You can have Banjo in with you, if you want him.'

'He'll get up on the bed.'

'That's grand. As long as he doesn't wet it.'

Trey says, 'How long can I stay?'

Lena looks at her. 'Go home tomorrow,' she says. 'See what

you're dealing with, for a day or two or three. Then we'll take it as it comes.'

Trey doesn't bother arguing. Lena is hard to budge. 'Then can I come back?'

'Probably, if you want. Wait and see.'

'I'll wax this,' Trey says, nodding at the bed. 'Needs a fresh coat.'

Lena smiles. 'It could do with one, all right,' she says. 'Go on and get some sleep now. I'll get you a T-shirt.'

The T-shirt smells of sun-drying and of Lena's washing powder, which is different from Trey's mam's. Trey lies awake for a while, listening to the muffled bumps and rustles of Lena getting ready for bed in the next room. She likes the width of the bed, and not having Maeve a few feet away, snuffling and kicking out and having irritable conversations with herself. Even in her sleep, Maeve is discontented about most things.

The night sounds different down here. Up the mountain, there's always a bullying wind shoving at the loose windowpanes and making an uneasy mutter in the trees, smudging any other noises. Here Trey can hear things clearly: the crisp snap of a twig, an owl on the hunt, young foxes squabbling far off across the fields. Banjo turns over, on the foot of the bed, and lets out a deep luxurious sigh.

In spite of the bed and the peace, Trey can't sleep. She feels like she needs to be ready, just in case. The feeling is familiar and strange at the same time. Trey is good at noticing things outside herself but uninterested in noticing things inside, so it takes her a while to recognise that this is the way she felt most of the time, up until a couple of years ago and Cal and Lena. It faded away so gradually that she forgot it, till now.

Trey is very clear on what she likes and doesn't like, and she liked her life a lot better the way it was this morning. She lies still in the bed, listening to creatures moving outside the window and to the night wind making its way down from the mountain.

2

The next day is the same as the last, dew burning off quickly under a blue empty sky. Cal checks in with Lena, who reports that Trey is grand and eating everything in the house bar the dog food, and then spends the morning up in his back field, where he has a vegetable patch. Last year the vegetables more or less grew themselves; about all Cal had to do was keep the rooks, the slugs and the rabbits off them, which he did with a combination of beer traps, chicken wire, Rip, and a scarecrow. The scarecrow went through various phases. Cal and Trey originally made it out of an old shirt and jeans of Cal's. Then Lena dug out a bunch of old scarves to give it some extra flutter, but then Mart, Cal's nearest neighbour, objected that it looked like it was doing the dance of the seven veils and it would distract all the old bachelors around, leading to crop failures and neglected sheep. He averted disaster by coming up with what looked like a genuine priest robe, which he put on the scarecrow. A couple of weeks later Cal got home from the store to find that someone, still unidentified, had given the priest inflatable armbands and a My Little Pony swim ring with a pink unicorn head. Regardless of costume changes, by the end of summer the rooks had cottoned on to the scarecrow, and made this clear by using it as a combined play structure and toilet. This spring, when the early lettuce started coming up, Cal and Trey got creative and rebuilt the scarecrow using a plastic zombie that Cal found online. It's motion-activated; whenever anything comes close, its eyes flash red, its teeth chatter, and it waves its arms and makes growling noises. So far it scares the shit out of the rooks. Cal expects them to take a well-constructed and elaborate revenge when they finally figure it out.

This year the growing is different, with the heat. The plants need endless watering and a considerable amount more weeding, which is what Cal is doing this morning. The earth is different from last summer, too, less rich and restful; it pours between his fingers instead of sticking to them, and it has a harsher, almost feverish smell. Cal knows from the internet that this weather is going to mess with the flavour of his parsnips, but the tomatoes are thriving on it. Some of them are the size of cooking apples, and reddening already.

Rip, who has been snuffling along rabbit trails, suddenly lets out a bark that belongs on a St Bernard. Rip has never come to terms with his size. In his mind, he's something that chases down escaped prisoners and eats them whole.

'Whatcha got?' Cal asks, turning.

He's expecting a fledgling or a field mouse, but Rip's head is up. He's pointing and quivering at a man strolling across the field.

'Stay,' Cal says. He straightens up and waits while the man comes towards them. The sun is overhead; his shadow is a small black thing puddling and flickering around his feet. The heat blurs his edges.

'That's a beauty of a dog you've got there,' the man says, when he gets close enough.

'He's a good dog,' Cal says. He knows this guy has to be around his own age, touching fifty, but he looks younger. He has a wistful, fine-boned face that makes him seem like something more than a hardscrabble guy from the back end of Ireland. In a movie, he'd be the wronged gentleman who deserves his title back and the prettiest girl to marry. Cal is startlingly, savagely glad that he looks nothing like Trey.

'Johnny Reddy,' the man says, offering Cal his hand.

Cal holds up his own palms, which are thick with dirt. 'Cal Hooper,' he says.

Johnny grins. 'I know, sure. You're the biggest news in Ardnakelty since PJ Fallon's ewe dropped the lamb with two heads. How's the place treating you?'

'Got no complaints,' Cal says.

'Ireland of the welcomes,' Johnny says, giving him a boyish smile. Cal doesn't trust grown men with boyish smiles. 'I hear I've to thank you. The missus says you've been awful good to our Theresa.'

22

'No thanks needed,' Cal says. 'I wouldn't've got this place fixed up half as quick without her help.'

'Ah, that's great to hear. I wouldn't want her being a nuisance to you.'

'She's no trouble,' Cal says. 'She's turning into a pretty handy carpenter.'

'I saw that coffee table the two of ye made for the missus. Lovely delicate legs on it. I wouldn't mind seeing legs that good on a young one.' Johnny's grin widens.

'All the kid's work,' Cal says. 'I didn't lay a finger on it.'

'I don't know where she gets it from, at all,' Johnny says, switching tack nimbly when he doesn't get the man-to-man guffaw he was angling for. 'If I tried, I'd land myself in hospital. The last time I did any woodworking was back in school. All I got outa that was ten stitches.' He holds up a thumb to show Cal the scar. 'And a slap across the head off the teacher, for bleeding on school property.'

'Well,' Cal says. 'We can't all have the same gifts.' Johnny gives him the urge to pat him down and ask him where he's headed. There are guys like that, who flunk the sniff test just going to the store; it's a good cop's job to work out whether they're actually doing something hinky, or whether it's just that they will be sooner or later, probably sooner. Cal reminds himself, which he hasn't needed to do in a long time, that hinkiness, imminent or otherwise, is no longer his problem. He motions to release Rip, who's twitching to investigate. Rip circles Johnny at a distance, deciding whether he needs destroying.

'And now here's Theresa making coffee tables,' Johnny says, offering Rip a hand to smell. He shakes his head, marvelling. 'When I was a young fella, people woulda broke their hearts laughing at that. They'd have said you were wasting your time teaching a girl, when she oughta be learning to cook a roast dinner.'

'That so?' Cal inquires politely. Rip, who is a creature of sense, has taken one sniff of Johnny and decided that nibbling his own ass for fleas is a better use of his time.

'Ah, yeah, man. Do the lads not slag you for it, down the pub?'

'Not that I know of,' Cal says. 'Mostly they just like getting their furniture fixed.'

'We've come a long way,' Johnny says, promptly switching tack again. Cal knows what he's doing: testing, aiming to get a handle on what kind of man Cal is. Cal has done it himself, plenty of times. He doesn't feel any need to do it now; he's learning plenty about Johnny as it is. 'It's great for Theresa, having the opportunity. There's always room for a good carpenter; she can go anywhere in the world with that. Is that what you did yourself, before you came here?'

There is not a chance in hell that Johnny doesn't know what Cal used to do. 'Nope,' Cal says. 'I was a police officer.'

Johnny raises his eyebrows, impressed. 'Fair play to you. That's a job that takes guts.'

'It's a job that pays the mortgage,' Cal says.

'A policeman's a great thing to have handy, in an outa-the-way place like this. Sure, if you'd an emergency, you'd be waiting hours for them eejits up in town to get to you – and that's if they bothered getting up off their arses at all, for anything less than murder. There was a fella I knew one time – naming no names – he took a bit too much of a bad batch of poteen and went mental altogether. He got lost on the way home, ended up on the wrong farm. He was roaring at the woman of the house, wanting to know what she'd done with his missus and his sofa. Smashing all round him.'

Cal does his part and laughs along. It's easier than it should be. Johnny tells a story well, with the air of a man with a pint in his hand and a night of good company ahead.

'In the end he hid under the kitchen table. He was waving the salt shaker at her, yelling that if she or any other demon came near him, he'd sprinkle them all to death. She locked herself in the jacks and rang the Guards. Three o'clock in the morning, that was. It was afternoon before they were arsed sending anyone out. By that time the fella had slept it off on her kitchen floor, and he was busy begging the poor woman to forgive him.'

'Did she?' Cal asks.

'Ah, she did, o' course. Sure, she'd known him since they were babas. But she never forgave the Guards up in town. I'd say the townland's over the moon to have you.'

Neither is there a chance in hell that Johnny believes Ardnakelty was over the moon about a cop moving in. Like most nowhere places, Ardnakelty is opposed to cops on general principle, regardless of whether anyone is currently doing anything that a cop might take an interest in. It allows Cal, but that's in spite of his job, not because of it. 'I'm not much good to them in that department,' Cal says. 'I'm retired.'

'Ah, now,' Johnny says, smiling roguishly. 'Once a policeman, always a policeman.'

'So I've been told,' Cal says. 'Myself, I don't police unless I'm getting paid for it. You hiring?'

Johnny laughs plenty at that. When Cal doesn't join in this time, he settles down and turns serious. 'Well,' he says, 'I suppose that's good news for me. I'd rather Theresa got a taste for carpentry than for policing. No harm to the job, I've a great respect for anyone who does it, but it's got its risks – sure, who am I telling? I wouldn't want her putting herself in harm's way.'

Cal knows he needs to make nice with Johnny, but this plan is undermined somewhat by his urge to kick the guy's ass. He's not going to do it, obviously, but just allowing himself to picture it gives him some satisfaction. Cal is six foot four and built to match, and after spending the last two years fixing up his place and help-ing out on various neighbours' farms, he's in better shape than he's been since he was twenty, even if he still has a certain amount of belly going on. Johnny, meanwhile, is a weedy little runt who looks like his main fighting skill is convincing other people to do it for him. Cal reckons if he got a running start and angled his toe just right, he could punt this little shit straight over the tomato patch.

'I'll try and make sure she doesn't saw off a thumb,' he says. 'No guarantees, though.'

'Ah, I know,' Johnny says, ducking his head a little sheepishly. 'I'm feeling a wee bit protective, is all. Trying to make up for being away so long, I suppose. Have you children of your own?'

'One,' Cal says. 'She's grown. Lives back in the States, but she comes over to visit me every Christmas.' He doesn't like talking about Alyssa to this guy, but he wants Johnny to know that she hasn't cut him off or anything. The main thing he needs to get across, in this conversation, is harmlessness.

'It's a fine place to visit,' Johnny says. 'Most people'd find it a bit quiet-like to live in. Do you not find that?'

'Nope,' Cal says. 'I'll take all the peace and quiet I can get.'

There's a shout from across Cal's back field. Mart Lavin is stumping towards them, leaning on his crook. Mart is little, wiry, and gap-toothed, with a fluff of grey hair. He was sixty when Cal arrived, and he hasn't aged a day since. Cal has come to suspect that he's one of those guys who looked sixty at forty, and will still look sixty at eighty. Rip shoots off to exchange smells with Kojak, Mart's black-and-white sheepdog.

'Holy God,' Johnny says, squinting. 'Is that Mart Lavin?'

'Looks like,' Cal says. At the start, Mart used to stop by Cal's place every time he got bored, but he doesn't come around as much any more. Cal knows what brought him today, when he's supposed to be worming the lambs. He caught sight of Johnny Reddy and dropped everything.

'I shoulda known he'd still be around,' Johnny says, pleased. 'You couldn't kill that aul' divil with a Sherman tank.' He waves an arm, and Mart waves back.

Mart has acquired a new hat from somewhere. His favourite summer headgear, a bucket hat in orange and khaki camouflage, disappeared from the pub a few weeks ago. Mart's suspicions fell on Senan Maguire, who had been the loudest about saying that the hat looked like a rotting pumpkin, brought shame on the whole village, and belonged on a bonfire. Mart put this down to jealousy. He believes adamantly that Senan succumbed to temptation, took the hat, and is sneaking around his farm in it. The pub arguments have been ongoing and passionate ever since, occasionally coming close to getting physical, so Cal hopes the new hat will defuse the situation a little bit. It's a broad-brimmed straw thing that, to Cal, looks like it should have holes in it for a donkey's ears.

'Well, God almighty,' Mart says, as he reaches them. 'Look what the fairies left on the doorstep.'

'Mart Lavin,' Johnny says, breaking into a grin and holding out a hand. 'The man himself. How's the form?'

'Fine as frog hair,' Mart says, shaking hands. 'You're looking in great nick yourself, but you always were a dapper fella. Put the rest of us to shame.'

'Ah, will you stop. I couldn't compete with that Easter bonnet.'

'This yoke's only a decoy,' Mart informs him. 'Senan Maguire robbed my old one on me. I want him thinking I've moved on, so he'll drop his guard. You couldn't watch that fella. How long are you gone now?'

'Too long, man,' Johnny says, shaking his head. 'Too long. Four years, near enough.'

'I heard you were over the water,' Mart says. 'Did them Brits not appreciate you well enough over there?'

Johnny laughs. 'Ah, they did, all right. London's great, man; the finest city in the world. You'd see more in an afternoon there than you would in a lifetime in this place. You should take a wee jaunt there yourself, someday.'

'I should, o' course,' Mart agrees. 'The sheep can look after themselves, sure. Then what brought a cosmopolitan fella like yourself back from the finest city in the world to the arse end of nowhere?'

Johnny sighs. 'This place, man,' he says, tilting his head back becomingly to look out over the fields at the long tawny hunch of the mountains. 'There's no place like it. Doesn't matter how great the big city is; in the end, a man gets a fierce longing on him for home.'

'That's what the songs say,' Mart agrees. Cal knows Mart has despised Johnny Reddy for most of his life, but he's watching him with lively appreciation just the same. Mart's personal boogeyman is boredom. As he's explained to Cal at length, he considers it to be a farmer's greatest danger, well ahead of the likes of tractors and slurry pits. Boredom makes a man's mind restless, and then he tries to cure the restlessness by doing foolish shite. Whatever Mart

27

may think of Johnny Reddy, his return is likely to relieve boredom.

'There's truth in the old songs,' Johnny says, still gazing. 'You don't see it till you're gone.' He adds, as an afterthought, 'And I'd left the family on their own long enough.' Cal finds himself disliking Johnny Reddy more by the minute. He reminds himself that he was primed to do that, no matter what the man turned out to be like.

'C'mere till I tell you who died while you were off gallivanting,' Mart says. 'D'you remember Dumbo Gannon? The little fella with the big ears?'

'I do, o' course,' Johnny says, coming back from the wide open spaces to give this the full attention it deserves. 'Are you telling me he's gone?'

'Took a heart attack,' Mart says. 'Massive one. He was sat on the sofa, having a bit of a rest and a smoke after his Sunday dinner. His missus only went out to get the washing off the line, and when she came back in, he was sitting there stone dead. The aul' Marlboro still burning away in his hand. If she'd been a bit longer with that washing, he coulda taken the whole house with him.'

'Ah, that's sad news,' Johnny says. 'God rest his soul. He was a fine man.' He has his face composed in the appropriate mixture of gravity and sympathy. If he had a hat, he'd be holding it to his chest.

'Dumbo ran you off his land once,' Mart says, fixing Johnny with a reminiscent gaze. 'Bellowing and roaring out of him, so he was. What was the story there, bucko? Did you ride his missus, or what did you do at all?'

'Ah, now,' Johnny says, winking at Mart. 'Don't be giving me a bad name. This fella here might believe you.'

'He will if he's wise,' Mart says, with dignity.

They're both looking at Cal, for the first time in a while. 'Too wise to fall for your guff,' Johnny says. This time he winks at Cal. Cal keeps gazing at him with mild interest till he blinks.

'Mr Hooper always takes me at my word,' Mart says. 'Don't you, Sunny Jim?'

'I'm just a trusting kinda guy,' Cal says, which gets a grin out of Mart at least.

'There's a few of the lads coming up to my place tomorrow night,' Johnny says casually, to Mart and not Cal. 'I've a coupla bottles in.'

Mart watches him, bright-eyed. 'That'll be nice,' he says. 'A lovely homecoming party.'

'Ah, just an aul' chat and a catch-up. I've a bit of an idea going.'

Mart's eyebrows jump. 'Have you, now?'

'I have. Something that could do this place a bitta good.'

'Ah, that's great,' Mart says, smiling at him. 'That's what this townland needs: a few ideas brought in. We were getting stuck in the mud altogether, till you came back to rescue us.'

'Ah, now, I wouldn't go that far,' Johnny says, smiling back. 'But a good idea never hurts. Let you come up to my place tomorrow, and you'll hear all about it.'

'D'you know what you oughta do?' Mart asks, struck by a thought.

'What's that?'

Mart points his crook at the mountains. 'D'you see that aul' lump of rock there? I'm fed up to the back teeth driving them roads every time I wanta get over that mountain. The potholes'd rattle the eyeballs right outa your head. What we need is one of them underground pneumatic railways. London had one right back in aul' Victoria's time, sure. A tunnel with a train carriage in it, just like the Tube, only they'd a big fan at each end. One would blow and the other would suck, and that carriage'd fly straight through the tunnel like a pea out of a peashooter. Twenty-five mile an hour, it went. Sure, you'd be through that mountain and out the other side in no time at all. You put your mind to it and get us one of those. If the Brits can do it, so can we.'

Johnny is laughing. 'Mart Lavin,' he says, shaking his head affectionately. 'You're the same as ever.'

'Theirs went wrong in the end, though,' Mart informs him. 'One day they shut it down, just like that; sealed off the tunnel, no word of an explanation. Fifty or a hundred years later, an explorer found the tunnel again, deep down under London. The carriage was still sealed up inside. A dozen men and women still sitting in their seats, in their top hats and hoop skirts and pocket watches, every one of them nothing but bones.' He smiles at Johnny. 'But, sure, yours wouldn't go wrong. We've all the finest technology these days. Yours'd be only great. You get onto that, now.'

After a moment Johnny laughs again. 'You oughta be the ideas man, not me,' he says. 'Come on up to my place and you'll hear it all. See you tomorrow night.' To Cal, he says, 'Good to meet you.'

'You too,' Cal says. 'See you round.' He has no desire to be invited over to drink to Johnny's return, under a roof he fixed himself, but he does have an ingrained dislike for rudeness.

Johnny nods to him, touches his temple to Mart, and heads off towards the road. He walks like a city boy, picking his way around anything that might dirty his shoes.

'Worthless little fecker,' Mart says. 'The best part of that fella ran down his mammy's leg. What did he want from you?'

'Check out the guy who's hanging out with his kid, I guess,' Cal says. 'Don't blame him.'

Mart snorts. 'If he gave a damn about that child, he wouldn'ta run off on her. That fella never did anything in his life unless he was after a few bob or a ride, and you're not his type. If he dragged his lazy arse down here, he wanted something.'

'He didn't ask for anything,' Cal says. 'Yet, anyway. You going to his place tomorrow night, get in on his big idea?'

'I wouldn't have one of Johnny Reddy's ideas if it was wrapped in solid gold and delivered by Claudia Schiffer in the nip,' Mart says. 'I only came down here to let him know not to be trying to get his hooks into you. If he wants to mooch, he can mooch offa someone else.'

'He can try all he wants,' Cal says. He doesn't want any favours from Mart. 'Did he hook up with Mrs Dumbo?'

'He did his best. That lad'd get up on a cracked plate. Don't you be letting him around your Lena.'

Cal lets that go. Mart finds his tobacco pouch, pulls out a skimpy rollie, and lights it. 'I might go on up to his place tomorrow night,'

30

he says reflectively, picking a shred of tobacco off his tongue. 'Whatever he's at, there's some eejits around here that'd fall for it. I might as well have a good view of the action.'

'Bring your popcorn,' Cal says.

'I'll bring a bottle of Jameson, is what I'll bring. I wouldn't trust him to have anything dacent in, and if I've to listen to that gobshite, I'd want to be well marinated.'

'I figure I'll stick with ignoring him,' Cal says. 'Save myself the booze money.'

Mart giggles. 'Ah, now. Where's the entertainment in that?'

'You and me got different ideas of entertainment,' Cal says.

Mart draws on his rollie. His face, creased against the sun, is suddenly grim. 'I'm always in favour of paying heed to the sly fuckers,' he says. 'Even when it's an inconvenience. You never know when there might be something you can't afford to miss.'

He nudges one of Cal's tomatoes with the point of his crook. 'Them tomatoes is coming along great,' he says. 'If you have a few going spare, you know where to find me.' Then he whistles for Kojak and starts off back towards his own land. When he crosses Johnny Reddy's trail, he spits on it.

Ignoring Johnny turns out to be harder than Cal expected. That evening, when Lena has sent Trey home and come over to his place, he can't settle. Mostly his and Lena's evenings are long, calm ones. They sit on his back porch drinking bourbon and listening to music and talking, or playing cards, or they lie on the grass and watch the expanse of stars turn dizzyingly above them. When the weather is being too Irish, they sit on his sofa and do most of the same things, with rain padding peacefully and endlessly on the roof, and the fire making the room smell of turf smoke. Cal is aware that this puts them firmly in boring-old-fart territory, but he has no problem with that. This is one of the many areas where he and Mart don't see eye to eye: being boring is among Cal's main goals. For most of his life, one or more elements always insisted on being interesting, to the point where dullness took on an unattainable end-of-the-rainbow glow. Ever since he finally got his hands on it, he's savoured every second.

Johnny Reddy is, just like Mart spotted from all the way over on his own land, a threat to the boringness. Cal knows there's nothing he can do about the guy, who has more right to be in Ardnakelty than he has, but he wants to do it anyway, and quick, before Johnny starts in fucking things up. Lena is drinking her bourbon and ginger ale, comfortable in the back-porch rocking chair that Cal made for her birthday, but Cal can't sit. He's throwing a stick for Rip and Nellie, who are surprised by this departure from routine but not about to turn down the opportunity. Daisy, Rip's mama, who doesn't have a sociable nature, has ignored the stick and gone to sleep beside Lena's chair. The fields have sunk into darkness, although the sky still has a flush of turquoise above the treeline in the west. The evening is still, with no breeze to take away the day's leftover heat.

'You fed her dinner, right?' he asks for the second time.

'Enough to fill a grown man,' Lena says. 'And if she needs more, I'd say Sheila might have the odd bitta food lying around the house. D'you reckon?'

'And she knows she can come back to your place if she needs to.'

'She does, yeah. And she can find her way in the dark. Or in a snowstorm, if one comes up.'

'Maybe you should go home tonight,' Cal says. 'In case she comes back and you're not there.'

'Then she'll know where to look for me,' Lena points out. Lena spends maybe two nights a week at Cal's place, which naturally the entire village has known since the day it began and probably before. At the start he suggested tentatively that she might walk, or he could walk to hers, to avoid people seeing her car and making her a target of gossip, but Lena just laughed at him.

Rip and Nellie are having a ferocious tug-of-war with the stick. Rip wins and gallops triumphantly over to drop it at Cal's feet. Cal hurls it back into the darkness of the yard, and they disappear again.

'He was nice to me,' Cal says. 'What was he nice to me for?'

'Johnny is nice,' Lena says. 'He's got plenty of faults, but no one could say he's not nice.'

'If Alyssa was hanging around some middle-aged guy when she was that age, I wouldn't've been nice to him. I'da punched his lights out.'

'Did you want Johnny to punch your lights out?' Lena inquires. 'Because I could ask him for you, but it's not really his style.'

'He used to hit them,' Cal says. 'Not often, from what the kid's said, and not too bad. But he hit them.'

'And if he tried it now, she'd have somewhere else to go. But he won't. Johnny's in great form. He's the talk of the town, he's buying the whole pub drinks and telling them all the adventures he had over in London, and he's loving it. When the world's being good to Johnny, he's good to everyone.'

This fits with Cal's assessment of Johnny. Except on the most immediate level, he isn't reassured.

'He told Angela Maguire he was at a party with Kate Winslet,' Lena says, 'and someone spilt a drink down the back of her dress, so he gave her his jacket to cover up the stain, and she gave him her scarf in exchange. He's showing the scarf all around town. I wouldn't say Kate Winslet would go near that yoke for love nor money, but it makes a good story either way.'

'He told Mart he had an idea,' Cal says, also for the second time. 'What kind of idea does a guy like that come up with?'

'You'll know day after tomorrow,' Lena says. 'Mart Lavin'll be straight down here to spill the beans. That fella loves being first with a bitta gossip.'

'Something that'd be good for this place, he said. What the hell would that guy reckon would be good for a place? A casino? An escort agency? A monorail?'

'I wouldn't worry about it,' Lena says. Daisy whimpers and twitches in her dream, and Lena reaches down to stroke her head till she settles. 'Whatever it is, it won't get far.'

'I don't want the kid around a guy like that,' Cal says, knowing he sounds absurd. He's aware that gradually, over the past two years, he's come to think of Trey as his. Not his in the same way as Alyssa, of course, but his in a specific, singular way that has no relation to anything else. He sees it in the same terms as the drystone walls that define the fields around here: they were hand-made rock by rock as the need arose, they look haphazard and they have gaps you could stick a fist through, but somehow they have the cohesion to stand solid through weather and time. He hasn't seen this as a bad thing; it's done no one any harm. He can't tell whether he would have done anything differently if he had expected Johnny to come home, bringing with him the fact that Trey is not, in reality, Cal's in any way that carries any weight at all.

'That child's no fool,' Lena says. 'She's got a good head on her shoulders. Whatever Johnny's at, she won't go getting sucked into it.'

'She's a good kid,' Cal says. 'It's not that.' He can't find a way to express, even to himself, what it is. Trey is a good kid, a great kid, on track to make herself a good life. But all of that seems so vastly against the odds that to Cal it has an aura of terrifying fragility, something incredible that shouldn't be disturbed until the glue has set hard. Trey is still too little for anything to have set hard.

Lena drinks her bourbon and watches him hurl the stick with all his force. Normally Cal has the innate calm of a big man or a big dog, who can afford to let things alone for a while and see how they play out. Regardless of the situation, a part of her welcomes seeing this different side of him. It lets her know him better.

She could settle his mind, temporarily at least, by bringing him to bed, but she decided right from the beginning that she wasn't going to make Cal's moods her responsibility – not that he has many, but Sean, her husband, was a moody man, and she made the mistake of believing that was her problem to fix. The fact that Cal never expects her to do that is one of the many things she values in him. She has no intention of wrecking it.

'Mart says all Johnny's ever looking for is women and cash,' Cal says. 'I could give him cash.'

'To leave, like?'

'Yeah.'

'No,' Lena says.

'I know,' Cal says. There are far too many ways Johnny Reddy could misread that, or make use of it, or both.

'He wouldn't take it, anyway,' Lena says. 'It's not the money Johnny's after, or not only. He's after a story where he got the money by being the big hero. Or the dashing bandit, at least.'

'And for that,' Cal says, 'he's got his big idea. Whatever it is.' Rip makes his way back up the garden, hauling the stick by one end, with Nellie dragging off the other. Cal detaches it from the pair of them, throws it, and watches them vanish into the dark again. The last of the light is ebbing out of the sky, and the stars are starting to show.

Lena is trying to decide whether to tell him the thought she had, the day before, as she watched Johnny saunter away. She'd like to have Cal's views on it – not only because, having been a detective, he has a wider knowledge of trouble and its many forms, but also because of the way he considers things, without hurry or strain. Before he even says a word, that makes the thing seem more manageable, susceptible to being held still and examined at leisure.

His restlessness is stopping her. She has only a guess, based on nothing but a scruffy haircut and old memories. Unsettled as Cal is, it would be unfair to put that on him, just for her own convenience. Lena herself is wary and watchful, but she's not unsettled. She isn't by nature a peaceful woman; her calm is hard-won, and Johnny doesn't have enough force in him to shake it. She's not altogether convinced that he has enough force to bring any trouble bigger than a debt-collection notice in his wake, but Cal, knowing less of Johnny and more of trouble, might see it differently. Then, too, she knows the stakes here aren't the same for Cal as they are for her.

She adds the tightness in Cal's face, and the fact that she finds herself shielding him, to the list of reasons she despises Johnny Reddy. The man hasn't been in town long enough to muddy the shine on those pretty shoes or that pretty smile, and already, without even aiming to, he's making problems where there were none.

'Come on,' Cal says suddenly, turning to her and holding out a hand. Lena thinks he wants to go inside, but when she takes his hand and lets him pull her out of the rocking chair, he leads her down the porch steps, onto the grass.

'I figure I oughta mind my own beeswax for a while,' he says. 'When was the last time we took a nighttime walk?'

Lena tucks her hand through his elbow and smiles. Rip and Nellie follow them, Rip taking big bounds over the long grass just for the fun of it, as they head for the road that twists away between the fields, faint and pale in the starlight. The night flowers have the rich, honeyed scent of some old cordial. Daisy opens one rolling eye to watch them on their way, and then goes back to sleep.

───────

Even though Cal tries not to say it, Trey knows he doesn't like her being out on the mountain in the dark. When she's at his place for dinner, he keeps one eye on the sky and orders her home as soon as the west starts to glow gold. He worries about her falling into a ditch and injuring herself, or straying off the path and getting sucked down in a bog, or running into one of the scattering of people who live high on the mountain and who have the reputation of being half wild. None of these things worry Trey. She's been on the mountain her whole life, which means her body knows it better than her mind does; the slightest unexpected shift in the consistency of the earth under her feet, or the slope of it, is enough to warn her if she's going wrong. The mountainy men have known her since she was a baby, and sometimes give her a few quid to do their messages at Noreen's shop, or to bring a few eggs or a bottle of poteen to a neighbour a mile or two up the road. She's considering being one of them when she's grown up.

She's spent the last few hours on the mountainside, waiting to be fairly sure her dad will be either in bed or down the village at Seán Óg's pub. Trey is good at waiting. She sits with her back against a drystone wall, in its shadow, rubbing Banjo's ears. She has a pocket torch, but she likes both the invisibility and the feeling of power that she gets from not using it. It's a bright enough night, anyway – the sky is crowded with stars, and there's a big, close half-moon; Trey can see down the ragged slopes of heather and sedge to the fields, bleached by the moonlight and misshapen by the shadows of their walls and trees. Up here the air has a thin fitful breeze, but

Lena lent her a hoodie, which is too big and smells of the same washing powder as Lena's sheets. Now and then there's a sharp, furtive rustle out on the bog or up among the trees, but those don't bother Trey either. She stays still and watches for the hare or fox to show itself, but whatever creatures are out there, they smell Banjo and stay clear. A few times, before she had Banjo, she saw hares dancing.

When the lights in the farmhouses below start to blink out, she heads home. The front of the house is dark, but there's a haze of yellow light spilling out behind it: someone is still awake. As Trey pushes open the gate, Banjo stiffens and lets out a low warning bark. Trey stops, ready to run.

'Call off the dogs,' says a voice not far away, light and amused. 'I'm harmless.'

A shadow peels itself off a tree trunk and comes towards her at a leisurely saunter. 'Wouldja look at this night,' her dad says. 'Isn't it only gorgeous?'

'Mam knows where I was,' Trey says.

'I know, sure. She said you were down at Lena Dunne's, polishing up an aul' bed. You're great to give her a hand.' Johnny takes a deep breath, smiling a little up at the stars. 'Smell that air. My God, there's nothing in all of London that'd compare to that smell.'

'Yeah,' says Trey, to whom the air smells much the same as usual. She heads for the house.

'Ah, come here,' her dad calls after her. 'Don't be wasting a night like this. We'll stay out here a bit. Alanna won't go asleep – overexcited, like. We'll let your mammy settle her in peace.' He beckons with his head to Trey and arranges himself comfortably, leaning his arms on the barred metal gate. Trey's dad likes being comfortable, and he's good at it; he can make anywhere look like he belongs there.

Trey remembers what Cal said about not pissing him off. She thinks it's stupid and knows he's right, both at the same time. She goes over and stands by the gate, an arm's length from her dad, with her hands in the hoodie pockets.

'I've missed your mammy,' Johnny says. 'She's still a beautiful woman – you're too young to see that, maybe, but it's the truth. I'm lucky to have her. Lucky she waited for me all this time, and didn't run off with some fancy man that came knocking at the door selling notions.'

Trey can't picture her mam having the energy to run off with anyone, and anyway no one ever comes knocking at their door. She had forgotten his smell, cigarettes and soap and an aftershave with some rich spice in it. Banjo is sniffing it too, and glancing up at her for clues on how to classify it. 'Sit,' she says.

'I can't get over the size of you,' her dad says, smiling at her. 'Just a little biteen of a thing that'd run from her own shadow, you were, when I saw you last. And now look at you: near grown up, working away, in and outa houses all over this townland. I'd say you know half the people round here better than I would. D'you get on with them all right?'

'Lena's sound,' Trey says. She can feel him wanting something from her, but she doesn't know what.

'Ah, yeah. Lena's grand. And I called in to your friend Cal Hooper. I reckoned if you're going down there on the regular, I oughta get to know him a bit. Make sure he's all right.'

Trey goes cold straight through with outrage. He said it like he was doing her a favour. He had no right anywhere near Cal. She feels like he stuck his hand in her mouth.

'He seems like a dacent-enough fella. For a policeman.' Johnny laughs. 'Jaysus, a child of mine hanging around a Guard. Did you ever hear the like?'

Trey says nothing. Her dad grins at her. 'Is he a nosy bollox, yeah? Always asking questions? Where were you on the night of the fifteenth?'

'Nah,' Trey says.

'I'd say he has the whole place afraid to put a toe outa line. If he caught the lads drinking poteen, heaven help us, he'd have them hauled up to the Guards in town before they'd know what hit them.'

'Cal drinks poteen,' Trey says. 'Sometimes.' She thinks about punching her dad in the face, or running away and sleeping in an abandoned cottage somewhere on the mountainside. A couple of years back she would probably have done both. Instead she just stands there, with her fists in the pockets of Lena's hoodie. Her anger is too dense and tangled to find a way out of her.

'Well, that's something, anyway,' her dad says, amused. 'He can't be too bad if he can handle Malachy Dwyer's stuff. I'll have to bring some down to him one day, and we can make a night of it.'

Trey says nothing. If he does that, she'll get Cal's rifle and blow his fucking foot off, and see can he make his way down the mountain to Cal's after that.

Johnny rubs a hand over his head. 'Are you not speaking to me?' he asks ruefully.

'Got nothing to say,' Trey says.

Johnny laughs. 'You always were quiet,' he says. 'I thought it was only that you couldn't get a word in edgewise, with Brendan about.'

Brendan has been gone more than two years. His name still feels like a jab to Trey's throat.

'If you're annoyed with me for going away, you can go on and say it. I won't get angry with you.'

Trey shrugs.

Johnny sighs. 'I went because I wanted to do better for you,' he says. 'All of ye, and your mammy. You might not believe that, and I wouldn't blame you, but at least have a think about it before you decide it's only rubbish. There was nothing I could do for you here. You know yourself: this shower of gombeens act like the Reddys are nothing but shite on their shoes. Am I wrong?'

Trey shrugs again. She doesn't feel like agreeing with him, but he's right, or near enough. People are nicer to her and her family, the last couple of years, but the note underneath hasn't changed, and she wouldn't want their niceness even if it was real.

'There wasn't one of them would give me a chance. Everyone knows my daddy was a waster, and his daddy before him, and that's all they want to know. There's a hundred jobs I'd be able for around here, but I was lucky to get a day shovelling shite. I'd go up for a factory job I could do in my sleep, and be turned away before

I could open my mouth – and the job'd go to some feckin' eejit that could barely tie his own shoelaces, but his daddy drank with the manager. And there was no point in trying Galway, or Dublin. This bloody country's too small. Someone woulda known someone whose mam was from Ardnakelty, and they'da scuppered my chances just like that.' He snaps his fingers.

Trey knows the dark edge to his voice. It used to mean he was going to slam out and come home drunk, or not at all. It's fainter now, just an echo, but her calf muscles still twitch, ready to run if she needs to.

'That wears a man down. It wears him till he loses sight of himself. I was turning bitter, taking it out on your mammy – I never usedta have a cruel bone in my body, but I was cruel to her, those last coupla years. She didn't deserve that. If I'da stayed, I'da only got worse. London was the nearest I could be and still have a chance to get somewhere.'

He looks at her. His face is pulled into the taut lines she remembers from those same nights, but those are fainter too. 'You know I'm telling the truth, am I right?'

'Yeah,' Trey says, to make him leave it. She doesn't give a shite why her dad went. Once he was gone, Brendan was the man of the family. He felt like it was his job to look after the rest of them. If their dad had stayed, Brendan might still be there.

'Don't be holding it against me, if you can help it. I done my best.'

'We've done grand,' Trey says.

'You have, of course,' Johnny agrees warmly. 'Your mammy says you've been a great help to her. We're proud of you, the pair of us.'

Trey doesn't respond. 'It musta been hard on you,' her dad says sympathetically, switching tone. She can feel him circling her, looking for ways in. 'I'd say it didn't help that Brendan went. The two of ye were always fierce close.'

Trey says, keeping her voice flat, 'Yeah.' Brendan was six years older than her. Up until Cal and Lena, he was the only person who ever appeared to think about Trey by choice, rather than because he had to, and the only person who regularly made her laugh. Six months before Trey met Cal, Brendan walked out of the house one afternoon and never came back. Trey doesn't think about those six months, but they're layered into her like a burn ring inside a tree.

'Your mammy said he went looking for me. Is that what he said to you?'

'He said nothing to me,' Trey says. 'I heard he went to Scotland, maybe.' This is true.

'He never found me, anyway,' her dad says, shaking his head. 'I never thought he'd take it that hard, me leaving. Do you ever hear anything from him?'

The wind fingers restlessly through the trees behind them. Trey says, 'Nah.'

'He'll be in touch,' her dad says confidently. 'Don't you worry. He's only off sowing his wild oats.' He grins, out to the slopes of dark heather. 'And praying for a crop failure.'

Brendan is buried somewhere in these mountains, Trey doesn't know where. When she's out there she keeps watch for any sign – a rectangle of mounded earth, a space where the brush hasn't had time to grow tall again, a tatter of cloth brought to the surface by weather – but there's more of the mountains than she could look at in a lifetime. There are people in the townland who know where he is, because they put him there. She doesn't know who they are. She watches for signs in people's faces, too, but she doesn't expect to find them. People in Ardnakelty are good at keeping things hidden.

She gave Cal her word that she'd say nothing and do nothing about it. Trey, seeing as she doesn't have much else, puts a fiercely high value on her word.

'I came back,' Johnny points out cheerfully. 'See? Brendan'll do the same.'

Trey asks, 'Are you gonna stay?'

It's a plain question – she wants to know what she's dealing with – but her dad takes it as a plea. 'Ah, sweetheart,' he says, giving her a soft-eyed smile. 'I am, of course. I'm going nowhere. Daddy's home now.'

Trey nods. She's no wiser. She can tell he believes it, but he always does; it's one of his gifts, taking every word out of his own mouth as gospel. She had forgotten what it's like talking to him, how misty and muddy.

Johnny leans in a little closer, his smile widening. 'I've no need to go anywhere, sure,' he says confidentially. 'Will I tell you something?'

Trey shrugs.

'I've a plan,' Johnny says. 'When I'm through, the only place we'll be going is a lovely new house with a big bedroom for each one of ye. And you won't have to be walking around with holes in your jeans, neither.'

He waits for her to ask. When she doesn't, he settles his arms better on the gate, preparing to tell the story anyway. 'There's a fella I met,' he says, 'over in London. I was in an Irish pub, having a pint with a few mates and minding my own business, when this lad came over to me. English fella. I was wondering what he was at in a place like that – the pub's a bit rough, now, and he was the type you'd expect to see drinking brandy at a fancy hotel. The coat on him, and the shoes: you could tell they cost more than I'd see in a month. He said he'd been asking around for an Ardnakelty man, and I was pointed out to him.'

Johnny rolls his eyes whimsically. 'Course I reckoned this was bad news, one way or another. I'm no pessimist, but Ardnakelty never worked in my favour before. I was about to tell him to fuck off for himself – which woulda been the worst mistake of my life – only he offered to get me a pint, and I was a bit short of a few bob that day. And then didn't it turn out his granny was from Ard- nakelty. One of the Feeneys, she was. She went over to London before the war, doing the nursing, and married a big-shot doctor. She usedta tell this fella stories about the place, how beautiful it was, how she'd run wild on the mountains – same as you do, sure.' He smiles at Trey. 'And she told him something else, as well. You know there's gold somewhere at the bottom of these moun- tains, don't you?'

'Teacher said that,' Trey says. 'In Geography.'

He points a finger at her. 'Fair play to you, paying attention in school. You'll go far. Teacher was right. The men that lived here thousands of years ago, they knew where to look for it. There's more ancient gold pieces found in this country than anywhere in the whole of Europe, did Teacher tell you that? Bracelets as wide as your hand, collars bigger than dinner plates, round bits like coins that they sewed onto their clothes. Your great-great-granddads and great-great-grannies woulda been dripping with it, at feasts. They'da been out on this mountain, round their fires, shining so bright you could hardly look at them. They were digging it up by the handful, musta been, big nuggets of it, as easy as we'd cut turf.'

He mimes grabbing a fistful and holding it high. His voice has caught alight, rising. His excitement tugs at Trey, but she doesn't like it. It doesn't fit in the still night. She feels like he's drawing notice, in ways that aren't safe.

'Only then the Brits came,' Johnny says, 'and that land was taken away from our people, and they emigrated, or they starved – and, bit by bit, the knowledge got lost. Except . . .' He leans in closer. His eyes are bright. 'It wasn't lost altogether. There were still a few families that passed it down, all those hundreds of years. This fella in the pub – Cillian Rushborough, his name is – his granny's granddad told her where to look. And she told Cillian.'

He cocks his head at her, teasing, waiting for her to ask more. In the moonlight, with his eyes shining and a half-smile on his face, he looks barely older than Brendan.

Trey says, cutting to the end, 'And your man Cillian told you, and now you're gonna dig up the gold.' That's all he came home for: money. The realisation is a sweep of relief. She's not stuck with him forever. If he finds nothing, and his novelty value in the village wears off, he'll be gone.

Johnny laughs. 'Ah, God, no. Only a fool would hand over a treasure map to a man he doesn't know from Adam, and Cillian's no fool. But he needed a man from Ardnakelty. The directions his granny gave him, they're all Greek to him: "In the old riverbed that's dried up now, just by the northwest corner of that field the

Dolans bought offa Pa Lavin . . ." He needs someone that knows his way around the place. And if he blew in here on his own, there's not a man that would let him go digging on their land. But with me on board . . .'

He leans in closer. 'I'll tell you a secret,' he says, 'that I've learned along the way. The best thing you can have in life is a bit of a shine on you. A bitta possibility; a bitta magic. A shine. People can't stay away from that. Once you've got it, it doesn't matter a tap whether they like you, or whether they respect you. They'll convince themselves they do. And then they'll do whatever you want from them. D'you know where I was last night?'

Trey shrugs. Only a few points of yellow light are left among the dark fields below them, and the chill of the breeze is sharpening.

'I was down at Seán Óg's, having the crack with half this townland. Four years ago, if I was on fire, there's not a one of them lads woulda pissed on me to put me out. But when I walk in there wearing this' – he flicks the lapel of his leather jacket – 'and buying the drink and telling them about the life in London, they're all crowded round me, laughing at my jokes and patting me on the back for being a great fella altogether. Because I've got the shine of a bitta cash and a bitta adventure on me. And that's nothing. Wait till they see what I've got up my sleeve.'

Trey hasn't been around anyone who talked this much since Brendan went. Brendan's stream of chat and messing made her want to be part of it, even when all she could think of to do was grin at him. Her dad's talk bombards her. It makes her feel more silent than ever.

'The one and only Mr Cillian Rushborough arrives from London in a few days' time, as soon as he's wrapped up some important business affairs, and then . . .' Johnny nudges Trey's arm with his elbow. 'Then, hah? We'll be on the pig's back. You'll have dresses outa Giorgio Armani, or VIP tickets to meet Harry Styles; take your pick. This fella here can have a diamond collar. Where d'you fancy going on holiday?'

Trey can feel him wanting her to put all her hope on him.

She can't remember when she first knew that he's too puny to take that weight. She thinks of Brendan, before he went out the door for the last time, promising her a new bike for her birthday, and meaning it.

'What if he doesn't find gold?' she asks.

Johnny grins. 'He'll find it,' he says.

Away among the trees, up the mountainside, there's a rattle of wings in branches and a bird's harsh alarm call. Trey wants, suddenly and sharply, to be inside.

'Gonna go in,' she says.

Her dad looks at her for a second, but then he nods. 'Go on,' he says. 'Tell your mammy I'll be in soon.' When Trey glances back at him as she rounds the house, he's still leaning on the gate, with his face tilted up to the moon.

Sheila is wiping down the kitchen counters. She nods when Trey comes in, but she doesn't look up. Trey finds a slice of bread, butters it, rolls it up and leans against the fridge to eat it. Banjo slumps heavily against her leg and lets out an extravagant sigh. He wants to go to bed.

'He's outside,' Trey says. 'He says he'll be in soon.'

Her mam says, 'Where'd you get that hoodie?'

'Lena.'

Sheila nods. Trey says, 'Are you gonna let him stay?'

Sheila keeps wiping. She says, 'He lives here.'

Trey pinches off a bit of her bread for Banjo and watches her. Sheila is a tall woman, rangy and rawboned, with thick red-brown hair starting to grey and pulled back in a ponytail. Her face is like old wood, worn shiny in some places and rough in others, and immobile. Trey is looking for the beauty her dad talked about, but she's seen her mother's face too many times; she doesn't know how to interpret it in those terms.

She says, 'Didja tell him Bren went off looking for him?'

It's been almost two years since they said Brendan's name to each other. Sheila knows what Trey knows, give or take. Trey hears her breath hiss through her nose.

She says, 'I did.'

'How come?'

Sheila swipes crumbs off the table into her hand. 'I know your daddy well. That's how come.'

Trey waits.

'And I told him the whole lot of ye missed him something fierce. Cried your eyes out every night, and wouldn't go to school because ye were ashamed of not having a daddy. And ashamed that I couldn't afford dacent clothes.'

'I didn't give a shite that he went,' Trey says. 'Or about the clothes.'

'I know that.'

The kitchen smells of bacon and cabbage. Her mam moves slowly and steadily, like she's making her energy last.

'If he gets to feeling bad enough in himself,' she says, dusting the crumbs off her hand into the bin, 'he'll run from it.'

Sheila wants him gone, too. Trey isn't surprised, but the knowledge doesn't offer her much comfort. If Sheila had enough force to move Johnny, she'd have done it already.

A sleepy wail comes from down the hall: 'Mammy!'

Ever since their dad left, Alanna has slept in with their mam, but her cry comes from Liam's room. Sheila wipes her hands on the dish towel. 'Finish that table,' she says, and she goes out.

Trey stuffs the last of her bread in her mouth and scrubs down the table. She listens to Alanna's fretful murmuring, and to the restless stirring of the trees. When she hears footsteps crunching out front, she snaps her fingers for Banjo and heads for bed.

3

Lena walks homewards in a morning that's already hot and zipping with insects. Sometimes she leaves her car at home when she goes to Cal's, specifically so that she can have this walk the next morning, sauntering lazily in her rumpled clothes, with the sun on her face and Cal's smell on her skin. It makes her feel young and a little reckless, as if she should be carrying her shoes in her hand, as if she's done something wild and enjoyed every minute. It's been a long time since Lena ran across something wild that she actually wanted to do, but she still likes the taste of it.

She was planning to stay clear of Noreen for a while. Lena gets on well with her sister, mainly by letting Noreen's flood of advice and suggestions wash right over her, but she would prefer to wait a while longer before she discusses Johnny Reddy, and Noreen has a low tolerance for waiting. Being nosy goes with Noreen's job. Lena suspects that she married Dessie Duggan at least in part to get her arse behind that shop counter, the gravitational centre to which is drawn every piece of information from Ardnakelty and beyond. When they were kids, the shop was run by Mrs Duggan, Dessie's mam. She was a big, slow-moving, heavy-lidded woman who smelled of Vicks rub and pear drops, and Lena never liked her. She was nosy, but she was a hoarder with it: she sucked up everything she heard and then kept it stored away, for years sometimes, bringing it out only when it could wield the most force. Noreen, by contrast, is generous-natured and gets her satisfaction not from stockpiling or using information but from dispensing it by the armload, to anyone who'll listen. Lena has no quarrel with that – in her view, Noreen has earned every bit of satisfaction she can get, by looking after Dymphna Duggan, who is now massive, almost housebound from sciatica, a flat cold-eyed face at her sitting-room window watching the village go by. And it means that if anyone has an inkling of what kind of trouble Johnny might have picked up in London, it's Noreen.

Lena stays out of other people's business. She came to that decision the same day she decided to marry Sean Dunne. Up until then, she was planning on freeing herself from Ardnakelty's mesh by the traditional method of getting the hell out of Dodge: she was going to Scotland to train as a vet, and not coming back except for Christmases. Sean, though, was going nowhere off his family's land. When she decided he was worth staying for, she had to come up with a different way to keep the townland from poking its tendrils into every crevice of her. For thirty years she's held it at arm's length: no having opinions on Oisín Maguire's planning permission, no giving Leanne Healy advice on her daughter's dodgy boyfriend, no joining the Tidy Towns or coaching the girls' Gaelic football; and, in exchange, no giving anyone a single word about the farm's finances, or the workings of her and Sean's marriage, or the reasons why they never had children. Minding your own business isn't a trait that's prized in Ardnakelty, especially not in women, and it's brought Lena a reputation for being either up herself or just plain odd, depending on who's talking. She quickly discovered she doesn't care. Sometimes it amuses her, watching how desperate people get for a handle to grab her by.

She doesn't like the feeling that Johnny Reddy, of all people, is her business now. What she wants to do about Johnny is watch this place work itself into a tizzy about him until he hightails it out of town, pursued by the debt collectors or whoever it is he's pissed off, and then dismiss him from her mind all over again. But there's Cal, unsettled, and there's Trey, with no choice about being smack in the middle of it all.

The dogs have bounded ahead of her towards home, working off the day's first burst of energy. Lena calls them back with a whistle and turns for the village.

Ardnakelty's two brief lines of square-set, mismatched old buildings have their windows open to catch breezes – windows that had been shut for decades have been pried open, this summer. Everyone who has the option is outdoors. Three old men, settled on the wall around the Virgin Mary grotto, nod to Lena and hold out their hands to her dogs. Barty, who runs Seán Óg's pub, has been inspired by the dry weather to do something about the walls, which have needed a coat of paint for at least five years; he's press-ganged a couple of Angela Maguire's lads, who are hanging off ladders at precarious angles, armed with buckets of paint in a violent shade of blue and a radio blasting Fontaines DC. Three teenage girls are leaning against the wall of the shop eating crisps, turning their faces up to the sun and all of them talking at once, all manes and legs like a bunch of half-wild colts.

Lena remembers the shop from her childhood as dark and never quite clean, stocked with drab rows of things that nobody actively wanted, but that you bought anyway because Mrs Duggan wasn't about to change her stocking practices to suit the likes of you. When Noreen took over, she marked her territory by scrubbing the place to within an inch of its life and rearranging it so that now, somehow, the same undersized space fits three times as many things, including everything you might need and plenty that you might actually want. The bell gives a brisk, decisive ding as Lena opens the door.

Noreen is down on her knees in a corner of the shop, with her arse in the air, restocking tins. 'You dirty stop-out,' she says, identifying Lena's second-day clothes with one glance. She doesn't say it disapprovingly. Noreen, having introduced Cal and Lena with intent, takes full credit for their relationship.

'I am,' Lena acknowledges. 'D'you want a hand?'

'There's no room down here. You can tidy the sweets.' Noreen nods to the front of the counter. 'Bobby Feeney was in buying chocolate. Mother a God, that fella's like a child with pocket money to spend: he has to touch everything in the shop, to make sure he's getting the best one. He has the place in tatters.'

Lena goes to the counter and starts realigning the chocolate bars and rolls of sweets. 'What'd he get in the end?'

'Packet of Maltesers and one of them fizzy lollipops. D'you see what I mean? Them's sweeties for a child. Grown men get the Snickers, or maybe a Mars bar.'

'See, I was right to turn him down,' Lena points out. Before Cal arrived, Noreen felt that Lena should consider Bobby as an option, if only so that his farm didn't go to waste by being left to his Offaly cousins. 'I couldn't spend the rest of my life watching that fella suck fizzy lollies.'

'Ah, there's no harm in Bobby,' Noreen says promptly. Noreen is still determined to put Bobby to use, if she can just find the right woman. 'He has himself all worked up because of Johnny Reddy coming home, is all. You know what Bobby's like: any change'd send him into a spin.' She throws a glance at Lena, over her shoulder. Noreen and Lena look nothing alike: Noreen is short, round, and quick-moving, with a tight perm and sharp dark eyes. 'Did you see Johnny yet?'

'I did. He came strolling by to show off his tail feathers.' Lena swaps the Maltesers around to be front and centre, so Bobby can get at them without ruining Noreen's day.

'Don't you go falling for Johnny's rubbish,' Noreen says, pointing a tin of beans at Lena. 'You're well sorted with Cal Hooper. He's ten times the man Johnny is, any day of the week.'

'Ah, I don't know. Cal's all right, but he never got a scarf off Kate Winslet.'

Noreen lets out a scornful *pfft*. 'Didja see that scarf yoke? Wee bitta chiffon that wouldn't keep a baba warm. That's Johnny all over: anything he's got looks lovely, but it's pure useless. What was he saying to you?'

Lena shrugs. 'He didn't make his fortune over in London, and he missed the fields. That's as far as he got before I ran him off.'

Noreen snorts and smacks a tin of peas onto the top of a stack. 'The fields. Feckin' state of him. That's tourist talk. Missed having someone to do his washing and cooking, more like.'

'You don't reckon Kate Winslet can cook a roast dinner?'

'I'd say she can, all right, but I'd say she'd have better sense than to do it for the likes of Johnny Reddy. No: that lad got his arse dumped, is what happened him. Didja see the hair on him? That fella would only leave himself get that scruffy if he'd some poor foolish one wrapped round his little finger. If he was single, he'd be done up to the nines, for going out on the prowl. I'm telling you: he had a one, she found out what he was made of and kicked him to the kerb, and he came home sooner than fend for himself.'

Lena straightens Twix bars and thinks this over. It's an angle she hadn't previously considered. It's both plausible and reassuring.

'And Sheila'd better not get used to having him about the place,' Noreen adds. 'If he convinces the bit on the side to take him back, we won't see him for dust.'

'The bit on the side won't have him back,' Lena says. 'Johnny's one of them fellas that are outa sight, outa mind. He's making a big splash coming home, but when he was gone, no one thought twice about him. I didn't hear one word about him, the whole four years. There was no one saying their nephew ran into him in a pub, or their brother was working with him on the building sites. I don't know what he was at, even.'

Noreen instantly takes up the challenge. 'Ah, I heard the odd word. A year or two back, Annie O'Riordan, you know her, from up towards Lisnacarragh? Her cousin in London saw him in a pub, with some young one bet into a pair of black leather leggings laughing her arse off at his jokes. D'you see what I mean? That fella couldn't make it through a wet weekend without a woman to look after him and tell him he's only amazing.'

'Sounds like Johnny, all right,' Lena says. Sheila used to think Johnny was only amazing. Lena doubts she does any more.

'And d'you remember Bernadette Madigan, that I usedta do the choir with? She's got a wee little antique shop in London now, and didn't Johnny come in trying to sell her a necklace that he said was diamonds, with some sob story about his wife running off and leaving him with three starving childer. He didn't recognise her – Bernadette's after putting on the weight something awful, God love her – but she recognised him, all right. She told him to stick his fake diamonds up his hole.'

'Did she ride him, back in school?' Lena asks.

'That's her business, not mine,' Noreen says primly. 'I'd say so, though, yeah.'

The spark of reassurance in Lena's mind is fading. Johnny was never crooked, exactly, but it was hard to tell whether that was just happenstance. If he's happened to drift over that line, who knows how far he might have drifted, and what he might have brought back on his trail. 'When'd she see him?' she asks.

'Back before Christmas. The feckin' eejit – Johnny, not Bernadette. She said a blind man coulda told you those were no diamonds.'

'You never said anything.'

'I hear a lot more than I say,' Noreen informs her with dignity. 'You've some notion that I'm the biggest gossip in the county, but I can keep my mouth shut when I want. I said nothing to anyone about Johnny's goings-on, because I knew yourself and Cal were working your arses off to keep that child on the straight and narrow, and I wasn't going to scupper that by giving her family a worse name than they've already got. Now.'

'Now,' Lena says, grinning at her. 'That's me told.'

'It'd better be. How's the child getting on, anyway?'

'Grand. She's been over putting a new coat of wax on Nana's old bed.'

'Ah, that'll be nice. What does she think of her daddy coming home?'

Lena shrugs. 'Trey, sure. She said he was back, and then she said the dog needed feeding, and that was the end of that.'

'That dog's mad-looking,' Noreen says. 'Like it was put together outa bits of other dogs that got left over. Your Daisy needs better taste in fellas.'

'She should've consulted you,' Lena says. 'You'd've had her set up with a gorgeous stud with a pedigree as long as my arm, before she knew what hit her.'

'I don't see you complaining,' Noreen tells her. Lena tilts her head, acknowledging the hit, and Noreen goes back to work with a little nod of victory. She says, 'I heard the child stayed over at yours, after Johnny came home.'

'Fair play to you,' Lena says, impressed. 'She did, yeah. Cal gets nervous about her walking up that mountain in the dark. He thinks she'll fall in a bog. She won't, but there's no convincing him.'

Noreen darts Lena a sharp glance. 'Pass me over that box there, with the jam. What about Cal?'

Lena nudges the cardboard box along the floor with a foot. 'What about him?'

'What does he think about Johnny?'

'Sure, he's hardly met the man. He hasn't had a chance to come up with much of an opinion.'

Noreen whips jam jars onto the shelf with expert speed. She says, 'Are you planning on marrying that fella?'

'Ah, God, no,' Lena says, going back to the Fruit Pastilles. 'White doesn't suit me.'

'Sure you wouldn't wear white the second time around anyway, and that's not the point. What I'm telling you is, if you're planning on marrying him, there's no reason to wait. Go on and get the job done.'

Lena looks at her. She inquires, 'Is someone dying, are they?'

'Jesus, Mary and Joseph, what are you on about? No one's dying!'

'Then what's the rush?'

Noreen gives her a prickly stare and goes back to the jam. Lena waits.

'You can't trust a Reddy,' Noreen says. 'No harm to the child, she might turn out grand, but the rest of them. You know as well as I do, you wouldn't know what notion Johnny'd get into his head. If he took against Cal and decided to make trouble . . .'

Lena says, 'He'd better not.'

'I know, yeah. But if he did. Cal'd be safer if he was married to you. Moved in with you, even. People'd be less likely to believe things.'

Lena has had her temper managed for so long that the blaze of rage catches her off guard. 'If Johnny gets anything like that in his head,' she says, 'he'd want to watch himself.'

'I'm not saying he would, now. Don't go giving him hassle, or—'

53

'I'm not giving him hassle. When was the last time I gave anyone fucking hassle? But if he goes starting anything—'

Noreen sits back on her haunches, glaring. 'For feck's sake, Helena. Don't be biting my head off. I'm only looking out for the pair of ye.'

'I'm not bloody getting *married* just in case Johnny Reddy is even more of a tosser than I thought.'

'All I'm saying is have a think about it. Can you just do that, instead of flying off the handle?'

'Right,' Lena says, after a second. She turns back to lining up Kit Kats. 'I'll be sure and do that.'

'Feck's *sake*,' Noreen says, not quite under her breath, and smacks a jam jar into place.

The shop is hot, and Noreen's stacking has stirred up dust motes that eddy in the broad bands of sunlight through the windows. Nellie whines discreetly at the door, and then gives up. Outside, one of the boys gives a startled shout, and the bunch of girls burst into helpless, happy laughter.

'Now,' Lena says. 'That's done.'

'Ah, you're great,' Noreen says. 'Would you ever give me a hand with that top shelf? You've the height for it, if you take the stool; I'd have to get the stepladder, and there's all them clothes from the clear-out in front of it.'

'I left the dogs outside,' Lena says. 'I've to get them home and get some water into them, before they shrivel up on me.' Before Noreen can offer to bring the dogs water, she gives a Dairy Milk a last tap into line and goes out.

Lena's visit didn't settle Cal's mind. He was half-hoping that, knowing Johnny and this place as she does, she would have some easy, reassuring thing to say about Johnny's return, something that would clarify the whole situation and relegate the guy to a minor temporary nuisance. The fact that he himself can't think of anything doesn't mean much – after more than two years in Ard-nakelty, Cal sometimes feels like he actually understands the place less than he did on his first day. But if Lena doesn't have reassurance to offer, that means there isn't any.

He deals with his unsettledness in his usual way, which is by working. He puts the Dead South on his iPod and turns the speakers up loud, letting the expert, nervy banjo set a fast rhythm, while he puts his back into planing down pine boards for Noreen's new TV unit. He's trying to work out what to charge her for it. Pricing in Ardnakelty is a delicate operation, laycred with implications about both parties' social position, their degree of intimacy, and the magnitude of previous favours in both directions. If Cal gets it wrong, he could end up discovering that he's either proposed to Lena or mortally offended Noreen. Today he feels like telling her to just take the damn thing.

He's decided that he's not going to ask Trey any questions about Johnny. His first instinct was to start steering and nudging conversations, but all the deeper part of him revolts against using Trey the way he would use a witness. If the kid wants to talk to him, she can talk by her own choice.

She arrives in the afternoon, banging the front door behind her to let Cal know she's there. 'Been over at Lena's,' she says, when she's got herself a drink of water and joined him in the workshop, wiping her mouth on her arm. 'Waxing up the spare bed. 'Cause she let me stay over.'

'Good,' Cal says. 'That's a fine way to say thanks.' He's been trying to provide the kid with some manners, to temper her general air of having been raised by wolves. It's working, to some extent, although Cal feels she may be getting the hang of the technique more than of the underlying principle. He suspects that, to her, manners are mainly transactional: she doesn't like being under an obligation to anyone, and an act of politeness allows her to write off the debt.

'Yeehaw,' Trey says, referring to the Dead South. 'Ride 'em, cowboy.'

'You're a barbarian,' Cal says. 'That's bluegrass. And they're Canadian.'

'So?' Trey says. Cal raises his eyes to the ceiling, shaking his head. She's in a better mood today, which reassures him. 'And I'm not a barbarian. Got my school results. Didn't fail anything, only Religion. A in Wood Technology.'

'Well, would you look at that,' Cal says, delighted. The kid is no dummy, but two years ago she gave so few shits about school that she was failing just about everything. 'Congratulations. You bring them along for me to see?'

Trey rolls her eyes, but she pulls a crumpled piece of paper out of her back pocket and hands it over. Cal props his rear end on the worktable to give it his full attention, while Trey starts in on the chair to make it clear that this is no big deal to her.

There's an A in Science, too, and a bunch of Cs with a couple of Bs thrown in. 'So you're a heathen as well as a barbarian,' Cal says. 'Good work, kid. You oughta be pretty proud of yourself.'

Trey shrugs, keeping her head down over the chair, but she can't stop a grin from tugging at one corner of her mouth.

'Your mama and your dad proud too?'

'My mam said well done. My dad said I'm the brains of the family, and I can go to Trinity College and graduate with a cap and gown. And be a rich Nobel Prize scientist and show all the begrudgers.'

'Well,' Cal says, keeping it carefully neutral, 'he wants the best for you, just like most mamas and dads do. You want to go into science?'

Trey snorts. 'Nah. Gonna be a carpenter. Don't need any stupid gown for that. I'd look like a fuckin' eejit.'

'Well, whatever you decide,' Cal says, 'work like this is gonna give you all the options you could ask for. We gotta celebrate. You want to go catch some fish, fry 'em up?' Ordinarily he would take the kid out for pizza – Trey, after going almost fourteen years without encountering pizza, discovered an overwhelming passion for it when Cal introduced her to the concept, and would eat it every day given the chance. No place delivers to Ardnakelty, but on special occasions they make the trip into town. Now, all of a sudden, he's wary. Ardnakelty in general approves of their relationship as the thing that likely prevented Trey from turning into a troubled youth who would break their windows and hotwire their motorbikes, but Johnny Reddy is a different matter. Cal doesn't have a handle on Johnny yet, or on what he wants. He feels the need to examine little things, ordinary things like a trip to town for pizza, for what they might look like from outside and how they could be used, and he resents this. Apart from anything else, Cal has a low tolerance for indulging in self-examination at the best of times, and he doesn't appreciate it being forced on him by some twinkly-eyed little twerp.

'Pizza,' Trey says promptly.

'Not today,' Cal says. 'Another time.'

Trey just nods and goes back to rubbing down the chair, without pushing or questioning, which pisses Cal off even more. He's put a lot of work into teaching the kid how to have expectations.

'Tell you what,' he says. 'We'll make our own pizza. I've been meaning to show you how to do that.'

The kid looks dubious. 'Easy as pie,' Cal says. 'We even got a pizza stone: we can use those tiles left over from the kitchen floor. We'll invite Miss Lena, make it a party. You go down to Noreen's and pick up ham, peppers, whatever you want on there, and we'll get started on the dough.'

For a minute he thinks she's going to turn it down, but then she grins. 'Not getting you pineapple,' she says. ''S disgusting.'

'You'll get whatever I say,' Cal says, disproportionately relieved. 'Make it two cans, just for that. Now git, before you smell of vinegar so bad that Noreen won't let your stinky self in her store.'

———

Trey goes all out on the toppings, which relieves Cal's mind a little bit: a kid who comes home with pepperoni, sausage, and two kinds of ham, as well as peppers, tomatoes, onions, and his pineapple, can't have restrained her expectations too thoroughly. She loads stuff onto her pizza like she hasn't eaten in weeks. The dough appears to have turned out OK, although their stretching game is weak and the pizzas aren't shaped like anything Cal's ever seen.

Lena is curled on the sofa at her ease, reading Trey's report card, with the four dogs dozing and twitching in a pile on the floor beside her. Lena doesn't do much cooking. She'll bake bread and make jam, because she likes those made her way, but she says she cooked a good meal from scratch every night of her marriage, and now if she wants to live mainly off toasted sandwiches and ready meals, she has the right. Cal takes pleasure in making her the best he can come up with, for variety. He wasn't in the habit of doing much cooking himself, when he first got here, but he can't feed the kid nothing but bacon and eggs.

'"Meticulous,"' Lena says. 'That's what you are, according to this Wood Technology fella. Fair play to you. And to him. That's a great word; it doesn't get out enough.'

'What is it?' Trey asks, considering her pizza and adding more pepperoni.

'Means you do things right,' Lena says. Trey acknowledges the justice of this with a nod.

'What'll you have?' Cal asks Lena.

'Peppers and a bitta that sausage. And tomatoes.'

'Read what the Science teacher said,' Cal tells her. '"An intelligent inquirer with all the necessary determination and method to find answers to her inquiries."'

'Well, we knew that already,' Lena says. 'God help us all. Well done; that's great stuff.'

''S just Miss O'Dowd,' Trey says. 'She's nice to everyone. Long as they don't set anything on fire.'

'You want some pizza on that pepperoni?' Cal asks her.

'Not of yours. Pineapple all over it. Dripping.'

'I'm gonna put chilli flakes on it, too. Right on top of the pineapple. You wanna bite?' Trey makes a face like she's gagging.

'Jesus,' Lena says. 'Mr Campbell's still there? I thought he'd be dead by now. Is he still fluthered half the time?'

'Here I'm trying to teach the kid to respect her elders,' Cal says.

'With all due respect,' Lena says to Trey, 'is he mostly fluthered?'

'Probably,' Trey says. 'Sometimes he falls asleep. He doesn't know any of our names 'cause he says we depress him.'

'He told us we were making his hair fall out,' Lena says.

'You did. He's bald now.'

'Ha,' Lena says. 'I'll have to text Alison Maguire. She'll take that as a personal victory. She hated him 'cause he said her voice gave him migraines.'

'Head on him like a golf ball,' Trey says. 'A depressed golf ball.'

'You be mannerly to Mr Campbell,' Cal tells Trey, sliding pizza off a cookie sheet onto the leftover floor tiles in the oven. 'Regardless of his golf-ball head.'

Trey rolls her eyes. 'I'm not gonna even see him. It's *summer*.'

'And then it won't be.'

'I'm mannerly.'

'Would I think you're being mannerly?'

Lena is grinning at them. Lena claims that Trey, on certain words she's picked up from Cal, has an American accent. 'Yeah yeah yeah,' Cal tells her. 'At least she knows the word. Even if she's kinda shaky on the meaning.'

'He's gonna shave his beard off,' Trey tells Lena, jerking a thumb at Cal.

'Sweet fuck,' Lena says. 'Are you serious?'

'Hey!' Cal says, aiming a swipe at Trey with the oven glove. Trey dodges. 'I only said I was thinking about it. What're you doing snitching on me?'

'Thought she oughta be warned.'

'And I appreciate it,' Lena says. 'I could've walked in here one day and seen your big naked face staring at me, right outa the blue.'

'I don't appreciate the tone of this conversation,' Cal informs them. 'What do you two think I'm hiding under here?'

'We don't know,' Trey explains. 'We're scared to find out.'

'You're getting fresh,' Cal tells her. 'That report card's gone to your head.'

'Probably you're gorgeous,' Lena reassures him. 'It's just that there's enough risks in life as it is.'

'I'm a hunk. I'm Brad Pitt's good-looking brother.'

'You are, o' course. And if you keep the beard, I won't need to worry about finding out different.'

'Who's Brad Pitt?' Trey wants to know.

'Proof that we're getting old,' Lena says.

'*Deadpool 2*,' Cal says. 'The invisible guy who gets electrocuted.'

Trey eyes Cal carefully. 'Nah,' she says.

'I liked you better back when you didn't talk,' Cal tells her.

'If you shave,' Trey points out, putting the last of the pepperoni in the fridge, 'you're gonna be two different colours. 'Cause of the tan.'

All three of them are tanned, this summer. Most people from around here, having evolved to suit Ireland's unemphatic weather, tan to a startled reddish shade that looks mildly painful, but Trey and Lena are exceptions. Lena goes a blonde's smooth caramel; Trey is practically hazelnut-coloured, and she has light streaks running through her hair. Cal likes seeing her that way. She's an outdoor creature. In winter, pale from school and short days, she looks unnatural, like he should be taking her to a doctor.

'You'll look like you're wearing a bandit mask,' Lena says. 'Seán Óg's would love that.'

'You've got a point,' Cal says. Him walking into the pub clean-shaven and two-toned would provide the regulars with months' worth of material, and probably land him with an unfortunate and unshakeable nickname. 'Maybe I oughta do it just out of neigh-bourliness. Spice up their summer a little bit.'

The words bring Johnny Reddy into his head. Johnny is spicing up this summer, all right. None of them has mentioned Johnny once, all evening.

'Fuck 'em,' Trey says. The flat, adamant note in her voice tightens Cal's shoulders another notch. She has every right to it, but it seems to him that a kid her age shouldn't have that cold finality in her armoury. It feels unsafe.

'That's some language out of a high-flier like you,' Lena tells her. 'You oughta say "Fuck 'em meticulously."'

Trey grins, against her will. 'So are you gonna leave the beard?' she demands.

'For now,' Cal says. 'As long as you behave yourself. You give me any sass, and you'll get an eyeful of my chin warts.'

'You don't have chin warts,' Trey says, inspecting him.

'You wanna find out?'

60

'Nah.'

'Then behave.'

The rich smell of the baking pizza is starting to spread through the room. Trey finishes putting things away and drops down among the dogs. Lena gets up, picking her way so as not to disturb any of them, and sets the table. Cal wipes down the counters and opens the window to let out the heat from the oven. Outside, the sun has relaxed its savagery and is laying a fine golden glow over the green of the fields; off beyond Cal's land, PJ is moving his sheep from one field to another, leisurely, holding the gate for them and swishing his crook to guide them through. Trey murmurs to the dogs, rubbing their jowls, while they close their eyes in bliss.

The oven timer goes off, and Cal manages to coax the pizzas onto plates without burning himself. Lena takes the plates from him to put on the table. '*Starving*,' Trey says, pulling up her chair.

'Hands off,' Cal says. 'The pineapple's all mine.'

He's thinking, out of nowhere, of his grandparents' house in backwoods North Carolina where he spent much of his childhood, and of how, before dinner every night, his grandma would have the three of them join hands round the table and bow their heads while she said grace. He has a sudden urge to do the same thing. Not to say grace, or anything else; just to sit still for a minute, with his hands wrapped around theirs, and his head down.

4

When Trey gets home, her dad is rearranging the sitting room. She stands in the doorway and watches him. He's cleared the clutter off the coffee table and brought in the kitchen chairs, and he's humming to himself as he spins them into place, stands back to get a better look, springs forward to adjust them. Outside the window behind him, the sun is still on the bare yard, but it's a loose, late sun, relaxing its grip. Liam and Alanna are taking turns throwing a rusty garden fork, trying to make it stick prongs-down in the dry ground.

Johnny never stops moving. He's wearing a shirt, faded blue with fine white stripes, in some rough material that looks fancy. He's had his hair cut, and not by Trey's mam – it tapers smoothly at the neck and ears, and the boyish flop in front has been expertly shaped. He looks too good for the house.

'Amn't I only gorgeous?' he says, sweeping a hand over his head, when he catches Trey looking. 'I took a wee spin into town. If I'm having guests, I oughta be in a fit state to welcome them.'

Trey asks, 'Who?'

'Ah, a few of the lads are calling in tonight. A few drinks, a few laughs, a bitta catching up. Bit of a chat about my idea.' He spreads his arms to the room. His eyes have the same lit-up, overexcited sparkle they had last night. He looks like he's had a drink or two already, but Trey doesn't think he has. 'Would you look at this, now? Fit for kings. Who says it takes a woman to bring out the best in a place, hah?'

Trey wanted to tell Cal about her dad's idea. She wanted to ask whether he reckoned it was a load of shite, or whether he thought it might actually come to something. But Cal never gave her an opening, and she couldn't find a way to make her own. As the day went on, she stopped trying. It occurred to her that Cal might be deliberately avoiding the subject of her dad because he has no desire to get mixed up in her family's mess. She doesn't blame him. He did that once before, when she made him, and got the living shite bet out of him for it. In certain lights, when it's cold, Trey can still see the scar on the bridge of his nose. She doesn't regret it, but she has no right to make him do it again.

She says, 'I wanta come.'

Her dad turns to look at her. 'Tonight?'

'Yeah.'

His mouth has an amused curl like he's about to laugh her out of it, but then he checks himself and looks at her differently.

'Well,' he says. 'And why not, I suppose. You're no baba, these days; you're a big girl that might be able to give your daddy a hand. Can you do that?'

'Yeah,' Trey says. She has no idea what he wants from her.

'And can you keep quiet about what you hear? That's important, now. I know Mr Hooper's been good to you, but what's going on here tonight is Ardnakelty business. He's got no part in it. Can you promise me you'll say nothing to him?'

Trey looks at him. She can't think of a single thing that he could beat Cal at. 'Wasn't gonna anyway,' she says.

'Ah, I know. But this is serious stuff, now; grown-up stuff. Promise me.'

'Yeah,' Trey says. 'Promise.'

'Good girl yourself,' Johnny says. He props his arms on the back of a chair to give her his full attention. 'These lads that are coming,' he says. 'There's Francie Gannon, Senan Maguire, Bobby Feeney, Mart Lavin, Dessie Duggan – I'd rather not have him on board, with the mouth on his missus, but there's no way round it. Who else, now?' He considers. 'PJ Fallon. Sonny McHugh, and Con as well, if that missus of his'll let him off the leash. That's a fine bunch of hairy-arsed reprobates, amn't I right?'

Trey shrugs.

'Have you had any dealings with any of them? Mended an aul' window frame for them, built them a wee table or two?'

'Most of 'em,' Trey says. 'Not Bobby.'

'Not Bobby, no? Has he got anything against you?'

'Nah. He just mends his own stuff.' He makes a pig's arse of it. When Bobby helps out a neighbour, Cal and Trey get called in to repair the damage.

'Ah, sure, that's grand,' Johnny says, dismissing Bobby with a sweep of his hand. 'Bobby'll do what Senan does, in the end. Now, here's what you'll do tonight. When this bunch of fine lads start arriving, you'll answer the door. Bring them through to here, all lovely and polite' – he mimes ushering people into the room – 'and make sure you ask how they got on with whatever bit of a job you did for them. If they've any complaints, you apologise and promise you'll make it right.'

'They don't have complaints,' Trey says flatly. She doesn't like doing work for Ardnakelty people. It always has a taste of patronage about it, them patting themselves on the back for being noble enough to throw her the job. Cal says to do it anyway. Trey gives them the finger by making sure they can't fault her work, no matter how hard they try.

Johnny reels back, laughing and holding up his hands in mock apology. 'Ah, God, I take it back, don't hurt me! No harm to your work – sure, haven't I seen it myself, don't I know you wouldn't get finer anywhere in this country? Go on, we'll say anywhere north of the equator. Is that better?'

Trey shrugs.

'Once they're all here, you can sit yourself down over in that corner, out of the way. Get yourself a lemonade or something to drink. Say nothing unless I ask you a question – sure, that'll be no bother to you, you've a talent for that.' He smiles at her, his eyes crinkling up. 'And if I do, you just go on and agree with me. Don't worry your head about why. Can you do that?'

'Yeah,' Trey says.

'Good girl yourself,' Johnny says. Trey thinks he's going to pat her shoulder, but he changes his mind and winks at her instead. 'Now let's put a shine on this place. Them dollies in the corner, bring them into Alanna's room, or Maeve's, or whoever owns them. And whose runners are those under the chair?'

Trey picks up dolls' clothes, toy cars, crisp packets and socks, and puts them away. The shadow of the mountain is starting to slide across the yard, towards the house. Liam and Alanna have got a bucket of water and are slopping it on the ground to soften it, so their garden fork will stick in better. Sheila shouts to them, from the kitchen, to come in for their baths. They ignore her.

Johnny buzzes around the room, setting out saucers for ash-trays with stylish flicks of his wrist, skimming dust off surfaces with a kitchen cloth, leaping backwards to admire his work and then forwards to fine-tune it, whistling through his teeth. The whistle has a tense jitter to it, and he never stops moving. It comes to Trey that her dad isn't excited; he's nervous, that this might not work out. More than that: he's afraid.

Trey sets her mind to coming up with a polite way to ask how the McHughs are liking their new patio benches. She wants her dad to need her in on this. The other thing she was going to ask Cal, if he reckoned her dad's plan might not be a load of shite, was how to scupper it.

The men fill up the room till it feels airless. It's not just the size of them, broad backs and thick thighs that creak the chairs when they shift; it's the heat off them, the smoke of their pipes and cigarettes, the smell of earth and sweat and animals from their clothes, the outdoors swell of their deep voices. Trey is crammed into a corner by the sofa, with her knees pulled up out of the way of sprawling feet. She's left Banjo out in the kitchen, with her mam. He wouldn't like this.

They arrived as the long summer evening was seeping away, slanting the mountain's shadow far across the fields and filtering tangles of sunlight through the trees. They came separately, as if the gathering was accidental. Sonny and Con McHugh swept in on a wave of noise, arguing about a call the ref made in last weekend's hurling match; Francie Gannon slouched in silently and took a chair in the corner. Dessie Duggan made a crack about not being able to tell whether Trey is a girl or a boy, which he thought was so funny that he repeated it all over again to Johnny, in the exact same words and with the exact same giggle. PJ Fallon wiped his feet twice on the mat and asked after Banjo. Mart Lavin handed Trey his big straw hat and told her to keep it out of Senan Maguire's reach. Senan took the opportunity to tell Trey, loudly, how she and Cal did a mighty job fixing the shambles Bobby Feeney had made of the Maguires' rotted window frame, while at his shoulder Bobby puffed up with offence. Their faces have the pucker of constant low-level worry – all the farmers' do, this summer – but tonight has brightened them: for a few hours, anyway, they can think about something other than the drought. Their cars, parked at angles that take no notice of each other, crowd the bare yard.

Trey has seen all these men since she was a baby, but she's seen them giving her a brief neutral glance on the road or in the shop, or – the last couple of years – discussing furniture repairs over her head with Cal. She's never seen them like this, taking their ease together with a few drinks on them. She's never seen them here. Her dad's friends, before he went away, were quick-moving men who picked up bits of work here and there, on other men's farms or in other men's factories, or who didn't work at all. These are solid men, farmers who own their land and work it well, and who four years ago would never have thought of coming up the mountain to sit in Johnny Reddy's front room. Her dad was right in this much, anyway: he's brought a change with him.

The tight-wound, glittery buzz that was coming off him earlier is gone; he's breezy as spring. He's poured the men lavish drinks, and put ashtrays at the smokers' elbows. He's asked after their parents by name and by ailment. He's told stories about the wonders of London, and stories that make the men bellow with laughter, and stories where he has to skip bits with a wink to the men and a tilt of his head at Trey. He's charmed stories out of each one of them, and been enthralled or impressed or sympathetic. Trey's feeling towards him, which was pure anger, is becoming shaded over by scorn. He's like a performing monkey, doing his tricks and somersaults and holding out his cap to beg for peanuts. She preferred her fury clean.

She did her own tricks for the men when they arrived, just like her dad wanted, showing them into the sitting room and asking after their furniture, nodding and saying *That's great thanks* when they praised it. Her anger towards them is untouched.

Johnny waits till halfway into the third drink, when the men have relaxed deep into their chairs but before their laughter takes on an uncontrolled edge, to thread Cillian Rushborough into the conversation. Bit by bit, as he talks, the room changes. It becomes focused. The overhead bulb isn't bright enough, and the fringed lampshade gives its light a murky tinge; when the men stay still to listen, it smears deep, tricky shadows into their faces. Trey wonders how well her father remembers these men; how many of the fundamental and silent things about them he's forgotten, or overlooked all along.

'Well, holy God,' Mart Lavin says, leaning back in his armchair. He looks like Christmas just came early. 'I underestimated you, young fella. Here I thought you'd be offering us some shitey music festival, or bus tours for Yanks. And all the time you've got the Klondike waiting at our doors.'

'Jesus, Mary and Joseph,' Bobby Feeney says, awed. Bobby is little and round, and when his eyes and mouth go round as well, he looks like a toy that's meant to roll. 'And me out in them fields every day of my life. I never woulda guessed.'

PJ Fallon has his gangly legs wound around the legs of his chair, to help him think. 'Are you positive, now?' he asks Johnny.

'Course he's not fuckin' positive,' Senan Maguire says. 'A few bedtime stories, is all he has. I wouldn't cross the road for that.'

Senan is a big man, with a ham of a face and a low tolerance for shite. Trey reckons Senan is her dad's main obstacle. Bobby Feeney and PJ Fallon are both easily led, Francie Gannon goes his own way and lets other people be fools if they want, nobody listens to Dessie Duggan, everyone knows Sonny McHugh would do anything for a few quid, and Con McHugh is the youngest of eight so it doesn't matter what he thinks. Mart Lavin disagrees with everything he encounters, often purely for the pleasure of arguing about it, but everyone is used to that and discounts it. Senan has no patience. If he decides this is foolishness, he'll want to stamp it out altogether.

'That's what I thought, at the start,' Johnny agrees. 'Some aul' story his granny heard, and maybe misremembered, or maybe just made up to keep a child entertained; sure, that's not enough to go on. Only this lad Rushborough, he's not a man you'd write off. Ye'll see what I mean. He's a man you'd take seriously. So I said I'd sit down with him and a map of the townland, and listen to what he had to say.'

He looks around at the men. Francie's bony face is expression- less and Senan's is pure disbelief, but they're all listening.

'Here's the thing, lads. Whatever's at the bottom of this story, it's not made up outa thin air. And if it's been misremembered along the way, it's funny how it's been misremembered to add up awful neat. Them spots Rushborough's granny told him about, they're actual places. I can pin down every one of them, within a few yards. And they're not just scattered around here, there and everywhere. They're in a line, give or take, from the foot of this mountain down through all your land to the river. Rushborough reckons there usedta be another river there, that's dried up now, and it washed the gold down from the mountain.'

'There was another river there, all right,' Dessie says, leaning forward. Dessie always raises his voice a little too loud, like he expects someone to try and talk over him. 'The bed of it goes across my back field. Gives me a pain in the hole with the plough- ing, every year.'

'There's dried-up riverbeds everywhere,' Senan says. 'That doesn't mean there's gold in them.'

'What it means,' Johnny says, 'is there's something in Rushbor- ough's story. I don't know about the rest of ye, but I wouldn't mind finding out how much.'

'Your man sounds like a fuckin' eejit,' Senan says. 'How much will this cost him, hah? Machinery, and labour, and fuck knows what else, and no guarantee that he'll get a cent out of it.'

'Don't be codding yourself,' Johnny says. 'Rushborough's no fool. A fool wouldn'ta got where he is. He can afford to indulge himself, and this is what he fancies. The way another man might buy a race-horse, or go sailing his yacht around the world. It's not about the cash – although he wouldn't turn down a bit more of that. This fella's mad on his Irish roots. He was reared on rebel songs and pints of porter. He'd get tears in his eyes talking about how the Brits tied James Connolly to a chair to shoot him. He's after his heritage.'

'Plastic Paddy,' says Sonny McHugh, with tolerant scorn. Sonny is a large man, with a spray of dusty-looking curls and a spreading belly, but he has a small man's quack of a voice; it sounds stupid coming out of him. 'We've a cousin like that. In Boston. He came over for the summer, three or four years back, d'ye remember? The young fella with the big thick neck on him? He brought us a digital camera for a present, in case we hadn't seen one before. Couldn't believe we knew *The Simpsons*. Shoulda seen the look on the poor fucker when he saw our house.'

'There's nothing wrong with your house,' Bobby says, perplexed. 'You've the double glazing and all.'

'I know, yeah. He thought we'd be in a thatched cottage.'

'My land's not a tourist attraction,' Senan says. He has his feet planted wide apart and his arms folded. 'I'm not having some gobshite trampling all over it, frightening my ewes, just because his granny sang him "Galway Bay".'

'He wouldn't be trampling all over your land,' Johnny says. 'Not to start with, anyway. He wants to start off panning in the river; easier than digging. If he finds gold in that river, even a small little biteen, he'll be delighted to pay each and every one of ye a lovely chunk of cash for the opportunity of doing some digging on your land.'

That gets a brief, vivid silence. Con glances at Sonny. Bobby's mouth is wide open.

'How much digging?' Senan asks.

'Samples, he'd want, first off. Just stick a wee tube down into the soil and see what it brings up. That's all.'

'How much cash?' asks Sonny.

Johnny turns up his palms. 'That's up to yourselves, sure. Whatever you can negotiate with him. A grand each, easy. Maybe two, depending on what mood he's in.'

'For the samples, only.'

'Ah, God, yeah. If he finds what he's after, it'll be a lot more than that.'

Trey has been so focused on her dad, she hadn't thought about the fact that these men would be making money from his plan. The surge of helpless rage burns in her throat. Even if he knew about Brendan, Johnny would be grand with filling up Ardnakelty's pockets, as long as he got what he wanted. Trey isn't. As far as she's concerned, all of Ardnakelty can fuck itself to eternity and beyond. She would rather pull out her own fingernails with pliers than do anyone here a favour.

'If there's gold there . . .' says Con McHugh. He's the youngest of the men, a big lad with rumpled dark hair and a handsome, open face. 'My God, lads. Imagine that.'

'Ah, it's there,' Johnny says, as easily as if he was talking about milk in the fridge. 'My young one over there, she learned all about it in school. Didn't you, sweetheart?'

It takes Trey a second to realise he means her. She forgot he knew she was there. 'Yeah,' she says.

'What did Teacher say about it?'

All the men's faces have turned towards Trey. She thinks about saying the teacher told them the gold was round the other side of the mountains, or that it was all dug up a thousand years back. Her dad would beat her afterwards, if he could catch her, but she doesn't consider that worth factoring into her decision. Even if she said it, though, the men might not be swayed by what some teacher from Wicklow thought. Her dad is a good talker; he might still talk them round. And she would have wasted her chance.

'He said there's gold at the bottom of the mountain,' she says. 'And people usedta dig it up and make things out of it. Jewellery. It's in the museums in Dublin now.'

'I saw a programme about that on the telly,' says Con, leaning forward. 'Brooches the size of your hand, and big twisty necklaces. Beautiful, so they were. The shine offa them.'

'You'd look only gorgeous in one of them,' Senan tells him.

70

'He wants them for Aileen,' Sonny says. 'Great big lad like him fits in her pocket—'

'How'd you get out tonight, hah, Con?'

'She thinks he's off getting her flowers.'

'He went out the back window.'

'She's got one of them GPS trackers on him. She'll be banging on the door any minute.'

'Get in behind the sofa there, Con, we'll say we never saw you—'

They're not just having the crack. Each of them, even Con reddening and telling the rest to fuck off, has one eye sliding to Johnny. They're making time, to assess what they think of him and his story and his idea.

While they're doing it, Trey's dad gives her a tiny approving nod. She gives him a blank look back.

'I'm only saying,' Con says, when he's shaken free of the slagging and the other men have settled back, grinning, into their seats. 'I wouldn't say no to a shovelful or two of that stuff.'

'Would any of ye?' Johnny asks.

Trey watches them picture it. They look younger when they do, like they could move faster. Their hands have gone still, letting their cigarettes burn away.

'You'd have to keep a bit,' Con says. His voice has a dreamy hush. 'A wee bit, only. For a souvenir, like.'

'Fuck that,' Senan says. 'I'd have a Caribbean cruise for my souvenir. And a nanny to mind the kids on board, so the missus and meself could drink cocktails outa coconuts in peace.'

'California,' Bobby says. 'That's where I'd go. You can go round all the film studios, and have your dinner at restaurants where your woman Scarlett Johansson does be sitting at the next table—'

'Your mammy wouldn't have any of that,' Senan tells him. 'She'll want to go to Lourdes, or Medjugorje.'

'We'll do the lot,' Bobby says. His colour is up. 'Feck it, why not? My mammy's eighty-one, how many more chances will she have?'

'And this drought can go and shite,' Sonny says, on a rising burst of exuberance. 'Bring it on, hah? If there's no grass and no hay, I'll buy in the best feed, and my cattle can eat like lords all year round. In a brand-new barn.'

'Jesus, will you listen to this fella,' Mart says. 'Have you no sense of romance, boyo? Get yourself an aul' Lamborghini, and a Russian supermodel to ride in it with you.'

'A barn'll last longer. A Lamborghini'd be bolloxed in a year, on these roads.'

'So would a Russian supermodel,' says Dessie, snickering.

'The Lamborghini's for your road trip across America,' Mart explains. 'Or Brazil, or Nepal, or wherever puts a glint in your eye. I wouldn't say the roads in Nepal are much better than ours, mind you.'

Johnny is laughing, topping up Bobby's whiskey, but Trey catches his watchful eye on Mart. He's trying to figure out whether the encouragement is sincere, or whether Mart is playing at something. Obviously he remembers this much, at least: Mart Lavin is always playing at something.

He remembers Francie, too. Francie is saying nothing, but Johnny leaves him to it without so much as a glance. Francie doesn't like being nudged, even a little.

Trey adjusts her thoughts on her father. With her, he's so ham-fisted he doesn't even realise it, but with other people he's deft. Scuppering his plan is likely to be harder than she thought. Trey has little practice trying to be deft with anyone.

'I'd have the finest ram in this country,' PJ says with decision. 'I'd have that young fella from the Netherlands that went for four hundred grand.'

'Sure, you'd have no need to wear yourself out raising sheep any more,' Mart tells him. 'You could just sit back and watch the gold pop up outa your land. With a butler bringing you food on toothpicks.'

'Jesus, hold your horses there, lads,' Johnny says, raising his hands, grinning. 'I'm not saying ye'll be millionaires. We won't know how much is in there till we start looking. It might be enough for butlers and road trips, or it might only be enough for a week in Lanzarote. Don't be getting ahead of yourselves.'

'I'd have the sheep anyway,' PJ tells Mart, after some thought. 'I'm used to them, like.'

'We'd have all the newspapers coming down here,' Dessie says. The thought makes him glow a bit, all over his baldy head. Dessie, as Mrs Duggan's son and Noreen's husband, has always been one step away from the centre of things. 'And the lads off the telly, and the radio. To interview us, like.'

'You'd make a mint offa them,' Mart tells him. 'They'd all buy their lunches outa your missus's shop. They'd be Dubs, sure. The Dubs would never think of bringing their own sandwiches.'

'Would I have to be interviewed?' PJ asks, worried. 'I never done that before.'

'I'd do it,' Bobby says.

'If you go shiteing on about aliens on national telly,' Senan tells him, 'I'll take a fuckin' hurley to you.'

'Hang on a fuckin' second here,' Sonny says. 'What do we need this plastic Paddy fella for, at all? If there's gold on my land, I'll dig it up myself. I don't need some eejit walking off with half the profit. And singing "Come Out Ye Black and Tans" at my cattle while he does it.'

'You haven't a clue where to look, sure,' Johnny points out. 'Are you going to dig up every acre you've got?'

'You can tell us.'

'I could, but it'd do you no good. There's laws. You can't use machinery, unless you've a licence from the government; you'd be digging away with nothing but your bare hands and a spade. And even if you found gold, you wouldn't be allowed to sell it. Young Con here might be happy enough to make the lot into brooches for his missus, but I'd say the rest of us want something more to show for it.'

'I've farmed my land my whole life,' Francie says. 'And my father and my grandfather before me. I never seen or heard of a single speck of gold. Never once.'

Francie has a deep voice that lands heavily in the room. It leaves a ripple of silence.

'I found an aul' coin in the back field, one time,' Bobby says. 'With your woman Victoria on it. That was silver, though.'

'What feckin' use is that?' Senan demands. 'If your man goes panning in the river, he'll find himself a whole, what d'you call it, a seam of shillings, is it?'

'Fuck off. I'm only saying—'

'D'you know what'd be mighty? If you only said nothing till you've something to say.'

'Did you ever find any gold?' Francie asks the room. 'Any one of ye?'

'You mightn't know, sure,' Con says. 'It might be deeper down than we'd be ploughing.'

'I don't be ploughing at all,' Mart points out obligingly. 'The whole of King Solomon's mines could be under my land, and I wouldn't have a bull's notion. And how hard do any of ye look at the dirt you plough up? Are ye inspecting every inch of it for nuggets, are ye? Come to that, would any of ye know a nugget if it was handed to ye on a plate?'

'I'd look,' Con says, and reddens when their grins turn towards him. 'Sometimes. Not for gold, like. In case I'd find something, only. You'd hear stories about people finding mad yokes, Viking coins—'

'You're a fuckin' sap,' his brother tells him.

'Didja ever find any gold?' Francie repeats.

'Not gold,' Con admits. 'Bits of pottery, but. And a knife one time, an old one, like, handmade—'

'Now,' Francie says, to the rest of them. 'Indiana Jones here found nothing. There's no gold.'

'The fish outa that river,' PJ says, having thought it over long enough to reach a solid opinion, 'are the same as any other fish.'

'Lads,' Johnny says, with a slow grin that blooms with mischief. 'Let's get something straight. I'm not guaranteeing the gold is where your man thinks it is. It might be, or then again, it might not. What I'm saying is, the bold Cillian has no doubt it's there.'

'His granny was a Feeney, sure,' Senan points out. 'The Feeneys'd believe anything.'

'Ah, now, hang on,' says Bobby, offended.

'Sure, you believe there's UFOs up the mountains—'

'I don't *believe* in them. I *seen* them. D'you believe in your sheep?'

'I believe in the prices they fetch. When you bring an alien into the mart and get six quid a kilo for it, then I'll—'

'Hold your whisht, the pair of ye,' says Francie. 'Maybe the bold Cillian has no doubts, but I have. He'll paddle about in the river and find fuck-all, and then he'll go off home to cry into his pint of porter. And that'll be the end of it. What the fuck are we here for?'

All of them are looking at Johnny. 'Well,' he says, with mischief lifting the corners of his mouth again. 'If Mr Rushborough wants gold, then we'll have to make sure he finds gold.'

There's a silence. Trey finds herself unsurprised. She resents this: it makes her feel too much her father's daughter. Cal's Alyssa, whom Trey has come to like, would have been at least a little shocked to hear this out of nowhere.

After a moment of stillness, the men move again. Sonny reaches for the whiskey bottle; Dessie stubs out his cigarette and rummages for a new one. Mart is leaning back in the armchair with a rollie in one hand and a glass in the other, enjoying himself. They wait, before coming out with anything at all, for Johnny to say more.

'I know the spot in the river where he wants to do his panning,' Johnny says. 'He's dying to believe in this; all he needs is a sniff of it, and he'll be off like a fuckin' greyhound.'

'Have you got a few handfuls of gold lying around spare, have you?' Mart inquires.

'Jesus, man,' Johnny says, holding up his hands, 'cool the jets. Who's talking about handfuls? We'll give him a wee little sprinkle of the stuff here and there, is all. Just enough to make him happy. A coupla grand's worth, only, at today's prices.'

'And you've got a coupla grand lying around spare?'

'Not any more. I'm after investing it into Rushborough's mining company, that he's set up to get the licences and all. If each of ye puts in three hundred quid, that oughta do it.'

The room smells of smoke. In the smudgy yellow light, shadows shift on the men's faces as they tilt their glasses, hitch at their waistbands, glance briefly at each other and away again.

'What do you get out of it?' Senan asks.

'I'll get a cut of anything Rushborough finds,' Johnny says. 'And twenty percent of anything he pays you. Finder's fee.'

'So you'll be getting a cut on each side. Whatever happens.'

'I will, yeah. Without me, ye'd be getting nothing and neither would Rushborough. And I've put my money where my mouth is already. I'm after investing more than the lot of ye put together; I want that back, whether there's gold there or no. If it wasn't that ye're putting in a bit as well, I'd be asking fifty percent of whatever he gives you.'

'Fuck me,' Sonny says. 'No wonder you won't say where the gold is.'

'I'm the middleman,' Johnny says. 'That's what a middleman does. I'm delighted to help all of ye towards your barns and your cruises, but I'm not in this outa the goodness of my heart. I've a family to look after. That child over there could do with a home that's not falling to bits, and maybe a dacent pair of shoes while she's at it. Are you telling me to pass that up so you can put better rims on that Lamborghini?'

'What's to stop you pocketing our few grand and skedaddling off into the sunset?' Mart inquires with interest. 'And leaving us with nothing to show for it but an annoyed tourist? If your man Rushwhatsit exists at all.'

Johnny stares at him. Mart looks cheerfully back. After a moment, Johnny gives a short chagrined laugh and sits back, shaking his head.

'Mart Lavin,' he says. 'Is this because my daddy bet you at cards back in the last century? Are you still sore about that?'

'A card cheat's a terrible thing,' Mart explains. 'I'd rather have dealings with a murderer than a card cheat, any day. A man could become a killer by happenstance, if his day didn't go to plan, but there's no such thing as an accidental card cheat.'

'When I've a bitta free time,' Johnny says, 'I'll be happy to defend my daddy's skill at cards. That man could read your hand from one twitch of your eyelid. But' – he aims a finger at Mart – 'I'm not getting myself sucked into one of your arguments tonight. We've a business opportunity here, and it's not one that'll last forever. Are you in or are you out?'

'You're the one that started in jibber-jabbering about your daddy and his spare aces,' Mart points out. 'I'd a question. A legitimate question.'

'Ah, for fuck's sake,' Johnny says, exasperated. 'Lookit: I won't lay a finger on the cash. Ye can buy the gold yourselves – I'll tell ye what type we'll need, and I'll show ye where to get it and where to sow it. D'you feel better now?'

'Oh, begod, I do,' Mart says, smiling at him. 'That's done me a power of good.'

'And ye can meet Rushborough yourselves, before ye ever put your hands in your pockets. I'm after telling him already that ye'll want to look him over before ye let him on your land, see if ye like the cut of him. That gave him a laugh – he thinks ye're a bunch of muck savages that don't know how a deal's done in the real world – but sure, that's all to the good, amn't I right?' Johnny smiles around the room. No one is smiling back at him. 'He'll be here the day after tomorrow. I'll bring him down to Seán Óg's that night, and ye can decide if he looks real enough for you.'

'Where'll he be staying?' Mart inquires. 'Here on that luxury sofa, is it? For the local atmosphere?'

Johnny laughs. 'Ah, God, no. I'd say he would, if he'd no other choice. The man's desperate to get his hands on that gold. But Sheila's cooking wouldn't be what he's used to. He's found himself a wee cottage over towards Knockfarraney – Rory Dunne's mammy's old place, at the foot of the mountain. They have it on Airbnb since the mammy died.'

'How long'll he be here?'

Johnny shrugs. 'That depends, sure. I'll tell you one thing: once ye've had a look at him, ye can't be hemming and hawing any longer. We'll need to get that gold into the river. I can keep Rushborough distracted for a few days showing him the sights, but after that, he'll want to go panning. First thing Tuesday morning, I'll need to know who's in and who's out.'

'And what happens after?' Francie Gannon demands. 'When he finds nothing on our land?'

'Ah, God, Francie,' Johnny says, shaking his head tolerantly, 'you're an awful pessimist, d'you know that? Maybe his granny was right all the way, and he'll find enough to make us all millionaires. Or' – he raises a hand as Francie starts to say something – 'or maybe his granny was half right: the gold goes through your land, but it never made it as far down as the river, or it's after washing away. So when Rushborough goes panning in the river, instead of finding nothing and giving up, he'll find our little biteen, and go digging on your land. And then he'll find enough to make us all millionaires.'

'And maybe I'll shite diamonds. What happens if he doesn't?'

'Grand, so,' Johnny says, with a sigh. 'Let's say, only because you're never happy unless you're miserable, let's say there's not a speck of gold anywhere in this county. Rushborough'll make himself a fine tie pin, with a harp and a shamrock on it, outa the bit we put in the river. He'll reckon the rest is stuck under this mountain somewhere, too deep for him to get at. And he'll go off back to England to show off his bitta heritage to his pals, and tell them all about his adventures on the old sod. He'll be only delighted with himself. And ye'll all be a grand or two richer, and so will I. That's the worst-case scenario. Is that so terrible that you're going to sit there all night with a puss on you?'

Trey watches the men turn this over in their minds. They watch each other as they do it, and Johnny watches them all watching. Every trace of the nervousness Trey saw in him earlier is gone. He's spread in his chair, as easy as the king of the mountain, smiling benevolently, giving them all the time they need.

They're not dishonest men, or anyway not what they or Trey would consider dishonest. Not one of them would ever rob so much as a packet of mints from Noreen's, and between any of them, a spit and a handshake would be as solid as a legal contract. An Englishman wanting to reap from their land falls under different rules.

'Let's see your man Rushborough,' Senan says. 'I want a look at this fella. Then we'll see what we're at.'

There are nods from the other men. 'That's settled, so,' Johnny says. 'I'll bring him down to Seán Óg's on Monday night, and ye can see what you think of him. Don't be ripping the piss outa the poor lad, is all I ask. He's used to highfalutin types; he wouldn't be able for ye at all, at all.'

'Ah, musha, God love him,' Dessie says.

'We'll be gentle,' Mart assures Johnny. 'He won't feel a thing.'

'Like fuck ye will,' Sonny says. 'I wouldn't bring that poor bastard anywhere near this shower, if I was you. D'you know what a few of them did to my Yank cousin? They told him Leanne Healy's young one fancied him – Sarah, the good-looking one with the arse on her—'

'Mind your tongue,' Senan says to Sonny, tilting his head at Trey, but he's started to chuckle, remembering. All of them have. The gold, by unanimous agreement, is no longer a subject for discussion. It's a thing to be turned over in private, until Rushborough comes.

'Go on outa that, now,' Johnny says to Trey. 'It's past your bedtime.'

Johnny wouldn't know what Trey's bedtime was even if she had one, which she doesn't. He's just got no more use for her tonight, and he wants to let the men relax into conversations they won't have with her there. She unfurls herself from her corner and picks her way between outstretched legs, saying good night politely to the men, who nod as she passes.

'Are you not going to give your daddy a hug?' Johnny asks, smiling up at her and reaching out an arm.

Trey leans over to him, puts one hand stiffly on his back, and lets him wrap his arm around her and give her a playful little shake. She holds her breath to keep out his spice-and-cigarettes smell. 'Look at you,' he says, laughing up into her face and ruffling her hair. 'Getting too big and dignified to hug your aul' daddy good night.'

'Night,' Trey says, straightening up. She wants a look at Rushborough, too.

5

Cal spends the next morning dicking around in his house, waiting for Mart to show up. He has no doubt that Mart will in fact show up, so there's no point in getting his teeth into anything serious. Instead he does dishes and wipes various stuff that looks like it could use it, with one eye on the window.

He could dick around in his vegetable patch instead, and let Mart come talk to him there, but he wants to invite Mart in. It's been a long time since Mart's been in this house. This was by Cal's choice: what happened to Brendan Reddy lies between them, cold and heavy. Cal accepted the boundaries Mart drew around it – he doesn't ask for names, he keeps his mouth shut, he keeps Trey's mouth shut, and everyone gets to live happy ever after – but he wasn't going to let Mart pretend it away. But the Johnny Reddy situation – Cal is starting to think of it as a situation – means that, regardless of how little he likes it, things need to shift.

Mart shows up halfway through the morning, smiling up at Cal on the doorstep like he comes over every day. 'Come on in,' Cal says. 'Outa the heat.'

If Mart's surprised, he doesn't show it. 'And why not, sure,' he says, knocking the dirt off his boots. His face and arms are burned a rough red-brown; under the sleeves of his green polo shirt, edges of white show where the sunburn stops. He rolls up his straw hat and stuffs it in a pocket.

'The mansion's looking well,' he observes, glancing around. 'That lamp adds a touch of style. Was that Lena?'

'Can I get you some coffee?' Cal asks. 'Tea?' He's been here long enough to know that tea is appropriate regardless of the weather.

'Ah, no. I'm grand.'

Cal has also been here long enough that he knows better than to take this as a refusal. 'I was gonna make some anyway,' he says. 'You might as well join me.'

'Go on, then; I can't let a man drink alone. I'll have a cuppa tea.'

Cal switches on the electric kettle and finds mugs. 'Another hot one,' he says.

'If this keeps up,' Mart says, taking a chair and arranging himself around his worst joints, 'I'll have to start selling off my flock because I haven't the grass to feed them. And come spring, the lamb crop'll be fuckin' atrocious. Meanwhile, what are them eejits on the telly showing? Pictures of childer ating ice creams.'

'The kids are a lot cuter than you are,' Cal points out.

'True enough,' Mart concedes, with a cackle. 'But them telly lads give me the sick all the same. Going on about the climate change as if it's news, big shocked faces on them. They coulda asked any farmer, any time these last twenty year: the summers aren't the same as what they were. They turned tricky on us, and they've only got trickier. And meanwhile all them fools are lying on the beaches, burning the pasty arses off themselves, like it's the greatest thing that ever happened to them.'

'What do the old guys reckon? It gonna break soon?'

'Mossie O'Halloran says it'll be lashing rain by the end of the month, and Tom Pat Malone says it won't break till September. Sure, how would they have any notion? This weather's like a dog that's turned rogue: you wouldn't know what it's capable of.'

Cal brings the tea stuff and a packet of chocolate chip cookies over to the table. Mart adds lavish amounts of milk and sugar and stretches out his legs with a luxurious sigh, putting the weather aside and settling in for the main business of the day.

'Will I tell you what never ceases to amaze me about this townland?' he asks. 'The level of feckin' eejitry.'

'This to do with Johnny Reddy?' Cal asks.

'That lad,' Mart informs him, 'would bring out the eejit in Einstein. I don't know how he does it, at all. 'Tis a gift.' He takes his time choosing a cookie, to build up the suspense. 'Guess what he's after picking up in London,' he says. 'Go on, guess.'

'A social disease,' Cal says. Johnny doesn't bring out his best side, either.

'More than likely, but as well as that. Johnny's after finding himself a Sassenach. Not a bit on the side, now; a man. Some plastic Paddy with a loada cash and a loada rosemantic notions about his granny's homeland. And Paddy Englishman's got it in his head that there's gold all through our fields, just waiting for him to come along and dig it up.'

Cal came up with a large number of possibilities for Johnny's bright idea, but this wasn't among them. 'What the fuck?' he says.

'That was my first thought, all right,' Mart agrees. 'He got the story offa his granny. She was a Feeney. The Feeneys are a terrible lot for getting ideas into their heads.'

'And she figured there was *gold* around here?'

'More like her granddaddy said his granddaddy said his granddaddy said there was. But Paddy Englishman took it as gospel, and now he wants to pay us for the chance to sniff it out. Or so Johnny says, anyhow.'

Cal's instinct is to automatically disbelieve in anything that comes out of Johnny Reddy, but he's aware that even a career bullshitter could accidentally stumble across something that has substance. 'You're the geology expert,' he says. 'Any chance it's true?'

Mart picks a cookie crumb out of a tooth. 'That's the mad part, now,' he says. 'I wouldn't rule it out altogether. There's been gold found in the mountains up on the border, not too far from here. And the bottom of this mountain, where the two different kinds of rock rub up against each other, that's the kind of spot where you'd get gold being melted by the friction and pushed up towards the surface, all right. And there's an aul' riverbed, sure enough, that coulda brought the gold down through all our land to the river beyond the village, once upon a time. It could be true.'

'Or it could be just the Feeneys and their ideas,' Cal says.

'More than likely,' Mart agrees. 'We pointed that out to the bold Johnny, but it didn't faze him one bit. He's one step ahead of the likes of you and me, d'you see. He wants us to bunce in three hundred quid each and buy a bitta gold to sprinkle in the river, so Paddy Englishman'll think it's popping outa the fields like dande-lions, and give us a grand or two each to let him take samples on our land.'

Even after only a few minutes' acquaintance with Johnny, Cal can't find it in himself to be surprised. 'And then what?' he says. 'If there's no gold in the samples?'

'Francie Gannon inquired about the very same thing,' Mart says. 'Great minds think alike, hah? According to Johnny, Paddy Englishman won't see anything amiss about that at all, at all. He'll prance off home with his pinch of gold, and we'll all live happily ever after. I wouldn't insult Sheila Reddy's virtue, but I don't know where that child got her brains from, because she got none from her daddy.'

'So you're not gonna get involved,' Cal says.

Mart tilts his head noncommittally. 'Ah, I didn't say that, now. I'm having a great aul' time, so I am. This is the best entertainment that's come to town in years. It'd almost be worth throwing in the few bob, just to have a front-row seat.'

'Get Netflix,' Cal says. 'Cheaper.'

'I've got the Netflix. There's never anything on it, only Liam Neeson battering people with snowploughs, and sure he's only from up the road. What else am I going to spend my life savings on? Silk velvet boxers?'

'You're gonna give Johnny three hundred bucks?'

'I am in my arse. That flimflam merchant's not getting his hands on a penny of mine. But I might go in with the other lads to buy the bitta gold. For the crack, like.'

'They're gonna do it?' Cal asks. This doesn't jibe with what he knows of Ardnakelty people, or of their views on Reddys. 'All of them?'

'I wouldn't say all of them. Not for definite. They're wary – specially Senan and Francie. But they haven't said no. And the more of them that say yes, the more the rest won't want to miss their chance.'

'Huh,' Cal says.

Mart watches him wryly, over his mug. 'You thought they'd have better sense, hah?'

'I didn't think those guys would put money on Johnny Reddy's say-so.'

Mart leans back in his chair and takes a pleasurable slurp of his tea. 'Like I'm after telling you,' he says, 'Johnny's got a great gift for bringing out the eejitry in people. Sheila was no eejit, sure, till he came sniffing around, and now look at her. But 'tis more than that. What you haveta keep in mind about every man jack in this townland, Sunny Jim, is that he's the one that stayed put. Some of us wanted to and some didn't, but once you've got the land, you're going nowhere. 'Tis all you can do to find someone to mind the farm for a week while you head for Tenerife to admire a few bikinis.'

'You can sell land,' Cal says. 'Lena sold hers.'

Mart snorts. 'That's not the same at all, at all. She's a woman, and that wasn't her land, 'twas her husband's. I'd sell my own kidneys before I'd sell my family's land; my father'd come outa the grave and take the head off me. But we can go the whole year round without seeing a new face, or a new place, or doing anything we haven't done all our lives. Meanwhile we've all got brothers WhatsApping us photos of wallabies, or posting on Facebook how they're baptising childer in the jungles of Brazil.' He smiles at Cal. 'It doesn't bother me, sure. When I get to feeling restless, I do a bitta reading about something new, to keep my mind on an even keel.'

'Geology,' Cal says.

'Sure, that was years ago. These days I do be looking into the Ottoman Empire. They were some boyos, them Ottomans. You'd want to get up early to take them on.' Mart adds an extra half-spoon of sugar to his tea. 'But some of the lads haven't got the same resources. They balance along grand most of the time – they're used to it, sure. But we're all a wee bit off-kilter, this summer, waking up every morning to fields that need rain worse and worse and aren't getting it. We're on edge, is what we are; our balance is upsetted already. And then along comes the bold Johnny, prancing in here with his stories about film stars and millionaires and gold.' He tastes the tea and nods. 'Look at PJ, now, over the wall. Do you reckon he's got the resources to keep his mind on an even keel when Johnny's offering him the sun, moon, and stars?'

'PJ seems pretty down-to-earth to me,' Cal says.

'No harm to PJ,' Mart says. 'He's a fine man. But he's worn to a frazzle, fretting day and night about what he's going to feed his sheep if this weather doesn't break, and he's got nothing else in his head to distract him when he needs a bit of a rest from that. No wallabies and no Ottomans, only the same aul' life he's had since he was born. And now Johnny's after bringing him something brand-new and shiny. PJ's bedazzled, and why wouldn't he be?'

'I guess,' Cal says.

'And even the rest of them, that mightn't be as easily bedazzled as PJ: they're allured, is what they are. They've got a bad case of allurement.'

'Fair enough,' Cal says. He doesn't feel he's in a position to judge them for that. He supposes what brought him to Ardnakelty could be described, from some angles, as a bad case of allurement. That got knocked out of him good and hard. The landscape still holds the power to bedazzle him, simply and wholly, but when it comes to everything else about the place, he sees too many of its layers for that. He and it have reached an equilibrium, amicable even if not particularly trusting, maintained with care and a certain amount of caution on all sides. All the same, taking everything into account, he can't bring himself to regret following where that allurement led him.

'And here's the thing of it,' Mart says, pointing the spoon at Cal. 'Who's to say they're wrong? You're sitting there thinking PJ's a fool for getting mixed up with Johnny, but even if Paddy English-man was to change his mind about the samples, maybe 'tis well worth the few hundred quid to PJ, to have something new to think about for a while. The same as it's worth it to me for the entertainment. Maybe it'll do him a lot more good than spending that money on a psychologist who'd tell him he's suffering from stress because his mammy took him outa nappies too early. Who's to say?'

'You're the one that was calling them all a bunch of eejits, five minutes ago, for wanting to get involved,' Cal reminds him.

Mart wags the spoon at him vigorously. 'Ah, no. Not for getting involved. If they go into this the way they'd put a few bob on an outsider in the Grand National, there's no eejitry in that. But if they're believing they'll be millionaires, that's a different thing. That's eejitry. And that's where it could all go a bit pear-shaped.' He throws Cal a sharp glance. 'Your young one told them her teacher says the gold is there.'

Cal says, 'Trey was there? Last night?'

'Oh, she was. Sitting in the corner like a wee angel, not a peep outa her till she was spoken to.'

'Huh,' Cal says. He thinks less and less of his chances of making it through this summer without punching Johnny Reddy's teeth out. 'Well, if she says her teacher said that, he probably did.'

'A year or two back,' Mart says meditatively, 'that wouldn'ta made a blind bitta difference. But now there's plenty of people around here that reckon your young one's worth listening to. It's great what a mended table can do, hah?'

'She's not mine,' Cal says. 'And this gold story's got nothing to do with her.'

'Well, if you're feeling technical,' Mart acknowledges, 'she's not. And maybe it hasn't. But in the lads' minds, it has, and she's having an effect. Isn't that a turn-up for the books altogether? Who woulda thought a Reddy would ever have that much credit in this townland?'

'She's a good kid,' Cal says. He's clear that Mart is giving him a warning, although a delicate one, for now.

Mart is reaching for another cookie, absorbed in picking the one with the most chocolate chips. 'She doesn't go running around looking for trouble, anyway,' he agrees. 'That's a great thing.' He selects a cookie and dunks it in his tea. 'D'you know something? The things these lads have planned for the gold, if it shows up, would give you the pip. Cruises, and barns, and tours of Hollywood. There's not a one of them came up with a single iota of originality.'

'What're you gonna spend yours on?' Cal asks.

'I won't believe in that gold till I get my hands on it,' Mart says. 'But if I do, I'm telling you now, I won't be spending it on any feckin' Caribbean holiday. I might put in a space telescope on my roof, or get myself a pet camel to keep the sheep company, or a hot-air balloon to bring me into town. Watch this space, boyo.'

While he listens to Mart, one part of Cal's mind has been picturing the wandering line Johnny is talking about, from the foot of the mountain through all those men's land to the river. 'If there's gold on your land and PJ's,' he says, 'it's gotta run through my back field.'

'I was thinking the same, all right,' Mart agrees. 'Imagine that: you mighta planted them tomatoes on a gold mine. I wonder will they taste any different.'

'So why didn't Johnny invite me along last night?'

Mart slants a look towards Cal. 'I'd say this is some class of fraud, what Johnny's got planned for Paddy Englishman. You'd know better than I would.'

'Not my department,' Cal says.

'If you were planning anything that might be fraud, would you invite a Guard along?'

'I'm a carpenter,' Cal says. 'If I'm anything.'

Mart's eyebrows twitch at an amused angle. 'A Guard and a blow-in. Johnny doesn't know you the way I do, sure. You've a dacent respect for the way things are done here, and you can keep your mouth shut, when that's the wisest thing to do. But he doesn't know that.'

That answers the question of why Johnny came running over to Cal's place to shoot the breeze before he even got his stuff unpacked. Not to check out the guy who was hanging around his kid; to find out whether the ex-cop was the kind who would screw with his scam.

Cal says, before he plans to say it, 'He'd know it if you vouched for me.'

Mart's eyebrows leap. 'What's this, now, Sunny Jim? Are you looking to get in on the action? I wouldn'ta had you down as the prospecting type.'

'I'm full of surprises,' Cal says.

'Are you getting restless already, or have you been turning up gold nuggets with the parsnips?'

'Like you said. There's nothing on Netflix.'

'For God's sake don't be telling me Johnny Reddy's after bringing out the eejitry in you, as well. I've enough of that to be dealing with. You're not feeling an urge to dust off the aul' badge and haul the bold fraudsters up to the Guards by the scruffs of their necks, now, are you?'

'Nope,' Cal says. 'Just reckon if my land's involved anyway, I might as well find out what's going on.'

Mart scratches meditatively at a bug bite on his neck and considers Cal. Cal looks back at him. All his gut rebels against asking Mart Lavin for favours, and he's pretty sure Mart knows that.

'You want entertainment,' he points out, 'watching Johnny try to figure out what to do about me oughta up the ante.'

'That's a fact,' Mart acknowledges. 'But I wouldn't want him getting an attack of nerves and whisking Paddy Englishman away from under our noses before things have a chance to get interesting. That'd be a waste.'

'I won't make any sudden moves,' Cal says. 'He'll hardly know I'm there.'

'You're great at being harmless, all right,' Mart says, smiling at Cal so that his whole face crinkles up engagingly, 'when you want to be. All right, so. Let you come down to Seán Óg's tomorrow night, when Johnny's bringing Paddy Englishman in for inspection, and we'll see where we get. Is that fair enough?'

'Sounds good,' Cal says. 'Thanks.'

'Don't be thanking me,' Mart says. 'I'd say I'm doing you no favours, getting you mixed up with that fella's nonsense.' He drains his tea and stands up, unsticking his joints one by one. 'What'll you spend your millions on?'

'Caribbean cruise sounds good,' Cal says.

Mart laughs and tells him to get away to fuck with that, and stumps out the door, pulling his straw hat down over his fluff of hair. Cal puts away the cookies and takes the mugs over to the sink to wash them out. It occurs to him to wonder why Mart decided to tell a Guard and a blow-in about a plan that might be fraud; unless, for reasons of his own, he wanted Cal on board.

The main talent Cal has discovered in himself, since coming to Ardnakelty, is a broad and restful capacity for letting things be. At first this sat uneasily alongside his ingrained instinct to fix things, but over time they've fallen into a balance: he keeps the fixing instinct mainly turned towards solid objects, like his house and people's furniture, and leaves other things the room to fix themselves. The Johnny Reddy situation isn't something that he can leave be. It doesn't feel like something that needs fixing, though, either. It feels both more delicate and more volatile than that: something that needs watching, in case it catches and runs wild.

———

Trey has to go to the shop for her mam because Maeve is a lick-arse. It's Maeve's turn, but she's snuggled up on the sofa with their dad, asking one stupid question after another about the Formula 1 on the telly, and hanging off his answers like they're the secret of the universe. When their mam told her to go, she pouted up at their dad, and he laughed and said, 'Ah, sure, leave the child be. We're happy here, aren't we, Maeveen? What's the big emergency?' So, since the emergency is that they have nothing in for the dinner, Trey is trudging down to the village dragging a wheeled shopping trolley behind her. She doesn't even have Banjo for company: she left him sprawled on the coolest part of the kitchen floor, panting pathetically, rolling an agonised eye at her when she snapped her fingers to him.

Trey dislikes going to the shop. Up until a year or two back, Noreen used to stare her out of it whenever she went in, and Trey robbed something every time Noreen shifted the glare away to serve a customer. These days Trey generally pays for the things she wants, and Noreen nods to her and asks after her mam, but occasionally Trey still robs something, just to keep the parameters clear.

She has no intention of robbing anything today; she just wants to buy potatoes and bacon and whatever other shite is on the list in her pocket, and go home. By now Noreen will have extracted every detail of last night from Dessie, with ruthless expertise, and will be on the hunt for more. Trey doesn't want to talk about any of it. The men stayed late into the night, getting louder and louder as they got drunker, and laughing in great eruptions that brought Alanna stumbling into Trey's room, confused and scared, to climb in with her and breathe wetly on the back of her neck. Johnny has them eating out of his hand. Trey is starting to feel like a fool for ever thinking she could do anything about any of them.

Noreen – of course – has company. Doireann Cunniffe is nestled up to the counter, where she can lean in to Noreen to catch every word first, and Tom Pat Malone is settled well into the corner chair that Noreen keeps for people who need a rest before they start home. Mrs Cunniffe is little and excitable, with funny teeth and a head that sticks forward, and she wears pink cardigans even in this heat. Tom Pat is a curled scrap of a man, well into his eighties, who can tell the weather and is the hereditary possessor of a recipe for wool-fat salve that cures everything from eczema to rheumatism. He was named after his grandfathers and has to be called by both names in order to avoid offending either, even though they've both been dead for fifty years. Mrs Cunniffe has a packet of boring biscuits on the counter and Tom Pat has the Sunday paper on his lap, to add legitimacy to their presence, but neither of them is there to buy things. Trey keeps her head down and starts collecting what she needs. She is under no illusion that she's going to get out of here easily.

'Begod, Noreen, 'tis like Galway station here today,' Tom Pat says. 'Is there anyone in this townland that hasn't been in to you?'

'They're only following your good example, sure,' Noreen points out smartly. She's dusting shelves – Noreen is never not doing something. 'How's your daddy today, Theresa?'

'Grand,' Trey says, finding ham slices.

'Jesus, Mary and Joseph, it's well for some. He must have a head made of titanium. What were they drinking, at all? I asked Dessie, but he couldn't turn his head on the pillow to answer me.'

Mrs Cunniffe giggles breathily. Trey shrugs.

Noreen shoots her a sharp bird-glance, over one shoulder. 'He was talking plenty when he came in, but, God help us all. Four in the morning, it was, and him shaking me outa the bed to tell me some mad story about gold nuggets and beg me to make him a fry-up.'

'Didja make it for him?' Tom Pat inquires.

'I did not. He got a piece of toast and an earful about waking the kids, is what he got. Come here, Theresa: is it true, what he said, or was it just the drink talking? There's some English fella coming to dig up gold on everyone's land?'

'Yeah,' Trey says. 'He's rich. His granny came from round here. She told him there was gold.'

'Holy Mary, mother a the divine,' Mrs Cunniffe breathes, clasping her cardigan together. ''Tis like a film. Honest to God, I'd palpitations when I heard. And will I tell you something awful strange? Friday night, I dreamed I found a gold coin in my kitchen sink. Just lying there, like. My granny always said the second sight ran in our—'

'That'll be ating cheese too late at night,' Noreen advises her. 'Once we had a baked Camembert at Christmas, and I dreamed I was after turning into a llama in a zoo, and I was annoyed 'cause my good shoes wouldn't fit on the hooves. Leave the cheese alone and you'll be grand. Now, Theresa' – Noreen abandons her dusting to lean over the counter and point the duster at Trey – 'did your daddy say who this fella's granny was?'

'Nah,' Trey says. 'Don't think he knows.' She can't see the jam they normally get. She grabs some weird-looking apricot thing instead.

'That's men for you,' Noreen says. 'A woman woulda thought to ask. Myself and Dymphna, that's Mrs Duggan, we spent half the morning trying to get it straight who she mighta been. Dymphna reckons she musta been Bridie Feeney from across the river, that went over to London before the Emergency. She never wrote back. Dymphna says her mammy always thought Bridie had gone over to have a baba and was hiding the shame, but I suppose it might be that she just didn't bother her arse writing at first, and then she married some fancy doctor and got too many notions to write to the likes of us. Or both,' she adds, struck by the idea. 'The baba first, and then the doctor.'

'Bridie Feeney's sister was married to my uncle,' Tom Pat says. 'I was only a wee little lad when she went off, but they always said she'd do well for herself. She was that kind. She coulda married a doctor, all right.'

'I know Anne Marie Dolan,' Mrs Cunniffe says triumphantly, 'whose mammy was a Feeney. Bridie woulda been her great-aunt. I rang Anne Marie straightaway, as soon as I got my breath back, didn't I, Noreen? She says neither her granddad nor her mammy ever said a word to her about any gold. Not a peep outa them. Would you credit that?'

'I would,' Tom Pat says. 'I'd say that's only typical. Anne Marie's granddad was aul' Mick Feeney, and Mick had no use for girls. He thought they were awful talkers, the lot of them, couldn't hold their water – no harm to the present company.' He smiles around at them all. Mrs Cunniffe titters. 'And he'd only daughters. I'd say he told no one, and waited for Anne Marie's young lad to get old enough that he could pass it on. Only didn't Mick take a heart attack and die, before he got the chance.'

'And no surprise to anyone but himself,' Noreen says tartly. 'I heard his back room was that full of bottles, they had to get a skip in. No wonder he never done nothing about the gold. He'd other things to keep him occupied.'

'And if it wasn't for this English chap,' Mrs Cunniffe says, a hand to her face, 'the secret woulda been lost and gone forever. And us walking over the gold our whole lives, without a notion.'

'That's what you get when people do nothing,' Noreen says. Having stood still for as long as she's capable of, she goes back to her dusting. 'God knows how many generations of Feeneys, every one of them doing feck-all about that gold. At least this English lad got sense enough from somewhere to do something. About feckin' time.'

'You'll be meeting this English chap, won't you, Theresa?' Mrs Cunniffe asks, edging closer to Trey. 'Would you ever ask him if there's any of it in our bitta land? Noreen was telling me it's in the river, and sure we're only a few yards away. I couldn't be digging myself, my back does be at me something terrible, but Joe's a great man for the digging. He'd have the garden up in no time.'

Somewhere on its way down the mountain, the gold has apparently turned from a possibility into a solid thing. Trey isn't sure what she thinks of this.

She dumps her shopping on the counter and adds a packet of crisps, as her fee for taking Maeve's turn. 'And twenty Marlboro,' she says.

'You're too young to be smoking,' Noreen tells her.

'For my dad.'

'I suppose,' Noreen concedes, throwing her one more suspicious glance and turning to get the cigarettes. 'Cal'd malavogue you if he smelled smoke off you. Remember that.'

'Yeah,' Trey says. She wants to leave.

'Come here to me, *a chailín*,' Tom Pat orders Trey, beckoning. 'I'd come to you, only I used up all the strength in my legs getting here. Come over and let me have a look at you.'

Trey leaves Noreen to ring up the shopping and goes to him. Tom Pat takes hold of her wrist, to bend her down so he can see her – his eyes are filmed over. He smells like a hot shed.

'You're the spit of your daddo,' he tells her. 'Your mammy's daddy. He was a fine man.'

'Yeah,' Trey says. 'Thanks.' Her granddad died before she was born. Her mam doesn't talk about him much.

'Tell me something, now,' Tom Pat says. 'Yourself and that Yankee fella up at O'Shea's place. Do ye ever make rocking chairs?'

'Sometimes,' Trey says.

'I fancy a rocking chair,' Tom Pat explains, 'for in front of the fire, in the winter. I do be thinking about the winter an awful lot, these days, to keep myself cool. Would ye ever make me one? A small one, now, so these little legs of mine can touch the ground.'

'Yeah,' Trey says. 'Sure.' She says yes to just about any work that comes their way. She's aware that, for government reasons she doesn't understand and doesn't care about, Cal isn't allowed to get a job here. One of her fears is that he won't make enough money to live on and he'll have to move back to America.

'Good girl yourself,' Tom Pat says, smiling up at her. His few teeth look as big as horses' teeth in his fallen mouth. 'Ye'll have to come down to me, now, to sort the ins and outs of it. I can't see to drive any more.'

'I'll say it to Cal,' Trey says. His hand is still around her wrist, loose bony fingers with a slow tremor shaking them.

'Your daddy's doing a great thing for all this townland,' Tom Pat tells her. 'A thing like this doesn't stop with a few diggers in a few fields. A few years from now, we won't know ourselves. And all because of your daddy. Are you proud of him, now?'

Trey says nothing. She can feel silence filling her up like pouring concrete.

'Sure, when did the childer ever appreciate their parents?' Mrs Cunniffe says with a sigh. 'They'll miss us when we're gone. But you tell your daddy from me, Theresa, he's a great man altogether.'

'Listen to me now, *a stór*,' Tom Pat says. 'D'you know our Brian? My Elaine's young lad. The redheaded fella.'

'Yeah,' Trey says. She doesn't like Brian. He was in Brendan's class. He used to wind Brendan up till Brendan lost his temper, and then run to the teacher. No one ever believed a Reddy.

'Your man, the Sassenach, he'll be needing someone to help him go scooping about in that river. Hah? He won't want to get his fine shoes wet.'

'Dunno,' Trey says.

'Brian's not a big lad, but he's strong,' Tom Pat says. 'And it'd do him good. All that lad needs is a bitta hard work, to get his head on straight. His mammy's too soft on him. You say that to your daddy, now.'

'Brian's not the only one that'll want that work,' Noreen puts in, unable to stay silent any longer. 'There's plenty of lads around here that'd only love to get a foot in the door there. My Jack'll be in the pub tomorrow night, now, Theresa. You tell your daddy to introduce him to that English fella.'

'I dunno if he even needs anyone,' Trey says. 'I never met him.'

'Don't be worrying about that. All you've to do is say it to your daddy. Can you remember that?'

All of them are focused on Trey with an intensity she's not used to. Everything feels very weird, like some crap old film where people's bodies get taken over by aliens. 'I've to go,' she says, moving her wrist out of Tom Pat's hand. 'My mam needs the dinner.'

'That'll be thirty-six eighty,' Noreen says, neatly backing off. 'Them cigarettes are awful dear. Would your daddy not try the vaping instead? I've Dessie on the vape yokes a year now, and he's off the cigarettes altogether – don't be giving me that look, I know what he was at last night, I've the use of my nose. But mostly.'

The shop bell dings cheerily and Richie Casey comes in, smelling of sheep shite and scraping his boots on the mat. 'Fuckin' roasting,' he says. 'The sheep'll be coming up and begging to be sheared, if the wool doesn't melt offa them first. How's it going, Theresa? How's your daddy?'

Richie Casey has never said a word to Trey before in her life. 'Grand,' she says, shoving her change into her pocket, and escapes before anyone can get even weirder.

It takes her most of the walk up the mountain to get her head clear and understand what's happening. All these people want something from her. They need her help, the same way her dad needed her help last night.

Trey isn't used to anyone except her mam needing her help. What her mam needs is stuff like going to the shop or cleaning the bath, straightforward things about which Trey has no choice and which have no implications or consequences. This is different. All these people need her to do things for them that she can decide whether or not to do; things that, either way, have implications.

Trey has always preferred straightforward things. Her first instinct was to reject this new situation, but slowly, as she jolts the trolley behind her up the rocky path, it shifts in her mind. For one of the first times in her life, she has power.

She turns it over, testing the flavour. She's pretty sure Cal would consider her dad's plan, and her involvement in particular, to be a bad idea, but that doesn't seem relevant. Cal is separate. She doesn't waste much effort on wondering whether he'd be right, because he mostly is, and because it makes no difference.

The heat scorches the top of her head. Insects spin and whine above the heather. She remembers Tom Pat's fingers, frail and shaking, around her wrist, and Mrs Cunniffe's pop-eyes fixed on her hungrily. Instead of rejecting the situation, her mind moves to meet it. She doesn't know how yet, but she's going to use it.

6

Normally, on a Monday night, Seán Óg's would be close to deserted. Barty the barman would be leaning on the bar watching the racing on TV, having intermittent shreds of conversation with his scattering of daily communicants, old bachelors in faded shirts who come in from the far reaches of the townland to see another human face. A clump of them might be playing Fifty-Five, a card game to which Ardnakelty brings the level of ferocious dedication that Americans reserve for football, but that's as intense as the action would get. When Cal goes to the pub on Mondays, it's because he feels like having a pint in peace.

Tonight it's crammed. Word has spread, and everyone for miles around wants to check out Paddy Englishman. There are people in here whom Cal has never seen before, and who are either the wrong gender or decades younger than this place's usual clientele. Everyone is talking at once, and some people are wearing their going-out clothes. Bodies and excitement have turned the air so muggy that Cal feels like he's not breathing. He checks around for Lena, but she's not there. He didn't really expect her to be.

'Pint of Smithwick's,' he says to Barty, when he manages to reach the bar. 'You're doing some business tonight.'

'Jaysus, wouldja stop,' Barty says. His face is sweating. 'Hasn't been this packed since Dumbo's funeral. It's fuck-all good to me, but. Half of these are grannies or teenagers; they order one fuckin' sherry or a pint of cider, and take up space for the night. If you see any of these shams spill a drop, you tell me and I'll throw them out on their ear.' A couple of months ago Barty replaced the splitting bar stools and banquettes with new, shiny, bottle-green ones. Ever since then he's been, according to Mart, like a woman with a new kitchen, one step away from going over you with a duster before he allows you in. He didn't do anything about the worn-out red linoleum flooring, or the lumpy painted-over wallpaper, or the faded newspaper clippings framed on the walls, or the frayed fishing net draped from the ceiling and festooned with whatever random items people feel like throwing in there, so the place looks pretty much the same as always, but Barty doesn't see it that way.

'I'll make sure they mind their manners,' Cal says, taking his pint. 'Thanks.'

Cal can tell where Paddy Englishman is – in the back alcove where Mart and his buddies usually hang out – because it's the corner everyone's carefully ignoring. He makes his way through the crowd, shielding his pint and nodding to people he knows. Noreen waves to him from a corner, where she's squeezed in between two of her enormous brothers; Cal waves back and keeps moving. One girl is hopping around in a neon-pink dress not much bigger than a bathing suit, presumably in the hope that Paddy Englishman will notice her and whisk her off to a party on his yacht.

A sizeable proportion of the regular occupants of Seán Óg's have condensed themselves into the alcove. All of them are a little redder in the face than usual, but Cal figures this is heat rather than drink. They're here for a purpose tonight; they wouldn't let drink blunt them until that purpose was thoroughly accomplished. In the heart of the alcove, with his shoulder to Cal, laughing at some story of Sonny McHugh's, is a narrow fair-haired guy in a noticeably expensive shirt.

The guys are scrupulously, methodically providing Rushborough with a normal night out. Dessie Duggan is giving out loudly to Con McHugh about something to do with shearing, and Bobby is explaining his mother's latest blood tests to Francie, who doesn't appear to have registered that he's there. None of them have dressed up for the occasion. Bobby has washed till he's even pinker and shinier than usual, and Con has flattened down his unruly dark hair, or else his wife has, but they're all in their work clothes – except Mart, who has given free rein to his sense of the artistic and is wearing a flat tweed cap, a threadbare grandfather shirt, and a hairy brown waistcoat that Cal had no idea he even owned. He could do with a clay pipe, but apart from that, he's a tourist board's dream.

Mart and Senan are sitting next to each other so they can argue more conveniently. 'That hat,' Senan is telling Mart, in the voice of a man repeating himself for the last time, 'is no loss to you or anyone. You oughta be thanking God it's gone. Say there was a news reporter here, and he caught that yoke on camera—'

'What the hell would a news reporter be doing here?' Mart demands.

'A report about . . .' Senan lowers his voice a notch and tilts his head at the fair-haired guy. 'That, sure. And say he put you on the telly, wearing that yoke. This town'd be the laughingstock of the country. The world, even. It'd go viral on YouTube.'

'Because the rest of ye are a shower of fashion icons, is it? Linda Evangelista wore that there polo shirt on the catwalk? That hat of mine had more panache than anything you've ever been next nor near. If that news reporter ever arrives, I know what you'll be wearing to greet him.'

'I wouldn't wear that fuckin' offence against nature for—'

'You're both beautiful,' Cal says. 'How's it going?'

'Ah, 'tis yourself!' Mart says with delight, raising his pint high to Cal. 'Shift over there, Bobby, and make room for the big fella. Senan oughta thank you, Sunny Jim; I was working on him to give me my hat back, but now that'll have to wait. Mr Rushborough!'

Rushborough turns from laughing with Sonny, and Cal gets his first good look at the guy. He's somewhere in his forties, probably, with the kind of thin, smooth, pale face that's impossible to pin down any closer. Everything about him is smooth: his ears lie close against his head, his hair is slicked down neatly, his shirt falls cleanly with no bulges, and his light eyes are set flat in his face.

'Let me introduce you to Mr Cal Hooper,' Mart says, 'my neighbour. Cal's the man that lives in between myself and PJ over there.'

Johnny Reddy is a couple of seats down from Rushborough, in conversation with PJ. He doesn't look one bit pleased to see Cal sitting his ass down among them. Cal gives him a big friendly smile.

'A pleasure to meet you,' Rushborough says, leaning across the table to shake Cal's hand. Even his voice is smooth and flat, what Cal would consider fancy-type English. Against the rich sway and roll of the Ardnakelty accents all around, it's jarring enough to feel like a deliberate challenge.

'Likewise,' Cal says. 'I hear your people come from round here.'

'They do, yes. In a way I've always considered it my real home, but I've never managed to find the time to visit before.'

'Well, better late than never,' Cal says. 'What do you think of it now that you're here?'

'I haven't had a chance to explore properly yet, but what I've seen is really stunning. And these chaps have been giving me a wonderful welcome.' He has a rich man's smile, easy and understated, the smile of a man who isn't required to put in effort. 'Honestly, it's a better homecoming than I ever dreamed of.'

'Good to hear,' Cal says. 'How long are you planning to stay?'

'Oh, at least a few weeks. No point in doing things by halves. Possibly more; it all depends.' He cocks his head. His pale eyes are measuring Cal up, working fast and competently. 'You're American, aren't you? Do you have heritage here as well?'

'Nope,' Cal says. 'Just liked the look of the place.'

'Clearly a man of excellent taste,' Rushborough says, laughing. 'I'm sure we'll speak again,' and he nods to Cal and goes back to his conversation with Sonny. His eyes stay on Cal for one second too long, before he turns away.

'He's my third cousin,' Bobby says, round-eyed, pointing at Rushborough. 'Didja know that?'

'I heard his grandma was a Feeney,' Cal says. 'I figured you'd be related somehow.'

'You wouldn't know it to look at us,' Bobby says a little wistfully. 'He's better looking than I am. I'd say he does great with the women.' He tugs down his shirtfront, trying to live up to his new standards. 'I never woulda thought I had a rich cousin. All my cousins are farmers, sure.'

'If this works out,' Johnny says in an undertone, grinning over his shoulder, 'you'll be the rich cousin.' Cal has already noticed that Johnny, while giving PJ his total flattering attention, is keeping sharp track of every other conversation in the alcove.

'Holy God,' Bobby says, a bit overawed by the thought. 'I will, and all. And me up to my oxters in sheep shite every day of my life.'

'It's not sheep shite you'll be smelling of in a few months' time, man,' Johnny tells him. 'It's champagne and caviar. And I'm telling you now, there's not a woman on earth that can resist that smell.' He winks and turns back to PJ.

'Is that a fact?' Bobby asks Cal. Bobby considers Cal to be an authority on women, on the grounds that Cal has both an ex-wife and a girlfriend. Cal himself feels like a divorce isn't exactly evidence of proficiency in the field, but it would be unkind to point that out to Bobby. It seems to cheer Bobby to believe that he has access to an expert.

'I dunno,' he says. 'Mostly the women I've known didn't care if a guy was rich, as long as he paid his way and didn't mooch. Probably some do, though.'

'I'd love a wife,' Bobby explains. 'I worry about the mammy; she doesn't want to go into a home, but she's getting to be more than I can manage on my own, herself and the sheep. 'Tisn't only that, but. I can do without the ride, mostly, but I'd love a cuddle. With a woman that's nice and soft. Not one of them bony ones.' He blinks wistfully at Cal. Cal revises his previous assessment: Bobby, at least, is around three-quarters drunk. Bobby is the resident lightweight – Mart says, with resigned contempt, that he'd get drunk off a sniff of a beer mat – but he knows that, and allows for it. The fact that he's let himself reach this point means that he's made up his mind about Rushborough.

Rushborough, meanwhile, has finished with Sonny and moved on to Francie, propping his elbows on the table to ask questions and nod intently at the answers. Francie doesn't look like he's made up his mind, or anywhere near it. He's answering the questions, though, which for Francie counts as being sociable. He's not rejecting Rushborough and his grandma outright, or at least not yet.

'If I get my share of that gold,' Bobby says, with decision, 'I'll find myself a lovely big soft woman that likes the smell of caviar.

I'll buy her a whole stewpot full of it, and a pint of champagne to wash it down. I'll bring it to her in bed, and the whole time she's ating it, I'll lie right there and give her a cuddle.'

'Sounds like a win-win to me,' Cal says.

Mart has lost interest in needling Senan and is leaning across to cut in on Rushborough and Francie's conversation. 'Oh, begod,' he says, ''tis still there, o' course. There's not a man in the townland would dig up that mound.'

'Or even go near it after dark,' Dessie says.

'The fairy hill on Mossie's land?' Bobby asks, coming out of his vision. 'Mossie does plough around it. And even for that, he brings his rosary beads. Just in case, like.'

'Really?' Rushborough asks, enthralled. 'It wasn't just my grandmother, then?'

'Ah, God, no,' Senan assures him. 'My own mother, God rest her soul' – he crosses himself, and the rest of the guys follow promptly – 'she was coming home one night, past that field, from visiting her daddy that wasn't well. A winter night, and everything quiet as the grave, only then didn't she hear music. 'Twas coming from that same mound. The sweetest music you ever did hear, she said, and she stood there listening a minute, only then it put a great fear on her. She ran all the way home like the devil himself was at her heels. Only when she got in the door, didn't she find all of us childer outa our minds with worry, and my daddy putting on his coat to go look for her, because she shoulda been home hours before. A two-mile walk was after taking her three hours.'

'Mrs Maguire wasn't one of them women that do be imagining all sorts,' Sonny tells Rushborough. 'There was no nonsense about her. She'd fetch you a clatter round the ear as soon as look at you.'

'Our bedroom window does look out over that field,' Dessie says. 'Many's the time I've seen lights around that mound. Moving, like; circling round, and crossing back and forth. You couldn't pay me to go in that field at night.'

'Good heavens,' Rushborough breathes. 'Do you think the landowner would let me have a look at it? In the daytime, of course.'

'You'd have to tell Mossie who your granny was,' Con says.

'He wouldn't let some aul' tourist wander around his land. He'd run them off with his slash hook, so he would. But if he knows you're from round here, sure, that's different. He'd show you the place, right enough.'

'I'll bring you down there any day you like,' Johnny promises. Johnny has been staying detached from Rushborough, letting the other men explore him at will. Cal doesn't find this reassuring. It means the evening is unfolding right along the lines that Johnny wants it to.

'Would you?' Rushborough asks, thrilled. 'That would be wonderful. Should I bring anything? I have some vague memory of my grandmother mentioning an offering of some kind, but it's so long ago – might it have been cream? Possibly it sounds foolish, but—'

'That's what my granny woulda put there, all right,' Mart agrees. Cal can tell from the quizzical angle of his head that Mart is finding Rushborough very interesting.

'Just don't step on the mound,' Francie says ominously. 'Mossie's nephew stood on that mound, one time, to show he wasn't afraid of any aul' superstition. He got a tingling right up his legs, like pins and needles. Couldn't feel his feet for a week.'

'God between us and harm,' Mart says solemnly, raising his glass, and they all drink to that. Cal drinks along with them. He feels, more and more, like they could all do with something between them and harm.

He's seen these guys leprechaun up before, at innocent tourists who were proud of themselves for finding a quaint authentic Irish pub that wasn't in any of the guidebooks. They convinced one earnest American student that the narrow window in the corner had been blessed by Saint Leithreas and that if he could climb through it he'd be sure to get to heaven, and he was halfway through before an outraged Barty came out from behind the bar and hauled him down by the seat of his pants. They tried it on Cal, too, in his first couple of months here, but he declined to dress all in green in order to ingratiate himself with the local Little People, or to walk round the pub backwards to avert bad luck when he dropped his change. This is different. They're not heaping extravagant quantities of blarney down this guy's throat to see what he'll swallow. This is a subtler, meticulous operation, and a serious one.

'Now there's a mighty idea!' Johnny cries, turning from PJ to the alcove. 'PJ's after pointing out that we can't welcome a man home without a bit of a singsong.'

PJ looks like he didn't notice himself having any such idea, but he nods obligingly. 'Oh, my goodness,' Rushborough says, delighted. 'A singsong? I haven't been to one of those since I was a boy at my grandmother's house.'

'Get out the guitar there,' Sonny orders Con, and Con turns promptly to get it from the corner behind him: clearly this was in the plan. If Rushborough wants heritage, he's going to get it. 'Ah, begod,' Mart tells the table happily, 'there's nothing like an aul' singsong.'

The normal repertoire in Seán Óg's, on evenings that turn musical, is a mix of traditional Irish stuff and everything from Garth Brooks to Doris Day. Tonight it's wall-to-wall green, in a tasteful array of shades: homesickness, rebellion, booze, and pretty girls, mainly. PJ starts off with 'Fields of Athenry' in a rich, melancholy tenor, and Sonny follows up by bellowing out 'The Wild Rover' and slapping the table till the glasses jump. Rushborough is entranced. On the maudlin songs he leans his head back against the banquette, with his eyes half closed and his pint forgotten in his hand; on the rowdy ones, he beats time on his thigh and joins in the choruses. When the men invite him to take his turn, he sings 'Black Velvet Band' in a light, clear voice that almost fits in, except for the accent. He knows all the words.

The crowd in the pub shifts and eddies, without hurry but with method. People pause at the entrance to the alcove, listening to the singing, or swapping news, or waiting for the bar to clear; after a few minutes they move on, leaving the space for someone else. None of them intrude on the alcove. Cal didn't expect them to. Soon enough they'll want to meet Rushborough, but that can wait for another day. For now they're content to circle, collecting impressions to discuss at leisure: his clothes, his hair, his accent, his manner; whether he looks like a Feeney, whether he looks like a millionaire, whether he looks handy in a fight; whether he looks like a fool. Cal isn't sure what a millionaire is supposed to look like, but to him this guy looks like he could do plenty of damage in a fight, and he doesn't look like any kind of fool at all.

The singing comes round to Cal. He doesn't try to add to the greenery – even if he wanted to, it would make a dumb tourist out of him, and he's not aiming to be a tourist right now. He sticks with 'The House of the Rising Sun'. Cal has the right voice for pub singsongs, a big man's voice, nothing showy or impressive, but good to listen to. He spots Johnny noticing that he takes his turn as a matter of course, and not liking it.

When he's accepted his round of applause, and Dessie has launched into 'Rocky Road to Dublin', Cal heads for the bar. Barty, topping up two glasses at once, nods to him but can't take the breath to talk. His face is sweating harder.

'Women,' Mart says with deep disapproval, appearing at Cal's shoulder. 'This pub's full of women tonight.'

'They get everywhere,' Cal agrees gravely. 'You reckon they should stay home and take care of the kids?'

'Ah, Jaysus, no. We've the twenty-first century here now. They've as much right to a night out as anyone. But they change the atmosphere of a place. You can't deny that. Look at that, now.' Mart nods at the girl in the pink dress, who has started dancing with one of her girlfriends in a few square inches of space between the tables and the bar. A large guy in a too-tight shirt is hovering hopefully nearby, making spasmodic movements that are presumably intended to match theirs. 'Is that what you'd expect to see in this pub on a Monday night?'

'I don't think I've ever seen anything like that in here,' Cal says truthfully.

'That's disco behaviour, is what that is. That's what you get when there's women in. They oughta have pubs of their own, so they can have their pint in peace without some potato-faced fucker trying to get into their knickers, and I can have mine without your man's hormones getting in the air and spoiling the taste.'

'If they weren't here,' Cal points out, 'you'd be stuck looking at nothing better'n my hairy face for the evening.'

'True enough,' Mart concedes. 'Some of the women in here tonight are a lot more scenic than yourself, no harm to you. Not all of them, but some.'

'Enjoy 'em while you can,' Cal says. 'Tomorrow the scenery'll be back to normal.'

'Near enough, maybe. Not all the way back, as long as we've got Bono over there drawing the crowds.'

They both glance over at the alcove. Rushborough has launched into a song about some guy getting killed by the British.

'Whatever the Croppy Boy sounded like,' Mart says, 'he didn't fuckin' sound like that.'

'You show him how it's done,' Cal says.

'I will, in a while. I've to lubricate the vocal cords a bit more first.'

Cal, interpreting this correctly, catches Barty's eye and points to Mart. Mart nods, accepting his due, and goes back to watching Rushborough, between moving shoulders. All the men in the alcove are gazing at the guy. Cal is out of patience with them. As far as he's concerned, Rushborough has a face that would make any sensible man want to walk away, not sit there goggling at him like he hung the moon.

'Will I tell you something, Sunny Jim?' Mart says. 'I don't like the cut of that fella.'

'Nope,' Cal says. 'Me neither.' He's been trying to guess what this guy might do, if he figures out he's been taken for a ride. He finds he doesn't much like the possibilities.

'He's who he says he is, anyway,' Mart informs him. 'I thought he mighta been some chancer that spun Johnny a line, trying to scam a bitta cash outa the lot of us. Johnny's not as cute as he thinks he is. A real first-class scam artist could make mincemeat outa him, and be long gone before Johnny ever noticed a thing.'

'That's the impression I got,' Cal says. He hasn't decided which option he likes less: Trey's father being a good con artist, or being a bad one. He accepts the pints from Barty and hands Mart his Guinness.

'But this fella knows about that fairy mound, and putting cream by it. He knows about the time Francie's great-granddad fell down the well and it took two days to get him back up. He knows the Fallon women had a name for being the finest knitters in this county. And didja hear when he sang "Black Velvet Band"? I never heard anyone but Ardnakelty people sing "A guinea she took from his pocket". Everyone else has the girl robbing a watch. His people came from around here, all right.'

'Maybe,' Cal says. 'But he still doesn't strike me as the type to go misty-eyed when someone sings "The Wearing of the Green".'

'That article there,' Mart says, eyeing Rushborough over his glass, 'doesn't strike me as the type that's ever gone misty-eyed over anything in his life.'

'So what's he here for?'

Mart's bright glance swivels to Cal. 'A coupla year back, people were asking the same about you, Sunny Jim. A few of them still do.'

'I'm here because I landed here,' Cal says, refusing to bite on that. 'This guy's come looking.'

Mart shrugs. 'Maybe he doesn't give a shite about the heritage; 'tis gold he wants, pure and simple. And he thinks it'll be easier to slip a quare deal past us if we take him for a sap that'd be happy with a handful of shamrock.'

'If that guy believes there's gold out there,' Cal says, 'he's got more to go on than some story his granny told him.'

'I'll tell you this much, anyway,' Mart says. 'Johnny believes it's there. He wouldn't go to all this trouble, dragging himself away from the bright lights and the film stars back to an inferior environment like this, just for the grand or two he'll get if there's nothing in them fields.'

'You figure he knows something we don't?'

'I wouldn't put it past him. Maybe he's saving it up for the right moment, or maybe 'tis something he's planning on keeping to himself. But I'd say he knows something.'

'Then why's he fucking around salting the river?'

'Now that,' Mart says, 'I don't know. Maybe he's only aiming to be sure, to be sure. But I'll tell you what's occurred to me, Sunny

Jim. Anyone that gives Johnny that bitta cash is in deep. Psychologically, like. Once you've sunk a few hundred quid into this, you won't back out; you'll let Paddy Englishman take whatever samples he wants, and dig up any field he chooses. Getting the lads to salt that river might be Johnny's wee bitta insurance, against anyone changing his mind.'

It occurs to Cal that the insurance won't just be psychological. Like Mart figured, salting the river is probably some kind of fraud. Anyone who gives Johnny that money will be giving him something he can hold over their heads, or at least try to.

Trying to hold anything over these guys' heads would not be a smart move. Johnny ought to know that, but Cal reached the conclusion, well before he met Johnny, that the guy is careful not to know anything that might make him uncomfortable.

'So you're out, huh?' he says.

'Ah, God, no,' Mart says, shocked. 'Sure, I'd be going in forewarned; my psychology wouldn't be running wild on me. I wouldn't stay in one minute longer than I wanted to. To be honest with you, if the rest of them shams decide they're on for it, I might haveta join in just outa the kindness of my heart. They'll make a pig's arse outa the whole operation if I'm not there to advise them.' He eyes the group in the alcove with tolerant scorn. 'They wouldn't have a baldy notion where the gold oughta lie in the river; they'll throw it in wherever takes their fancy. And I'd bet my life they'll just sprinkle in the dust as it is, the way half of it'll be washed downstream before it can sink to the bottom, and we'll never see it again. What they oughta do is roll the dust into little pellets of mud, the way it'll go straight to the bottom, and then the mud'll dissolve away and leave it ready for your man to find.'

'Sounds to me like you're in,' Cal says.

'I hate a botched job,' Mart says. He cocks his head at Cal. 'How about you, Sunny Jim, now you've had a look at His Lordship? Are you in or out?'

'I'm here,' Cal says. 'That's all I am, right now.' The sense of being in cahoots with Mart doesn't sit well with him. 'So,' he says, 'the fairy mound's real, huh?'

Mart flicks him a grin that says he knows what's in Cal's head and is enjoying it. ''Tis there, anyhow. And Mossie does plough around it, but that could just be outa laziness: his daddy and his granddaddy did it, so he hasn't the initiative to do anything different. Beyond that, I'm making no guarantees. You're welcome to go down there and look for the fairies any night you like. Tell Mossie I sent you.'

'And make sure I have a few shots of poteen first,' Cal says. 'To shorten my odds.'

Mart laughs and claps him on the shoulder, and turns to nod to a stout guy leaning on the bar. 'How's she cuttin'?'

'Not a bother,' says the guy. 'Your man's having a grand aul' night, anyhow.' He nods at Rushborough.

'Sure, who wouldn't, in a fine establishment like this,' Mart says. ''Tis a while since I saw you in here yourself.'

'Ah, I'd be in every now and again,' the guy says. He takes his pint from Barty. 'I've been thinking of selling a few acres,' he mentions. 'That field down near the river.'

'I'm not in the market,' Mart says. 'You could try Mr Hooper here. He could do with something to keep him occupied.'

'I'm not offering. I'm only saying. If there was gold on it, or even if your man went looking for gold on it, I could triple the price.'

'Out you go with a spade, then,' Mart says, smiling at him, 'and start digging.'

The guy's jowls set mulishly. 'Maybe your man's granny said there was gold on your land, but she never said there was none anywhere else. Johnny Reddy can't be keeping this to himself and his pals.'

'I'm no pal of Johnny Reddy's, bucko,' Mart says. 'But I'll say this for the man: he's wise to start small. Let you bide your time, and see what way the wind blows.'

The guy grunts, still dissatisfied. His eyes are on the alcove, where Dessie is putting plenty of bawdy winks into a song about a guy coming home drunk and finding various unexpected items in his house, and Rushborough is laughing. 'See you again,' he says, picking up his glass and giving Mart a brief nod. 'I'll be back in soon enough.'

'D'you know what Johnny Reddy's real failing is?' Mart asks, considering the guy's back as he wades through the crowd towards his table. 'He doesn't think things through. It wouldn't take a psychic to predict that fella, and plenty of others like him, but I'd put money on it that he never once occurred to Johnny.'

'That guy doesn't look like a happy camper,' Cal says.

'I did consider sending him in to have the chats with Mr Rushborough,' Mart says, 'just to watch what wee Johnny made of that. But that fella has no subtlety about him. He'd go putting a sour taste in Paddy Englishman's mouth, and then where would we be at all?'

'Do people know?' Cal asks. And, when Mart cocks his head inquiringly: 'That Johnny's aiming to salt the river.'

Mart shrugs. 'There's no telling who'd know what, around here. I'd say there's a dozen different stories going around this same pub, and a few dozen different ways that people wanta get in on the action. We're in for an interesting wee while. Now come on back, before that chancer robs our seats on us.'

The night proceeds. Gradually the singing runs out of momentum; Con puts his guitar back in the corner, and Rushborough buys him and everyone else in the alcove a double whiskey. The pub has started to run out of momentum, too. The non-locals have reached the maximum level of drunkenness at which they still consider it reasonable to drive home on unfamiliar roads. The old people are getting tired and heading for their beds, and the young ones are getting bored and taking bags of cans back to each other's houses, where they'll have more scope. The girl in pink leaves with the potato-faced fucker's arm around her waist.

By midnight, all that's left in the pub is a dense fug of sweat and beer breath, Barty wiping down tables with a rag, and the men in the alcove. The ashtrays have come out. Rushborough smokes Gitanes, which lowers him further in Cal's esteem: Cal feels that, while people are entitled to their vices, anyone who isn't a dick finds a way to pursue those vices without giving everyone in the room a sore throat.

'I'm proud,' Rushborough informs them all, throwing an arm around Bobby's shoulders, 'I'm proud to claim this man as my cousin. And all of you, of course all of you, I'm sure we're all cousins of some degree. Aren't we?' He looks about half drunk. His hair is ruffled out of its sleek sweep, and he's tilting a little bit, not drastically, off centre. Cal can't get a good enough look at his eyes to decide whether it's real.

"Twould be a miracle if we weren't,' Dessie agrees. 'All this townland's related, one way or another.'

'I'm this fella's uncle,' Sonny informs Rushborough, pointing his cigarette at Senan. 'A few times removed. Not far enough for me.'

'You owe me fifty years' worth of birthday presents, so,' Senan tells him. 'And a few quid in communion money. I don't take cheques.'

'And you owe me a bitta respect. Go on up there and get your uncle Sonny a pint.'

'I will in me arse.'

'Look,' Rushborough says, with sudden decision. 'Look. I want to show you all something.'

He lays his right hand, palm down, in the middle of the table, among the pint glasses and the beer mats and the flecks of ash. On the ring finger is a silver band. Rushborough turns it around, so that the bezel is visible. Set into it is a pitted fragment of something gold.

'My grandmother gave me this,' Rushborough says, with a wondering reverence in his voice. 'She and a friend found it, when they were children digging in the friend's garden. About nine years old, she says they were. Michael Duggan was the friend's name. They found two of these, and kept one each.'

'My great-uncle was Michael Duggan,' Dessie says, awed enough to talk quietly for once. 'He musta lost his.'

The men lean in, bending low over Rushborough's hand. Cal leans with them. The nugget is about the size of a shirt button, polished by time on the high surfaces, ragged in the crevices, studded with small chunks of white. In the yellowish light of the wall lamps, it shines with a worn, serene glow.

'Here,' Rushborough says. 'Take it. Have a look at it.' He pulls the ring off his finger, with a reckless little laugh like he's doing something wild, and passes it to Dessie. 'I don't really take it off, but . . . God knows, it could have been any of yours as easily as mine. I'm sure your grandparents were digging away in the same gardens. Side by side with mine.'

Dessie holds up the ring and peers at it, tilting it this way and that. 'Holy God,' he breathes. He lays one fingertip on the nugget. 'Wouldja look at that.'

''Tis beautiful,' Con says. Nobody makes fun of him.

Dessie passes the ring, held over a cupped hand, to Francie. Francie, giving it a long stare, nods slowly and unconsciously.

'That'll be quartz,' Mart informs them all. 'The white stuff.'

'Exactly,' Rushborough says, turning eagerly towards him. 'Somewhere in that mountain, there's a vein of quartz, shot through with gold. And over thousands of years, much of it was washed down out of the mountain. Onto Michael Duggan's land, and all of yours.'

The ring passes from hand to hand. Cal takes his turn, but he barely sees it. He's feeling the change in the alcove. The air is drawing in, magnetised, around the shining fragment and the men who surround it. Till this moment, the gold was a cloud of words and daydreams. Now it's a solid thing between their fingers.

'The thing is,' Rushborough says, 'the important thing is, you see, my grandmother didn't just discover this by chance. The one thing that frightens me, the one thing that's been giving me pause about this whole project, is the possibility that her directions are no good. That they've been passed down over so many generations, they got warped along the way, to the point where they're not accurate enough to lead us to the right spots. But you see, when she and her friend Michael found this' – he points to the ring, cupped like a butterfly in Con's big rough hand – 'they weren't digging at random. They picked the spot because her grandfather had told her his father said there was gold there.'

'And he was right,' Bobby says, starry-eyed.

'He was right,' Rushborough says, 'and he didn't even know it.

That's one of the marvellous aspects: her grandfather didn't actually believe in the gold. As far as he was concerned, the whole thing was a tall tale – something invented by some ancestor to impress a girl, or to distract a sick child. Even when my grandmother found this, he thought it was just a pretty pebble. But he passed the story on, all the same. Because, true or false, it belonged to our family, and he couldn't let it disappear.'

Cal takes a glance at Johnny Reddy. Johnny hasn't said a word to him all evening. Even his eyes have stayed carefully occupied, far from Cal. Now, he and Cal are the only people who aren't gazing at the scrap of gold. While Cal is watching Johnny, Johnny is watching the other men. His face is as intent and consumed as theirs. If this ring is what Johnny was keeping up his sleeve, it's having all the impact he could have hoped for.

'The gold is out there,' Rushborough says, gesturing at the dark window and the hot night outside, thrumming with insects and their hunters. 'Our ancestors, yours and mine, they were digging it up thousands of years before we were born. Our grandparents were playing with it in those fields, just as they'd play with pretty pebbles. I want us to find it together.'

The men are still. Their land is changing from a thing they know inside out to a mystery, a message to them in a code that's gone unsuspected all their lives. Out in the darkness, the paths they walk every day are humming and shimmering with signals.

Cal feels like he's not in the room with them, or like he shouldn't be. Whatever's on his land, it's not the same thing.

'I feel incredibly lucky,' Rushborough says quietly. 'To be the one who, after all these generations, is in a position to salvage this story and turn it into a reality. It's an honour. And I mean to live up to it.'

'And no one but this load of gobshites to give you a hand,' Senan says, after a moment of silence. 'God help you.'

The alcove explodes with a roar of laughter, huge and uncontrolled. It goes on and on. There are tears rolling down Sonny's face; Dessie is rocking back and forth, barely able to breathe. Johnny, laughing too, reaches over to clap Senan on the shoulder, and Senan doesn't shrug him off.

'Oh, come on,' Rushborough protests, slipping his ring back onto his finger, but he's laughing too. 'I can't imagine better company.'

'I can,' Sonny says. 'Your woman Jennifer Aniston—'

'She'd be no good with a shovel,' Francie tells him.

'She wouldn't need to be. She could just stand at the other end of the field, and I'd dig my way over to her like the fuckin' clappers.'

'Here, you,' Bobby says, digging a finger into Senan's solid arm, 'you're forever giving me shite about why aliens would want to come to the back-arse of Ireland. Does this answer that for you, does it?'

'Ah, whisht up, wouldja,' Senan says, but his mind isn't on it. He's watching Rushborough's hand, the turn and pulse of light as he gestures.

'Aliens need gold now, do they?' Mart inquires, taking up Senan's slack.

'They need something,' Bobby says. 'Or otherwise why would they be here? I knew there hadta be something out there that they were after. I reckoned it was plutonium, maybe, but—'

'Fuckin' *plutonium*?' Senan bursts out, goaded out of his thoughts by this level of idiocy. 'You reckoned the whole mountain was about to blow up in a big mushroom cloud—'

'Your trouble is you don't fuckin' listen. I never said that. I only said they're bound to need fuel, if they're coming all this—'

'And they're using gold for fuel now, is it? Or are they trading it for diesel on the intergalactic black market—'

Cal leaves them to it and goes back up to the bar. Mart joins him again, in case Cal should forget by whose favour he's here tonight.

'Hey,' Cal says, motioning to Barty to make it two pints.

Mart leans on the bar and works a knee that's stiff from sitting. He has an eye on the alcove, over Cal's shoulder. 'Didja ever hear the story of the three wells?' he asks.

'Well, well, well,' Cal says. He's not in the right frame of mind to humour Mart.

'That's the one,' Mart says. 'Well, well, well.'

He's watching, not Rushborough, but Johnny. Johnny has his head bent sideways over a lighter, flicking it hard. In that unguarded second his face is slack, almost helpless, with some emotion. Cal thinks it might be relief.

'Like I told you,' Mart says. 'We're in for an interesting wee while.'

Cal says, 'What'll you do if it all goes wrong?'

Mart's forehead crinkles. 'What d'you mean, like?'

'If Rushborough starts smelling a rat.'

''Tisn't my place to do anything, Sunny Jim,' Mart says gently. 'This is Johnny Reddy's wee enterprise. I'm only here for the view. The same as yourself. Remember?'

'Right,' Cal says, after a second.

'Don't worry,' Mart reassures him. He pulls out his tobacco pouch and starts rolling a cigarette on the bar, with leisurely, expert fingers. 'If you forget, I'll remind you.'

Barty swears bitterly at a rip in one of his new bar stools. In the alcove, someone whistles, high and shrill, cutting through the laughter and the voices like an alarm.

7

Over breakfast, Cal does some hangover-related calculations. He wants a talk with Johnny Reddy, as early as possible, to prevent Johnny from claiming he's too late; but that requires Johnny to be awake, and he was still going strong when Cal left the pub at midnight. He doesn't want Rushborough there, and while Cal figures Johnny won't want to leave Rushborough unsupervised, Rushborough looked a lot drunker than Johnny did, so he's likely to take longer to surface. Cal also doesn't want to encounter Trey, but she has football training on Tuesday mornings and mostly hangs out with her friends afterwards, so she should be out of his way at least until she gets hungry.

In the end he reckons ten-thirty should find Trey gone, Johnny conscious, and Rushborough not yet functional. At a quarter to ten he gets three hundred euros out of his emergency-cash envelope, puts it in his pocket, and starts off towards the mountain. He leaves Rip at home. As far as Cal is concerned, Rip made his opinion of Johnny plain on their first meeting, and shouldn't be subjected to a second one.

The mountain is sly. From far off, its low, rounded curves look almost harmless, and even as you go up the trail, every step seems gentle enough, until all of a sudden you realise your leg muscles are juddering. The same goes for straying: the path is clear, until you look down after a minute's distraction and find yourself with one foot slowly pressing deeper into watery bog. It's a place whose dangers only come into focus when you're already engaged with them.

Cal, knowing that, takes it slow and steady. The heat is already starting to build. On the purple bogland, the bees fill up the heather with a ceaseless, intent hum and a rustle so tiny that only their sheer numbers make it audible. The view shifts with the twists of the path, over crumbling stone walls and stretches of tall moor grass, to the spread of trim, busy fields far below.

In the Reddys' front yard, Liam and Alanna have found a broken-handled spade and are building earthworks in the shade of a bedraggled tree. They come running over to explain their construction to Cal and investigate him for candy bars; finding he's brought none today, they zoom back to their project. The sun is drawing a rich, restless scent from the spruce grove behind the house.

Sheila Reddy answers the door. Cal makes a point of finding chances to speak with Sheila often enough that she doesn't feel her daughter is off with a stranger. Mostly she smiles and seems pleased to see him, and tells him how well the mended roof has held up to the weather. Today, her face has the same shuttered wariness it wore years ago, when he first came here. She holds the door like a weapon.

'Morning,' he says. 'Looks like another hot one coming.'

Sheila barely glances at the sky. 'Theresa's at football,' she says.

'Oh, I know that,' Cal says. 'I was hoping to speak to Mr Reddy, if he's free.'

Sheila looks at him for a minute, expressionless. 'I'll get him,' she says, and shuts the door behind her.

Liam starts kicking at a corner of the earthworks, and Alanna yells at him. Liam kicks harder. Alanna yells louder and shoves him. Cal resists the urge to tell them both to knock it off.

Johnny takes his time coming to the door. Today the first thing about him that irks Cal is his shirt, which is a blue pinstripe, freshly ironed, with the cuffs neatly rolled. It's set to be another sizzling day, the kind where even the shrivelled old ladies who arrange flowers in front of the Virgin Mary grotto dig out short sleeves, but this little schmuck feels the need to express that he's too fancy for everything about Ardnakelty, right down to the weather.

'Mr Hooper,' he says pleasantly. This time he doesn't try to shake hands. 'Did you enjoy last night? You were an addition to the party: you've a fine voice on you.'

The guy's not even outside his door and he's managed to irk Cal a second time over, acting like last night was his personal party and Cal was some gatecrasher he decided to humour. 'Thanks,' Cal says. 'You sounded pretty good yourself.' Johnny, inevitably, sang

"The West's Awake", in a poignant tenor with plenty of grandeur on the big notes.

Johnny laughs that off. 'Ah, I can carry a tune, is all. It's in the blood, sure: everyone from around here can hold their own in a singsong.'

'Sure sounded like it,' Cal says. 'You got a minute?'

'I do, of course,' Johnny says graciously. He strolls across the yard towards the gate, letting Cal follow and leaving the door open, to make the point that this can't take long. In the sunlight, his hangover shows; there are bags under his eyes, and redness in them. It sits poorly with his boyish mannerisms, giving them a tawdry, used-up air. 'What can I do for you?'

It's been Cal's experience that men like Johnny Reddy don't deal well with being taken off guard. They're used to picking the easiest victims, so they're used to being the ones who set the agenda, the pace, and everything else. If someone takes that away from them, they flounder.

'I hear you're looking for investors to get some gold into the river,' Cal says. 'I'm in.'

That wakes Johnny up. He stops walking and stares for a second. Then: 'Holy God,' he says, bursting into extravagant laughter. 'Where'd that come out of?'

'The buy-in's three hundred bucks. Right?'

Johnny shakes his head, grinning, blowing out air. 'My God, Theresa musta got the wrong end of the stick altogether. What's she after saying to you, at all?'

'She hasn't said a word,' Cal says. 'About that or any of it. And I haven't asked her.'

Johnny hears the edge in his voice and backs off fast. 'Ah, I know you wouldn't do that,' he assures Cal. 'Only you have to understand, man. This'll be a wonderful opportunity for Theresa, I'll be able to give her all kinds of things that she's never had up till now – music lessons, she'll be able to have, and horseback riding, and whatever she fancies. But I won't have her put in the middle of it all. Being quizzed about what she knows, having to worry about what she should and shouldn't say. 'Twouldn't be fair on her.'

'Yeah,' Cal says. 'I'm with you on that.'

'I'm glad to hear it,' Johnny says, nodding gravely. 'It's great to be on the same page.' He brushes off the gate rail and leans his forearms on it, narrowing his eyes to gaze out over the mountain slope. 'Then, if you don't mind me asking, who was it said this to you?'

'Well,' Cal says, settling his back against the gate, 'I gotta admit I was kinda surprised you didn't mention it to me yourself. What with my land being right on the gold line, and all.'

Johnny's face registers a twinge of embarrassed reproach, like Cal has committed a social error. 'I'da loved to bring you on board,' he explains. 'I need a chance to repay a wee biteen of all the kindness you've shown Theresa, while I was away. But that'll have to wait a little longer. Man, no harm to you and no offence meant, but this is Ardnakelty business. Mr Rushborough's going to stick to taking his samples on land that's owned by Ardnakelty men. You heard him last night: where to find the gold, that's been passed down through his ancestors, and ours. Not yours.'

Cal is out of practice. He let Johnny use Trey as a sidetrack, and now Johnny's had enough talking time to recover his footing and come up with an angle.

'Well, I can see why you'd take that into account,' he says, smiling at Johnny. 'But it was an Ardnakelty guy that told me the whole story, and invited me along last night. He said I oughta remind you about me and my land being involved, just in case you'd forgotten. Does that set your mind at ease?'

Johnny laughs, his head going back. 'Go on, let me guess. Mart Lavin, is it? He's always been a terrible man for stirring the pot. I thought he'da outgrown it by now, but some people never learn.'

Cal waits. He's had squirrelly little conversations like this with squirrelly little fucks like this before, hundreds of times: two-layer conversations where everyone knows what's going on, and everyone knows that everyone knows, but they all have to keep playing dumb for the squirrelly little fuck's convenience. The wasted energy always irritated him, but at least back then he was getting paid for it.

Johnny sighs and turns serious. 'Man,' he says ruefully, rubbing at his face, 'let me tell you what I'm dealing with. I'm in a bit of a delicate position here. I can't take a step offa this mountain without people coming up to me asking why they've been left out, why your man won't be digging on their land. That's people I've known since I was a wee baba. I've tried to explain to them that I'm not the one that decides where there's gold and where there isn't, and if they just let the hare sit, there'll be plenty of opportunities to go round. But . . .' He spreads his hands and gives Cal a world-weary eye-roll. 'Sure, you can't make people hear what they don't want to hear. What would they all think if I let a stranger in on this, while I'm keeping them out? Half the townland would go mental on me. I've enough on my plate without that.'

'Well,' Cal says. 'I sure wouldn't want you inconvenienced.'

'It's not just that,' Johnny explains. 'Mr Rushborough's not looking for a lucrative business venture. He's looking to get in touch with his heritage. No harm to you, but an American who blew in with a few grand in his pocket to buy up Irish land . . . that's not the buzz he's after. He wants to hear that there'll be no outsiders in this, because then he knows he's no outsider. If it starts to look like a free-for-all, the whole idea might turn sour on him, and then where would we all be?'

'Hate to think,' Cal agrees. He looks over the house, at the thick grove of trees rising up the mountainside. Even in this weather, a breeze nudges among the branches, languid but not restful, saving its force.

'Like I said,' Johnny reassures him, 'there'll be plenty to go round, all in good time. You just sit tight. You'll get your share. You never know: Mr Rushborough might even fancy having his own wee bit of Ardnakelty, and come looking to buy your land.'

'Gee whiz,' Cal says. 'Imagine little ol' me being bought out by a millionaire.'

'The sky's the limit,' Johnny tells him.

'What happens if the guy decides to head out panning first thing this morning?' Cal inquires. 'Once his hangover wears off.'

Johnny laughs, shaking his head. 'You've some mad ideas about all this, man. D'you know that? You talk like Mr Rushborough's only here to grub up all the gold he can get his hands on. He's here to see the land where his ancestors lived and died. He's got plenty to do before he gets around to the river.'

'Let's hope so,' Cal says. 'Be a shame if your gold rush was over before it even got going.'

'Listen to me, man,' Johnny says indulgently. 'This story about putting gold in the river, or however it went. I don't know who told you that, but whoever he was, he was taking the mickey – having you on, that means; having a wee joke with you. We've a fierce mischievous sense of humour around here; it takes a while to get used to. Don't you be doing anything foolish with that story, now, like maybe bringing it to Mr Rushborough. Because I can tell you right now, he won't believe a word of it.'

'You don't think?' Cal inquires politely. He has no intention of discussing this with Rushborough. He's under no illusion that he has Rushborough's measure yet.

'Ah, God, no. I'll tell you what to do. Don't let on you fell for the story – don't be giving Mart Lavin, or whoever 'tis, the satisfaction. Go back home and say nothing about this morning. And when he comes asking how you got on with me, you laugh in his face and ask him if he takes you for a fool.'

'That's an idea, all right,' Cal agrees. He turns around to lean his arms on the rail, shoulder to shoulder with Johnny. 'I got a better one. You cut me in for my share, and I won't go up to town and tell Officer O'Malley what kind of scam you're running on his patch.'

Johnny looks at him. Cal looks back. They both know Officer O'Malley would get a great big handful of nothing out of Ardna-kelty, but that doesn't matter: the last thing Johnny needs right now is a cop all up in his business, making everyone wary.

Johnny says, 'I'm not sure I oughta let Theresa hang around a man that'd want in on a scam like that one.'

'You're the one that came up with the idea,' Cal says. 'And let her hang around to hear it.'

'Didn't happen, man. And if it had, I'm her daddy. That's why

I want her around me. Maybe I oughta look a little harder at your reasons.'

Cal doesn't move, but Johnny flinches anyway.

Cal says, 'You don't want to try that, Johnny. Trust me on this one.'

The heat is building. The sun up here is different; it has a scouring quality, like it's scraping your skin raw to make it easier to burn. Liam and Alanna have started chanting something giggly and triumphant, but the high air of the mountain thins it to a wisp of sound.

Cal takes the three hundred bucks out of his pocket and holds it out.

Johnny glances at it, but doesn't move to take it. After a moment he says, 'That's nothing to do with me. If you want to do something with it, talk to Mart Lavin.'

Cal more or less expected this. Mart said no one wants to trust Johnny with cash, so they're buying the gold themselves. Johnny is keeping his hands clean, and making the men think it's their smart idea.

'I'll do that,' he says, pocketing the cash. 'Good talk.'

'Daddy!' Liam yells, and he starts pointing at the earthworks and calling out some long excited story. 'I'll see you round,' Johnny says to Cal, and he saunters over to Liam and Alanna's construction, where he squats down and starts pointing at things and asking interested questions. Cal heads off all the way back down the mountain, to find Mart.

———

Pissing Noreen off comes at a price. Lena is the last person in several townlands to hear about Johnny Reddy's Englishman's granny's gold. Contrary to Noreen's opinion, Lena is not a hermit and in fact has a respectable number of friends, but the close ones are women from the book club she did in town a few years back, or people from work – Lena does the accounts, and whatever else needs doing, at a stable out the other side of Boyle. She can go for days without talking to anyone from Ardnakelty, if she feels like it, which under the circumstances she has. She hasn't been into the shop, on the grounds that if Noreen starts shoving her down the aisle again, Lena might tell her to fuck off and mind her own business, which would be satisfying but unproductive. She hasn't been round to Cal's, either. The easeful rhythm they've established, over the past two years, has them meeting a few times a week; and Lena, who has never before felt the need to worry about what Cal might read into her actions, doesn't want him thinking she's hovering and fretting over him because Johnny bloody Reddy is back in town. She expected Trey to come back looking to stay the night again, but there's been no sign of her.

So the first Lena hears of the gold is when she calls round to Cal on Tuesday to give him some mustard. Lena likes finding small gifts for Cal. He's not a man who wants many or fancy things, so she enjoys the challenge. At the food market in town, on her way back from the morning's work, she came across a jar of mustard with whiskey and jalapeños, which should both please Cal and give Trey's face the look of mingled suspicion and determination that he and Lena enjoy.

'Fuck me,' Lena says, when Cal has put her abreast of the situation. They're on the back porch, eating ham sandwiches for lunch – Cal wanted to try the mustard straightaway. A few of the rooks, who zeroed in on the food before Lena and Cal even sat themselves down, are stalking the grass at a safe distance, turning their heads sideways to keep an eye on the prize. 'Didn't see that one coming.'

'I thought Noreen would've told you before now,' Cal says.

'We annoyed each other, the other day. I was giving it some time to wear off. I shoulda known. I miss two days of Noreen, and I miss the biggest news in years.'

'Go tell her you just found out now,' Cal says. 'She'll be so smug, she'll forgive you anything.' Rip is twitching to go after the rooks. Cal runs a hand down the back of his head, settling him.

Lena is thinking back to Johnny lounging on her gate, telling her about his fortune under construction. 'Ha,' she says, struck by a thought. 'Here I thought that little fecker was calling round to me trying to get his leg over. And all the time it was my wallet he had his eye on, not my pretty face. That'll teach me to flatter myself.'

'He's only looking for cash from people whose land is on this line,' Cal says. 'So far, anyway. I reckon what he mostly wanted from you was someone to tell people he's a great guy and they oughta back him up.'

'He was barking up the wrong tree here,' Lena says, tossing a scrap of bread to the rooks. 'I reckon anyone that gets involved with that eejit wants his head examined.'

'That'd be me,' Cal says. 'I gave Mart three hundred bucks this morning, for my share of the gold.'

Lena forgets about the rooks and turns to look at him.

'Probably I need my head examined,' Cal says.

Lena says, 'Is that fucker getting Trey mixed up in this?'

'He had her in the room while he talked the guys into it,' Cal says. 'Had her telling them how her teacher says the gold's there. Beyond that, I dunno.'

He sounds calm, but Lena doesn't mistake that for taking it lightly. 'So you're going to keep an eye on him,' she says.

'Not much else I can do, right now,' Cal says. He pulls a chunk of crust off his sandwich, avoiding the mustard, and throws it to the rooks. Two of them get into a tug-of-war over it. 'If something does come up, I want to be there to catch it.'

Lena watches him. She says, 'Like what?'

'I don't know yet. I'm just gonna wait and see. That's all.'

Lena has only ever known Cal to be gentle, but she's not under the illusion that he has no other side. She doesn't underestimate his anger. She can almost smell it off him, like heat off metal.

'What's Johnny think of having you on board?' she asks.

'Doesn't like it one little bit,' Cal says. 'But he's stuck with me. Specially if he doesn't want me.'

Even if Lena had any inclination to try and turn him from this, she would get nowhere. 'It'll do him good,' she says. 'He's too fond of getting his own way, that fella.'

'Yeah, well,' Cal says. 'Not this time.'

Lena eats her sandwich – the mustard is good and strong – and examines what she's learned. Her first guess was right, and Noreen's was wrong. Johnny didn't just drift home because his girlfriend had dumped him and he couldn't figure out how to work himself on his own. Johnny needs money, badly. For him to go to this much trouble, it's not just rent arrears or an unpaid credit card. He owes someone; someone dangerous.

Lena doesn't give a shite what Johnny personally is facing. What she wants to know is whether the danger is going to stay over in London, waiting trustingly for him to show up with the cash, or whether it's coming after him. Lena wouldn't trust Johnny to come back with her cash from down the road, let alone from over the water. If she wanted the money, she'd be going after him.

Cal, not knowing Johnny as she does, is unlikely to have reached the same conclusions yet. Lena considers sharing hers with him, and decides against it for the moment. It's one thing to refuse responsibility for Cal's moods; it's another to deliberately whip up his fears and his anger, when she has nothing to go on but conjecture.

'Next time I see Trey,' she says, 'I'll ask her to come stay with me for a few days.'

Cal throws the rooks another piece of crust and shifts, trying to get the sun to attack a different part of his face. 'I don't like this weather,' he says. 'Back on the job, this kind of heat was when we knew things were gonna get messy. People lose their minds, do the type of crazy stuff where you figure they must've been high on half a dozen things at once, till the tests come back and nope, stone-cold sober. Just hot. Whenever it stays hot for too long, I'm just waiting for things to get messy.'

Lena, although she doesn't say this, has been liking the heat wave. She appreciates the change it brings to the townland. It transforms the muted blues and creams and yellows of the village houses, lifting them to an expansive brightness that barely seems real, and it rouses the fields from their usual soft somnolence to a spiky, embattled vividness. It's like seeing Cal in a new mood: it lets her know the place better.

'That's a different class of heat, sure,' she says. 'From what I've heard, the summer in America'd melt your brains. This is just the kinda heat you'd get on holiday in Spain, only for free.'

'Maybe.'

Lena watches his face. 'I suppose there's a few people getting edgy, all right,' she says. 'Last week Sheena McHugh threw Joe outa the house, because she said she couldn't stand the way he chews his food one minute longer. He had to go to his mammy's.'

'Well, there you go,' Cal says, but his mouth has quirked in a smile. 'You'd have to be losing your mind to dump anyone with Miz McHugh. Did Sheena let him back in yet?'

'She did, yeah. He went into town and bought one of them fans, the big tower ones. It's got an app and all. She'da let in Hannibal Lecter if he was carrying one of those.'

Cal grins. 'The heat'll break,' Lena says. 'Then we'll all be back to giving out about the rain.'

The two rooks are still fighting over Cal's sandwich crust. A third one sneaks up on them, gets within a couple of feet, and lets loose an explosion of barking. The first two shoot into the air, and the third one grabs the chunk of crust and heads for the hills. Lena and Cal both burst out laughing.

Late at night, Trey's parents are arguing in their room. Trey extracts herself from the sweaty tangle of sheets and Banjo and Alanna, who's come into her bed again, and goes to the door to listen. Sheila's voice, low and brief, but sharp; then a load of Johnny, with a note of outrage, controlled but building.

She goes out to the sitting room and turns the telly on, to give herself an excuse for being there, but muted so she can keep an ear out. The room smells of food and stale smoke. The mess has started to silt up again, since she and her dad tidied it the other night – half the carpet is taken up by an arrangement of small staring dolls, and there are a bunch of Nerf bullets and a dirty sock stuffed with sweet wrappers on the sofa. Trey throws them in a corner. On the telly, two pale women in old-fashioned clothes are looking upset about a letter.

Cillian Rushborough came for dinner. 'I can't be cooking for some fancy fella,' Sheila said flatly, when Johnny told her. 'Bring him into town.'

'Make Irish stew,' Johnny said, catching her round the waist and planting a kiss on her. He'd been in great form all day, kicking a football around the yard with Liam, and getting Maeve to teach him Irish dancing steps on the kitchen floor. Sheila didn't kiss him back, or turn away, just kept moving like he wasn't there. 'Heavy on the aul' spuds. He'll love it. Sure, your stew's fit for a billionaire, never mind a millionaire. That's what we'll call it from now on, won't we, lads? Millionaire stew!' Maeve jumped up and down and clapped her hands – ever since their dad got home, she's been acting like a four-year-old – and Liam started banging his chair legs and chanting something about millionaire stew being made of goo. 'Come on, Maeveen,' their dad said, grinning, 'get your shoes on, and you and me'll go down to the shop and get the finest ingredients. Millionaire stew for everyone!'

The little ones had to eat in the sitting room in front of the telly, but Trey and Maeve were let eat in the kitchen with the adults, so Trey got her look at Rushborough. He praised the stew to the skies, went into raptures about his day wandering around the boreens ('Is that how you pronounce it? Honestly, you must correct me, you can't let me make a fool of myself'), asked Maeve about her favourite music and Trey about carpentry, and told a funny story about getting chased by the Maguires' goose. Trey has an aversion to charm, which she's encountered on only a few occasions, mostly in her father. Rushborough is more skilled at it. When he asked her mam about the little watercolour landscape that hangs on the kitchen wall, and got nothing out of her but a few brief words, he backed off instantly and gracefully, and went back to discussing Taylor Swift with Maeve. His deftness makes Trey more wary of him, not less.

She didn't expect to like Rushborough, and doesn't consider that to be important. What matters is what she can do about him.

She was expecting him to be, not thick, but like Lauren in her class, who believes stupid things because she doesn't bother to check them enough in her mind. One time Trey's mate Aidan told Lauren that one of Jedward was his cousin, and she went around telling people that for a whole day, till someone called her a fucking eejit and pointed out that Jedward are twins. But Rushborough checks things. Maeve would say something meant to be funny, and Rushborough would laugh his arse off and then move on; only a minute later Trey would catch his eye resting on Maeve, just for a second, checking what she said against things in his mind.

What Trey reckons is that he wants the gold to be real so badly that he's decided not to check too hard. If he finds out it's fake, or at least partly fake, he'll be raging double, because he'll be raging at himself as well. But he won't find out, unless he has no choice. She could tell him straight out what her dad said the other night, and he'd brush her off as a contrary teenager trying to stir shite.

The voices in the bedroom gain in intensity, although not in volume. Trey is weighing up whether she needs to do anything when her parents' door opens, hard enough to bang off the wall, and Johnny comes down the hall and into the sitting room, buttoning his shirt. Trey knows from the looseness of his movements that he's about half drunk.

'What are you doing awake?' he demands, when he sees her.

'Watching the telly,' Trey says. She doesn't think there's any immediate danger – when her dad hit her before, he mostly went for their mam or Brendan first, and for her only as an afterthought, if he had some left over; and none of the sounds from the bedroom implied that. Her muscles are ready to run if she needs to, all the same. She feels a sudden, savage anger at her body for still having the habit. She had come to believe she was done with this.

Johnny drops into an armchair with a sigh that's close to a snarl. 'Women,' he says, wiping his hands over his face. 'Honest to God, they're the fuckin' divil.'

He appears to have forgotten that Trey is a girl. People sometimes do. It doesn't bother her from them, and it neither bothers her nor surprises her from her father. She waits.

'All a man needs from a woman,' Johnny says, 'is for her to have a bitta faith in him. That's what puts the strength into you, when things are tough. A man can do anything in the world, once he knows his woman's behind him all the way. But her . . .'

He flicks his head in the direction of the bedroom. 'God almighty, the whinging out of her. Oh, she'd a terrible time altogether while I was away, all alone, afraid for her life, ashamed to walk into the shop with the women looking sideways at her, the Guard coming down from town trying to make ye go to school, having to borrow money for the Christmas— Did she do that, even? Or was she just saying it to make me feel guilty?'

'Dunno,' Trey says.

'I said to her, sure what's there to be afraid of, all the way up here, and what do you care what them bitches say – and if that Guard's got nothing better to do than give out to kids for mitching, then fuck him anyway. But there's no talking to a woman that's looking to make a big fuckin' deal outa nothing.'

He digs through his pockets for his smokes. 'She's never satisfied, that one. I could bring her the sun, moon, and stars, and she'd find something wrong with them. She wasn't happy when I was here, and she wasn't happy when I was gone. And sure' – Johnny's hands fly up in outrage – 'sure, I'm back now. Here I am. Sitting here. I've a plan to put the lot of us on the pig's back. And she's still not fuckin' happy. What the fuck does she want from me?'

Trey isn't sure whether he wants her to answer or not. 'Dunno,' she says again.

'I even brought your man Rushborough here for her to meet. Does she think I wanted to bring him into this kip? I did it anyway, just so's she could see I wasn't talking shite. That man who complimented your mammy's stew, he's eaten at the finest restaurants in the world. And she looked at him like he was some latchico I picked out of a ditch. Did you see that?'

'Nah,' Trey says. 'I was eating the stew.'

Her dad lights a cigarette and pulls hard on it. 'I asked her for her opinion and all. Told her the whole plan – what d'you reckon, says I, that oughta make for a better Christmas this year, amn't

I right? D'you know what she did?' Johnny stares past Trey's ear and gives an exaggerated shrug. 'That's it. That's what I got offa her. All I needed was for her to look at me and say, *It's great, Johnny, well done.* Maybe give me a smile, even, or a kiss. That's not a lot to ask. And instead I get—' He does the stare and shrug again. 'I swear to fuck, women are only put on this earth to wreck our fuckin' heads.'

'Maybe,' Trey says, feeling that some response is required of her.

Johnny looks at her then, taking a second to focus his eyes, and appears to recall who she is. He makes the effort to smile at her. Tonight, with the spring and shine taken off him, his boyish look is gone; he seems small and wispy in the armchair, as if his muscles are already starting to shrivel towards old age. 'Not you, sweetheart,' he reassures her. 'Sure, you're Daddy's great girl. You've all the faith in the world in me, haven't you?'

Trey shrugs.

Johnny looks at her. For a second Trey thinks she's going to get a slap. He sees her ready to bolt, and closes his eyes. 'I need a fuckin' drink,' he says, under his breath.

Trey sits there looking at him, slumped with his head leaned back and his legs splayed at random. There are purple shadows under his eyes.

She goes out to the kitchen, takes the whiskey bottle from its cupboard, and puts some ice in a glass. When she gets back to the sitting room, her father hasn't moved. A thin trail of smoke trickles upwards from his cigarette. She squats beside his chair.

'Daddy,' she says. 'Here you go.'

Her dad opens his eyes and looks blankly at her for a second. Then he spots the bottle and lets out a small harsh burst of laughter. 'God,' he says, softly and bleakly, to himself.

'I'll get you something different,' Trey says. 'If you don't want that.'

Johnny stirs himself, with an effort, and sits up straight. 'Ah, no, sweetheart, that's lovely. Thanks very much. You're a great girl altogether, looking after your daddy. What are you?'

'Great girl,' Trey says obediently. She pours some whiskey and hands him the glass.

Johnny takes a deep swig and lets his breath out. 'Now,' he says. 'See? All better.'

'I've got faith in you,' Trey says. 'It's gonna be great.'

Her dad smiles down at her, pinching the top of his nose like his head hurts. 'That's the plan, anyhow. And sure, why shouldn't it be? Don't we deserve a few nice things?'

'Yeah,' Trey says. 'Mam'll be delighted once she sees it. She'll be all proud of you.'

'She will, o' course. And when your brother comes home, it'll be great for him to have a nice surprise to come back to. Isn't that right? Can't you just see the face on him, when he steps outa the car and gets an eyeful of a house the size of a shopping centre?'

Just for a second, Trey does see it, as vividly as if it could actually come true: Brendan's head tilted up to the shining rows of windows, his mouth opening, his thin mobile face exploding like a firework with delight. Her dad is good at this.

'Yeah,' she says.

'He'll never want to go roaming again,' Johnny says, smiling at her. 'He'll have no need.'

'Mrs Cunniffe says can you ask Mr Rushborough is there any gold on their land,' Trey says. 'And Tom Pat Malone says can their Brian help dig the gold outa the river.'

Johnny laughs. 'There you go. See? Everyone's dying for a hand in this, except your mammy, and we'll get her there in the end. You just tell Mrs Cunniffe and Tom Pat that Mr Rushborough appreciates their interest, and he'll keep them in mind. And you keep on telling me who comes looking to get in on this, just like you've done now. Can you do that?'

'Yeah,' Trey says. 'Sure.'

'Good girl,' Johnny says. 'Where would I be without you?'

Trey says, 'When are you gonna put the gold in the river?'

Johnny takes another swig of the whiskey. 'It'll arrive sometime tomorrow,' he says. 'Not here – sure, the courier'd get lost on the mountain, amn't I right? He'd end in a bog, him and the gold, and we don't want that. It's going to Mart Lavin's. The next day, first thing in the morning, we'll put it in. Then we'll be all ready for Mr Rushborough to go treasure hunting.' He cocks his head at Trey quizzically. The whiskey has braced him up. 'Do you want to come along, is that it? You're going to give us a hand?'

Trey definitely doesn't want to go along. 'What time?' she asks.

'We'll have to go bright and early. Before the farmers are up, even. We don't want anyone spotting us, sure we don't? It'll be daylight by half-five. We'll want to be down at the river by then.'

Trey makes a horrified face. 'Nah,' she says.

Johnny laughs and ruffles her hair. 'My God, I should've known better than to ask a teenager to get up outa her bed before noon! You're grand; you get your beauty sleep. There'll be other ways you can give me a hand, won't there?'

'Yeah,' Trey says. 'Just not that early.'

'I'll find you something,' Johnny assures her. 'Sure, with the brains on you, there'll be a million things you can do.'

'I can keep an eye on Rushborough for you,' Trey says. 'Tomorrow. Make sure he doesn't go down to the river before you have it ready.'

Her dad turns from his glass and looks at her. Trey watches him, slowed by the drink, trying to assess this idea.

'He won't see me,' she says. 'I'll stay hid.'

'D'you know something, now?' her dad says, after a moment. 'That's a great idea. I'd say all he'll do is wander around seeing the sights, and you'll be bored to bits – but sure, no need to put your whole day into it. I'm bringing him to see Mossie O'Halloran's fairy hill in the afternoon; you just mind him for the morning. If you see him heading down towards the river, you go up to him and say hello, nice and polite like, and offer to show him that aul' bit of a stone tower off the main road. You tell him it belonged to the Feeneys, and he'll go along with you like a lamb.'

'OK,' Trey says. 'Where's he staying?'

'He's in that grey cottage over towards Knockfarraney, on Rory Dunne's farm. You go down there first thing tomorrow morning, once you drag yourself outa the bed, and see what Rushborough does with himself. Then you can come tell me all about it.'

Trey nods. 'OK,' she says.

'That's great,' her dad says, smiling at her. 'You're after doing me a power of good, so you are. That's all I needed: my own wee girl on my side.'

'Yeah,' Trey says. 'I'm on your side.'

'You are, o' course. Now go get some sleep, or you'll be fit for nothing tomorrow morning.'

'I'll get up,' Trey says. 'Night.'

This time he doesn't try to hug her. As she turns to close the door behind her, she sees his head go back again and his fingers pinch at his nose. She reckons possibly she should feel sorry for him. The only thing she feels is a cold spark of victory.

Trey is not, by nature, one to go at people or things sideways. Her inclination is to go in straight, and keep going till she gets the job done. But she's open to learning new skills when the necessity arises. She's learning them from her dad. The part that surprises her isn't how fast she's picking this up – Cal always says she's a quick study – but how easily her dad, who's never gone at anything straight in his life, can be taken in.

8

Until Trey shows up at his door on Wednesday afternoon, Cal doesn't realise how much of him has been fretting that Johnny would keep her away. He feels bad for not having more faith in her, when he has personal experience of how hard it is to keep Trey away from anything she wants; but then again, he would have to be a serious dumbass to assume that he knows what Trey wants right now, when she might not even know that herself. Cal's own daddy bounced in and out of his life a bunch of times, when he was growing up. He was funnier and a lot less dapper than Johnny Reddy, and he made more of an effort when he was around, but he gave the same impression that his actions had surprised him as much as anyone, and that it would be both uncouth and unfair for anyone to rake them up. By the fifth or sixth go-round, Cal and his mama would have had every right to tell the guy to get fucked, but somehow it was never that simple. He had enough bad habits that Cal presumes he's dead by now.

They've finished cleaning the fixer-upper chair, which under all the layers of dirt and grease turns out to be a muted, autumny golden-brown. They dismantle it carefully, taking photos on Cal's phone as they go, and measure up the broken pieces for replacements. Cal leaves plenty of silences where Trey could bring up her dad and Rushborough and the gold, but she doesn't.

Cal tells himself this is normal. She's fifteen, right around the age when Alyssa stopped telling him stuff. Trey has very little in common with Alyssa, a gold-hearted girl who sees potential good in the most unlikely people and has solid, methodical plans for letting them see it too, but in some ways fifteen is always fifteen. When Alyssa stopped talking to him, Cal reckoned at least she was talking to her mama, and let it be. He's no longer sure that was the right call, but even if it was, he has no such easy out when it comes to Trey.

Nothing, of course, says he can't bring up the subject himself and just tell her straight out that he knows the story – which presumably the kid has already guessed, Mart's mouth being what it is – and that he's bought in on the gold; but that has the feel of a bad idea. Trey is unlikely to believe that Cal feels any urge to scam money out of some random Brit, and he's nowhere near convinced that she'll appreciate the thought of him getting involved in order to look out for her. And if she's ashamed of the stunt Johnny is pulling, or if she just wants to keep her time with Cal separate from his shenanigans, she won't welcome Cal prying the topic open. Trey has various levels of silence. The last thing Cal wants to do is nudge her into a deeper one.

'That'll do for today,' he says, when they've cut and planed pieces of the oak sleeper to roughly the right sizes, ready for turning. 'Spaghetti Bolognese sound good?'

'Yeah,' Trey says, dusting her hands on her jeans. 'Can I borrow your camera?'

Not long after Cal moved to Ireland, he splashed out on a high-end camera, so he could send Alyssa photos and videos. His phone would have done the job just fine, but he wanted better than fine: he wanted to offer her every shade and detail, the full fine range of subtleties that make up the place's beauty, so he could maybe tempt her to come see it for herself. Trey used the camera for some school project on local wildlife, last year. 'Sure,' Cal says. 'What for?'

'Just for a coupla days,' Trey says. 'I'll look after it.'

Cal has no desire to push her till she comes up with a lie. He goes into his bedroom and finds the camera, on one of the neat array of shelves they built into the closet.

'Here,' he says, coming back out to the living room. 'You remember how to use it?'

'Sorta.'

'OK,' Cal says. 'Let's find you something good to practise on. We've got a while, unless you're about to starve to death.'

Trey turns out to have definite ideas about what she wants to photograph. It needs to be outdoors, and at a distance of about fifty yards, and she needs video, and she needs to know how to adjust the camera for low light. Cal can't provide the low light – at past five o'clock, the air is still swollen with sun – but they head out to his back field and use the scarecrow for a model. Someone has been bringing out its hidden potential again. It's been out hunting: it has a water pistol in one hand and a big teddy bear dangling upside down from the other.

'Mart,' Trey says.

'Nah,' Cal says. He starts to count off fifty paces from the scarecrow, which, activated by their approach, is growling at them and brandishing the teddy bear menacingly. 'Mart would've told me. He likes to take credit.'

'Not PJ.'

'Hell no. Senan, maybe, or his kids.'

'We could get a security camera. The Moynihans have one they can watch off their phones. Lena said Noreen said one time Celine Moynihan stayed home from mass 'cause she said she felt sick, and halfway through the homily Mrs Moynihan looked at her phone and saw Celine in the garden shifting her fella. Let such a squawk outa her that the priest lost his place.'

Cal laughs. 'Nah,' he says. 'I don't wanna scare off whoever it is. I'd rather see what they come up with next. How 'bout here? This far enough?'

The dogs, with a rawhide bone each to keep them from getting restless, gnaw and mumble contentedly in the grass. While he shows Trey how to move her autofocus point and how to switch between stills and video, Cal tries to figure out what Johnny could want her to photograph. The best theory he can come up with is that Johnny wants footage of the guys planting the gold in the river, in case at some point he needs to do a little arm-twisting to keep them on board. Cal doubts he'll even stir his scrawny ass to take his own footage; it looks like that's going to be Trey's responsibility, specially since he doubts her personal moral code would allow for putting his camera in Johnny's hands. And of course Johnny wouldn't bother to consider what might happen to her, if she should get caught.

Come dawn, Cal is going to be at that river. If he wants the men to keep him abreast of any developments, he can't sit back like

Johnny and let other people do the dirty work. He has to be right in there beside them, the whole way.

If Trey shows up and sees him standing there, up to his knees in water and gold dust and intrigue, she'll feel like he's been lying to her. He revises his ideas. At some point this evening, he needs to bring up the subject.

'Need to zoom closer,' Trey says. 'He's not clear enough.'

'It's got face detect,' Cal says. 'Not sure it works on zombies, but if you've got people in the frame, it'll automatically focus in on their faces.'

Trey doesn't respond to that. She fiddles with dials, tries another shot, and examines the display critically. The scarecrow gapes out at them, in such precise detail that they can see the drips of fake blood on its teeth. Trey nods, satisfied.

'The buttons can light up,' Cal says, 'if it's dark. So you can see what you're doing. You gonna want that?'

Trey shrugs. 'Dunno yet.'

'It's this key here,' Cal says. 'You oughta try it out in the dark somewhere, before you actually go out shooting. Just in case the buttons light up brighter'n you might want them to be.'

Trey turns to look at him, a sharp questioning look. For a second Cal thinks she's going to say something, but then she nods and turns back to the camera.

''S heavy,' she says.

'Yeah. You need to make sure you're settled somewhere you can keep your hand good and steady.'

Trey tests out different ways of bracing her elbow on her knee. 'Might need a wall,' she says. 'Or a rock or something.'

'Listen,' Cal says. 'You remember when we talked about what if someone tries to make you do stuff you don't want to do?'

'Go for the nads,' Trey says, squinting through the viewfinder. 'Or the eyes.'

'No,' Cal says. 'I mean, yeah, sure, if you need to. Or the throat. But I mean if people try to get you to do drugs or booze. Or dumb shit like, I dunno, breaking into old buildings.'

'I'm not gonna do drugs,' Trey says flatly. 'And I'm not gonna get drunk.'

'I know that,' Cal says. He notices automatically that Trey didn't say she's not planning to drink, or for that matter break into abandoned buildings, but those can wait. 'But remember we talked about what if people try to pressure you?'

'They don't,' Trey reassures him. 'They don't give a shite. More for them. And my mates don't do drugs anyway, only hash sometimes, 'cause they're not fuckin' thick.'

'Right,' Cal says. 'Good.' Somehow this conversation seemed a lot simpler the last time they had it, a year or so ago, fishing in the river. Now, with Johnny Reddy all over everything, it feels like rocky and complicated territory. 'But if anyone ever does. You could handle that, right?'

'I'd tell 'em to fuck off,' Trey says. 'Look at this.'

Cal looks at the photo. 'Looks good,' he says. 'If you want the trees in the background clearer, you can play around with this a little bit. What I'm saying about pressure is, you can do the same thing with adults. If an adult ever tries to rope you into something you don't like the looks of, you've got every right to tell him to fuck off. Or her. Whoever.'

'Thought you wanted me to be mannerly,' Trey says, grinning.

'Right,' Cal says. 'You can tell them to kindly fuck off.'

'I never like the looks of my Irish homework,' Trey points out. 'Can I tell the teacher—'

'Nice try,' Cal says. 'People fought and died so you could learn your own language. I don't know the ins and outs, but that's what Francie tells me. So you do your Irish.'

'I've loads of Irish,' Trey says. '*An bhfuil cead agam dul go dtí an leithreas.*'

'That better not be Irish for "kindly fuck off".'

'Find out. Say it to Francie next time.'

'I bet it doesn't mean anything,' Cal says. He's slightly reassured by the fact that Trey is in a good mood, but only slightly. Trey's sensors for danger are miscalibrated, or not hooked up right, or something: she can identify a dangerous situation without

138

necessarily recognising any need to back away from it. 'You just made it up.'

'Did not. It means "Can I go to the toilet?"'

'Damn,' Cal says. 'That sounds fancier'n it has any right to. You could tell someone to kindly fuck off in Irish, and they'd probably take it as a compliment.'

Rip lets out a bark that has a growl mixed in. Cal turns fast. He feels Trey tense beside him.

Johnny Reddy is walking out of the late sun towards them. His long shadow across the stubbled field makes him look like a tall man, moving closer at a slow glide.

Cal and Trey get to their feet. Cal says, before he knows he's going to, 'You don't have to go with him. You can stay here.'

Rip lets out another bark. Cal puts a hand on his head. 'Nah,' Trey says. 'Thanks.'

'OK,' Cal says. His throat hurts on the words. 'Just so you know.'

'Yeah.'

Johnny lifts his arm in a wave. Neither of them waves back.

'Well, fancy meeting you here,' Johnny says happily, when he gets close enough. 'I'm after bringing Mr Rushborough to see Mossie O'Halloran's fairy hill. God almighty, the excitement; he was like a child at its first panto, I'm not joking you. He'd a bottle of cream with him, and a wee bowl to put it in, and he was fussing about like an aul' one with her doilies, trying to pick the perfect spot for it. He wanted to know what side of the hill would be traditional.' Johnny gives an extravagant, humorous shrug and eye-roll. 'Sure, I hadn't a notion. But Mossie said the east side, so the east side it was. Mr Rushborough was all for staying out there till it was dark and hoping we'd get a sound-and-light show, but I want my dinner. I told him we'd be better off coming back another day, so we can see did the fairies take the cream.'

'Foxes'll eat it,' Trey says. 'Or Mossie's dog.'

'Shhh,' Johnny says, waving a finger at her reproachfully. 'Don't be saying that around Mr Rushborough. 'Tis a terrible thing to crush a man's dreams. And you never know: the fairies might get to it before the foxes do.'

Trey shrugs. 'Have you been down there yourself?' Johnny asks Cal.

'Nope,' Cal says.

'Ah, you oughta go. Regardless of what you think about the fairies, 'tis a beautiful spot. Tell Mossie I said you were to get the full tour.' He winks at Cal. Cal suppresses the urge to ask him what the fuck he's winking about.

'So I'm after dropping Mr Rushborough home,' Johnny says. 'He's had enough excitement for one day. I saw the two of ye out and about, and I thought, since I've the car' – he waves an arm at Sheila's beat-up Hyundai, whose silver roof shows over the roadside wall – 'I'd save my wee girl the walk home. Make sure you're in time for whatever feast your mammy's cooked up tonight.'

Trey says nothing. She switches the camera off.

'Here,' Cal says, handing Trey the camera case. 'Remember to charge it.'

'Yeah,' Trey says. 'Thanks.'

'What's this, now?' Johnny inquires, cocking his head at the camera.

'Taking a lend of it,' Trey says, fitting the camera carefully into the case. 'Summer homework. We've to photograph five kindsa wildlife and write about their habitat.'

'Sure, you can use my phone for that. No need to be risking Mr Hooper's lovely camera.'

'I'm gonna do birds,' Trey says. 'The focus isn't good enough on a phone.'

'Holy God, you don't make life easy for yourself, do you?' Johnny says, smiling down at her. 'Would you not do bugs? You could find yourself five different bugs in ten minutes, just out the back of the house. Job done.'

'Nah,' Trey says. She loops the camera strap across her body. 'Everyone's gonna do bugs.'

'That's my girl,' Johnny says affectionately, ruffling her hair. 'Don't follow the herd; do things your own way. Say thank you to Mr Hooper for the lend.'

'Just did.'

Cal discards his earlier ideas. Whatever Trey is planning to do with that camera, she doesn't want her father knowing about it. He has no idea what the kid is up to, and he doesn't like that one bit.

At least there's no longer any urgency about explaining to Trey how he's mixed up in all this, if she's not going to be at the river to see him. Cal's instinct, in terrain as misty and boggy as this, is to take as few steps as possible. He might still need to have that conversation at some point, but he's considerably happier leaving it till he can pick up some sense of where Trey stands.

'It might be a while before you get that back, now,' Johnny warns Cal. 'Theresa won't have as much time for the aul' carpentry, the next while. She's going to be giving me a hand with a few bits and bobs. Isn't that right, sweetheart?'

'Yeah,' Trey says.

'I'm in no hurry,' Cal says. 'I can wait as long as it takes.'

Trey whistles for Banjo, who comes lolloping over with his head cocked at a goofy angle to manage his bone. 'Seeya,' she says to Cal.

'Yup,' Cal says. To Johnny he says, 'See you round.'

'Ah, you will,' Johnny assures him. 'Sure, in a place this size, you can't escape anyone. Are you ready, missus?'

Cal watches them head across the field towards the car. Johnny is yakking away, tilting his face to Trey, gesturing at things. Trey is watching her sneakers kick through the grass. Cal can't tell whether she's answering.

———————

In the dark before dawn, the men don't look like men. They're only snatches of disturbance at the edges of Trey's senses: smudges of thicker shadow shifting on the riverbank, flickers of muttering through the rush and gabble of the water, which is raucous in the silence. The stars are faint enough that the surface of the river barely shimmers; the moon is a bare cold spot, low on the horizon, giving no light. The tiny orange glow of a cigarette butt arcs out over the water and vanishes. One man laughs.

Dawn comes early in July. Trey, who has the knack of waking when she wants, was dressed and out her window before four, waiting in the trees beside the road for her father to pass her by. He was harder to follow than she expected. She was thinking of him as a city blow-in who would crash through undergrowth, trip over rocks, and take half an hour to pick his way half a mile. It had slipped her mind that he has more years on this mountain than she does. He went down it like a fox, nimble and silent, shortcutting over walls and through groves. A few times Trey, hanging back for safety, lost him; but he has a small torch that he switched on for a second whenever he needed to get his bearings, and she watched for that.

He brought her to a bend in the river, not far from where she and Cal sometimes fish. Trey is in among the beech trees on the bank's elbow, crouched low behind a fallen trunk that will both mask her and steady the camera. The ground beneath her has a warm, living smell. Below the bend, where the river widens and shallows, the men have gathered.

Slowly the darkness thins. The men take shape, at first not human, just tall standing stones spaced irregularly at the water's edge. As the sky blooms deep blue they come alive. Trey recognises Mart Lavin first, the hunch of his back over his crook. She spots her dad by his quick restlessness, shifting and turning, and PJ by his walk when he takes a few paces forward to peer into the river – PJ gives the impression of having a limp, till you realise that he drags both feet, not just one; his legs are too gangly for him to keep them supervised all the way to the ends. She thinks the biggest man there, a little apart from the rest, must be Senan Maguire, until he turns to glance up at the coming dawn, and by the movement of his shoulders she knows him for Cal.

Trey goes stiller among the underbrush. It doesn't enter her mind for a moment that Cal might be there to con Rushborough. She takes for granted that he, like her, has reasons for what he's doing, and that they're likely to be solid ones.

She's angered, and stung hard, regardless. Cal knows she can keep her mouth shut. He knows, or ought to know, that she's not a child to be shielded from the big people's doings. Whatever he's at, he should have told her.

She slides the camera up her hoodie to muffle the chirp when she turns it on. Then she finds it a stable spot on the fallen trunk and starts adjusting her settings, the way Cal taught her. The sky is lightening. Sonny McHugh and Francie Gannon, the two most dedicated fishermen, are pulling on thigh-high waders and rolling up their shirtsleeves.

Trey, down on one knee squinting over the tree trunk, imagines that the viewfinder of the camera is the sight on Cal's big Henry rifle. She imagines picking off the men one by one, Mart crumpling forward over his crook, Dessie Duggan bouncing on his fat belly like a kid's ball, until the only two left are Cal, standing motionless amid it all, and her dad, running like a rabbit while she lines up the sights on his back.

The morning is coming to life. On the opposite bank, a colony of small birds in a massive oak tree are waking up and yammering all at once, and the rush of the river has settled in among the rising morning sounds. The light has brightened enough for filming. Trey presses Record.

Mart takes something from inside his jacket, a big Ziploc bag. The men close in around him, swiftly, to peer at it. Trey hears Con McHugh laugh, a quick crow of incredulous delight like a boy's. Bobby Feeney reaches to touch the bag, but Mart slaps his hand away. Mart is talking, jabbing a finger at the bag and explaining something. Trey tries to keep Cal out of her picture, but he's mixed in among the rest and she can't avoid him.

Mart gives the Ziploc to Francie, and he and Sonny wade into the river. It's low; they have to stretch to step down from the bank, and the water swirls and eddies around them only knee-deep. Sonny has a long stick that he uses to prod all around him, testing depths. They bend and feel under the water. Then they take handfuls from the bag. Their closed fists go deep into the water, and come up empty.

Mart gestures to them with his crook, giving instructions. Johnny talks, swivelling his head among the other men; sometimes

143

they laugh, the sound coming up to Trey as a rough murmur rising above the noise of the river. Trey keeps the camera steady. Once she sees Cal's head lift and turn, scanning. She freezes. For half a second she thinks his eyes catch hers, but then they slide on.

When Francie and Sonny straighten up and turn to wade out of the river, Trey fits the camera into its case and starts inching carefully backwards through the undergrowth. As soon as she's out of view, she runs, holding the camera against her body with one hand to stop it jolting. On her way back up the mountain she takes a load of photos of every bird she can spot, just in case.

By the time she gets home, Alanna and Liam are out in the yard, trying to teach Banjo to walk on his hind legs, which Banjo has no intention of doing. Trey goes in through the front door, so she can hide the camera before anyone sees it. Then she goes looking for breakfast.

Sheila is in the kitchen, ironing Johnny's shirts. 'There's no bread left,' she says, without looking up, when Trey comes in.

The room is already hot; the sun comes full through the window, singling out Sheila's rough hands moving across the blue of the shirt. Steam from the iron rises up through its beam.

Trey finds cornflakes and a bowl. 'Where's my dad?' she asks.

'Out. I thought you were with him.'

'Nah. Just out.'

'Emer rang,' Sheila says. 'I told her.'

Emer is the oldest. She went off to Dublin a few years ago, to work in a shop. She comes home for Christmas. Trey doesn't think about her much in between. 'Told her what?' she asks.

'That your daddy came back. And about the English fella.'

'Is she gonna come home?'

'Why would she?'

Trey shrugs one shoulder, acknowledging the justice of this.

'I thought you were going to stay a while at Lena Dunne's,' Sheila says.

'Changed my mind,' Trey says. She leans against the counter to eat her cornflakes.

'Go to Lena's,' Sheila says. 'I'll give you a lift down in the car, the way you won't have to carry your clothes.'

Trey says, 'Why?'

Sheila says, 'I don't like this English fella.'

'He's not staying here.'

'I know that.'

Trey says, 'I'm not scared of him.'

'Then you oughta be.'

'If he tried to do anything to me,' Trey says, 'I'd kill him.'

Sheila shakes her head, one brief twitch. Trey stays silent. What she said sounds stupid, now it's out of her mouth. The iron hisses.

Trey says, 'What's my dad doing today?'

'Something with the English fella. Seeing the sights.'

'How about tonight?'

'Francie Gannon has a card game.'

Trey refills her bowl and thinks about this. She considers it unlikely that Rushborough will be invited to Francie's game. Unless he goes down to Seán Óg's for a pint, he'll be home, on his own.

Sheila arranges the shirt on a hanger and hooks it onto the back of a chair. She says, 'I shoulda picked ye a better father.'

'Then we wouldn't exist,' Trey points out.

Sheila's mouth twists in amusement. 'No woman believes that,' she says. 'No mother, anyhow. We don't say it to the men, so as not to hurt their feelings – they're awful sensitive. But you'd be the same no matter who I got to sire you. Different hair, maybe, or different eyes, if I'da went with a dark fella. Wee little things like that. But you'd be the same.'

She shakes out another shirt and examines it, tugging creases straight. 'There was other lads that wanted me,' she says. 'I shoulda got ye any one of them.'

Trey thinks this over and rejects it. Most of the men in the town-land appear to an outside eye to be better bargains than her father, but she wants nothing to do with any of them. 'Why'd you pick him, so?' she asks.

'I can't remember that far back. I thought I'd reasons. Maybe I just wanted him.'

Trey says, 'You coulda told him to fuck off. When he came home.'

Sheila presses the tip of the iron along the shirt collar. She says, 'He said you're giving him a hand.'

'Yeah.'

'What way?'

Trey shrugs.

'Whatever he's promised you, you won't get it.'

'I know. I don't want anything offa him.'

'You know nothing. D'you know where he is? He's out hiding gold in the river for that English fella to find. Did you know that?'

'Yeah,' Trey says. 'I was there when he said it to the others.'

For the first time since Trey came in, Sheila lifts her head to look full at her. The sunbeam shrinks her pupils so that her eyes look one hot, clean blue.

'Go to Lena's,' she says. 'Pretend Cal Hooper's your daddy. Forget this fella was ever here. I'll come down and get you when you can come back.'

Trey says, 'I wanta stay here.'

'Pack your things. I'll bring you now.'

'I've to go,' Trey says. 'Me and Cal have that chair to do.' She goes to the sink and rinses her bowl under the tap.

Sheila watches her. 'Go on, so,' she says. She bends over the iron again. 'Learn your carpentering. And remember, your daddy has nothing to give you that's worth half as much. Nothing.'

9

Trey takes it for granted that there are unseen things on the mountain. The assumption has been with her from as far back as she can remember, so that the edge of fear that comes with it is a stable, accepted presence. The men who live deeper in the mountain's territory have told her about some of the things: white lights luring from the heather at night, savage creatures like great dripping otters snaking out of the bogs, weeping women who once you get close aren't women at all. Trey asked Cal once if he believed in any of these. 'Nope,' he said, between delicate hammer-taps on a dovetail. 'But I'd be a fool to rule them out. It's not my mountain.'

Trey has seen none of them, but when she's on the mountain at night, she feels them there. The sensation has changed in the last year or two. When she was younger she felt herself glanced over and dismissed, too slight to be worth any time or focus, just another small animal going about its business. Now her mind is a denser, more intricate thing. She feels herself being noted.

She sits with her back to an old wall, watching dusk fill up the air with hazy purple. Banjo is slouched comfortably against her calf, his ears and nose up to track the progress of the evening. Farmhouse windows are sprinkled, neat and yellow, among the dimming fields below them. A lone car curves down the road, its headlight beams long in the emptiness. The small grey cottage where Rushborough is staying stands alone in the shadow of the mountain, unlit.

Whatever lives here, Trey expects to meet it in the next week. She's used some of her carpentry money to buy five days' worth of supplies, mainly bread, peanut butter, biscuits, bottled water, and dog food. She's stashed them, and a couple of blankets and some toilet roll, in an abandoned house up the mountainside. Five days should be more than enough. Once she does what she's about to do, Rushborough will be gone as fast as he can pack. And once the men find out he's left, her dad will be gone in no time. All she needs to do is stay out of his way till then.

She doesn't trust Rushborough, but she can't see any reason why he would rat her out. To her dad, maybe, but not to the other men. If anyone asks why she was gone, she'll say her dad came home raging because he'd slipped up and Rushborough got suspicious, and she ran for fear he'd take it out on her, which is close to true. She's left a note in her bed saying 'Have to go somewhere. Back in a few days' so her mam won't worry.

She even remembered a knife for the peanut butter. She grins, thinking how proud Cal will be of her manners, till she remembers she can't tell him.

Trey has been thinking about Brendan. She doesn't think about him as much, these days. When she first learned what had happened to him – by accident, Cal said it happened, things just went bad that day, with the implication that that should make some kind of difference – she never stopped. She spent hours going back and redoing things in her mind so that she kept him from leaving the house that afternoon, warned him what to look out for, went along with him and shouted the right words at the right moment. She saved him a million times over, not because she believed it would change anything, just for respite from a world where he was dead. She stopped when she realised Brendan was starting to feel like someone she had made up. After that she thought only, ever, about the real him: she went over every word and expression and movement she could recall, tattooing them on her mind and pressing deep so the marks would stay sharp. Every one of them hurt. Even when she was doing something, working with Cal or playing football, what happened to Brendan was a cold fist-sized weight below her breastbone, dragging downwards.

Over time it's eased. She can do things free of that weight, see things without that blackness blotting out part of her vision. Sometimes this makes her feel like a traitor. She's thought of cutting Brendan's name into her body, only that would be stupid.

What she hopes to meet on the mountain is ghosts. She has no idea whether she believes in them or not, but if they exist, Brendan's will be here. She doesn't know what form he might take, but none of the possibilities are enough to deter her.

Bats are out hunting, quick deft swoops and shrills. The first stars are showing. Another car sweeps down the road and stops at Rushborough's cottage, barely visible now in the thickening dark. After a moment it sweeps away again, and the cottage lights flick on.

Trey unfolds herself and starts to make her way down the mountainside, with Banjo at her heel. She has the camera zipped under her hoodie, to leave her hands free in case she trips, but she won't.

She watched Rushborough all yesterday morning, just like she'd promised her dad. Mostly he just wandered around the lanes and took photos of stone walls, which to Trey seem like an idiotic thing to photograph; once he scraped around in the dirt for a while, held something up to squint at it, and then put it in his pocket. He stopped a few times to chat to people he came across: Ciaran Maloney, moving sheep between fields; Lena, out walking her dogs; Áine Geary, watering plants in the garden with her kids pulling at her. Once or twice Trey thought she saw his head turn towards her, but it always kept on turning. It was worth a wasted morning to find out where he's staying. When she reported back to her dad, at first he looked like he'd forgotten what she was talking about. Then he laughed and told her she was a great girl, and gave her a fiver.

Rushborough, when he opens the door, looks taken aback to see her. 'My goodness,' he says. 'Theresa, isn't it? Your father's not here, I'm afraid. He very kindly took me to see a few sights, and then dropped me back here. He'll be sorry to have missed you.'

Trey says, 'Got something to show you.'

'Oh,' Rushborough says, after a second. He steps back from the door. 'In that case, do come in. You're welcome to bring your friend.'

Trey doesn't like this. She meant to show him there on the doorstep. It seems to her that Rushborough should be warier of a kid he doesn't know. Her dad said Rushborough is an innocent who thinks all of Ardnakelty is leprechauns and maidens dancing at the crossroads, but Rushborough is no innocent.

The sitting room is very clean and very bare, just a few bits of pine furniture arranged in unnatural spots and a painting of flowers on the wall. It smells like no one has ever lived there. Rushborough's coat, hanging on a coat tree in the corner, looks faked.

'Won't you have a seat?' Rushborough asks, gesturing to an armchair. Trey sits, measuring the distance to the door. He arranges himself on the flowery sofa and cocks his head at her attentively, his hands clasped between his knees. 'Now. What can I do for you?'

Trey wants to be out of there. She doesn't like the way his teeth are too little and even, or the disconnect between his pleasant voice and the expert way he watches her, like she's an animal he's deciding whether to buy. She says, 'No one hasta know it was me that told you.'

'My goodness,' Rushborough says, his eyebrows going up. 'How mysterious. Of course: my lips are sealed.'

Trey says, 'You're going out tomorrow to look for gold in the river.'

'Oh, your father let you in on the secret?' Rushborough smiles. 'I am, yes. I'm not getting my hopes up too high, but wouldn't it be wonderful if we found some? Is that what you have to show me? Have you found a bit of gold of your own?'

'Nah,' Trey says. She unzips her hoodie, takes the camera out of its case, pulls up the video, and hands it over.

Rushborough gives her a look that's somewhere between amused and quizzical. As he watches, it fades off his face till there's nothing there at all.

'That's gold,' Trey says. All her instincts are pulling towards silence, but she makes herself say it. 'That they're putting in the river. For you to find.'

'Yes,' Rushborough says. 'I see that.'

Trey can feel his mind working. He watches the video to the end.

'Well,' he says, with his eyes still on the display. 'Well well well. This is unexpected.'

Trey says nothing. She stays ready for any sudden move.

Rushborough glances up. 'Is this your camera? Or do you have to give it back to someone?'

'Gotta give it back,' Trey says.

'And do you have this backed up anywhere?'

'Nah,' Trey says. 'Don't have a computer.'

'In the cloud?'

Trey gives him a blank look. 'Dunno about the cloud.'

'Well,' Rushborough says again. 'I do appreciate you looking out for me. It's very kind of you.' He taps his front teeth with a fingernail. 'I think I need to have a conversation with your father,' he says. 'Don't you?'

Trey shrugs.

'Oh, definitely. I'll give him a ring and ask him to pop round now.'

'I've to go,' Trey says. She gets up and holds out her hand for the camera, but Rushborough doesn't move.

'I need to show this to your father,' he explains. 'Are you afraid that he'll be angry? Don't worry. I won't let him do anything to you. I'm delighted that you brought me this.'

'I said. No one hasta know it was me. Just say someone told you.'

'Well, he's hardly going to spread this around,' Rushborough points out reasonably. He pulls a phone out of his pocket and dials, keeping his eyes on Trey. 'This won't take long,' he tells her. 'We'll clear everything up in no time. Johnny? We've got a bit of a situation. Your lovely daughter is here, and she's brought me something that you ought to see. When can you be here? . . . Marvellous. See you then.'

He puts the phone away. 'He'll just be a few minutes,' he says, smiling at Trey. He sits back on the sofa and flicks through the other photos on the camera, taking his time over each one. 'Did you take all of these? They're very good. This one wouldn't look out of place in a gallery.' He holds up a photo Cal took of the rooks in their oak tree.

Trey says nothing. She stays standing. Banjo, getting restless, nudges her knee with his nose and makes the ghost of a whine; she puts a hand on his head to quiet him. Something is wrong. She wants to make a run for the door, but she can't leave without Cal's camera. Rushborough keeps scrolling, examining the photos with interest, giving one of them a little smile every now and then. The windows are black and she feels the distances outside them, the spread and the silence of the fields.

Her dad is there faster than he should be. The car speeds up the drive with a rip of spraying gravel. 'There we are,' Rushborough says, getting up to open the door.

'What's the story?' Johnny demands, his eyes skittering back and forth between Trey and Rushborough. 'What are you doing here?' he asks Trey.

'Shh,' Rushborough says. He hands Johnny the camera. 'Have a look at this,' he says pleasantly.

Johnny's face as he watches the video gives Trey a savage flare of exultation. He's white and blank, like the thing in his hand is a bomb and he's helpless against it; like he's holding his death. He lifts his head once, his mouth opening, but Rushborough says, 'Finish watching.'

Trey puts a hand on Banjo and gets ready. She puts no store in Rushborough's talk about not letting her dad be angry with her; she'd rather put her faith in the mountain. The minute her dad loosens his hold on the camera to start coming up with excuses, she's going to grab it, shove her dad into Rushborough, and run for her abandoned house. You could look for someone all year, on this mountain, and never find a sign. And once the townland learns that Rushborough is gone, her dad won't have a year.

When the video ends and Johnny lowers the camera, Trey waits for him to start spinning whatever story he thinks Rushborough's thick enough to believe. Instead he lifts his hands, still holding the camera, its strap swinging crazily.

'Man,' he says. 'It's not a problem. Honest to God. She'll say nothing. I guarantee it.'

'First things first,' Rushborough says. He takes back the camera. He asks Trey, 'Who have you told about this?'

'No one,' Trey says. She doesn't get why Rushborough is acting like the boss, giving her dad orders. None of this makes sense. She has no idea what's going on.

Rushborough looks at her with curiosity, his head to one side. Then he backhands her across the face. Trey is flung sideways, trips over her feet, slams into the arm of the chair and falls. She scrambles up, putting the chair between herself and Rushborough. There's nothing to grab for a weapon. Banjo is on his feet, growling.

'Call your dog,' Rushborough says. 'Or I'll break his back.'

Trey's hands are shaking. She manages to snap her fingers, and Banjo reluctantly eases back to her side. He's still growling, low in his chest, ready.

Johnny hovers, his hands fluttering. Rushborough asks again, in the same tone, 'Who have you told?'

Trey says, 'I never said a word. Them bastards can all go fuck themselves. Alla this place.' Blood comes out when she talks.

Rushborough lifts his eyebrows. Trey can tell by him that he knows she means it. 'Well,' he says. 'Why?'

Trey lets her eyes slide over his shoulder to her dad, who's trying to find something to say. 'If it hadn'ta been for them treating you like shite,' she says, 'you wouldn'ta gone.'

It comes out perfect, raw with just the right mix of anger and shame, something she would never have said unless it was ripped out of her. Her dad's face opens and melts.

'Ah, sweetheart,' he says, moving forward. 'Come here to me.'

Trey lets him put his arms around her and stroke her hair. Under the spices, he smells like burnt rubber from fear. He says stuff about how he's home now and they'll show those bastards together.

Rushborough watches. Trey knows he isn't fooled. He knew when she was lying, just like he knew when she was telling the truth, but he doesn't seem to care.

Trey doesn't fear easily, but she's afraid of Rushborough. It's not that he hit her. Her dad has hit her before, but that was just because he was angry and she happened to be there. This man has intention. She can feel his mind working, a glinting efficient machine ticking along dark tracks she doesn't understand.

He gets bored and flicks Johnny's arm away from Trey. Johnny moves back fast. 'What about the American bloke?' Rushborough asks Trey.

'Said nothing to him,' Trey says. Her cut lip has left blood on her dad's shirt. 'He'd tell the others.'

Rushborough nods, acknowledging this. 'This is his camera, right? What did you tell him you wanted it for?'

'School project. Wildlife photos.'

'Oh, the birds. That's not bad. I like that. Actually,' he says to Johnny, 'this could all work out very very nicely.'

He points Trey back to the armchair. Trey sits, taking Banjo with her, and blots her lip on the neck of her T-shirt. Rushborough takes his place on the sofa again.

'Just making sure I've got this right,' he says. 'Your idea was, I'd see this' – he taps the camera – 'and I'd piss off back to England. These blokes would be left with their dicks in their hands, no cash payout, buggering about in the river trying to get some of their gold back. Is that right?'

His accent has changed. It's still English, but it's not posh any more; he just sounds ordinary, like someone that would work in a shop. It makes him more frightening, not less. He feels nearer this way.

'Yeah,' Trey says.

'Because you don't like them.'

'Yeah.' Trey presses her hands on her thighs to still them. Bit by bit, things are coming together.

'I'da been run outa town,' Johnny says, outraged, the thought suddenly occurring to him. 'Without a cent to show for any of this.'

'Didn't think that far,' Trey says.

'For fuck's sake,' Johnny says. All his other feelings are getting turned into anger, for ease of use. 'The fuckin' ingratitude. Here was me promising you anything you want—'

'Shut up,' Rushborough says. 'I'm not upset about that. I'm upset that I'm working with a fucking cretin who got the wool pulled over his eyes by a fucking child.'

Johnny shuts up. Rushborough turns back to Trey. 'It's not a bad plan,' he says. 'I've got a better one, though. How would you like to make those blokes lose a few grand each, instead of a few hundred quid?'

'Yeah,' Trey says. 'Maybe.'

'Wait here,' Rushborough says. He goes into the bedroom. He takes the camera along, with a small knowing smile at Trey.

'You'll do whatever he says,' Johnny tells Trey, under his breath. She doesn't look at him. Banjo, disturbed by the smell of blood and fear, licks at her hands, looking for reassurance. She rubs his jowls. It helps her hands stop shaking.

Rushborough comes back carrying a little click-sealed plastic bag. 'The original idea was that I found this, yesterday morning,' he says. 'You saw me, didn't you? You'd have been able to tell people you saw me find it. But it'll be much better coming straight from you.'

He hands the bag to Trey. In it is what looks like a bit of gold foil, off a bar of chocolate or something, that's been squashed in a pocket for too long. It's about the size of a nail head, the big old handmade ones that are bastards to replace when they rust. There are bits of white rock and dirt mashed in with it.

'You found it just at the foot of the mountain,' Rushborough says, 'about half a mile east of here. You overheard me talking to your dad, you recognised the place I was describing, and you went off to do a little private gold-mining of your own. You can be cagey about the exact spot, because you shouldn't have been digging without the landowner's permission, but you're dead pleased with yourself, and you can't resist showing this around. Have you got all that?'

'Yeah,' Trey says.

'Has she got it?' Rushborough asks Johnny. 'Can she pull it off?'

'Oh, God, yeah,' Johnny assures him. 'The child's smart as a whip. She'll do a great job. If you think about it, this is all for the—'

'Good. That's all you have to do,' Rushborough says to Trey, 'and you'll be taking thousands straight out of those blokes' pockets. Won't that be fun?'

'Yeah.'

'Don't lose it,' Rushborough says. He smiles at her. 'If you do a good job, you can keep it. Little present. Otherwise, I'm going to want it back.'

Trey rolls up the bag and tucks it in her jeans pocket. 'There,' Rushborough says. 'See? All on the same side here. It's all going to be lovely-jubbly, and it's going to make us all happy.' To Johnny he says, 'And you're not going to give her any shit. Stay focused.'

'Ah, God, no,' Johnny assures him. 'I wouldn't. Sure, everything's grand, man. All coola-boola.' He's still white.

'Eyes on the prize,' Rushborough says.

'I gotta give back the camera,' Trey says.

'Well, not yet,' Rushborough says reasonably. 'I'll hold on to it for a little while, just in case it might come in useful. There's no reason your school project shouldn't take a few days.'

'All sorted, so,' Johnny says, heartily and too fast. 'All tickety-boo. Let's get this girl home to bed. Come along, sweetheart.'

Trey knows she's not getting the camera back, at least not tonight. She stands up.

'Let me know how it goes,' Rushborough tells her. 'Don't make a balls of it.' He brings his heel down on Banjo's paw.

Banjo yelps wildly and snaps at him, but Rushborough is already out of range. Trey grabs Banjo's collar. He whimpers, holding his paw high.

'Come on,' Johnny says. He gets a grip on Trey's arm and pulls her towards the door. Rushborough moves out of the way, politely, to let them pass.

When the door shuts behind them, Trey shakes off her dad's hand. She's not worried that he'll hit her for taking the video. He's too afraid of Rushborough to step out of line.

Sure enough, all he does is blow out his breath in a comical puff of relief. 'Christ almighty,' he says, 'life's full of surprises, all the same. I haveta hand it to you, I never saw that one coming. I'd say you got a bit of a shock yourself, hah?' He's managed to get some of the whimsical note back into his voice. In the heavy moonlight Trey can see him grinning at her, trying to make her grin back. She shrugs instead.

'Is your lip sore?' her dad asks, ducking his head to peer at her face. He's doing his gentlest, most sympathetic voice. 'Sure, it'll heal in no time. You can say you tripped over.'

'It's grand.'

'Are you upset that I didn't tell you the whole story? Ah, sweetheart. I just didn't want to get you mixed up in this, any more than I hadta.'

'Don't give a shite,' Trey says. Banjo lets out a whimper every time he puts that paw to the ground. She strokes his head. She doesn't want to stop and look him over till they're out of Rushborough's sight.

'You'll be a big help to us now, but. You'll do a great job with that wee yoke. All you've to do is give one or two people a look at it – pick people that'll talk, now – and the rest'll do itself. I'd pay to see Noreen's face when you pull that out.'

Trey heads past the car, towards the road. 'Where are you going?' Johnny demands.

'Gonna get Banjo's paw seen to,' Trey says.

Johnny laughs, but it has a forced sound. 'Get away outa that. The dog's grand; not a bother on it. You're carrying on like he took its leg off.'

Trey keeps going. 'Come here,' Johnny snaps after her.

Trey stops and turns. Once he has her, Johnny doesn't seem to know what to say to her.

'That all turned out well, hah?' he says in the end. 'I won't lie to you, I was worried there. But he likes you. I can tell.'

'He's got no granny that's from here,' Trey says. 'Right?'

Johnny moves, looking back at the house. The windows are empty. 'He's a mate of mine. Not a mate exactly, like, but I know him from around.'

'And there's no gold.'

'Ah, you never know,' Johnny says, wagging a finger at her. 'Sure, didn't your own teacher say it's out there?'

'Somewhere. Not here.'

'That's not what he said. He just never said it is here. It might be. Here's as good as anywhere.'

It strikes Trey with a new clarity that she hates trying to have conversations with her father. She says, 'And your man's not rich.'

Her dad makes himself laugh again. 'Ah, now, depends what you mean by rich. He's no billionaire, but he's got more than I've ever had.'

'What's his name?'

Johnny comes closer to her. 'Listen to me,' he says, keeping his voice down. 'I owe that lad money.'

'He lent you money?' Trey says. She doesn't bother to conceal the disbelief. Rushborough isn't thick enough to lend her dad money.

'Ah, no. I was doing a bitta driving for him, here and there. Only then I was driving something up to Leeds, and I got robbed. 'Twasn't my fault, someone musta set me up, but he doesn't care.' Johnny is still moving, his feet shifting in the gravel of the drive, making little crunching noises. Trey wants to punch him to make him stop. 'I had no cash to pay him back. I was in big trouble, d'you get how much trouble I was in?'

Trey shrugs.

'Big trouble. D'you get what I mean? Big trouble.'

'Yeah.'

'Only I'd this idea. I'd had it in the back of my mind for years, bouncing it around, like – I had it all mapped out in my head where the gold oughta be, I knew whose land it hadta be on, I'd a wee ring with a nugget in that I picked up in an antique shop for proof . . . I'd to beg himself to give it a go. He didn't want me coming over here alone, he said he'd never see hide nor hair of me again. So I said he could come with me if he wanted, be the other fella.' Johnny shoots a glance over his shoulder at the cottage. 'I never thought he'd do it. Him stuck in a tip like this, for weeks, no nightlife, no women? But he likes something new. He gets bored awful easy. And he likes keeping people on their toes, the way you never know what he'd do next. I'd say 'twas that.'

Trey thinks of Rushborough, or whatever his name is, sitting at their kitchen table, smiling at Maeve, asking her about Taylor Swift. She knew then he was all wrong. She feels like a fool for not having seen the rest.

'I wouldn'ta chosen it,' Johnny says, with an injured note like she accused him. 'Having him around you and your mammy, and the wee ones. But I had no choice. I couldn't tell him no, could I?'

Cal would have, Trey knows. Cal wouldn't have got himself into this in the first place.

'It'll be grand,' Johnny assures her. 'It's all going great guns. You just do your wee bit, so the lads know there's gold out there for the taking. Next thing, after himself finds the stuff in the river, he's going to give them a choice: they can have a grand each to let him take samples on their land, or they can invest a few grand in his mining company and be in for a share of everything he finds. He's got other people back in London looking to be investors, we'll say, but he wants to give first shot to the boys from the auld sod. Only they have to decide quick, 'cause the London lads are at him. Keep things moving, bish bosh boom, keep them excited, keep the pressure on, d'you see? If all of them go for the investment, I'm paid off. Free and clear. If we can get more people on board after that, it's all profit.'

'They're not gonna give him money,' Trey says. 'Not just 'cause they hear I found that thing.'

'They've already thrown in a few hundred, sure. That's what they'll be thinking of. Why not go that one extra step and be in for the big prize?'

''Cause they're not thick,' Trey says. 'And they don't trust you.' The way the evening has gone gives her a freedom that takes her by surprise. She doesn't need to lick up to her dad any more.

Johnny doesn't argue with that. He smiles a little, looking out over the dark fields. 'I forget you're only a child,' he says. 'You haveta understand men. These lads around here, they've been hardworking men all their lives. Everything they've got, they earned. A man's supposed to be proud of that, but the truth is, he can get awful weary of it. He gets to craving something he didn't

159

have to earn; something that fell into his hands, for no reason at all. That's why people play the lottery. 'Tisn't the money they want, even if they think it is; 'tis that moment when they'd feel like they're one of God's own handpicked winners. These lads want to feel lucky, for once. They want to feel like God and the land are on their side. They might not give five grand for the chance of fifty, but they'll give it for the chance to feel lucky.'

Trey doesn't know what he's on about and doesn't care. She says, 'Leave Cal outa it.'

'I never wanted him in it to start with,' Johnny says, offended. 'I wouldn't take a penny off a man that's been good to you. I turned him down flat. D'you know what that fella did? He threatened to go to the Guards if I didn't let him in. That's what you get for hanging off a Yank. Would any man from around here do that?'

Trey says, 'Leave him outa it or I'll throw this yoke in a bog.'

'You'll do what you're told,' Johnny says. He sounds like everything about him has worn thin. 'Or I'll beat the living shite outa you.'

Trey shrugs.

Johnny rubs a hand down his face. 'Right,' he says. 'I'll do what I can. Just get your bit right. For Jesus' sake.'

Trey heads off down the road. 'Where d'you think you're going?' Johnny calls after her. 'There's no vet open at this hour.'

Trey ignores him.

'Are you headed to your man Hooper's?'

Trey wants to speed up, but she has to wait for Banjo. He isn't whimpering any more, but he's limping heavily, favouring the hurt paw.

'Ah, come back here,' Johnny calls. She hears the car door open. 'I'll give the pair of ye a lift.'

'Get fucked,' Trey calls back to him, without turning her head.

Trey cuts across fields till she's sure her dad can't have followed her. Then she finds a moonlit spot, near enough a wall that she won't stand out too clearly, and squats down to examine Banjo's paw. Her heart is still going hard.

The paw is swollen. When Trey tries to feel for lumps or breaks, Banjo whimpers, moans urgently, and finally growls, although he follows that up with a frenzy of licking to apologise. Trey sits back and rubs his neck the way he likes best. She isn't going to push him till he snaps at her. It would break his heart.

''S OK,' she says. 'You're grand.' She wishes she had kneed Rushborough in the goolies.

Rushborough and everything he's brought with him are so alien to her that she can't translate the evening into any terms she can comprehend. It feels like something that didn't happen. She sits, trying to spread it out in her mind till she can see it straight. On the other side of the wall, cows chew in a steady, dreamy rhythm.

As far as Trey can see, she has two choices. She can stick to her original goal, which was to scupper her dad's plan and set him running. That would be easy. She could take the scrap of gold to Cal, or to any of the men, and tell them where she got it. They're suspicious of her dad already, by reflex. They'd have him and his Englishman run out of town within a day. Rushborough may be hard, but he's outnumbered and off his patch: he'd be gone.

Against this is the fact that Trey would cut off her own hand sooner than do any of those men a favour. What she wants to do with them is splay open their rib cages and pull out their hearts. She wants to break her teeth on their bones.

This urge has never troubled her, morally speaking. She's accepted it as something she can never act on, even if she somehow learned exactly where it should be directed, but she's clear that she would have every right to act. What's stopped her, too adamantly for the slightest questioning, is Cal. They made a deal: Cal found out for her what had happened to Brendan, as near as he could, and in exchange she gave him her word to do nothing about it, ever. But her dad's doings have no connection to Brendan. She can do whatever she wants with them.

She could do what her dad and his Englishman need from her. Against that is the fact that she has no desire to do them any favours, either: her dad can fuck himself, and after what Rushborough did to Banjo, he can fuck himself a million times over. But their plan, if she helps them, could hit half of Ardnakelty. Somewhere in there, it's bound to hit the people who did that to Brendan.

And her dad will be gone soon enough that way, too. Even if the plan goes perfectly, sooner or later it'll run up against the fact that there's no gold. He and Rushborough will grab as much cash as they can, and go.

It surfaces in Trey's mind only gradually that her dad never had any intention of staying around. It seems like an obvious thing, something she knew all along, if she had bothered looking. She could have just fucked off to Lena's and waited him out, without ever thinking twice about the shite he's brought with him.

She would have done that, if she'd realised. She's glad she didn't. She sits in the field a little longer, running Banjo's soft ears between her fingers and weighing up her different revenges in her mind.

'Come on,' she says to Banjo, in the end. She hoists him up in her arms and gets him draped over her shoulder, like a huge baby. Banjo is delighted with this. He snuffles at her ear and gets drool in her hair. 'You weigh a fuckin' ton,' Trey tells him. 'I'm gonna put you on a diet.'

The warm, smelly weight of him is welcome. Trey feels, all of a sudden, savagely lonesome. What she wants to do is bring all this to Cal, dump it at his feet, and ask him what to do with it, but she's not going to. Whatever Cal is at, he's made it plain that he doesn't want her in it.

'Salad,' she tells Banjo, as she starts down the road. 'That's all you're getting.' He licks her face.

Trey was worried Lena would have gone to bed, but her windows are still lit. When she opens the door, music comes out from behind her, a woman with a throaty voice singing something restless and melancholy in a language Trey doesn't recognise. 'Jesus,' Lena says, raising her eyebrows. 'What happened to you?'

Trey had forgotten her lip. 'Tripped over Banjo,' she says. 'He went under my feet. I stood on his paw. Will you have a look at it?'

Lena's eyebrows stay up, but she doesn't comment. 'No problem,' she says, pointing Trey to the kitchen. 'Bring him in here.'

At the sight of Nellie and Daisy, Banjo starts wriggling to get down, but when his paw touches the floor he lets out a pitiful yelp. 'Ah, yeah,' Lena says. 'That's at him, all right. Out,' she says to Nellie and Daisy, opening the back door. 'They'll only distract him. Now. Sit, fella.'

She turns off the music. In the sudden silence, the kitchen feels very still and restful. Trey has an urge to sit down on the cool stone floor and stay there.

Lena kneels in front of Banjo and makes a fuss of him, rubbing his jowls while he tries to lick her face. 'You get behind him,' she says. 'Stand over him and hold up his jaw, in case he snaps. If he cuts up rough we can muzzle him with a bitta bandage, but I'd rather not.'

'He won't,' Trey says.

'He's hurt. Even the best dog in the world changes when it's hurt. But we'll try it this way first. Come here, fella.'

She takes up Banjo's paw, very gently, and feels her way around it. Banjo squirms against Trey's hand, goes through his full repertoire of whines and moans and yelps, and finally brings out his deepest, most impressive bark. 'Shh,' Trey says softly, into his ear. 'You big aul' baby. You're grand.' Lena, running her fingers over his other paw for comparison, doesn't look up.

'I wouldn't say anything's broken,' she says in the end, sitting back on her heels. 'Bruised, only. Don't let him do much, the next few days.'

Trey releases Banjo, who goes in circles trying to lick them both at once, to show he forgives them. 'Thanks,' she says.

'He oughta stay here for the night,' Lena says. 'He shouldn't walk all the way up that mountain.'

'I'll carry him,' Trey says.

Lena gives her a look. 'In the dark?'

'Yeah.'

'And if you trip once, the pair of ye'll be in worse shape than you already are. Leave him where he is. Anyhow, if it's worse in the morning, we'll have to bring him to a vet for X-rays. You can stay too. The bed's still made up from last time.'

Trey thinks of the wide cool bed, and of her dad waiting at home to fidget and nudge at her. She asks abruptly, 'Do you know who done that on my brother?'

They've never talked about this before. Lena doesn't show any surprise, or pretend not to understand her. 'No,' she says. 'No one was about to tell, and I wasn't about to ask.'

'You could guess.'

'I could, yeah. But I might be wrong.'

'Who d'you guess?'

Lena shakes her head. 'Nah. Guessing games are for who's messing with your scarecrow, or who done a shite on the Cunniffes' front step. Not this.'

'I already hate all of 'em round here,' Trey points out. ''Cept you and Cal.'

'There's that,' Lena acknowledges. 'If you knew who done what, would you hate the rest of 'em any less?'

Trey considers that. 'Nah,' she says.

'Well then.'

'I'd know what ones to hate more.'

Lena tilts her chin, conceding the justice of this. 'If I knew for definite,' she says, 'I'd probably tell you. It might be a bad idea, but there you go. But I don't.'

'Reckon that was Donie McGrath,' Trey says. 'The Cunniffes' step, not the scarecrow. 'Cause Mrs Cunniffe gave out about him playing his music loud.'

'Sounds about right,' Lena says. 'That's different, but. You're on solid ground there. There's not a lot of people around here that would leave shite on a doorstep, and most of them'd use cow shite; Donie's an exception. But there's plenty of people here that'd hide things away if they go wrong, no matter how bad. I'd only be guessing blind.'

'Yeah,' Trey says. She wants to say that the real difference is that they have no right or need to know about the Cunniffes' step, while she has both a right and a need to know about Brendan, but fatigue has suddenly hit her like a rock to the head. She loves Lena's kitchen, which is worn and the right kind of messy and full of warm colours. She wants to lie down on the floor and go to sleep.

She has a third choice. She could walk away from all of this. Go up the mountain, and stay there till this all blows over: live in her abandoned cottage, or go to one of the mountainy men. They're not talkers; they wouldn't ask questions, and they wouldn't rat her out, no matter who came looking. They're not scared of the likes of Rushborough.

Lena is looking at her steadily. 'What brought this on?' she inquires.

Trey looks blank.

'How come you're asking me tonight, two years on?'

Trey didn't expect this. Lena is the least nosy person she knows, which is among the reasons Trey likes her. 'Dunno,' she says.

'Feckin' teenagers,' Lena says. She gets up from the floor and goes to let the dogs in. They skid over to check out Banjo and sniff his paw. 'Did that fella have his dinner yet?'

'Nah,' Trey says.

Lena finds an extra bowl and takes a bag of dog food from a cupboard. All three dogs forget about Banjo's paw and close in on her, writhing around her legs and giving her the full blast of desperate beagle starvation.

'When I was sixteen,' she says, 'one of my mates got pregnant. She didn't want her parents knowing. So d'you know what I did? I kept my mouth shut.'

Trey nods in agreement.

'I was a feckin' eejit,' Lena says. She nudges dogs out of the way with her knee so she can pour out their food. 'Your woman needed a doctor keeping an eye on her; there coulda been something wrong. But all I thought was, adults would make a big fuss about it, make it all complicated. Simpler to leave them outa it, and handle it ourselves.'

'What happened?'

'One of our other mates had better sense. She told her mam. Your woman got to see a doctor, she had the baby, everything was grand. But she coulda ended up having it in a field and the pair of them dying. All because we reckoned adults were more hassle than they were worth.'

Trey knows what Lena is getting at, but it seems to her that, like with the Cunniffes' step, Lena is overlooking differences that matter. She feels lonelier than ever. She almost wishes she hadn't come to Lena's, seeing as Banjo is grand anyway. 'Who was it?' she asks.

'Feck's sake,' Lena says. 'That's not the point.'

Trey picks herself up off the floor. 'Can you keep him tonight?' she says. 'I'll come get him in the morning.'

Lena puts the dog food bag back in its cupboard. 'Listen to me, you,' she says. 'Me and Cal, we'd do anything for you. You know that, yeah?'

'Yeah,' Trey says, acutely embarrassed, staring at the dogs eating. 'Thanks.' The idea does give her a kind of comfort, but a confusing, messy kind. It would be more solid if she could find something that she wanted them to do.

'Then remember it. And you need to wash your face and put something over that T-shirt, unless you want people asking what kinda wars you've been in.'

The mountain is busier on the way home, a busyness that keeps itself on the edge of perception, crowded with movements and rustles that might or might not be there. Its night activities are in full swing. Trey feels bare, without Banjo at her heel.

She's not worried for Lena. If her dad tries convincing Lena to put money into Rushborough's imaginary gold mine, he'll be wasting his time. What Trey is worried about is Cal. He's doing something, she can't tell what, and he doesn't know what Rush-borough is. Cal has sustained enough damage through getting mixed up with her and hers. The whole of her mind balks at the thought of him taking any more. The fact that she's pissed off with him only intensifies this: right now, in particular, she has no wish to be deeper in his debt than she already is.

She'll find something to do about Cal. Somewhere along the way, her decision has clarified itself. Her dad and Rushborough are the only weapons she has, or is ever likely to get, against this townland. They're locked and loaded, ready to her hand. She didn't go looking for them; something laid them in front of her, the same something that brought Cal to Ardnakelty when she needed to find out what had happened to Brendan. She was scared to talk to Cal, then. She did it anyway because she could feel, the same way she can feel now, that walking away would be spitting in the face of that something.

Cal told her a long time back that everyone needs a code to live by. Trey only partway understood what he meant, but in spite of or because of that, she thought about it a lot. Her code has always been a rudimentary, inchoate thing, but since her dad came back, it's been coalescing and sharpening, pointing ways and forming demands of its own. If she can't kill anyone for what they did to Brendan, or even send them to prison, she needs a blood price.

10

Occasionally Lena has mild second thoughts about not having children, mainly when the even predictability of her life starts to chafe at her, but today she's thanking God for it. Trey isn't even hers, and she still has Lena's head melted.

Something is happening in Trey's world. Lena assumes it was Johnny who hit her and hurt Banjo, but from the way Trey was talking, it wasn't just a drunk tantrum; it had something to do with Brendan. Lena has gathered the gist of what happened to Brendan, though she's been careful not to know the details, but she can't make any of it connect up with Johnny or his Englishman or their gold. She was almost hoping Banjo's paw would get worse overnight, so she would have the drive to the vet's and back to take another shot at talking to Trey, but by this morning the swelling had gone down and he could put weight on the paw, although he still felt he deserved extra fuss and food as compensation for the experience. Trey showed up before Lena left for work and took him away, with barely a word beyond a careful thank-you speech that she'd obviously been practising. Lena had no idea what to do about her.

This is a skill she's never learned. She loves her nieces and nephews, she's played with them and listened to their troubles and given the odd opinion if they asked for one, but any tricky bits of handling they require fall on their mothers, or occasionally their fathers. Probably she could have done more if she had chosen to, but she never did. It never seemed necessary: their parents had things well in hand. Whatever things are going on in Trey's life, no one has them in hand.

Lena is, at last, unsettled. Trey put the capper on it, but it's not just Trey. It's Cal, electric with edginess, anger smoking under his calm; and it's Rushborough, who stopped her to make small talk about scenery when she was out walking the dogs, and whom she liked even less than she expected to. Waiting and watching aren't enough any more. She bit her tongue and rang Noreen to make amends for their spat the other day, but Noreen, while her fund of conjecture and rumour is considerably more impressive than Lena's, had nothing solid either. So, against most of her own instincts, Lena is headed to the one place where she might get a hint as to what the fuck is going on. She's fairly sure that this is a bad idea, but she hasn't got a better one.

The heat has thickened. The early-afternoon sun grips the village into immobility; the main street is empty, only the old men sitting slumped on the grotto wall, too hot to move indoors, one of them fanning himself with sluggish flaps of his newspaper.

Mrs Duggan is in her window, as always, having a smoke and trawling the street for anything of value. Lena catches her eye and nods, and Mrs Duggan arches an eyebrow at her. When Lena knocks at the door, there's no movement inside, but after a moment a heavy, slow voice calls, 'Well, in you come, so.'

The house smells like Noreen's cleaning, with a thick undercurrent of something sweaty and sweet. The front room is cluttered with old brown furniture, ruffly porcelain objects, and framed photos of popes from a while back. Mrs Duggan is settled deep into her armchair, overflowing onto the arms. She's wearing a purple dress and battered fleece slippers; her hair, dyed a shiny black, is pulled back in a tight bun. She has the air of something geological, like the house was built around her because no one was willing to move her.

'Well, would you look at that, now,' she says, inspecting Lena with amused, hooded eyes. 'Lena Dunne paying me a visit. 'Tis strange times around here, all right.'

Mrs Duggan is one of the reasons Lena never had children. She's a dense, ripe fermentation of all the things about Ardnakelty that Lena wanted to leave behind. In the end Lena made her own terms with the place, but she was never willing to give a child into It's hands.

'I'm after making blackberry jam,' Lena says. 'I brought you a jar.'

'I'd eat that,' Mrs Duggan says. She leans forward, grunting with effort, to take the jam from Lena and examine it. 'That'd go nice with a bitta soda bread. I'll have Noreen make some tonight.' She finds space for the jar on the small table at her elbow, amid tea mugs and ashtrays and playing cards and biscuits and tissues, and gives Lena a glance. 'Are you pitying your sister, now, running around making soda bread for an old woman in this heat?'

'Noreen has what she wanted,' Lena says. 'I've no reason to pity her.'

'Most of us get what we wanted,' Mrs Duggan agrees. 'For better or worse. Sit you down.' She nods to the chair on the other side of the window. 'Like you got yourself that American fella up at O'Shea's place. How's he turning out?'

'He suits me,' Lena says. 'And it looks like I suit him.'

'I knew you'd have him,' Mrs Duggan says. 'The first time I saw him walk past that window, I made a wee bet with myself: Lena Dunne'll take him. I had a glass of sherry on the strength of it, when I heard I was right. Are you going to keep him?'

'I don't plan ahead,' Lena says.

Mrs Duggan gives her a cynical look. 'You're too old to be coming out with that foolishness, trying to sound like some featherheaded young one. O' course you plan ahead. You're right not to marry him yet. Let him keep on feeling like you're a fling a while longer. They like that, at his age. It makes them think the wildness isn't gone outa them.' She takes a last deep drag off her cigarette and mashes it out. 'Out with it, now. What d'you want?'

Lena says, 'You'll have heard about Johnny Reddy and his Englishman looking for gold.'

'Sure, the dogs in the street have heard about that.'

'Was there ever any word of gold here, before this?'

Mrs Duggan leans back in her chair and laughs, a deep, throbbing wheeze that sets all her folds moving in slow tectonic rolls.

'I was wondering when someone would think to ask me that,' she says. 'I'd a wee bet on with myself, who it'd be. I was wrong. No glass of sherry for me tonight.'

Lena doesn't ask who she was betting on. She's giving Mrs Duggan no more satisfaction than she has to. She waits.

'Didja ask Noreen?'

'If Noreen had ever heard anything, I'd know already.'

Mrs Duggan nods, her nostrils flaring a little with contempt. 'That one can't hold her piss. Why are you bothering asking me, if her ladyship's got nothing to give you?'

'Things get lost,' Lena says. 'There mighta been someone thirty or forty or fifty years ago that knew about the gold, that's dead now. And Noreen doesn't get as deep as you did. If anyone knows, it'd be you.'

'It would, all right. You won't flatter me by telling me what I already know.'

'I wasn't aiming to flatter you,' Lena says. 'I'm telling you why I'm here.'

Mrs Duggan nods. She takes another cigarette from her packet, fumbling a bit with swollen fingers, and lights it.

'My Dessie's down at the river now,' she says, 'with a loada the other lads. Helping the English fella take out the gold they put in. Is your fella with them?'

'I'd say he is, yeah.'

'Like a buncha wee boys,' Mrs Duggan says, 'grubbing about in the muck, delighted with themselves.' She sits and smokes, her eyes moving over Lena's face. 'Here's what I'd loveta know,' she says. 'Why'd you go kissing Johnny Reddy when you were engaged to Sean Dunne?'

Lena has refused to blink for Mrs Duggan for a long time. She says, 'Johnny was a fine thing, back then. All of us fancied him.'

Mrs Duggan snorts. 'What would you want with a little scutter like that, when you'd a fine fella of your own? Sean was twice the man Johnny is.'

'He was, all right,' Lena says. 'But there's plenty of girls that fancy a last fling before they settle down. Plenty of lads, as well.'

'That's God's own truth,' Mrs Duggan acknowledges, with a private smile. 'Plenty. But you were never a slut. You always thought you were too great to follow the rules, but that's not the way it took you. If you'da wanted a last fling, you'da gone off backpacking round Australia.'

She's right, and Lena doesn't like that. 'That woulda been better crack, all right,' she says. 'But Johnny was quicker and cheaper.'

Mrs Duggan merely shakes her head again and waits, watching Lena and smoking. She looks amused.

Lena has a flash of the kind of naked powerlessness she hasn't felt in decades. This woman and this place are both so obdurately, monumentally what they are, down to bedrock, that it feels insane to go trying to outwit them. Their vastness allows her no space to manoeuvre, or even to breathe. For one sharp instant she remembers this feeling, teetering on mindless panic, and Johnny's hand sliding up her back.

'If Sean had found out,' she says, 'he mighta broke it off. And then I'da gone off to college.'

Mrs Duggan leans back in her armchair and laughs again. The sound goes on for a long time. 'Would you look at that, now,' she says, when she's taken her full enjoyment from it. 'That's what it was all along: the bold Helena wanted more than the likes of poor aul' Seaneen Dunne and poor wee Ardnakelty could offer her. And you were hoping I'd do your dirty work for you.'

'Not hoping,' Lena says. 'I wanted Sean, or else I'da done my own dirty work. I just felt like rolling the dice, just the once.'

'You thought you were awful smart,' Mrs Duggan says. 'But I won't be used.'

'I wasn't thinking of you,' Lena says. 'I didn't even know you'd find out. I was just thinking of anyone that happened to pass by.'

'You knew,' Mrs Duggan says. 'I hear things. But I'll have my will with them, not yours or anyone's.'

Lena is done; she's paid her fee. She says, 'You'll have heard whether there's gold out there or not, so.'

Mrs Duggan nods, accepting the transaction. She blows out smoke and watches it curl against the windowpanes.

'In all my days,' she says, 'I never once heard a whisper about any gold. People are saying aul' Mick Feeney knew and kept it to himself, but there's been times when Mick Feeney woulda given me anything he had in exchange for what he wanted offa me, and he never said a word about that. I've known every Feeney around for eighty year now, and if any one of them had a notion of any gold, I'll ate this ashtray.' She puts out her cigarette, pressing down hard, and watches Lena. 'I can't tell you if there's gold out there, but I can tell you no one ever thought there was, not till Johnny and his Englishman came in here talking big. What d'you think of that?'

'Anything outa Johnny Reddy's mouth,' Lena says, 'I'd be more surprised if it hadda turned out to be true.'

Mrs Duggan snorts, acknowledging this. 'Now you have it. What are you going to do with it?'

'I haven't thought of that yet,' Lena says. 'Nothing at all, maybe.'

'There's going to be trouble,' Mrs Duggan says, with slow, pleasurable anticipation. 'I know you tried to tell me you don't be planning ahead, but if I was you, I'd make an exception this time.'

Lena says, 'You never said this to Noreen, or Dessie, no?'

'If they hadda asked me right,' Mrs Duggan says, 'I mighta, maybe. But they never thought to ask me at all. They think your sister's the one that knows things now. I'm only some aul' biddy that's gone past her sell-by date.' She leans back, the chair creaking, her wide mouth stretching in a smile. 'So I'm just sitting here at my ease and watching them all run mad. 'Tis nothing to me if Dessie wants to make a fool of himself. I'll be gone soon enough. While I'm here, I'll take what I can get.' She nods at the ashtray. 'Empty that, on your way out. Don't be getting it in with the recycling. Your sister does be awful fussy about that.'

Lena takes the ashtray into the kitchen and empties it into the bin. The kitchen is big and bright and ferociously clean, with rows of matching mugs hanging below the cupboards and a fruit-patterned oilcloth on the long table. On one wall is a whiteboard with a column for each of Noreen's children, to keep track of training times and orthodontist appointments and who needs a new hurling stick. Lena writes 'Do something nice for your mam' in each column, while she's there.

173

'Well, Sunny Jim,' Mart says, as he and Cal head up the lane towards their homes, taking it at an easy pace to spare Mart's joints. The sun is only just starting to gentle; it throws their shadows sharp and black onto the road, to leap up and flutter at their elbows along walls and hedges. 'I'd say that went well.'

'Everyone seemed pretty happy,' Cal says. This was the part that startled him: the men's spontaneous explosion of shouts and cheers when Rushborough held up the first glittering traces in the pan; the ring of genuine, wild amazement and delight, like they had all been holding their breath waiting to find out if anything was in there. The gold has taken on a reality outside themselves and their actions. They're like believers exalted by the holy truth underlying a relic, even though they know the relic itself is a shard of chicken bone.

'I wasn't banking on that,' Mart explains. 'When you're dealing with the likes of Johnny Reddy, you'd always allow for things going a bit arseways. But I'll give the lad this much: there's been none a that. Everything smooth as butter.'

'So far,' Cal says.

'So far,' Mart acknowledges. 'I'll tell you one thing that took me by surprise, but. I wasn't reckoning on putting my whole day into this.' He tries to arch his back, and grimaces as it cracks. 'I thought all you had to do was give the pan an aul' shake and tip out the muck, and away you go to the next spot. I wasn't bargaining for all that fussing and foostering. Standing still that length of time is grand for you and the rest of the spring chickens, but it's a whole other kettle of fish for the likes of me.'

'You should've gone home,' Cal says. 'Left me and the other spring chickens to it.'

'I coulda,' Mart concedes, 'only there's not enough action around here that I can afford to miss out on any. And besides, anyone that takes his eye off Johnny Reddy deserves whatever he gets.' He cracks his back again and suppresses a wince. 'I'll be grand, sure. Are you coming down to the celebrations? You can't be skipping those, now. We can't have Paddy Englishman wondering if something's wrong.'

'I doubt he'd miss me,' Cal says. 'I don't think that guy likes me much.' Rushborough was civil to him, with the pinch-lipped, flickery-lidded civility that Brits save for people they dislike, and looked at him as little as possible. Cal could see Johnny getting twitchy over it. He likes Johnny twitchy.

'To be honest, I wouldn't say he'd notice either way,' Mart says. 'He's other things on his mind. Did you see the face on him? Like a child that just saw Santy.'

'Yeah,' Cal says. He thinks of Rushborough thigh-deep in the river, the pan held high as a trophy and his teeth bared in an exultant grin, sunlight splintering all around him and water streaming down his arms. He didn't look like a kid to Cal. 'I'm just gonna get some food and a shower, and I'll be there. I've been sweating like a sinner in church.'

'You'll have someone to give you a hand with both of those,' Mart says, grinning and pointing at Cal's front yard with his crook, as they round the bend. 'You might not end up any less sweaty after, but.'

Lena's car is parked in the yard. Without meaning to, Cal quickens his pace. Normally Lena's old blue Skoda is one of his favourite sights, but these days everything unexpected has the queasy shimmer of bad news about it. 'Holy God, you're in a hurry,' Mart says, grinning more broadly. Cal slows down.

He's been getting edgier and edgier, the last few days. There are too many little things he doesn't like. He doesn't like it, for example, that Johnny came down to the river yesterday to help sow the gold. Cal had it all figured that Johnny was staying well clear of that part of the operation, but Johnny was right there on the riverbank with the rest of them, and Cal isn't sure why. He doesn't like his own enforced inaction, either: in normal times he's happy to direct his fixing instinct towards old chairs, but these aren't normal times, and the situation calls for a lot more than standing in mud watching some dumbass Brit play treasure hunter. He doesn't like the way Johnny is cutting Trey away from him, as nimbly as Mart's dog cutting out a sheep he has use for, and he doesn't like the fact that he can't work out what use Johnny might have for the kid. Most of all he doesn't like Trey keeping things from him, although he knows she's under no obligation to tell him anything at all.

'I won't stop in to say hello,' Mart says. 'Your missus isn't mad about me, didja spot that? I never done anything on her that I can think of, but she's not a fan.'

'There's no accounting for tastes,' Cal says.

'When we're all rolling in gold, maybe I'll buy her a great big hamper of treats for them dogs of hers, and see if she changes her tune. Meanwhile, I'll leave ye to it.'

'See you at Seán's,' Cal says. Another thing he doesn't like is the sense of alliance with Mart that's somehow been thrust on him. He had the boundary between the two of them carefully and clearly mapped out, and it held firm for two years, although Mart sometimes poked at it just out of devilment. Now it's lost its solidity. Johnny himself may be nothing but a yappy little shitbird, but he's somehow brought with him enough force to pull the whole townland off true.

'Don't be rushing,' Mart says. 'I'll tell the lads you've a good excuse for being late.' He lifts his stick in farewell and trudges off, the heat from the road making his legs waver like he's about to dissolve into thin air. Cal heads round to the back of his house, over the withering lawn.

Lena is in her rocker on the back porch, where Cal knew she would be. She has a key to his house, but walking in when he's not there is a borderline she hasn't yet been willing to cross. Sometimes Cal wishes she would. He likes the idea of coming home to find her curled on his sofa, absorbed in a book, with a mug of tea in her hand.

Lena came as a complete surprise to Cal. When his wife left him, he planned on being done with women for good. He had been with Donna since he was twenty; she was the only woman he had ever wanted, and the last thing he intended was to ever start wanting another one. He was planning on being one of those guys who are happy to have a good-natured flirtation in the bar, maybe a one-night stand every now and then, but nothing more. He knows from Lena that she felt a little differently, maybe because her husband died rather than walking out on her. It wasn't that she was set against ever taking another man; it was just unimaginable. And yet, somehow, here they are, wherever here is. The fact of them still startles Cal sometimes. He feels like he has no right to it, after how adamantly he ruled out anything of the kind.

'Hey,' he says. 'Everything OK?'

'Grand,' Lena says, which lets Cal take a breath. 'I let Rip out, before he et the door off the hinges; he's down the back field, with mine. And I'd murder a glass of that tea, if you've any in the fridge.'

This summer has finally converted Lena to Cal's sweet tea, which previously both she and Trey viewed with extreme suspicion. Cal fixes each of them a tall glass, with ice and a wedge of lemon, and picks sprigs of mint from the pot on the porch.

'I heard this was the big day,' Lena says, raising her glass to thank him. 'All of ye down at the river, getting the gold back out from where ye put it yesterday. The circle of life.'

'Does the whole place know?' Cal asks, dropping into his chair.

'Noreen had it from Dessie, and myself and herself are speaking again, so I had it from her. I wouldn't say she's told the world, but; she only said it to me because she reckoned I'd already have heard it from you. How'd it go?'

'Went according to plan, I guess. That Rushborough guy, he had all kinds of equipment – a pan and a screen thing to go over it, and a magnet and a thing that puffed air and I don't know what-all. He talked the whole time. Placer gold, re-stratifying, alluvial channels. I felt like there was gonna be a pop quiz at the end.'

Cal sinks half his glass and wishes he had put bourbon in it. Mart is right, it was a longer day than he'd bargained for. The sun struck off the water at bewildering angles, so that he had to keep squinting and turning, trying to make sense of it. He suddenly feels a little bit heat-sick, or sun-sick, or something-sick.

'The whole time,' he says, 'I was thinking: maybe we did something wrong. Like we put the gold at the wrong depth, or in the wrong part of the river, or whatever. And Rushborough would catch it and back out; shut down the whole thing and take off back to London. If he went, Johnny'd go too, before the guys give him a beat-down for making them waste their money.' He presses the cold glass to his temple and feels the blood throb against it. 'I guess Mart must know his stuff too, though, 'cause Rushborough acted like everything was perfect. Gabbing away about how proud his grandma would be. Happy as a pig in shit.'

Lena says nothing. She's turning her glass in her hands, watching the ice cubes swirl. Cal can feel her examining the best ways to tell him something. His muscles are tightening again. Like most guys he knows, he finds few things as nerve-racking as a woman with something on her mind. He knocks back more of his tea, hoping the cold will brace up his brain for whatever's on the way.

'I went to see Mrs Duggan,' Lena says. 'D'you know her? Noreen's mother-in-law. The big woman that sits at her window all day watching the street.'

'I've seen her,' Cal says. 'Never met her.'

'She doesn't get out much, only for mass. Sciatica, she's got. Up until maybe fifteen years back, but, she ran the shop. She knew everything that went on around here. Even more than Noreen does. You could get up to some mischief with no one but your best mate, that'd never say a word to anyone, but the next day Mrs Duggan'd know.'

Lena is rocking the chair easily and her voice is level, but Cal can hear the charge in it. Going to see this woman cost her.

'There was one of them around where my granddaddy lived,' he says. 'Most places'd be better off without them.'

'Mostly I'd say the same,' Lena says. 'Today, I'm not sure yet. Mrs Duggan says she never heard a word about any gold around here. She's eighty, so she never knew your woman Bridie Feeney that was Rushborough's granny, but she woulda known Bridie's brothers and sisters. And Michael Duggan, that Rushborough said found that bitta gold along with his granny, he was Mrs Duggan's uncle-in-law. If she never heard of any gold, then neither did any of them.'

Cal sits still, trying to fit this in among the other things he knows or suspects or fears. The sickly haze has seared right off him; he's as alert as he's ever been in his life. 'You figure she's telling you the truth?' he asks.

'Ah, yeah. That's the worst about Mrs Duggan: she's always right. There's no point being the one that knows everything, unless people know to believe what you tell them.'

'Then where the hell—'

Cal can't stay put. He gets up and walks a circle around the porch. 'Where the hell did all that crap come from? Rushborough just pulled the gold straight out of his ass, threw in a bunch of stuff his gramma told him about this place, and used that dumb shit Johnny to get him in the door?' He could kick himself for not figuring this out days ago. Rushborough never looked like a sucker; always, from the first glance, he looked like the guy fleecing the suckers for all they were worth. Everyone else has an excuse for missing that. Cal has none.

'No,' Lena says. 'I reckon there's the two of them in it. I'll tell you one other thing: when Johnny got back here, he needed a haircut. That's a little thing, but it wasn't like him. He always liked making a fancy entrance. I thought then, he came running. 'Cause he was in trouble.'

Cal says, 'You didn't tell me that.'

'No,' Lena says. 'I didn't. It mighta been nothing.'

'So Johnny and this Rushborough guy,' Cal says. He makes himself sit down again, to hold his thoughts to a steady pace. 'They ran themselves into some kinda hot water, over in England. They cooked up this story and came over here to scam a few quick bucks, to get themselves outa trouble.'

He doesn't underestimate the level of trouble Johnny could be in. By nature Johnny is clearly small-time, but he's made up of nothing but a shit-ton of talk and a useful smile; he's light. If he got caught up by something with force, he could roll a long way from where he naturally belongs.

'How, but?' Lena says. 'They pulled, what, a grand or two worth of gold outa the river today? It wouldn't be worth their while doing all this just for that.'

'Nope,' Cal says. He remembers Mart, in the pub, gabbing

about psychology. 'This was just the start. Now they've got the guys all worked up, they're gonna come up with some reason they need more money. Mining licences, or equipment, or something. The guys, Mart and PJ and the rest, have they got enough cash to make them worth scamming?'

The movement of Lena's rocking chair has stilled. 'They'd have a bit put away, all right,' she says. 'Maybe not Con McHugh, he's only young, but the rest. And they've the land. Sixty or seventy acres each – Senan has a hundred. That's family land, all of it, owned free and clear. Any of them could walk into a bank tomorrow and mortgage a few of those acres for maybe five grand each, or put them up as collateral for a loan.'

'Those guys are knee-deep in this thing already,' Cal says. He never worked Fraud, but he had buddies who did; he knows how it goes. 'If Johnny talks a good enough game, they'll figure it'd be a waste not to go that one step deeper.'

Lena has started rocking her chair again, slowly, thinking. 'They'd do it,' she says. 'Most of them, anyway. If they think there's gold on their own land, or even that there might be, they can't just turn away from it. If it was up on the mountain, they'd play safe and leave it, maybe. But not on their land.'

Cal finds himself strangely and deeply outraged for the men who were on the riverbank today. He has his own beef with these men, or some of them, but he remembers their faces in the pub when Rushborough brought out the ring: their stillness as their land transformed and ignited, blazing with fresh constellations and long-hidden messages from their own blood. Compared to what Rushborough and Johnny are doing, their salting the river seems like kid mischief: shoplifting beer, shaving the drunk guy's eyebrows. Cal has lived in Ardnakelty long enough to be conscious that the tie between them and their land is something he can't fathom, cell-deep and unvoiceable. Johnny, at least, should have known better than to fuck with that, and much better than to let some guy with an English accent fuck with it.

'If they find out,' he says, 'there's gonna be trouble.'

Lena watches him. She says, 'You reckon they should find out?'

'Yeah,' Cal says. An immense tide of relief is rising inside him. At last, he can do something. 'And I reckon the sooner the better. We're all heading down to Seán's, to celebrate. They can all find out at once.'

Lena's eyebrows go up. She says, 'That'll get messy.'

'The longer I wait, the messier it'll get.'

'You could say it to Johnny on his own. Walk home with him after the pub, tell him you'll be saying it to the lads tomorrow, so he's got till then to pack his bags. Keep things from getting outa hand.'

'Nah,' Cal says.

'Tell him there's other people that know as well. In case that Rushborough gets any funny ideas.'

'People round here,' Cal says, 'they think about the kid like she's half mine.' It comes out with difficulty, because he's never said it before and because he has no idea how much longer it will hold any kind of truth; he's sorely aware that he hasn't seen Trey in days. But for now, at least, it can still have some worth to her. 'If I call out Johnny in front of God and everybody, so the whole place knows it was me that tanked his plan, then no one's gonna go thinking she was in on his bullshit. So, once he's gone, she can go on living here without anyone giving her hassle.'

There's a small silence. Off by the vegetable patch, the dogs have triggered the zombie scarecrow and are losing their minds, threatening all manner of extravagant destruction from a safe distance. The tomato plants are burgeoning; even from here, Cal can see the bursts of red shining among the green.

'This Rushborough fella,' Lena says. 'I met him, the other morning. I was out walking the dogs, and he stopped for a wee chat.'

'About what?'

'Nothing. Aren't the mountains lovely, and this isn't the weather he expected from Ireland. Whatever you do, watch that fella.'

'I'm not gonna say anything when Rushborough's there,' Cal says. 'He's smarter'n Johnny; he might manage to talk his way out. But I bet you a hundred bucks Rushborough's gonna leave after a couple of drinks, to give Johnny and the guys some space to gloat about how good they fooled him. That's where I come in.'

'Still,' Lena says. 'Watch him, after. I don't like him.'

'Yeah,' Cal says. 'Me neither.'

He wants to tell Lena that these days he feels like he can't find Trey, that for three nights running he's had nightmares where she disappeared somewhere on the mountainside, that he wishes he had bought her a phone and put a tracker app on it so he could spend his days just sitting still and watching her bright dot go about its business. Instead he says, 'I gotta go shower and eat something. We're heading down to Seán's at six.'

Lena looks at him. Then she comes over to him, cups her hand around the back of his neck, and kisses him full and strong on the mouth. It feels like a baton-pass, or like she's sending him into battle.

'Right,' she says, straightening up. 'I'll leave you to it, so.'

'Thanks,' Cal says. The smell of her is in his nose, clean and sunny as drying hay. 'For talking to Mrs Duggan.'

'That woman's a feckin' nightmare,' Lena says. 'If I was Noreen I'da poisoned her tea years ago.' She puts a finger and thumb in her mouth and whistles for her dogs, who abandon their war with the scarecrow and head across the field in long, happy bounds. 'Let me know how you get on,' she says.

'Will do,' Cal says. He doesn't watch her to her car. He's already picking up the glasses and heading into the house, thinking about the right words to use when the time comes.

II

It's early enough that Seán Óg's is mostly empty, just a few old guys
eating toasted sandwiches and bitching at the racing on the TV;
most of the Friday crowd are still at home digesting their dinners,
laying the proper groundwork for the serious drinking ahead. Daylight still slants in at the windows, in long rays turned solid by the
lazy hang of dust motes. Only the alcove is full and raucous. The
guys are scrubbed and combed, buttoned into good shirts; their
faces and necks are reddened in odd spots, from the sun off the
river. Rushborough is holding court in the middle of it all, spread
wide on a banquette telling some story with sweeping arm gestures, and getting all the laughs he could want. On the table among
the pints and the beer mats, mottled rich red and green and yellow
by the drops of coloured sunlight through the stained glass, is the
little bottle of gold dust.

'Sorry I'm late,' Cal says to the alcove in general, pulling up a
stool and finding space for his pint on the table. He took his time
getting ready. He feels no urge to spend any longer with Rushborough and Johnny than he needs to.

'I was as well,' PJ tells him. PJ, like Bobby, has a tendency to con-
fide in Cal, possibly because Cal lacks the long familiarity to give
them shit. 'Listening to music, I was. I was all stirred up when I got
in; couldn't sit still. I tried to sit down to my tay, and wasn't I up and
down like a hoor's knickers, forgetting the fork and then the milk
and then the red sauce. When I do be like that, the only thing that'll
set me straight is a bitta music.'

Clearly the music only partly did its job. This is a very long speech
for PJ. 'What'd you listen to?' Cal asks. PJ sings to his sheep sometimes, mostly folk songs.

'Mario Lanza,' PJ says. 'He's great for settling the aul' spirits.
When I'm the other way, when I can't get outa the bed, I'd listen

to this English young one called Adele. She'd put enough heart in you for anything.'

'What the hell were you all stirred up for?' Mart inquires with interest, glancing across at Rushborough to make sure his voice is low enough. 'Sure, you knew what was in there all along.'

'I know,' PJ says humbly. 'But 'twas some day, all the same.'

'We don't get many like this,' Mart concedes.

Rushborough, taking a brief second to scan Cal as the rest of the men laugh at his punchline, has picked up on the tail end of this. 'My God, you must lead more exciting lives than I do, I've *never* had a day like this,' he says, laughing, leaning forward over the table. 'You do see what this means, don't you? It means we're on the right track. I knew the gold was out there, I always knew that. But what I was afraid of, what I was terrified of, was that my grandmother's instructions weren't good enough. It's not as if she gave me a map, you know, X marks the spot. She was playing a game of Telephone that had been going on for centuries, describing a place she hadn't seen in decades – all these directions like "And then follow the old streambed down to the west but if you reach Dolan's back field you've gone too far", my God' – he throws himself back on the banquette, arms flying wide – 'sometimes I wondered if I was stark raving bonkers to go chasing after something so vague. She could have been miles off target, literally miles. I was braced to find nothing but mud today, and go home with my tail between my legs – not that it would have been a waste of time, it's been entirely worth it just to meet you and see this place at last, but I can't deny it: I would have been heartbroken. Devastated.'

Cal has professional experience of shitbirds like this, whose lies take up so much space that people believe them just because disbelieving all of that would be too much work. He has no certainty that, when he says his own piece, the guys will be swayed. He's sharply aware that he's a stranger, no less than Rushborough, and one who's given them trouble before.

'But this' – Rushborough seizes the bottle of gold and clasps it between his hands, like he can't keep away – 'this is proof. My grandmother, God bless her – I'll have to, I don't know, lay flowers on her grave or light a candle in the church, to beg her forgiveness for doubting her. She led me straight as a, what am I looking for? not a die, a, an arrow, that's it, straight as an arrow to the spot—'

'Jaysus, man,' Johnny says, laughing and clapping Rushborough on the shoulder. 'You're bouncing off the walls here. You need something to settle you, before you give yourself a heart attack. Barty! Get this fella a brandy.'

'And the same for all of us!' Rushborough calls over his shoulder, laughing. 'I know, I know, I'm excited, but do you blame me? It's the gold at the end of the rainbow!'

The other thing that strikes Cal is how much the guy is putting into it. This is some Hallmark-level emotion he's got going on. For it to be worth this amount of effort, he and Johnny must be planning to take Ardnakelty for everything it's got.

The brandy goes down with a toast to Rushborough's granny and a scattering of cheers. Cal holds his, but doesn't drink it; he's not going to take anything from this guy. He sees Rushborough's eye slide over him again, noting.

'Well, chaps,' Rushborough says, putting down his glass and stifling a yawn, 'or lads, I should say, shouldn't I? Lads, I'm afraid I'm going to have to call it a night. I hate to break up a lovely party, and I don't know whether it's the adrenaline or simply my shameful city lifestyle taking its toll, but I'm exhausted.'

There's plenty of protest, but not the kind that risks making Rushborough change his mind and stick around. Just like Cal expected, the men want some time to themselves.

'Would you mind,' Rushborough says a little shyly, putting a finger on the bottle of gold dust, 'if I kept this? I'll get it properly weighed and pay each of you for your share, of course. But – I know it's sentimental, but . . . the first fruits, don't you know. I'd like to have something made out of this. A new setting for my grandmother's nugget, maybe. Would that be all right?'

Everyone thinks this is a wonderful idea, so Rushborough pockets the bottle and jabbers himself out. The place is starting to fill up; people turn to nod and lift their glasses as he goes by, and he doles out smiles and waves in exchange.

'He went for it,' Con says, leaning forward over the table, as soon as the pub door closes behind him. 'He did, didn't he? He went for it.'

'Et it up with a spoon,' Senan says. 'The fuckin' sap.'

'Ah, here,' Johnny says, pointing at him. ''Twouldn't take a sap. Ye were only magnificent, every one of ye. I almost believed ye myself. That's what done it. Not him being a sap. The lot of ye playing a fuckin' blinder.' He raises his pint to them all.

'Don't be getting all modest on us, young fella,' Mart says, smiling at him. 'Credit where credit's due: you did the heavy lifting. You're very convincing altogether, when you wanta be. Hah?'

'I know Rushborough,' Johnny assures him. 'I know how to handle the man. I won't let ye down.'

'What now, so?' Francie demands. Francie is looking stubbornly sceptical. His face naturally inclines that way, being bony and thin-lipped, heavy on the eyebrows, but its usual cast has intensified.

'Now,' Johnny says, relaxing back on the banquette, his face shining with glee, 'we've got him. That fella'll do whatever it takes to get stuck into the serious digging. All we haveta do is take the cash and let him at it.'

'If there's anything worth having on my land,' Francie says, 'and I'm not saying there is, I don't fancy waking up one morning and finding out I've handed over the rights to millions for a coupla grand.'

'Fuck's sake, Francie,' Johnny says, exasperated. 'What is it you want, at all? If you think there's millions on your land, then ask Rushborough can you buy into his company and get your share. If you believe there's nothing there, then take the few grand for the mining rights, and let him dig his wee heart out. You can't have it both ways. Which is it?'

Cal is becoming clearer on the next step in Johnny and Rushborough's plan. He stays quiet, letting things play out a little longer. The more Johnny says, the more the guys will have to chew on, after Cal throws his grenade.

'It's none a your business, is what it is,' Francie tells Johnny. 'Ye can all do whatever you want. I'm only saying, he can't walk onto my land and take what he likes.'

'Jesus fuck, you're some dose, d'you know that?' Sonny explodes at Francie. 'Here's everything going great guns, and you sitting there with a puss on you that'd sour milk, looking for holes to pick. Would you not shut your gob just for the one evening, and let the rest of us enjoy ourselves?'

'He's thinking a-fuckin'-head,' Senan snaps. 'You should try it yourself sometime.'

'He's being a fuckin' moan.'

'Arrah, shut the fuck up, wouldja, and let the men with sense do the talking—'

All of them are too loud and too quick off the mark. Cal can feel the electric charge jittering through the air. Someone is liable to get his ass kicked tonight. Cal is aware that, once he says his piece, there's a fair-to-middling chance it could be him.

'D'you know something?' Bobby demands suddenly, of Senan. 'You're awful fond of telling people to shut up. No one made you king of this place. Maybe you oughta shut up yourself, once in a while.'

Senan stares at Bobby like he just grew another head. Bobby, terrified by his own new daring but not about to back down, pulls himself up to his full height and stares back. Mart looks like he's having the night of his life.

'Sweet fuck,' Senan says. 'If this is what just the smell of gold does to you, I'd hate to see what you'll be like if anything's found on your land. You'll lose the run of yourself altogether. You'll be swanning around with a tiara and a big diamond ring on you, expecting people to kiss it—'

'I'm only saying,' Bobby tells him, with dignity. 'He's as much right to an opinion as you have.'

'Sir Bobby, will it be? Or Your Lordship?'

'Ah, lads, lads,' Johnny says soothingly, raising his hands to quell the argument and bring everyone back on track. 'Listen to me.

Francie here's got a point. The man just wants to be sure he'll get value. What's wrong with that? Don't we all?'

'Fuckin' right,' Senan says.

'Sure, I wouldn't want your man walking away with the lot, either,' Con says. 'Not off my land.'

A shift runs through the other men, a low mutter of assent.

'Do we haveta let him?' PJ asks, worried.

'You don't haveta do anything you don't wanta,' Johnny reassures him. 'Have a think about it. Take your time. The only thing you oughta keep in mind is, let's say you reckon there's gold there, and you decide to ask Rushborough can you invest in his company: you'd want to do it soon. Once he finds gold, them shares'll get an awful lot dearer.'

This silences PJ; he takes refuge in his pint while he tries to disentangle it. Sonny and Con glance at each other, questions passing between them.

'How much would it be?' Dessie asks. 'Investing, like.'

Johnny shrugs. 'Depends, man. On what percentage you want, how much he reckons he'll find, all that. I threw in a few grand and that got me a fair aul' chunk, but that was when all your man had was some fairy tale off his granny. He might rate it higher now, after today.'

'If we all stick together,' Senan says, 'he'll rate it at whatever we say, or he can do his digging in his own back garden.'

'I'm not promising he wants investors at all,' Johnny cautions them. 'He's got other lads sniffing around, back in London; he might not have the room for anyone else.'

'Like I said. If there's the lot of us in it, he can take it or leave it.'

'Who says I want to invest anything?' Francie demands.

Sonny throws himself back on the banquette with a roar of frustration. 'Fuck's *sake*, you're the one that started all this—'

'Lads, lads,' Johnny says, soothing again. 'No one needs to decide anything tonight. Just talk to Rushborough. Nice and delicate, now; don't go wading in like you're dealing with some aul' bull of a lad at the cattle mart. Just put out the feelers, and see what he says.'

Cal is done waiting. He figures this should be plenty to help the guys put the situation into a fresh perspective, once they have his two cents' worth to get them started.

'Johnny,' he says. He doesn't raise his voice, but he makes sure it takes up enough space that the guys fall silent. 'I got a question for you.'

For one blink, Johnny stares. Then: 'Oh, holy God,' he says, mock-terrified, putting a hand to his heart. 'This sounds awful serious altogether. Did I forget to pay my telly licence, Guard? Are the treads gone on that aul' banger of ours? Give us one more chance, I'm begging you, I'll be a good boy . . .'

Cal waits for him to run himself down. The other men are watching. Some of them, Sonny and Dessie and Bobby, are grinning along at Johnny's little song-and-dance routine. PJ merely looks bewildered. Senan and Francie aren't smiling.

'No, hang on,' Johnny says, lifting a finger like Cal tried to break in on him, which he didn't. 'Don't tell me. I've got it. I've been very bold, Guard. I crossed the road without—'

Then his eyes slip away, over Cal's shoulder, and Trey's voice says, 'Dad.'

Cal turns fast. Trey is standing at the entrance to the alcove. She's just standing like always with her feet planted and her hands shoved in her pockets, wearing an old blue T-shirt and her worn-out jeans, but out of nowhere Cal is slammed by the sight of her. Browned by the summer and muscled by their work, her features stronger and more marked than he remembers them being just a couple of days ago, she doesn't look like a kid; she looks like someone who could handle herself. Cal's heart squeezes so tight he can't breathe.

'Well, wouldja look who it is,' Johnny says, after a fraction of a second. 'What's the story, sweetheart? Is there something wrong at home?'

'Nah,' Trey says. 'Got something to tell you.'

Johnny's eyebrows go up. 'Well, holy God,' he says, 'isn't this all very mysterious. D'you want me to come outside, is it?'

'Nah. Here's good.'

Johnny is eyeing Trey with an indulgent half-smile, but Cal can see him thinking fast. He's not at sea, exactly, but something here has taken him by surprise. Something is going on.

'Are you after doing something a wee bit bold,' he says, 'and you're worried I'll be angry with you?' He wags his finger playfully at Trey. 'Ah, now. Daddy won't be angry. Sure, didn't I do plenty of bold things myself, when I was your age?'

Trey shrugs. PJ, trapped amid what looks like family complications, is shuffling his feet around and trying to come up with a conversation to have with Mart. Mart is ignoring him and unabashedly soaking up the drama.

'All right,' Johnny says, reaching a decision. 'Come sit here and tell me all about it.' He pats the banquette beside him. Trey moves over to him, but she stays standing. Her bottom lip looks swollen.

'When your man Rushborough called round, that evening,' she says. 'And he was telling you where his granny said there was gold. I listened in.'

'Ah, God. And you were worried I'd be angry with you for that?' Johnny laughs affectionately up into her face, giving her arm a pat. Trey doesn't move away. 'God love you, no one coulda resisted the temptation. Sure, any of these great big grown-up lads, if they'da been there' – he wags a finger teasingly around the table – 'they'da had an ear up against the door. Wouldn't they?'

'Dunno,' Trey says. Banter has never been Trey's strong suit.

'They would, o' course. Is that all you wanted? To get that off your chest?'

'Nah,' Trey says. She hasn't looked at Cal once; her eyes are on Johnny. 'I went out to where your man Rushborough said. Did a bitta digging around. Just to see, like.'

'Ah, now,' Johnny says reprovingly, waving a finger at her. 'You know better than that, missus. I won't give out to you this time, 'cause you came clean to me, but from now on, if you wanta—'

'Yeah,' Trey says. 'Found this.' She fishes in her jeans pocket and pulls out a small, squashed click-seal bag.

'What's this, now? Didja dig up something pretty?' Johnny takes it from her with a half-puzzled, half-amused glance, and bends his head to peer at it. Under the men's watching eyes, he turns it over and tilts it to the light.

Cal's muscles almost launch him before he knows it. He wants to flip the table in Johnny's face, get Trey by the shoulder, spin her around and march her straight out of all this. He holds himself still.

Johnny lifts his head to stare at Trey. 'Where'd you get this?' he asks.

'Told you,' Trey says. 'Where your man was saying. There at the foot of the mountain.'

Johnny looks around at the men's faces. Then he tosses the bag into the centre of the table, among the glasses and the beer mats.

'That's gold,' he says.

Out in the main bar, the TV commentator's voice gallops along with the horses. Someone swears, and someone else cheers.

Con, leaning in to gaze at the bag, starts to laugh first, then Dessie, then Sonny.

'What?' Trey demands, baffled and prickling up.

'Oh, Jesus,' Con gasps. Senan has started laughing too. 'And us feckin' about in that river at the crack of dawn, up to our oxters—'

Bobby is doubled up with giggles, beating his hands on the table. 'State of us—'

'And hundreds outa our pockets,' Sonny manages, 'and all the time, we coulda just sent out—' He points at Trey and dissolves into helpless wheezes.

'*What?*'

'Nothing,' Johnny says, chuckling, patting her arm. 'No one's laughing at you, sweetheart. We're laughing at ourselves, only.'

Trey still looks unconvinced and prickly. Cal takes a look at Mart. He's laughing along, but his eyes are sharp and steady, moving between Johnny and Trey.

''Tis 'cause we thought we were awful cute,' PJ explains to Trey, grinning. 'Only we were thick.'

Trey shrugs. ''F you don't want it,' she says, jerking her chin at the bag on the table, 'I'll have it back.'

'And why not,' Johnny says, catching up the bag and pressing it into her hand. 'No one'll grudge you that. You've earned it. Amn't I right?'

'Go on,' Dessie says, still giggling, flapping a hand at her. 'Plenty more where that came from.'

'Whatever,' Trey says, pocketing the bag. 'Thought you might wanta see it, is all.'

'Ah, sweetheart,' Johnny says remorsefully, catching her arm. Cal is starting to wonder if the guy even remembers her name. 'You done great. Daddy's only delighted with you, and so are all these other nice lads. OK? You go along home now and tell your mammy to put that somewhere safe, and we'll have it made into a lovely necklace for you to wear.'

Trey shrugs, detaches her arm from his hand, and leaves. Her eyes skid right over Cal.

'Well, God almighty, lads,' Johnny says, running his hands through his hair and gazing after her with a mixture of fondness and bemusement. 'Doesn't that beat Banagher? I didn't know whether to give her a hug or a skelp. That child'll be the death of me.'

'She's got good timing, anyway,' Mart says amiably. 'Isn't that a great talent to have?'

'Where was it she went digging?' Senan asks.

'Fuck's sake, man,' Johnny says, giving him a disbelieving stare. 'Are you serious? I'm handing nothing over for free. And even if I did, 'twouldn't do ye a blind bitta good: like I told you before, there's no use in heading out digging with no licence. No: we'll do this right.'

'Foot of the mountain, she said,' Sonny says to Con. 'That'll be our land.'

'Hang on,' Johnny says, turning to Cal, holding up a hand to silence the rest. 'Mr Hooper had a question for me, before my Theresa came in and interrupted him. Mostly I'd apologise for her, only this time I reckon what she had to say was worth hearing, amn't I right?'

'Jesus fuck,' Sonny says, from the heart, agreeing.

Johnny sits there smiling at Cal, waiting.

'Nope,' Cal says. 'Nothing.'

'Ah, there was. Something awful serious, going by the face on you. You put the heart crossways in me there, man; I was afraid maybe I'd run over your dog and never noticed.'

'Not that I know of,' Cal says. 'Can't've been that serious; it's gone right outa my head. It'll come back, though. I'll be sure and let you know when it does.'

'You do that,' Johnny says, giving him an approving nod. 'Meanwhile, lads, I think we all deserve another shot of the good stuff, amn't I right? This one's on me. We'll have a toast to that mad young one of mine.'

'Count me out,' Cal says. 'I'm gonna head home.'

'Ah, now,' Johnny says reproachfully. 'You can't stay for just the two; that's not the way we do things around here. Sit where you are a while longer and then I'll see you safe home, if you're worried about overdoing it. I reckon we could do with a chat anyway.'

'Nah,' Cal says. He drains his pint and stands up. 'I'll see you round.' As he leaves, he hears Johnny say something that gets a big old laugh.

The moon is almost full. It turns the mountain road white and treacherously narrow, a trickle of safety wavering upwards between the thick dark scribbles of heathery bog and the formless looming of trees. A fidgety breeze roams among the high branches, but it takes none of the heat out of the air. Cal keeps climbing, sweating through his shirt, till the road splits and he strikes off down the fork that leads to the Reddy place. It leaves him a little closer to the Reddys' than he'd like, but he doesn't need someone irrelevant passing by at the wrong time. He finds a boulder in the shadow of a low, gnarled tree, with a clear view of the path below him, and sits down to wait.

He's thinking of Trey, standing in the entrance of the alcove with her eyes on Johnny and her jaw set, close enough to touch and unreachable. He wonders where she is now, and what she's thinking, and what happened to her mouth. It aches right through him that he failed her: he didn't find a way to make her able to come to him with this.

He understands that it's not surprising. When Johnny first came home, she had no use for him, but the more Cal sees of Johnny, the more he figures there are ways Trey's brother Brendan took after his daddy. Trey idolised Brendan. If she saw in Johnny flashes of things she had thought were lost to her, she might find it hard to turn away.

Cal knows, not that it makes any difference, that Johnny isn't deliberately trying to put the kid in harm's way. He doubts that the extent of the possible harm has even crossed Captain Chucklefuck's mind. Johnny has a plan, and everything is going to plan, so in his head, everything is hunky-dory. He has no conception of the dangers of being the one with a plan, when your targets have no such thing and are willing instead to do whatever the situation demands.

The undergrowth ticks and twitches as things follow their accustomed trails among it; a weasel or a stoat streaks neatly across the path, fine as a brushstroke, and vanishes into the other side. The moon moves, shifting the shadows. Cal wishes, with a surge of something that feels like vast dawning grief, that Johnny had waited even one more year, till Cal had had just a little more time to shore up the kid's cracked places, before he came prancing into town breaking things.

He hears Johnny coming before he sees him. The dumb fuck is sauntering up the mountain singing to himself, softly and happily: 'But I'm tired of all this pleasure, so I'm off to take my leisure, and the next thing that you'll hear from me is a letter from New York . . .'

Cal stands up quietly, in the shadow of the tree. He lets Johnny get within ten feet before he steps out onto the path.

Johnny leaps and shies sideways like a spooked horse. Then he recognises Cal and recovers himself. 'Fuck, man, you nearly gave me a heart attack,' he says, hand to his chest, managing to pull out a laugh. 'You'd want to watch yourself, doing that. Another man woulda given you a clatter, if you took him by surprise like that. What are you doing out here, anyhow? I thought you were headed home to the bed.'

Cal says, 'You said you wanted to talk to me.'

'Jesus, man, cool the jets. 'Tisn't life-or-death. It can wait – I've been celebrating here, I'm in no state to be having delicate conversations. And neither are you, if you're out here getting brambles stuck in your arse at this hour; you musta got a touch of the sun on that river. Go on home. I'll buy you a straightener tomorrow, and we'll have a nice civilised chat then.'

Cal says, 'I been waiting here two hours to hear whatever you've got to say. Go ahead and say it.'

He watches Johnny eye him and the escape routes. Johnny isn't drunk, but he's considerably closer to it than Cal is, and the terrain has too many surprises to favour a quarry with no head start.

Johnny sighs, running a hand over his hair. 'All right,' he says, marshalling his resources to humour the pushy Yank. 'Here's the story. No offence, now, and don't be shooting the messenger, yeah?'

'Takes a lot to offend me,' Cal says.

Johnny grins automatically. 'That's a great thing, man. Listen: I hate to say it, but my friend Mr Rushborough, he's after taking against you. No reason that he's given me; he just doesn't like the cut of you. You make him nervous, he says. I'd say 'tis just that you don't fit the idea of the place that he's got into his head, d'you know what I mean? Them hairy aul' farm fellas that smell of sheep shite and tin whistles and forty shades of green, they're what he came looking for. A street-smart Chicago cop like yourself . . .' He turns up his palms. 'That doesn't fit the image at all, at all. 'Tisn't your fault, but you're upsetting the dream. And men get awful edgy if you upset their dreams.'

'Huh,' Cal says. 'You know what, I had a feeling it was gonna be something along those lines. Maybe I'm psychic.'

'Sure, you're a man of experience,' Johnny explains. 'A man that's seen as much of the world as you have, he can spot when another man's taken against him. It happens, sometimes, no rhyme nor reason to it. But you see where that leaves us, don't you? If you were to stay on board with this, Rushborough'd only keep getting edgier, till in the end he'd decide, *Ah, here, I'm not enjoying myself any more.* And off he'd go, back to London. So . . .' He gives Cal a regretful look. 'I'll need you to step back outa this, Mr Hooper. You won't be leaving empty-handed, now, don't be worrying about that; myself and the lads, we'll make up your share outa what we get. 'Tis fierce unfair, I know that, but we've a delicate situation on our hands, and 'tis this or lose the man altogether.'

'Yeah,' Cal says. 'Like I said, no surprises there. Now it's my turn. Run whatever con you want, I don't give a shit. Like you said, I'm not from around here. But you don't get to bring Trey into it. She has to live here, once you and Whatshisname are done and gone.'

He watches Johnny think about going into outraged-daddy mode, and then think better of it. He goes for baffled innocent instead. 'Man,' he says, spreading his hands, injured, 'I didn't bring her into anything. Maybe I shoulda checked that she wasn't listening in, but how was I supposed to know she'd go digging? And where's the harm in it, anyhow? There's plenty there for everyone, no need to grudge the child her bitta fun—'

'Johnny,' Cal says, 'I'm not in the mood. You gave the kid that piece of gold. There's nothing to find.'

'Ah, God,' Johnny says, rolling his eyes in exasperation, 'there's always one. The feckin' pessimist. Debbie Downer, isn't that what you Yanks call it? Here, I'll tell you what we'll do: I'll give you back your few quid, so you won't need to be worrying about what's out there, and you can jog on. That way we're all happy.'

'Nope,' Cal says. 'You're done here. Pack your stuff, pack your Brit, and get out.'

Johnny rears back in the moonlight, eyebrows going up. 'Ah, here. Are you joking me? You're trying to order me outa my own home place? You've got some brass neck on you, Hooper.'

'I'll give you two days,' Cal says. 'That oughta be long enough for you to come up with a story that'll keep the kid clear.'

Johnny laughs at him. 'Jesus, man, who d'you think you are? Vito Corleone? You're not in the States now; that's not how we do things round here. Relax on the fuckin' jacks. Get yourself some popcorn, sit back and enjoy the show. It'll all be grand. Rushborough'll go away happy, whatever we find or don't find—'

'Johnny,' Cal says. 'I'm trying real hard to be patient here, but you need to cut the bullshit. You're not running a con on Rushborough; you and him are running it on the guys. The more cash you scam out of them, the more flak the kid'll take when the shit hits the fan. You're done.'

Johnny looks at him with no expression at all. Then he lets out a short, meaningless laugh. He sticks his hands in his pockets and turns to scan the long slow curves of the mountains against the stars, giving himself time to pick his new tack. When he turns back to Cal, his tone has lost its lilting charm, turned crisp and businesslike.

'Or what, man? Quit throwing shapes and look at it straight for a minute. Or what? You'll go to the Guards and tell them you and the lads are trying to run a scam on some poor tourist, only it's not working out for ye? Or you'll go to the lads and tell them they're the ones getting conned? Here's you making out you care so much about Theresa: how d'you reckon that'll pan out for her?'

'There's no "or",' Cal says. He wants his gun. He wants to shoot the balls right off this little shitweasel for fathering the kid, when she deserves so much better. 'You got till Sunday night.'

Johnny looks at him for a minute and sighs. 'Man,' he says, in a new, simpler voice, 'if I could, I would. Believe me. D'you think I wanta be here? I'd be gone in a second, if I'd the choice.'

For the first time in their acquaintance, he doesn't sound like he's trying to bullshit Cal. He sounds tired and powerless. When he brushes his hair out of his eye, screwing up his face and catching a sudden breath like a kid, he looks like he wants to lie down right there on the path and sleep.

'There's four buses a day,' Cal says. 'Right up on the main road. Pick one.'

Johnny shakes his head. He says, 'I owe money.'

'That's your problem. Not the kid's.'

'She wanted to help. I never twisted her arm.'

'You shoulda said no.'

Johnny looks up at Cal. 'I owe your man Rushborough,' he says. His voice is so sodden with defeat and fear that it weighs down the night air. 'And he's not someone you wanta fuck around with.'

'Great. Him and me got something in common after all.'

Johnny shakes his head again. 'Nah, man,' he says. 'Talk tough all you want. I seen that fella hold a wee girl down and slice lines in her arm with a razor – a child, like, no bigger than my Alanna – till her daddy paid up.'

Cal says, no louder, 'So you brought him here.'

Johnny gives a shrug, wry and appealingly rueful: *Gee, man, what do you want from me, a guy's gotta do what a guy's gotta do.* Cal, at long last, punches him right in the mouth.

Johnny never saw it coming and he goes down hard, hitting the verge with a thud and a crunch of undergrowth. But he recovers fast, and by the time Cal comes after him he's got a foot up, aiming for Cal's stomach. He misses and gets Cal in the thigh, and Cal falls on him, full weight, hearing the breath retch out of him. Things turn messy then, crowded with grunts and elbows. Johnny is a better fighter than Cal expected. He fights desperate and dirty, jabbing for the eyes and scrabbling for fishhooks. Cal welcomes it. He doesn't want a clean fight, not with this guy.

Johnny is rolling them over and over among the rocks and brambles, trying not to let Cal get a solid purchase where his weight will tell, pressing close so Cal can't get the reach for a decent punch. He smells of shitty fake-fancy aftershave. Cal sees flashes of his bared teeth, the heather, the stars. It streaks across his mind that if they roll too far and land in a bog, the mountain will take them and no one will ever know.

He gets Johnny by his pretty haircut and mashes his face into the dirt, but Johnny finds Cal's ear, tries to rip it off, and twists away quick as a fox when Cal jerks backwards. Cal lunges after him, on hands and knees, blinded by the crisscross of moonlight and shadow, following Johnny's scrabbles and the painful whine of his breath. He grabs a limb and drags Johnny back towards him, punching at anything he can reach, taking a vicious heel to the forehead. Neither of them yells out. Cal has never been in a fight this close to silent. If anyone or anything else is out on the mountain, neither of them wants to draw its notice.

He tries to get hold of Johnny's arms, takes a thumb to the eyeball and sees a bright burst of stars, but the fresh shot of rage lets him force a knee up between their bodies and slam Johnny in the balls. While Johnny is curled up wheezing, Cal straddles him and lands one more punch to his nose, just to put a dent in his good looks, save a girl or two from falling for his wheedles. He forces himself to stop there. He wants to keep hammering the guy's face till there's nothing left of it, but he needs Johnny to hear what he has to say.

Johnny gets his breath back and tries to heave himself free, but Cal is a lot bigger than him. When Johnny goes for his eye, Cal catches his wrist and bends it backwards till Johnny yelps.

'If you're still in town Monday morning,' he says, so close to Johnny's face that he can smell the blood and booze, 'I'm gonna shoot you and dump your carcass in a bog where it belongs. We clear?'

Johnny laughs, which makes him cough blood. Fine droplets of it hit Cal's cheek. In the moonlight his face, stippled and smeared black and white, barely looks like a face at all; its edges blur into the black and white of the undergrowth, like he's dissolving away.

'No you won't, man. If you do that, Rushborough'll think I took off, and he'll come looking to get me back by going after my family. You think he'll stop at Theresa?'

Cal gives his wrist an extra twist, and Johnny catches his breath with a hiss. 'You don't give two shits about your family, fuckhead. He could shove 'em all in a wood chipper, and you wouldn't budge an inch outa cover. He knows that.'

'Then he'll do it just to get his money's worth. You don't know the man.'

'I'll worry about Rushborough. All you gotta worry about is packing your shit.'

'Are you planning on putting him in a bog as well? 'Cause I'll tell you something for nothing, boy: you won't catch him napping as easy as you caught me. Try anything on him, and you'll be the one lands in the bog.'

Johnny's voice is staticky, clogged with blood. 'I'll take my chances,' Cal says. 'All you need to know is, your chances are a lot better out of this place than in it. You got the whole world to dodge Rushborough in. You're not gonna dodge me. Are we clear?'

They are very close together. Johnny's eyes, made of fractured slashes of light and shadow, hold nothing but refusal, pure as an animal's. For a moment Cal thinks he's going to have to break Johnny's wrist. Then he sees the vivid flash of fear as Johnny reads that thought and realises that Cal means every word.

'Yeah!' Johnny yells, just in time. He jerks his head, trying to shake blood out of his eyes. 'Jesus, man, I get it. Get the fuck off me.'

'Great,' Cal says. 'About fucking time.' He picks himself up, starting to feel the throbbing in various parts of him, and hauls Johnny to his feet by his shirt collar.

'Bye, Johnny,' he says. 'It's been something.' The struggle carried them farther off the path than he realised; it takes him a minute to get his bearings, amid the maze of shadows, and aim Johnny in the right direction. He gives Johnny a good hard shove and Johnny stumbles off towards home, blotting his nose on his sleeve, with the autopilot obedience of a guy who's lost enough fights to know the protocol. Cal resists the urge to speed him on his way with a kick in the pants.

He hasn't worked out what, if anything, he's going to do about Rushborough. His instinct is that Johnny was just blowing smoke, and that if Johnny goes, Rushborough will go after him. Cal has encountered plenty of men, and women too, who hurt people for pleasure, but he doesn't get that scent off Rushborough. Rushborough smells like a different kind of predator, the ice-minded kind that locks on to his prey and doesn't turn loose unless you shoot him off it. Regardless of what he said, Cal doesn't rate Johnny's chances of giving Rushborough the slip, here or anywhere.

He knows he has to factor in the possibility that Johnny was telling the truth for once, but this seems like a problem for after he's washed off some of the blood. He also knows that Johnny may not be going anywhere. Johnny's fears right now are an intricate spread, and Cal has no idea how the odds are weighted, or what bets his private, desperate algorithms might finally land on.

The sounds of Johnny blundering away are slowly fading into the distance. Cal makes his way to the edge of the path and listens till he's sure the little shit is gone. He tests his injuries. There's a goose egg above his eyebrow and a swelling bruise on his jaw, his thigh hurts where Johnny's foot jabbed deep into the muscle, something has ripped through his shirt and dug a long gouge up his side, and about every part of him has small sharp grazes and bruises, but all of it seems minor enough to mend by itself. More importantly, he's damn sure Johnny is a lot worse off.

He wonders where Johnny is heading, whether Trey is home, what Johnny will tell her and what she'll make of it. He wonders whether he just fucked up bad. He has no qualms about having given Johnny a beat-down – it needed doing, and if anything he feels like he did well to hold out so long – but he's made uneasy by the fact that he did it because he lost his temper. It feels unmanaged, and this situation needs managing.

He starts homeward, listening for any movement in the shadows.

————

Trey knows she's not the only one still awake. Everyone else has gone to bed, Liam is snoring softly and Maeve is sleep-muttering her annoyances, but Trey can hear her mother moving about the bedroom, and the occasional loud heave and sigh as Alanna turns among the sheets, hoping someone will come see what's wrong. The house isn't at rest.

Trey is sprawled on the sofa, automatically rubbing Banjo's head propped on her knee. Banjo's paw is better, but he's still holding it up and looking pathetic when he wants treats and fusses. Trey is giving him plenty of both.

She's listening for her father to come home. She reckons most likely he'll be pleased with her, but with him you can never be sure. She's left her bedroom window open, in case he's raging and she needs to run.

She considered doing what he said, showing Noreen or Mrs Cunniffe the piece of gold and letting them talk. It wouldn't have worked. Trey, like anyone from Ardnakelty, has a gut-deep understanding of the ferocious power of talk, but it's the wrong kind of power for this: fluid, slippery, switchbacking, forging twisting channels you can't predict. She can see why her father went that way without a second thought. He's all those things distilled; regardless of what either he or the townland might like to think, he's Ardnakelty to the bone. Trey isn't and doesn't want to be, which means she sees angles that he misses. A solid thing appearing in front of the men's faces, brazen and undeniable, has a different kind of power, to which they're unaccustomed and against which they have few defences. She let the gold do its own talking.

Banjo jerks in his sleep, eyebrows twitching and paws starting to work. 'Shh,' Trey says, running his soft ear between her fingers, 'it's grand,' and he relaxes again.

She went to Cal's in the morning, to warn him. She wasn't clear on exactly how to do that, because she doesn't want Cal knowing too much about what way she's thinking; there's a chance he might consider this to be a breach of her promise to do nothing about Brendan, and tell her to back off. It made no odds in the end, anyway, because Cal wasn't home. Trey waited on his back porch for hours, her and Banjo eating the ham slices she'd brought to make sandwiches for lunch, but he didn't come. He was out with the men, going about the business he doesn't want her to know. In the end she left.

She doesn't underestimate what she's got into. The things she's done before, robbing off Noreen and breaking into abandoned houses with her mates and drinking their parents' booze, those were baby stuff. This is real. It feels good.

When she hears her dad at the door, she thinks at first, from the sounds of fumbling and staggering, that he's drunk. Then he comes into the sitting room, and she sees his face. She stands up, spilling Banjo off her lap.

Johnny's eyes go over Trey like she's not there. 'Sheila,' he says, and then, louder and more savagely, 'Sheila!' Blood is all round his mouth and chin like a bright beard, and a flood of it is stiffening his shirtfront. When he puts his right foot down, he flinches like Banjo.

Sheila comes to the doorway and looks him over. The state of him doesn't appear to cause her either surprise or upset. She seems like she's been expecting this to happen ever since he came back.

'Your nose is broke,' she says.

'I fuckin' know that,' Johnny snaps, with enough of a snarl in his voice that Trey goes up on her toes, but he's too focused on himself to take time out for anyone else. He dabs his fingers gingerly at his nose and examines them. 'Get me cleaned up.'

Sheila goes out. Johnny turns like he can't stay still, and his eyes catch on Trey. Before she can move, he's lunged across the room and grabbed her by the wrist. His eyes are dilated almost black, and there are bits of brush in his hair. He looks animal.

'You fuckin' squelt to that Yank. What the fuck are you—'

'I did not—'

'You'll get me kilt. Is that what you want? Is it?'

He jerks her wrist, hard, digging in to bruise her. 'I said fuckin' *nothing*,' Trey snaps, right in his face and not flinching. Banjo is whining.

'Then how the *fuck* does he know? No one knew, only you. What the fuck, what are you playing at—'

His hand on her wrist is shaking in sharp spasms. Trey wrenches herself free with such unexpected ease that she stumbles backwards. Johnny stares, and for a second she thinks he's going to come after her. If he does, she'll punch him bang in his broken nose. The only time she'll bow to her dad's will, from now on, is when it matches her own purposes.

Maybe Johnny sees that. Either way, he stays put. 'Lena Dunne,' he says. The injuries have turned his voice clotted and ugly. 'Didja talk to her? She'd squeal on me, no problem to her, uppity bitch—'

'I said *nothing*. To anyone.'

'How the fuck does Hooper know, so?'

'He coulda just guessed. He's not thick. Just 'cause the rest fell for it—'

Johnny spins away from her, lurching around the room, hands in his hair. 'This is what you get when you mess with fuckin' cops. I knew it, the minute I got a smell of him, I *knew* he was trouble— What the fuck are you doing hanging around with a cop? Are you fuckin' simple?'

'Don't wake the children,' Sheila says, in the doorway. She's holding a saucepan of water and an old red-checked dish towel. 'Sit down.'

Johnny stares at her for a second, like he's forgotten who she is. Then he drops onto the sofa.

'Get to bed,' Sheila tells Trey.

'You stay put,' Johnny says. 'I've use for you.'

Trey moves closer to the door, just in case, but she stays. Sheila sits on the sofa beside Johnny, dips the towel in the water, and squeezes it out. When she dabs at his face, he hisses. Sheila ignores it and keeps working, in short systematic swipes like she's getting a spill off the cooker.

'He's got nothing,' Johnny says, wincing as Sheila catches a sore place. He sounds like he's talking to himself. 'He can say what he wants. No one'll believe the likes of him.'

There's silence in the room, only the drip as Sheila wrings out the cloth. Alanna has stopped tossing. The water in the pan is turning red.

'You tell me,' Johnny says, twisting to get one eye on Trey. 'You know the man. Is Hooper going to run around this townland bleating it to everyone that there's no gold?'

'Dunno,' Trey says. 'He might not.' Cal's relationship with Ardnakelty baffles her. He would have every right to a handful of well-honed grudges, but he's easy and mannerly with everyone, to the point where she can't even spot where the grudges might lie. That doesn't mean they don't exist, though. Cal, even if he's pissed off with Johnny for fooling him, might accept this chance to sit back and let the townland walk into Johnny's trap. She knows, from stories he's told her about his childhood, that his code allows for revenge, and that he knows how to take his time.

'If he does, will the place believe him?'

'Dunno. Some of 'em will.'

'Francie fuckin' Gannon. That dry aul' shite's just looking for an excuse to wreck everything.' Johnny spits blood into the pan. 'I can do without Francie. Everyone knows what he's like, sure. How about the rest? Do they trust Hooper?'

The question is a complicated one, and Trey has no intention of going into the details. 'Sorta,' she says.

Johnny gives a harsh laugh. 'Look at that. A fuckin' cop, and a Yank, and my own home place'd take his word over mine.' His voice is rising. 'Every fuckin' time, any chance they get, spitting in my face like I'm— Aah!' He flinches and slaps Sheila's hand away furiously. 'The fuck was that?'

'I said not to wake the children,' Sheila says.

They stare at each other. For a second Trey thinks he's going to hit her. She readies herself.

Johnny slumps back into the sofa. 'Sure, it's not the end of the world,' he says. His nose is still bleeding; Sheila mops up the trickle. 'No need to panic. Some of the lads'll stick. And they'll bring in more. We'll find a way. It might take a wee bit longer, but we'll get there in the end, so we will.'

'Course,' Trey says. 'It'll be grand. I'll help.' She's not going to let her dad give up and do a legger, when he's only taken a few hundred quid off each of those men. Brendan is worth more than that.

Johnny focuses on her and brings out a smile, which makes him wince. 'Someone's got faith in me, anyway,' he says. 'Daddy's sorry for giving out. I shoulda known better, isn't that right? I shoulda known you'd never say a word.'

Trey shrugs.

'That was only brilliant tonight, the way you walked into the pub. I shoulda thought of that. The faces on those great eejits, hah? I thought Bobby Feeney's big fat head was going to explode.'

'They fell for it,' Trey says.

'They fuckin' did. Hook, line, and sinker. 'Twas only beautiful; I'da watched that all night long. We'll teach them to fuck with the Reddys, hah?'

Trey nods. She expected to hate bringing out the gold in the pub, talking shite with everyone staring at her; she was unprepared for the burst of power. She had those men by the noses, to lead wherever she wanted. She could have made them get up out of their seats, leave their pints and traipse obediently around the mountain, along every trail she took when she was hunting for Brendan. She could have walked the lot of them straight into a bog.

Sheila turns Johnny's chin towards her so she can get at the other side of his face. 'Now,' he says, rolling an eye over his shoulder to catch Trey's, 'I've another wee job for you. Tomorrow morning, you go down to that smartarse Hooper and ask him, nice and polite like, to mind his own fuckin' business, as a favour to you. Can you do that for me?'

'Yeah,' Trey says. 'No problem.' She wants Cal out of this as much as her dad does. She doesn't like being on the same side as her dad. It leaves her with a strange, prickly sense of outrage.

'You explain to him that no one'll believe him. If he meddles, he'll do nothing but get you in trouble. That oughta do it.' Johnny smiles at her, lopsided. 'And after that, it's plain sailing all the way. Happy days, hah?'

The door creaks. Alanna stands half in, half out of the room, wearing an old T-shirt of Trey's, with her stuffed rabbit tucked under her arm. 'What happened?' she says.

'Go back to bed,' Sheila says sharply.

'Ah, sweetheart,' Johnny says, snapping alert to give Alanna a big smile. 'Your big silly daddy fell over. Wouldja look at the state of me? Your mammy's just tidying me up a wee bit, and then I'll be in to give you a good-night hug.'

Alanna stares, wide-eyed. 'Get her to bed,' Sheila says to Trey.

'Come on,' Trey says, steering Alanna back into the hall. Johnny waves to them both as they go, grinning like a fool through the blood and the dish towel.

'Did he fall over?' Alanna wants to know.

'Nah,' Trey says. 'He got in a fight.'

'With who?'

'None a your business.'

She's heading for Alanna and Liam's room, but Alanna balks and pulls at her T-shirt. 'Want to come in with you.'

'If you don't wake Maeve.'

'I won't.'

The bedroom is too hot, even with the window open. Maeve has kicked off her sheet and is sprawled on her stomach. Trey guides Alanna through the tangle of clothes and who knows what on the floor. 'Now,' she says, pulling the sheet over the two of them. 'Shh.'

'I don't want him to stay,' Alanna tells her, in what's meant to be a whisper. 'Liam does.'

'He won't stay,' Trey says.

'Why?'

''Cause. That's how he is. Shh.'

Alanna nods, accepting that. In no time she's asleep, snuffling into her rabbit's head. Her hair smells of gummy bears and is faintly sticky against Trey's face.

Trey stays awake, listening to the silence from the sitting room. The curtain stirs sluggishly in the feeble breeze. Once there's a sudden strangled roar of pain from Johnny and a sharp word from Sheila, which Trey reckons is her setting his nose back into line. Then the silence rises to wall them off again. Alanna's breathing doesn't change.

———————

It takes Cal a long time to get home. The adrenaline has leached out of him, leaving his limbs heavy and unwieldy as wet sandbags. The moon has sunk behind the mountains, and the night is dark and simmering hot. When he finally rounds the bend and his house comes into view, the living-room windows are lit, small and valiant against the black huddle of the mountains.

Cal stands still among the moths and rustles, leaning on the roadside wall with both hands, his mind groping for what intruder this might be and where he's going to find the force to drive them out. His thigh and his forehead are throbbing. For a second he considers just lying down and going to sleep under a hedge, and dealing with this in the morning.

Then a shape crosses the window. Even at this distance, Cal knows it for Lena, by the line of her back and by the moving sheen of the lamplight on her fair hair. He takes a breath. Then he straightens up and heads down the dark road, his big old sandbag feet catching in potholes, towards home.

The dogs signal his arrival early enough that Lena is at the door to meet him. She's barefoot, and the house smells of tea and toast. She's been waiting a while.

'Hey,' Cal says.

Lena's eyebrows go up, and she moves him into the light so she can examine his face. 'Johnny, yeah?' she inquires.

'He looks worse'n I do.'

'That's nice,' Lena says. She turns his head to one side and the other, assessing the damage. 'Dessie went home and told Noreen about Trey coming into the pub,' she says, 'and Noreen was on to me so fast she left skid marks. So I thought I'd call round and see what you made of it. I guessed right, or near enough.'

Cal takes her hand away from his cheek and wraps his arms around her. He stands there for a long time, with his face down in the warmth of her hair, feeling the steady thump of her heart against his chest and the strength of her hands on his back.

12

Mart, whom Cal has been expecting, shows up in the morning, as Lena is leaving. He hangs back at the gate, being discreet as obtrusively as possible and grinning his head off, while Lena kisses Cal goodbye on the doorstep. When she starts up her car, Mart opens the gate for her and gives a big wave as she drives past. Lena lifts a hand without looking at him.

Cal, not wanting to be obliged to invite Mart in, heads down to the gate. 'D'you see what I mean, now?' Mart says, sighing. 'That one's got no time for me. If I was the sensitive type, I'd be wounded right to the heart.'

'You were just aiming to see if you could fluster her,' Cal says. Rip and Kojak gallop off to inspect the perimeter together.

'I wouldn't waste my time,' Mart says. 'Lena Dunne's not easy flustered.'

'You'd have to do a lot better'n that,' Cal agrees.

Mart watches the car disappear behind the hedges. He's given no sign of noticing Cal's various injuries, which this morning are pretty tender and hard to miss. 'What would ye be talking about, the two of ye?' he inquires.

The question startles Cal. 'Like what?'

'That's what I'm asking you. One way or t'other, I've never had much opportunity for conversation with the women – apart from my mammy, and sure, I knew what she was going to say before she did. She was a fine woman, my mammy, but she'd no truck with variety; the same conversations she'd been having for seventy year were good enough for her. I don't count that. What would a man be talking about with a woman?'

'Jeez, man,' Cal says. 'I dunno.'

'I'm not asking you what sweet nothings you go whispering in her ear. I'm asking about conversation. What kinda chats you'd be having over a cuppa tea, like.'

'Stuff,' Cal says. 'Like I'd talk about with anyone. What do you talk about with the guys in the pub?'

'Stuff,' Mart acknowledges. 'Fair point there, bucko. Ah, well; if I get curious enough, I'll have to hunt out a woman that's willing to have a cuppa tea with the likes of me, and find out for myself.' He gazes meditatively after Lena's car. 'That's what Bobby's planning to do, if Johnny Reddy makes him a millionaire: get himself a woman. I don't know does he think he can order one off Amazon, like a DVD, but that's what he says.' He throws Cal a sharp glance. 'What d'you reckon there, boyo? Is wee Johnny going to make millionaires of us all?'

'Who knows,' Cal says. Rip comes zooming back from his circuit with Kojak and butts up against Cal's leg, looking for attention. Cal runs a hand over him. He's picked up a nice coating of burrs somewhere along the way.

'Johnny musta been drunker than he looked, last night,' Mart informs Cal. 'Didja see him yet today?'

'Nope,' Cal says.

'He was down at Noreen's, lolling about taking up space, when I went in. D'you know what he done last night, on his way home? Walked straight off the path and went arse over tip halfway down the mountainside. You oughta see the state of him. Like he got bet up by every rock on the way down.'

So Johnny has weighed up his various risks and has no intention of skipping town, and he wants to make that clear. 'He didn't look that drunk to me,' Cal says. 'Not when I left, anyway.'

'Isn't that what I'm saying to you? I wasn't counting the man's pints, but he musta been lashing them into him, to go astray on a path he's been walking half his life. What d'you reckon about that?'

'I don't rate Johnny's brainpower too high,' Cal says. 'Drunk or sober. I'm not gonna get surprised by any dumb thing he does.'

'True enough,' Mart acknowledges. 'I wouldn't rate you a fool, though, Sunny Jim. Did you fall down the mountainside too, didja?'

'Nope,' Cal says. 'Slipped in the shower. I musta been drunker than I thought, too.'

'The shower's a terrible man,' Mart agrees obligingly. 'My cousin up in Gorteen, he slipped in the shower and smacked his head. He's got a mad squint on him ever since. It does be fierce hard work talking to him; you wouldn't know which eye to look at.'

'Guess I got lucky,' Cal says. He squats down and starts picking burrs out of Rip's coat.

'So far,' Mart points out. 'I'd watch that shower if I was you. Once they get a taste of blood, there's no holding them.'

'Yeah,' Cal says. 'Maybe I'll get one of those non-slip mat things.'

'Do that. You wouldn't want matters getting outa control.' Mart squints meditatively up at the sky, apparently gauging the weather, which looks exactly the same as it has for the last two months. Cal is getting more and more resentful of the weather. He's coming to the conclusion that at least half of what he loves about Ireland is the smell of it under rain. Without that smell, complex and melancholy and generous, he feels obscurely ripped off.

'D'you know something,' Mart says, 'I might haveta find myself that woman to talk to. The men do be awful predictable.'

'Sorry 'bout that,' Cal says. Rip is squirming and licking at him, making the removal process as difficult as possible, not because it bothers him but just for kicks.

'D'you know another thing about men that drives me mental altogether?' Mart says. 'The way they'd hold a grudge. The women, now' – he settles his elbow on the gate, getting comfortable for some in-depth explaining – 'if a woman has a grudge against someone, the whole townland knows. You'd know what the person done, and why they had no right, and what they oughta do to clear the air, and what's on the cards if they don't do it. You'd be hearing about it on the regular for as long as it takes, and if it's not sorted in your lifetime, your childer'll hear about it when you're gone. But a man, sure: he'll hold a grudge for ten or twenty or thirty year, and never say a word to anyone. Even the fella he's got the grudge against mightn't have a notion. What's the point in that? What good does the grudge do you or anyone, if it never gets an airing?'

'Search me,' Cal says.

'And then,' Mart says, 'when 'tis after bubbling away all that time, and no one any the wiser, one fine day something goes a wee bit wrong – the man sees his chance, maybe, or maybe he just has a bad day or a bit too much drink – and it all boils over. I know a lad beyond Croghan that was at his own daughter's twenty-first, and he hit his brother-in-law a skelp to the head with a bottle, near kilt him. Outa nowhere, like. All they could get outa him was that the brother-in-law deserved it for something he'd said at that same daughter's christening.' He shakes his head. 'And him a lovely quiet lad that got on with everyone. That's not the kind of unpredictability I like. Revenge can be awful disconcerting, Sunny Jim, when it comes outa the clear blue sky.'

Rip has got bored and started dancing and curvetting, trying to make Cal's job difficult enough that he'll give up and let Rip go back to Kojak. 'Stay,' Cal says. Rip lets out a martyred sigh and flops down.

'There's exceptions, now,' Mart allows. 'Your young one's a girl, but I'd say she'd hold her tongue about any grudges she might have stored up. And myself, I like to get the good outa them; I haven't many, but I'll tell all the details to anyone who'll listen.'

'Hashtag, not all men,' Cal says, shoving Rip's nose out of his way. He's been in Ardnakelty long enough to understand that Mart isn't just shooting the shit here. He's trying to figure out whether Mart is telling him something, or asking him something, or both.

'Holy God, wouldja listen to that,' Mart says, delighted, poking Cal in the leg with his crook. 'We've Mr Social Media here, with the hashtags. Are you one of them influencers on the side, Sunny Jim? Are you on the TikTok shaking yourself to Rihanna? I'd watch that.'

'I'll get right on it,' Cal says. 'Soon as I can find a black leather dress that fits.'

Mart laughs. 'Tell us, Sunny Jim,' he says, settling back onto his crook. 'Where do you stand on the aul' grudges? If you had a coupla them, would I know all the details, or would you be keeping them to yourself? I'd say you're the strong silent type, are you?'

'I'm not from round here,' Cal says. 'You gotta be local to have grudges.'

Mart cocks his head to one side, considering that. 'Maybe,' he concedes. 'You'd know better than I would; I've been local all my life. You're telling me if someone done you wrong, or done wrong to someone you cared about, or just annoyed the holy bejaysus outa you, you'd turn the other cheek and forget the whole thing, just 'cause you're a Yank? That's very Christian of you altogether.'

'I just mind my own business,' Cal says. 'And aim to get along with people.' Things are getting a little bit clearer. Mart, in his own way and in his own sweet time, is inquiring about revenge. He's asking whether Cal, if he happened to have information that the gold was a load of hooey, would sit back and watch the guys sink their savings into it.

'You're an example to us all,' Mart informs him piously. 'I don't know how many'd follow it, but. I'll tell you one thing: there'll be some grudges held if that gold doesn't come through.'

'Yeah,' Cal says. 'I bet there would.' He gets the warning.

'Specially if the lads go investing in that company of Paddy Englishman's, on the strength of that bitta gold your young one found, and then the whole thing goes to shite.' Mart grins. 'Bobby won't be a happy man if he misses out on his internet woman.'

'Bobby's a good guy,' Cal says. 'There's plenty of women that'd be glad to run into someone like him.'

'None a them live round here, though. Now there's an example,' Mart adds, struck by a thought and pointing his crook at Cal to emphasise it. 'Everyone knew Bobby had his eye on Lena, till you came along and swept her off her feet – not that she woulda had him anyhow, but sure, he doesn't know that. Bobby doesn't act like he's holding any grudge against you, but you wouldn't know, would you?'

Cal has made up his mind. It sets that dark terror pumping through him, but he doesn't see that he has much choice. 'I don't give a shit who holds what against Johnny,' he says, straightening up from Rip. 'But I don't want to see the kid getting any blowback.'

Mart cocks an eye at him. 'Theresa that was in the pub last night, waving around bits of gold she's after digging up? That kid?'

'Yeah. That kid.'

'Sure, if there's any gold found at all, she'll be grand. Johnny'll get a bitta – what did you call it, now? – blowback, if there's not enough for the lads to break even. But your Theresa never made anyone any offers or any promises. The place won't hold her daddy's shite against her.' He flicks Cal a glance. 'Unless she's after doing something foolish herself, like. If that yoke she brought into the pub doesn't hold up, let's say. If there was no more gold found at all, or if Johnny was to take the lads' cash and run for the hills. That wouldn't be great news.'

Cal doesn't say anything. After a minute Mart nods and goes back to examining the sky, sucking meditatively on his teeth. 'If I was in your shoes, Sunny Jim,' he says, 'and I'm only delighted I'm not, but if. The first thing I'd do is explain to Johnny Reddy that him and his business associate need to saddle up their horses and get outa town.' His eyes pass briefly, with no change of expression, over Cal's bruised face. 'If the message didn't get through, then I'd drop a word in the ear of someone that might have a bit more firepower. And then I'd have a wee chat with that child. Set her straight on a few things. Tell her to keep the head down till this is all sorted. And for Jaysus' sake not to do anything else foolish.'

'And she wouldn't get any shit from anyone.'

'Ah, God, no. No harm, no foul. Like I said, Johnny's not her fault.' Mart smiles at Cal. 'As far as we're concerned, boyo, she's your young one, regardless of who made her. Once you're in good standing, so is she.'

Cal says, 'According to Mrs Duggan, there's never been any rumours about gold around here. Not till Johnny Reddy brought them in.'

That takes Mart by surprise. His eyebrows shoot up, he stares at

Cal, and then after a moment he starts to laugh. 'Dymphna Duggan,' he says. 'Jesus, Mary, and all the saints in the calendar, I shoulda known she'd have something to contribute. I'm kicking myself, so I am, for not thinking of her before you did. I couldn'ta talked to her myself, mind you, she hates the bones of me, but I shoulda got someone to do it – not that it woulda done any good, most likely: she'd get more entertainment outa watching the action than outa anything thcm big lumps coulda offered her. For the love a God, bucko, tell me, before I die of curiosity: how'd you get it outa her? Dymphna never in her life handed over that calibre of intel outa the goodness of her heart; she'd want some high-quality material in exchange. What'd you give her?'

'Trade secret,' Cal says. He thinks of Lena waiting for him on his back porch, the taut hum of tension coming off her. He's always known, and accepted without difficulty, that Lena has spaces she keeps private from everyone including him. The thought of her laying those bare to Mrs Duggan makes him wish he had been a lot more thorough with Johnny.

Mart eyes him, assessing. 'D'you know, now,' he says, 'I wouldn'ta thought you'da had anything she'd fancy. She's an awful fussy feeder, is aul' Dymphna. There's one or two things that I know you'd know better than to offer her, and apart from those, I can't see what you could have that'd tickle her taste buds.'

'That's just 'cause you think I'm predictable,' Cal says. 'Doesn't mean everyone else feels the same way.'

'Lena Dunne, now,' Mart continues thoughtfully, taking no notice of that. 'Your Lena. She's a woman of mystery, or as near as we'd get around here. I'd say she could get Dymphna Duggan's mouth watering, all right, if she wanted to bad enough.'

Cal rolls up his handful of Rip's burrs and shoves them into the hedge. 'Go on,' he says, giving Rip's flank a slap. 'Git.' Rip streaks off to find Kojak.

'Well,' Mart says, 'how and ever it was, if Dymphna says the story's a loada shite, then it's a loada shite. I haveta admit, I'm feel-ing a wee bit smug now. I got a whiff of nonsense off that story right from the start. 'Tis nice to know the aul' instincts are still in working order.'

'Johnny owes Rushborough money,' Cal says. 'And he's scared of the guy. That's why he doesn't want to skip town.'

'Is he, now,' Mart says. 'That wee shitemonger never did have the sense God gave an ass. This'll want a bitta thought put into it, Sunny Jim. If I go off half-cocked, there'll be holy war, and sure no one wants that. I'll get back to you. Till then, you just sit tight.'

He whistles for Kojak, who turns neatly in mid-run and comes flying across the field with Rip galloping in his wake, miles behind, ears flapping joyfully. Mart watches the sunlit long grass wave around them.

He says, 'If 'tis any help, man, you're after making the right call. That'll stand to your Theresa. No one around here wants to give the child any hassle. All we want to know is that she's in good hands and being brought up right. If she had a wee wobble, sure, that's natural enough, with that eejit bouncing in outa the blue. She just needs setting back on the right track, and she'll be grand. You have a word with her.'

'I'll do that,' Cal says. The pulse of the terror has slowed some. Mart is, to the bone, a practical man. He has no qualms about doing damage when he considers it necessary, but he would see no point in wasting energy doing it for punishment or for revenge. If Cal can talk Trey into line, she'll be safe. He has no idea when, or whether, he'll have the chance.

'You and me together,' Mart says, flashing him a sudden wicked grin, 'we'll have it all sorted in no time. Teamwork makes the dream work, boyo.'

'Keep me posted,' Cal says.

'There was me in the pub the other night,' Mart says reflectively, 'telling you to mind your business and stay outa Johnny's, d'you remember? And now, for once in my life, I reckon someone did the right thing, taking no notice of me. 'Tis a funny aul' world some days, Sunny Jim. It'd keep you on your toes, right enough.'

Cal watches him stump off up the road, absently whistling patches of some old tune. He wants to go inside and get to work on that chair, but he leans on the gate for a little while first. He feels the same way he did when Trey first told him Johnny had come home: like either the ground or his legs might not be solid enough to hold him. Cal is too old to like setting things in motion without having at least some idea of where they might go.

———————

It's been a long time since Lena went up the mountain. When she was a wild-blooded teenager hunting for ways to rove, she and her mates would go up there to do things they didn't want to be caught at; and in the bad months after Sean died, she walked up there half the night sometimes, trying to exhaust herself enough to sleep. At both ages she knew it had dangers, and welcomed them, in different ways. It occurs to her that, apart from visiting Sheila after each of the babies came, she may never have been up this mountain in her right mind before.

The sun and the heat make the mountain feel more dangerous, not less; as if it's emboldened, no longer keeping its risks hidden, instead flaunting them like dares. The heather on the bog rustles loudly at every twitch of breeze, making Lena turn fast for nothing; real trails and false ones look wickedly identical, twisting away among the trees; the drop-offs stand out starkly, revealed by the wilting undergrowth, too close to the path. Lena left the dogs behind because of the heat, but she's regretting it slightly. The mountain today feels like a place where a bit of company wouldn't be a bad thing.

She finds the Reddy place all right, though, and she's picked her time well. It's late morning; people are off about their own pursuits. Two messy-haired small kids whose names she can't remember are clambering around a makeshift climbing frame cobbled together out of scrap wood and metal, but there's no sign of Banjo, and when Lena asks the kids whether their dad or Trey is in, they shake their heads, hanging on to the climbing frame and staring unblinkingly.

Sure enough, Sheila answers the door, with a potato peeler in her hand and a wary look on her face. When she sees Lena, the wariness sharpens. It's not personal; it's an automatic response to anything that arrives without an explanation.

'I brought this,' Lena says, producing a jar of blackberry jam. Lena makes her own jam primarily because she likes it made her way, but she's well alive to its other useful properties. 'Your Trey had some at my place the other day and went mad for it, and I said I'd give her a jar, only I forgot. Did I catch you in the middle of something?'

Sheila looks down at the potato peeler. It takes her a second to remember the correct formula. 'Ah, no,' she says. 'You're grand. Come on in and have a cuppa tea.'

Lena sits at the kitchen table, asking harmless questions about the kids, while Sheila moves the potatoes out of the way and puts the kettle on. Half their lives ago, she would have taken up a knife and cut the spuds while Sheila peeled. She wishes she could; it would make the talk flow more easily. But they're not on those terms now.

She's not sure when she last saw Sheila. Sheila rarely comes down to the village; mostly she sends Trey or Maeve to Noreen's for what she needs. Lena assumed it was out of pride. Back in the day, Sheila was not just a beauty but a cheerful-natured one, making the most of every laugh and brushing away any worries on the grounds that it'd all turn out grand, and Ardnakelty is full of begrudgers who take optimism personally; Lena figured Sheila had no wish to let them pick smugly over the remains of all that. Now, looking at her, she reckons it might be just that Sheila hasn't the energy to make the trip.

Sheila brings the tea to the table. The mugs have old-fashioned prints of bunnies among wildflowers, faded from washing. ''Tis almost too hot for tea,' she says.

'Cal makes it iced these days,' Lena says. 'Not with milk, now; just made weak, with sugar and lemon, and kept in the fridge. I don't mind the heat, but I have to admit I appreciate the iced tea.'

'I hate this heat,' Sheila says. 'Everything's dry as a bone, up here; the wind rattles it all night long. I can't sleep for the noise.'

'Some people are after getting fans. I'd say that'd block out the noise, or some of it anyhow.'

Sheila shrugs. 'Maybe.' She sips at her tea, steadily and mechanically, like it's another job to be got through before the day can be over.

'Johnny's looking well,' Lena says. 'London suited him.'

'Johnny's the same as he always was,' Sheila says flatly. ''Tis nothing to do with London. He'd be the same anywhere he went.'

Lena's patience, which isn't at its fullest this week to begin with, has been further whittled down by the walk up the mountain. She gives up on the small talk, which in any case appears to be getting her nowhere.

'Here's what I wanted to say to you,' she says. 'If you need a hand with anything, ask me.'

Sheila raises her eyes to look at her full on. She says, 'What would I need a hand with?'

'I dunno,' Lena says. 'You might want a place to stay for a bit, maybe.'

The corner of Sheila's mouth lifts in something that could be amusement. 'You. Taking in me and the four kids.'

'I'd find room.'

'You don't want us.'

Lena isn't going to lie to her. 'I'd have you and welcome,' she says.

'Why would I go? He hasn't hit me. And he won't.'

'You might wanta be away from him.'

'This is my house. And he's my man.'

'He is, yeah. So you might wanta show everyone he's nothing to do with you.'

Sheila puts down her mug and looks at Lena. Lena looks back. She wasn't sure, till now, whether Sheila knew what Johnny is at. Presumably Sheila was wondering the same about her, if she was wondering anything at all. Lena welcomes the new clarity of the situation, regardless of its unpredictability. One of the main things that annoys her about the townland has always been the endless rolling game of who-knows-that-I-know-that-she-knows-that-he-knows.

Sheila says, 'Why would you have us?'

'I've got awful fond of your Trey.'

Sheila nods, accepting that. 'At first I thought you meant for old times' sake,' she says. 'I wouldn'ta fell for that. You were never like that.'

'I wasn't,' Lena agrees. 'I mighta gone that way in my old age, but I haven't checked.'

Sheila shakes her head. 'I'm grand where I am,' she says. 'I wanta have my eye on him.'

'Fair enough,' Lena says. 'I'll take the kids if you want.'

'The little ones are all right here. I told Trey to go down to you till he leaves.'

'I'll have her. No problem.'

'I know that. She wouldn't go.'

'Tell her again. And I'll ask her.'

Sheila nods. ''Tis great there's people that see it in her,' she says, 'that she's worth helping. She oughta make the most of that. No one ever thought that about me.'

Lena considers this. 'People thought you had what you wanted, maybe,' she says. 'I thought that. There's no point in trying to help someone outa what they want.'

Sheila shakes her head briefly. 'They thought I had what I deserved. That's different.'

'They're awful fond of thinking that, around here,' Lena agrees. 'I'd say there was plenty that thought the same about me when Sean died.'

'I liked Sean,' Sheila says. 'You picked right.' Out in the yard, one of the kids yells, but she doesn't look around. 'There's people that help me now, anyhow,' she says. 'The last coupla years. Bringing me a loada turf for the winter. Mending my fence that was falling down.'

Lena says nothing. She knows why the townland started giving Sheila help.

'I oughta spit in their faces,' Sheila says. 'Only I can't afford to.'

Lena says, 'Are you wanting to spit in my face?'

Sheila shakes her head again. All her movements have a spare, contained quality, like she's eking herself out to last the day. 'You're not doing it 'cause you think it'll clear your debt,' she says. 'You owe me nothing. And you're not doing it for me, anyhow. You're doing it for Trey.'

'Well then,' Lena says. 'If you want to bring the kids down to mine, bring them.'

This time Sheila looks at her differently, with something almost like interest. 'Everyone'd be asking you questions,' she says. 'You always hated that. People poking their noses in.'

It's the first time she's spoken like Lena is someone who used to be her friend. 'I'm older now,' Lena says. 'They can ask all they like. It'll do them good. Get the aul' circulation going.'

'What would you tell them?'

'Whatever we fancy, sure. The English fella's here hunting for Bobby's aliens, maybe, and him and Johnny are after bringing one into the house, and you're sick of cleaning alien shite off your floors.'

Sheila laughs. The laugh, clear and free and youthful, takes both of them by surprise. Sheila snaps her mouth closed and looks down into her mug like she's done something ill-judged.

'Doireann Cunniffe'd fall for it,' Lena says. 'As long as you kept a straight face.'

That pulls a faint smile out of Sheila. 'I was awful for that,' she says. 'You had the best poker face of any of us. I was always the one that'd start in giggling and give us away.'

'That was half the fun, sure. Talking our way outa trouble afterwards.'

One of the kids shrieks again. This time Sheila gives the window a brief glance. 'If I told them what we usedta get up to,' she says, 'they wouldn't believe it, to look at me now. The children. They wouldn't believe a word.'

The thought seems to chafe at her. 'Sure, that's the way it goes,' Lena says. 'I'd say our parents got up to plenty that we wouldn'ta believed, either.'

Sheila shakes her head. 'I'd like them to know,' she says. 'To warn them, like. One minute you're a bunch of mad wee messers, and then next thing you know . . . You tell Trey. She'll believe you.'

'She's fifteen,' Lena points out. 'We'll be lucky if she believes a word outa any adult, the next few years.'

'You tell her,' Sheila repeats. She picks at something stuck to her mug, which seems to irritate her. The shrieking outside has stopped. 'I left him one time,' she says. 'Middle of the night. He was asleep, drunk. I packed the kids into the car – the four of them, just, 'twas before Liam and Alanna – and I went. Mostly I remember how quiet it was: the rain on the windscreen, and not another soul on the roads. The kids went asleep. I drove for hours. In the end I turned around and came back. There was nowhere I could drive to that was far enough to be worth my while.'

Her fingers have stilled on the mug. 'I felt like a prize feckin' eejit,' she says. 'He never knew, anyway. I was glad of that. He woulda made fun of me.'

'If you think of something I could do,' Lena says. 'Say it to me.'

'Maybe,' Sheila says. 'Thanks for the jam.' She gets up and starts clearing away the tea things.

————————

Cal is doing the dishes after lunch when Trey and Banjo show up. The sound of the door banging open hits him with a surge of relief so disproportionate it almost knocks him off his feet. 'Hey,' he says. 'Long time no see.'

Trey gives his injured face one long, unreadable look, but then her eyes skid away. 'I came yesterday morning,' she informs him. 'You were out.'

The fact that she came at all has to be a good thing, but Cal can't tell by her whether she was just there for carpentry purposes, or whether she wanted to talk. 'Well,' he says, 'I'm here now.'

'Yeah,' Trey says. She crouches to meet Rip's welcome and rub his jowls.

She hasn't brought anything. Mostly Cal doesn't like it when Trey shows up with food – he doesn't require an entrance fee – but today he would have welcomed a packet of cookies or a hunk of cheese or whatever. It would mean she was planning to stick around a while.

'What's with his paw?' he asks, indicating Banjo.

'Fell over him,' Trey says, that little bit too promptly. 'That was days ago, but. He's grand. He's only looking for ham slices.'

'Well, we got those,' Cal says. He goes to the fridge and tosses Trey the packet. He doesn't try asking about her lip, which looks pretty much healed. Apparently today everybody is politely not asking anybody anything. 'You want something to eat?'

'Nah. Had lunch.' Trey drops onto the floor and starts feeding Banjo scraps of ham.

'No thank you,' Cal says automatically, before he can stop himself.

Trey rolls her eyes, which comforts him a little bit. 'No thank you.'

'Hallelujah,' Cal says, getting out the iced tea. His voice sounds fake to him. 'We got there in the end. Have some of this. This weather, if you don't keep drinking you'll shrivel up.'

Trey rolls her eyes again, but she downs the iced tea and holds out her glass for more. 'Please,' she adds, as an afterthought.

Cal gives her a refill and pours a glass for himself. He knows he needs to talk to her, but he allows himself a minute first, to just lean against the counter and look at her. The kid is outgrowing her jeans again; her ankles stick out. Last time it took Sheila months to notice and buy her new gear, while Trey refused to take Cal's charity and Cal tried to come up with a way of raising the issue to Sheila without being some pervert who looked at teenagers' legs. Back then he swore that next time he was just going to go into town and buy her some damn jeans, and if she didn't like it she could feed them to Francie's pigs.

'I saw my dad last night,' Trey says. 'When he got in.'

'Oh yeah?' Cal says. He keeps his voice neutral, even though that little shitbird clearly saw no downside to telling the kid who had done the damage, putting her right in the middle.

'You bet him up pretty good.'

Two years ago she would have said 'You bet the shite outa him,' or something. That 'pretty good' is all Cal. 'We went at it,' he says.

'How come?'

'We had a difference of opinion.'

Trey has her jaw set at the angle that means there's business to be dealt with. 'I'm not a fuckin' *baby*.'

'I know that.'

'So how come you fought him?'

'OK,' Cal says. 'I don't like your dad's game.'

'It's not a game.'

'Kid. You know what I mean.'

'What d'you not like?'

Cal finds himself where Trey regularly seems to put him: helplessly and desperately out of his depth, right when it's crucial not to fuck up. He has no idea what to say that won't make things worse.

'I'm not gonna bitch about your daddy to you, kid,' he says. 'That's not my place. But the stuff he's doing . . .' *That's not what I want for you,* is what he means, except that he has no right to want anything for Trey at all. 'People round here are gonna end up pretty pissed off.'

Trey shrugs. Rip is shouldering Banjo out of the way, looking for both shares of ham and attention. She disentangles them and uses one hand for each.

'When they do,' Cal says, 'it'd be a real good idea if you weren't smack in the middle of all this.'

That gets a swift flash of a glance from Trey. 'They can go and shite. All of 'em. I'm not scared of them.'

'I know that,' Cal says. 'That's not what I mean.' What he means is simple enough – *Things were good, that matters, don't go and fuck it all up* – but he can't find a way to say it. It seems laden with too many things that a kid Trey's age is incapable of knowing, even if he could explain them to her: the full weight and reach of choices, how unthinkingly and how permanently things can be forfeited. She's much too young to have something the size of her future in her hands. He wants to ditch this whole damn topic of conversation and argue with her over whether she needs a haircut. He wants to tell her she's grounded till she gets some sense.

'Then what?' Trey demands.

'He's your daddy,' Cal says, picking his words with difficulty. 'It's natural for you to want to help him out. But things are gonna get messy.'

'Not if you say nothing.'

'You figure that'll make a difference? Seriously?'

Trey gives him a look like if he was any dumber she'd have to water him. 'You're the only one that knows. How are the lads gonna find out, if you don't talk?'

Cal feels his temper rising. 'How the hell are they *not* gonna find out? There's *no fucking gold*. I don't care how dumb your dad thinks they are, sooner or later they're gonna notice that. And then what?'

'My dad'll come up with a story,' Trey says flatly. 'That's what he's good at.'

Cal bites back several comments that need to stay unsaid. 'Yeah, the guys won't give a shit how good his story is. What they'll want is their money. If you're hoping they'll cut your dad some slack if you're involved, just 'cause you've got some respect around here—'

'Never thought that.'

'Good. 'Cause they won't. All you'll do is drop yourself in the shit right alongside him. You want that?'

'I told you. They can all go and shite.'

'Listen,' Cal says. He takes a breath and brings his voice down to normal, or as close as he can get it. He looks at the mutinous set of Trey's shoulders and has a doomed sense that whatever he says is inevitably going to be the wrong thing. 'All I'm saying is, sooner or later, this is gonna be over. When it is, your dad and Rushborough are gonna have to leave town.'

'I know that.'

Cal can't tell, from what he can see of her face, whether that's true or not. 'And I'm saying you need to think about what happens after that. If you stay out of your dad's doings from now on, I can pretty much guarantee that you won't get any flak from anyone. But if—'

That gets a flash of anger from Trey. 'I don't want you sticking your nose in. I can look after myself.'

'OK,' Cal says. 'OK.' He takes another breath. He doesn't know how to highlight the things Trey values in order to make his argument, because right now he has very little sense of what those are, apart from Banjo, and apparently neither does she. 'Regardless of what I do, if you stay mixed up in this, things are gonna change after. This place thinks pretty highly of you, these days. You talk about wanting to go into carpentry when you're done with school; the way you've been going, you could start up your own shop tomorrow, and have more business'n you could handle.'

He thinks he sees her lashes flicker, like that caught her. 'If you keep on helping your dad,' he says, 'all that's gonna be out. People round here won't treat you the way they do now. I know you don't want to give a shit about them, but things aren't the same as they were two years ago. You've got stuff to lose now.'

Trey doesn't look up. 'Like you said,' she says. 'He's my dad.'

'Right,' Cal says. He rubs a hand over his mouth, hard. He wonders whether she's thinking that, when Johnny skips town, he'll take her with him. 'Yeah. But like you said, you're not a baby. If you don't want to be mixed up in his doings, you've got a right to make that call. Daddy or not.' He has a crazy impulse to offer her things, pizza, a fancy new lathe, a pony, whatever she wants, if she'll just step away from the lit fuse and come home.

Trey says, 'I wanta do it.'

There's a small silence in the room. Sunlight and the lazy burr of haying machines come in through the windows. Rip has rolled over to have his belly rubbed.

'Just remember,' Cal says. 'You can change your mind anytime.'

'How come you even care if those lads get fucked over?' Trey demands. 'They're nothing to you. And they done plenty on you, before.'

'I just want peace,' Cal says. All of a sudden he's exhausted, down to his bones. 'That's all. We had that, up to a couple of weeks ago. It was good. I liked it.'

'You can have peace. Just get outa it. Leave the rest of them to it.'

That leaves Cal stymied again. He can't tell Trey that he won't walk out while she's in; it would be unfair to put that on her. This barely even feels like a conversation, just a series of stone walls and briar patches.

'It's not that simple,' he says.

Trey blows out an impatient puff of air.

'It's not, kid. Say I pull out: what are the rest of them gonna think, when it all goes belly-up? They're gonna think I knew and didn't tell them. That's not gonna be any kind of peace.'

She says, still not looking up from the dogs, 'My dad said to tell you to back off and mind your own business.'

'Did he now,' Cal says.

'Yeah. He says you've got nothing, and if you go talking you'll only land me in shite.'

'Huh,' Cal says. He wishes he had just dumped Johnny in a bog while he had one handy. 'I guess that's one way to look at it.'

Trey shoots him one brief glance he can't read. She says, 'I want you outa it as well.'

'You do,' Cal says. He feels like a stone just dropped into his stomach. 'How come?'

'Just do. 'S not your business.'

'Right,' Cal says.

Trey watches him, rubbing Rip's belly and waiting for more. When Cal has nothing else to offer, she says, 'So will I say to my dad that you'll leave it?'

'Anything I've got to say to Johnny, I said last night. And,' Cal says, even though he knows he should shut his mouth, 'if I find something to add, I'll tell him myself. I won't use you as a god-damn go-between.'

For a minute he thinks Trey's going to argue. Instead she says abruptly, standing up and spilling dogs everywhere, 'Can we just do that chair?'

'Sure,' Cal says. Out of nowhere he feels, crazily, like tears might be stinging his eyes. 'Let's do that.'

They give the chair more care and delicacy than it really deserves, going back three times over the turning of the leg, sanding it finer and finer till a baby could suck on it. Mostly they work in silence. Summer air wanders in and out of the window, bringing the smells of silage and clover, picking up sawdust motes and twirling them idly in the wide bars of sunlight. When the sun moves off the window and the heat starts to mellow towards dinnertime, Trey dusts off her outgrown jeans and goes home.

13

That night the house is still: everyone is hard asleep, after last night's disturbances. Trey doesn't want to be in bed. Her life has stopped feeling normal; it's crowded with too many people and too many wants, till she doesn't feel safe taking her eye off it, even to sleep. Instead she stays on the sofa, being hot and watching worn-out late-night telly by the dirty yellow light of the standing lamp. Some smarmy tosser is trying to make an unhappy-looking couple build an extension shaped like a box even though they hate it. Trey is in no humour for the likes of him. She hopes the couple give him a kick up the hole and build whatever they want.

When light powerful as day ignites outside and floods in around the curtains, she doesn't move. Her mind is a blank; there's nothing in it to answer this. For a wild lurch of a second she thinks Bobby Feeney's UFOs are real and have landed, even though she doesn't believe in that shite. For another lurch she thinks she must have fallen asleep and it's morning, but on the telly the same tosser is still quacking away. Trey switches him off. In the sudden silence she hears engines revving, loud and deep.

She stands in the middle of the sitting room, listening. There's no movement from the rest of the house. Banjo, tucked away in his corner by the sofa, is snoring peacefully. In the blue-white glare the room looks like something in a nightmare, familiar objects suddenly incandescent and humming with menace. Outside, the engines pulse on.

Trey moves, very quietly, down the corridor towards her bedroom. She's thinking of the window, but before she even reaches the door she can see the same blue-white light spilling out through the opening. In the glow from the window Maeve's sleeping face is luminous and unnatural, like she's deep underwater, unreachable.

'Mam,' Trey says, not loud enough to be heard. She has no idea whether she wants her mam to wake up. She has no idea what she expects her mam to do.

Maeve turns sharply on the bed and makes a protesting sound. Trey doesn't want to deal with Maeve awake and demanding explanations. 'Mam,' she says, louder.

In her parents' room there's a stir and a murmur, and then quick footsteps. Sheila opens the door in a flowered nightie, hair messy on her shoulders. Behind her, Johnny, in boxers and a T-shirt, is pulling on trousers.

'There's something outside,' Trey says.

'Shhh,' Sheila says. Her eyes flick around the corridor. Maeve is sitting up, open-mouthed; Liam is calling.

Johnny pushes past Sheila and Trey and heads down the corridor, towards the front door. He stands still, his ear cocked to the door, listening. The rest of them gather behind him.

'Daddy,' Maeve says. 'What is it?'

Johnny ignores her. 'Come here,' he says to Alanna, straightening up, but she backs away with a high muffled whimper. 'You, then,' he says, catching Liam's arm. 'Don't be whinging, for fuck's sake; no one's going to hurt you. Come on.' He pushes Liam in front of him, opens the door, and stands in the doorway.

The light hits them full in the face from all directions. It turns the night air to a white haze. The rev of the engines is louder, a full deep snarl. On every side amid the haze, too blinding to look at straight, are circles of condensed light, paired like eyes. It takes Trey a minute to understand: high beams.

'What's the story, lads?' Johnny calls cheerily, raising his arm to shield his eyes. The note of his voice jars crazily against the scene. 'Is there a party on and no one told me?'

Silence; just the growl of the engines and a strange flapping sound, like wind-whipped washing on the line. Trey, craning past her dad's shoulder, sees flames. In the middle of the bare front yard is a galvanised metal barrel. Inside it is fire. The flames surge avidly, feet high, a tall ragged column swaying in the restless breeze.

'Ah, here, lads,' Johnny calls, shifting his voice to a mix of tolerance and exasperation. 'I've children trying to sleep. Go home to your beds. If ye've something to say to me, come up tomorrow and we'll have a chat like dacent men.'

Nothing. The breeze catches a flaming scrap from the barrel and scuds it away till it blinks out, high against the sky. Trey squints, trying to see the men or even the cars, but the lights are too bright; everything behind them is erased into darkness. The air is fever-hot.

'Shut that door,' Sheila says sharply. 'Whether you're in or you're out.'

Johnny doesn't look around at her.

'I said shut it.'

'Fuck's sake, lads,' Johnny calls reproachfully. 'Cop yourselves on. Go on outa that and sober up. We'll talk tomorrow.' He pulls Liam back inside and closes the door.

They stand in the cramped corridor, barefoot and ragtag in the odds and ends they wear for sleeping. No one wants to move. Around them, every doorway is alive with the blue-white glow.

'Who's out there?' Alanna whispers. She looks like she might cry.

'Lads messing,' Johnny says. His eyes are moving, assessing options. His bruises look like holes in his flesh.

'Why's there a fire?'

'They mean they'll burn us out,' Sheila says. She says it to Johnny.

'What's burn us out?'

Johnny laughs, throwing his head back. 'Christ almighty, would you ever listen to yourself,' he says to Sheila. 'The drama outa you, holy God. No one's burning anyone out.' He squats down to put a hand on Alanna's shoulder and the other on Liam's, grinning into their blank faces. 'Your mammy's only messing, sweethearts, and so are those lads out there. They've had a few too many pints, is what happened, and they reckoned it'd be funny to play a wee joke on us. Aren't they silly aul' fellas, acting the maggot at this hour?'

He smiles at Liam and Alanna. When neither of them responds, he says, 'I'll tell you what we'll do. Will we play a joke back on them?'

'Shoot 'em with my air gun,' Liam says.

Johnny laughs again, clapping him on the shoulder, but he shakes his head regretfully. 'Ah, no. I'd only love to, but we might give them a fright, and we wouldn't wanta do that, sure we wouldn't? No, I'll tell you what we'll do: we'll go back to bed and take no notice of them at all, at all. They'll feel like a right bunch of eejits then, won't they? Coming all the way up here for nothing?'

They look at him.

'Go to bed,' Sheila says. 'The lot of ye.'

For a few seconds the four of them don't move. Alanna's mouth is open; Maeve looks like she wants to argue but can't find an argument.

'Come on,' Trey says. She gives Alanna and Liam a shove towards their room and gets Maeve by the arm. Maeve pulls away, but after a glance at Johnny and Sheila, she shrugs extravagantly and follows Trey.

'You can't tell me what to do,' Maeve says, in their bedroom. Out in the corridor, their parents aren't talking.

Trey gets into bed fully dressed and turns her back on Maeve, pulling the sheet over her head to block out the light from the window. For a while she can feel Maeve standing still, watching her. Finally Maeve gives up, lets out a huffy sigh, and thumps into bed. The rev of the engines runs on outside.

After a long time, when Maeve's breathing has finally slowed into sleep, the light slides off the window and the room goes dark. Trey turns in bed and watches the corridor dim as, one by one, the other windows are released from their beams. She listens to the engines moving away, slowly, down the mountain.

———

'What happened in the night?' Alanna asks Sheila, at break-fast. Their dad is still in bed.

'Nothing happened,' Sheila says. She sets down a cup of milk in front of each of them.

'Who was outside?'

Liam is watching Sheila too, pulling the crusts off his toast.

'No one was outside,' Sheila says. 'Eat your breakfast.'

Sheila says the house needs cleaning and none of them can go out till it's done. 'I don't have to,' Liam says, looking up at Johnny for approval. 'Boys don't have to clean.' Johnny – just surfaced, rumpled and smelling of sweat – laughs and ruffles Liam's hair, but he says, 'You help your mammy.'

Sheila sets Maeve to tidy the sitting room and Trey and Alanna to clean the bathroom, while she and Liam do the kitchen. Maeve turns up the telly too loud, some idiot talk show with lots of whooping and laughing, as revenge for not being allowed to go meet her friends.

'Here,' Trey says, spraying cleaner around the sink. 'Wipe that down.'

Alanna takes the sponge. 'There were people outside,' she says, looking up sideways at Trey to check her response.

'Yeah,' Trey says. She expects more questions, but Alanna just nods and starts wiping the sink.

Johnny mostly stays in the bedroom. Some of the time he's on the phone; Trey can hear him pacing as he talks, fast and low, with the occasional flare of urgency quickly tamped down. He's talking to Rushborough, and Rushborough isn't happy. She tries listening in, for clues to how raging he is and what Johnny's telling him to calm him, but every time she reaches the bedroom door, Sheila comes out of the kitchen and sends her back to her work.

Johnny comes into the bathroom as Trey is scrubbing the walls. The walls looked OK to her anyway, but if she says she's finished here, Sheila will only find her something else to do. Alanna has got bored and is sitting in the bathtub singing to herself, a made-up chant with no beginning or end.

'How're ye getting on?' their dad asks, leaning in the doorway and smiling at them.

'Grand,' Trey says. She doesn't want to talk to him. Somehow or other, he fucked up. Between him and her and Rushborough, they had all of Ardnakelty hooked and ready to be reeled in, and somehow he managed to blow the whole thing.

'That's looking great,' Johnny says, scanning the bathroom approvingly. 'God almighty, we won't know this place when ye're done. We'll think we're living in a luxury hotel.'

Trey keeps scrubbing. 'C'mere to me,' Johnny says. 'You're the brains of this outfit, so you are; if anyone knows, it's you. Who was out there last night?'

'Dunno,' Trey says. Alanna is still singing, but Trey is pretty sure she's listening. 'Couldn't see.'

'How many of 'em d'you reckon?'

Trey shrugs. 'Eight, maybe. Maybe less.'

'Eight,' Johnny repeats, tapping his fingers thoughtfully on the door frame, like she said something deeply meaningful. 'That's not too bad, sure it's not? That leaves an awful lotta people who wanted nothing to do with it. D'you know, now' – his voice lifts, brightening, and he points a finger at Trey – 'this mightn't be a bad thing for us, when all's said and done. They're a contrary lot, around here. If there's a few grumpy aul' fellas banging on about what a terrible idea this is altogether, there's plenty of 'em that'll put it down to begrudgery and dig their heels in deeper.'

The way he says it, it sounds more than possible; it sounds obvious. Trey wants to believe him, and is furious with herself for it.

'All we need to do,' Johnny says, 'is find out which ones are which. Tomorrow you'll go down to the village, see what you can pick up. Hang around Noreen's, keep an eye on who's friendly and who's a bit off with you. Stop in to Lena Dunne. Talk to your Yank, see if he's heard anything.'

Trey sprays more cleaner on the wall. 'Not today, but,' her dad says, with a grin in his voice. 'Let the hare sit. Do 'em good to stew for a bit, amn't I right?'

'Yeah,' Trey says, without looking at him.

'Missed a bit up the top there,' her dad says, pointing. 'You're doing a great job. Keep it up. Perseverance is a virtue, hah?'

After lunch, Sheila and Trey and Maeve go out front to deal with the remains of the fire. They have the mop bucket and the stewpot, both full of water. The yard is noisy with grasshoppers, and the sun hits them like a solid blow. Sheila tells the little ones to stay inside, but they stray out onto the step and hang off the door, watching. Alanna is sucking on a biscuit.

The galvanised barrel was stuffed with rags and newspapers, now black and fragile, edges crumbling in on themselves. Wisps of smoke still curl from the heap. When Trey touches the side of the barrel, it's hot.

'Move,' Sheila says. She hefts her bucket with a hard grunt of effort, braces its lip on the barrel, and pours. The barrel lets out a vicious hiss and a puff of rising steam.

'More,' Sheila says. Trey pours in the water from the stewpot. The residue in the barrel is sinking into a sodden mess.

'Get the rake,' Sheila says. 'And the spade. Whatever's got a long handle.'

'Why?' Maeve demands. 'It's out.'

'One spark and we'll have the whole mountain on fire. Get the things.'

The shed, at the far edge of the yard, holds tools from a time before they were born, when Sheila tried to turn the yard into a garden. Trey and Maeve scuff their way through scattered scraps of black that disintegrate under their feet. 'I hate them lads,' Maeve says. 'They're a shower of fuckin' pricks.'

'They don't give a shite if you hate them,' Trey says. She and Maeve have never liked each other much, not since they got old enough to tell the difference, and today neither of them likes anyone much.

They heave aside a cobwebbed stepladder and a rust-ridden wheelbarrow to dig out a rake, a hoe, and a spade. 'It's not Daddy's fault,' Maeve says defiantly, as they get back to the barrel. Neither of them answers her.

They dig the handles of the tools into the barrel and stir, extinguishing any hidden smoulders. It gives off a thick, acrid reek. 'Stinks,' Maeve says, wrinkling her nose.

'Fuck up, you,' Trey says.

'You fuck up.'

Sheila swings round and catches each of them a slap across the face, in one move so neither of them has time to jump back. 'Now ye'll both fuck up,' she says, and turns back to the barrel.

The mess resists them, clogging and tangling the handles. In the end Sheila pulls the rake free and stands back, breathing hard. 'Get rid of that,' she says, nodding at the barrel. 'And come straight home, or I'll malavogue the pair of ye.' She picks up the bucket and the stewpot and heads back to the house.

Trey and Maeve take one side of the barrel each and drag it around the back of the house and up the mountainside. There's a ravine where they dump unwanted large things, broken bikes and Alanna's outgrown cot. The barrel is awkward to grip and heavy, scraping across the yard with a loud relentless grating, leaving a wide swathe of raw dirt and a leaking trail of black liquid in its wake. When they get in among the underbrush, they have to stop every minute to heave it over roots and brambles.

'You think you're so great,' Maeve says. She sounds like she's on the verge of tears. 'Now look what you done.'

'You haven't got a clue,' Trey says. Her arms ache from hauling the barrel; flies are whirling noisily at the sweat on her face, but she doesn't have a hand free to swat them away. 'You thick cow.'

The ravine drops out of the mountainside with lethal suddenness. Its sides are steep and rocky, blurred in patches by muscular, tenacious bushes and tangles of tall weeds. At the bottom, among the undergrowth in the dried-up streambed, Trey can see the flash of sun on something else discarded.

'You fucked it up on purpose,' Maeve says. 'You never wanted him back.'

They swing the barrel together, over the edge of the ravine. It bounces down to the streambed in great zigzagging arcs, letting out a deep ominous boom each time it hits the ground.

———

'I'm going out,' Trey says, as they clear the table after dinner. Sheila had nothing in, so dinner was a dispiriting stew of potatoes, carrots, and stock cubes. Johnny made a big production of praising the flavour and talking about fancy restaurants where traditional Irish cooking is all the rage. No one except Liam was hungry.

'You're going nowhere,' Sheila says.

'Going for a walk.'

'No. Wash them up.'

'I'll do it later.' Trey can't stick looking at their faces another second. The air feels like it's clamping in all round her. She needs to move.

'You'll do it now.'

'Sure, you can't go out anyway,' Johnny says, in a peacemaking voice. 'I'm off for a wee saunter myself, in a bit; you need to stay here and help your mammy while I'm gone.'

'I don't want you to go,' Maeve tells him, pouting. 'Stay.' She nuzzles up against Johnny's side. He smiles and smooths her hair.

'Quit acting like a baby,' Trey says.

'I'm not!' Maeve snaps, her lip trembling. 'I want Daddy!'

'You're fuckin' *eleven*.'

'I'm scared!'

'You make me wanta puke.'

Maeve kicks out and gets Trey in the shin. Trey shoves her hard enough that she staggers back against the counter. Maeve screeches and goes for her, raking at Trey's face with her nails, but Trey catches Maeve's wrist and punches her right in the gut. Maeve wheezes for breath and grabs for Trey's hair, but it's too short. Somewhere Liam is laughing too loud, like it's fake but he can't stop.

Their dad gets between them. He's laughing his arse off too. 'Whoa, whoa, whoa, cool the jets there,' he says, holding them apart with a hand on each one's shoulder. 'Holy God almighty, wouldja look at the pair of spitfires we've got here? None a that, now. Leave that stuff to the big rufty-tufty lads. Ye're both too gorgeous to go ruining those faces. Are you all right, Maeveen love?'

Maeve bursts into tears. Trey shakes her dad's hand off her

shoulder and goes to the sink to wash up. She feels like she's drowning, deeper in bog every second, the mountain sucking her down.

———————

On his way out, Johnny pokes his head into Trey's room, where she's shut herself to get away from the rest. Maeve is in the shower and has been for a while. Trey would bet money that she's using up all the hot water on purpose.

'There's my wee wild woman,' her dad says. He's all dolled up, with a fresh shirt on and his hair arranged in an appealing swoop; Trey can smell his aftershave. He looks like he's going on a date. 'Now, you do what your mammy says while I'm out, and look after the little ones. And don't be bickering with Maeve. She's a bit nervy, just. 'Tisn't her fault she's not as big and brave as you.'

Trey shrugs. She's brushing Banjo. Normally he basks in the attention, twisting to make sure she gets the best spots, but tonight he's too hot to do anything but lie there like he's melted. She thought about leaving the shed fur in Maeve's bed, but that kind of babyish shite doesn't fit in the place where they've found themselves.

'And don't you go worrying your head, now,' her dad says, waving a finger at her. 'No one'll do anything on anyone tonight. They've all gone for a nice sleep, after their shenanigans last night. You do the same.'

'Why can't I go out, so?'

'Ah, now,' Johnny says reprovingly. 'I know you're missing your pals, but a bitta responsibility won't do you any harm. 'Tis only for one night; you'll be out and about tomorrow.'

Trey doesn't answer. Johnny switches tone. 'Ah, sweetheart. 'Tis awful hard being the oldest, isn't it? It'll be only great when Brendan gets the rambling outa his system and comes home. You can be one of the little ones again, and have the poor lad's head wrecked.'

Trey doesn't want to think about Brendan. She keeps her eyes on Banjo.

'Meanwhile,' Johnny says, 'you just keep telling the rest

everything's grand. 'Cause it will be. I'll do my bit tonight, and you'll do your bit tomorrow, and we'll have the show back on the road in no time.'

'What's your bit?' Trey asks.

'Ah,' Johnny says, tapping the side of his nose, 'that'd be telling. This and that, and a bit of t'other. You just get some rest; you've a busy day ahead.' He gives Trey a wink and a thumbs-up, and he's gone.

———————

Trey doesn't want to sleep, but after last night and the night before, she can't stop herself. She moves in and out of a sweaty doze, jerking alert to things that could be real or dreams – a door closing, a strange voice snapping *Wait* in her ear, a flash of light, a sheep's insistent call – and getting dragged back down into the doze when they fade. Maeve tosses and mutters wretchedly.

When she half-wakes for the dozenth time and sees dawn light around the curtains, Trey forces herself to sit up. The house is silent. She doesn't want to be around for everyone getting up, her dad putting his arm around her and giving her instructions, Maeve pouting and whining for his attention. She carries her shoes out to the kitchen, feeds Banjo, and butters a few slices of bread while he eats. She'll find somewhere in the shade to eat them and wait for Ardnakelty to get underway, so she can start assessing the damage.

She still holds a thread of hope that her dad will actually get his plan back on track. Like she told Cal, making up stories and getting people to believe them is what Johnny is good at, and he's got desperation to spur him; he might pull it off. The thread is a thin one, and it frays every time she remembers the column of flame in the yard, but it's what she's got, so she keeps hold of it.

The bleating she heard in the night was real: a few black-faced sheep, each with a splotch of red spray paint on its right hip, are straggling around the yard, eating what they can. Malachy Dwyer's herd have found or made a gap in their paddock wall again. At Banjo's delighted howl, they startle and bound off into the trees. Trey revises her plans. She likes Malachy, who always gave her messages to do when she was a kid and who has the mountainy men's rule of asking no questions. Instead of shiteing around till people are awake, she'll go up the mountain and tell Malachy his sheep are out. By the time she's helped him round them up, it'll be late enough to head down to Noreen's.

Before she's out the gate, she's sweating. The sun is barely up, but today even the mountain breeze has been tamped down to a twitch, and the air is so heavy Trey can feel it pressing at her eardrums. What they need is a thunderstorm, but the sky is the same mindless blank it's been for weeks.

As they near the fork where their road merges with the one twisting from higher up the mountain, Banjo stiffens and stretches his nose forward. Then he gallops off ahead, around the bend and gone.

Trey hears his siren howl, the one that means he's found something, rise through the trees and the webs of sun. She whistles for him, in case he's run into more of Malachy's sheep, but he doesn't come back. When she rounds the bend, there's a dead man lying across her way.

14

The dead man is lying at the fork where the two paths meet. He's on his left side, his right arm and leg flopping awkwardly, with his curled back to Trey. Even though she's ten paces away and can't see his face, she has no doubt that he's dead. Banjo stands over him, legs planted wide, nose high, howling up into the trees.

'Banjo,' Trey says, not moving closer. 'Good boy. You done great. Come here, now.'

Banjo's howl fades to a moan. This time, when Trey whistles, he dashes over and presses his nose into her hand. She rubs him and talks softly to him, and looks past him at the dead man. There's something wrong with the back of his head. The shadows bend into it strangely.

Her first assumption, taken for granted without question, was that it's her dad. The narrow build is right, and the shirt is white and crisp. It's only on this longer look that she stops being sure. The crisscrossing shadows of branches and the low slant of dawn light make it hard to tell, but the hair looks too fair.

'Good boy,' Trey says again, giving Banjo one more pat. 'Sit, now. Stay.' She leaves him behind and moves cautiously, in a wide arc, around the dead man.

It's Rushborough. His eyes are half open and his top lip pulled up, so he looks like he's snarling at something behind Trey. The front of his shirt is dark and stiff.

Trey has never seen a dead person before. She's seen plenty of dead animals, but never a human being. Ever since she found out what happened to Brendan, she's had a deep, fierce need to see one. Not Brendan's. She needs to find where he's laid, but not in order to see him; so that she can go to the place, and so she can mark it, as a signal of defiance to whoever put him there. She's needed to see a dead body in the same way: so that she can place Brendan clearly in her mind, where she can lay her hand on him.

She squats by the body for a long time, looking at it. She understands this as a part of the interchange between her and whatever brought first Cal and then Rushborough to Ardnakelty. She didn't turn away from it, and in response it put this in her path.

The birdcalls and the light gain force as the day expands. It seems to Trey that the thing at her feet shouldn't be considered as a person any more. As a person, as Rushborough, it's incomprehensible, wrong in ways that her mind can barely take in without ripping. If she looks at it as just another thing on the mountain, it becomes simple. After a while the mountain will absorb it, as it does fallen leaves and eggshells and rabbits' bones, and transmute it into other things. Seen in this way, it makes clear and uncomplicated sense.

She stays put until the body has become natural to the mountain, and she can look at it without her mind bending. A few more of Malachy's sheep wander at the edge of the upper path, steadily crunching weeds.

The sound of a phone ringing goes off like a fire alarm. Trey and Banjo both leap. It's coming from Rushborough's pocket.

Trey takes it as a warning. The day is starting to gain momentum; sooner or later, someone will come along this path. Trey is well aware that other people aren't going to see the body as something that can be left to the mountain's slow processes, and that once she leaves this spot, neither will she. She has no problem with that. She, no less than the mountain, is well able to turn the body to good account.

The liberation it's brought with it is only starting to sink in. In the changed landscape this has created, she doesn't need to hang off her father any more. She doesn't have to twist herself around what he does and thinks and wants. He's meaningless; he'll be gone soon enough, and for her purposes, he's as good as gone already. She's on her own now, to do things her way.

She gets up, snaps her fingers for Banjo, and heads down the road, not at a run, but at a fast steady lope that she can keep up all the way. Behind her, Rushborough's phone rings again.

———————

Cal wakes early and can't get back to sleep. He doesn't like the way nothing at all happened yesterday. He hung around the house waiting for Lena, who didn't come, and Mart, who didn't come either, and Trey, who he knew wouldn't come. He went down to the shop, where Noreen gave him a new kind of cheddar and Senan's wife gave them both a blow-by-blow account of her oldest kid's wisdom-tooth removal. He watered his damn tomato plants. No one had even messed with the scarecrow. Cal knows good and well there was plenty happening somewhere. He doesn't like the skill and thoroughness with which it stayed out of sight.

And it's Monday morning. This is the deadline he gave Johnny to skip town. Regardless of what's been going on beyond his line of vision, sometime today he needs to go up the mountain and see if Johnny is still there, which he will be, and then decide what to do about him. Cal has never killed anyone and has no desire to start with Trey's daddy, but doing nothing isn't an option. His inclination is to haul Johnny's worthless ass into his car, drive him to the airport, buy him a ticket to wherever will have him, and watch him through security, using whatever measures are necessary to make him cooperate. He considers it possible that Johnny, spineless wimp that he is, will be relieved to have matters taken out of his hands, especially if Cal throws in a little extra cash. If that doesn't work out, he'll have to move on to methods with less room for disagreement. Either way, it promises to be a long day.

In the end Cal gives up on trying to sleep and starts making bacon and eggs, with the iPod speaker playing the Highwaymen good and loud, trying to distract his mind. The breakfast is just about ready when Rip jumps up and bounds to the door. Trey and Banjo are up early, too.

'Hey,' Cal says, aiming to keep the rush of glad astonishment out of his voice. He wasn't expecting to see the kid again till after her dad left town, if ever. 'You got good timing. Fetch another plate.'

Trey doesn't move from the doorway. 'Your man Rushborough's dead,' she says. 'Up on the mountain.'

Cal feels everything inside him go still. He turns from the stove.

He says, 'Dead how?'

'Someone kilt him.'

'You sure?'

'Yeah. His head's bashed in, and I reckon he was stabbed as well.'

'OK,' Cal says. 'OK.' He goes to the iPod and turns it off. The things speeding in his mind don't include surprise; he feels like some part of him has been taking this moment for granted, just waiting to get word. 'Where?'

'Below ours, where the road splits. He's there on the road.'

'The Guards there yet?'

'Nah. No one knows, only me. I found him. Came straight here.'

'Right,' Cal says. 'Good call.' He turns off the stove. He's breathless with relief that the kid came to him with this, but he can't gauge from her face how much she's not telling him, whether she came to him for refuge from the shock or for defence against something much bigger. She's had a shock, regardless, but that's going to have to wait. He feels a spurt of anger at the fact that, all Trey's life, any gentleness to her has had to wait till other business is dealt with.

'OK,' he says, dumping the bacon and eggs into Rip's dish, where the two dogs dive on them joyfully. 'We'll let these boys handle this here.' He opens the cupboard under the sink and pulls out a fresh pair of the latex gloves he uses occasionally for gardening or carpentry. 'Let's go see what we've got.'

In Cal's rickety red Pajero, Trey fishes a paper-towel bundle out of her back pocket, unwraps it to reveal several squashed slices of bread and butter, and gets to work. She seems surprisingly OK: not shaky, not white, shovelling food into her face. Cal doesn't entirely trust this, but he welcomes it anyway.

'How you doing?' he asks.

'Grand,' Trey says. She offers him a slice of bread and butter.

'No thanks,' Cal says. Apparently he and Trey are back to normal: all the complications between them appear to have been wiped away, like they never existed or like they're no longer relevant.

'It's a shock,' he says, 'seeing someone dead. I've done it plenty of times, and it still doesn't come easy. Specially when you're not expecting it.'

Trey considers this, methodically biting the crust off her bread to leave the soft middle for last. 'It was weird, all right,' she says in the end. 'Not like I woulda expected.'

'What way?'

Trey thinks that over for a long time. A few farmers are out in their fields, but the road is still empty; they've only passed one other car, some guy in an office shirt starting off early on a long commute. There's a good chance no one else has come across Rushborough yet.

When Cal's stopped waiting for an answer, Trey says, 'I thought it'd be worse. I'm not being hard or nothing, not like "Ah, no big deal to me." It was a big deal. Just not in a bad way.'

'Well,' Cal says. 'That's good.' He's finally put his finger on how she seems: calm. She's calmer than she's been since the day her dad showed up. He can't interpret this.

'He was only a shitehawk anyway,' Trey adds.

Cal swings the car off the road onto the mountain track. It's unpaved, narrow and gritty; gorse whips at the car windows, and puffs of dust rise around his tyres. He slows down.

'Kid,' he says. 'I gotta ask you something, and I don't want you flying off the handle.'

Trey looks over at him, chewing, her eyebrows twitching down.

'If you had anything to do with this – anything at all, like even if you kept watch for someone and you didn't know what he was gonna be doing – I need to know now.'

Trey's face shutters over instantly. Her wariness makes Cal sick to his stomach. 'How come?'

''Cause,' Cal says. 'We're gonna do things differently, depending on that.'

'Differently how?'

Cal figures maybe he should tell her a lie, but he's not going to do it. 'If you had nothing to do with it,' he says, 'we're gonna phone the Guards. If you did, we're gonna load the guy into the

245

back of this car, take him up the mountain, dump him in a ravine, and go on about our day.'

To his utter surprise, when he takes a sideways glance at Trey, her face has cracked into a huge grin. 'Some cop you are,' she tells him.

'Yeah, well,' Cal says. Several layers of relief flood through him with such force he can hardly drive. 'I'm retired; I don't have to behave myself any more. Lemme hear you say it: did you have anything to do with this?'

'Nah. Found him, just.'

'Well, damn,' Cal says. The relief has left him almost giddy. 'You gotta go and make things complicated. It would've been a lot simpler to dump the motherfucker up the mountain.'

'I can say I done it if you want,' Trey offers obligingly.

'Thanks, kid,' Cal says, 'but no thanks. I've got a little good behaviour left in me. I'll take a look, and then we'll hand him over to the Guards.'

Trey nods. The prospect doesn't seem to bother her.

'You're gonna have to tell them about finding him.'

'No problem,' Trey says. 'I wanta tell them.'

The promptness and certainty of that make Cal look over at her, but she's gone back to her breakfast. 'I know you don't want me sticking my nose in,' he says. 'But maybe, when you talk to the cops, don't say anything about gold. They're gonna hear about it sooner or later, but they don't need to hear that you were involved, at least not outa your own mouth. I'm not even certain what kinds of illegal were going on all up in there, what with everyone and his gramma trying to rip off everyone else, but I'd rather you didn't find out the hard way. I'm not saying lie to the police, kid' – when he catches Trey's widening grin – 'I'm just saying. If they don't bring it up, you don't need to either.'

The advice is almost definitely unnecessary – not bringing things up is one of Trey's main skills – but Cal feels like making sure. Trey eye-rolls so hard that her whole head gets involved, which reassures him.

They've come within view of the fork, with the unidentifiable huddle at its centre. Cal parks the car. The road here is a double dirt track, dry and pebbly, divided by a patchy line of dying grass.

'OK,' he says, opening the car door. 'Stay on the grass.'

'I went on the dirt before,' Trey says. 'Right up close to him. Are the Guards gonna give me hassle?'

'Nah. You did what was natural. There won't be any footprints for us to mess up anyway, not on this surface. I'm just playing it safe.'

They come to a stop ten or twelve feet from the body, where the road broadens out into the fork. Rushborough looks out of place to the point of impossibility, a thing with no relationship to this mountain, like he was dropped from one of Bobby's UFOs. His fancy clothes are awkwardly stretched and twisted by his curled pose. The air is too still even to lift his hair.

'Banjo found him first,' Trey says, at Cal's shoulder. 'He howled.'

'He's a good dog,' Cal says. 'He knows to tell you when something's important. This how you left the guy? Anything different?'

'Nah. There's flies on him now, just.'

'Yeah, well,' Cal says. 'That happens. You stay here. I'm just gonna take a closer look.'

Rushborough is dead, all right, and Cal can't argue with Trey's conclusion that someone killed him. The flies are thick on his chest; when Cal waves them away, they rise in a furious clump, and Cal sees the crust of blood blackening most of his shirtfront. They're clustered on the back of his head, too, and under those is a deep dent. Bone splinters and brain matter show for a second, before the flies settle again.

Trey is watching, keeping her distance. There's a dark stain of blood soaked into the dirt under the body, but nowhere near enough blood. The uppermost side of Rushborough's face is a clabbered white; the underside, next to the ground, is mottled purple. He was moved after he died, but not long after.

Cal knows better than to touch a victim, but he also knows it could be hours before a medical examiner gets way out here, and there's information that might not wait that long. He takes the latex gloves out of his pocket and puts them on. Trey keeps watching and says nothing.

Rushborough's skin is cold; it feels colder than the air, although Cal knows that's an illusion. His jaw hinge is clamped stiff, so is his elbow, but his finger joints and his knee still move. The medical examiner can factor in temperatures and whatnot to work out an approximate time of death. The flies, resenting Cal's intrusion, come at his face with a whine like bombers.

'We oughta cover him up,' Trey says. 'From them.' She motions with her chin at the flies. 'You've that tarp in the back of the car.'

'Nope,' Cal says, straightening up and peeling off the gloves. 'We do that, we'll get fibres and dog hair and what-have-you all over him. We just leave him.' He catches himself fumbling for his radio to call Dispatch. He pulls out his phone instead and dials 999.

The cop he gets put through to hasn't had his coffee yet and is clearly expecting some farmer bitching about his neighbour's bird-scarer, but Cal's tone wakes him up, even before the situation is laid out. Once Cal manages to get across where they are, which takes a while, the guy promises to have people at the scene inside half an hour.

'You sounded like a cop there,' Trey says, when Cal hangs up.

'I still got it when I need it,' Cal says, putting his phone away. 'It got his attention, anyway.'

'Have we gotta stay till they come?'

'Yeah. If we leave, someone else is gonna come along and mess up the scene some more, and call the cops all over again. We'll stick around.' He doesn't offer to stand guard and let Trey go home. He's not letting the kid out of his sight.

The heat is building. Cal was going to get back in the car, where the air-conditioning mostly works, but a couple of crows have set-tled on the higher branches of the trees overhanging Rushborough, eyeing the situation below with interest. Cal leans up against the hood of the car, where he can eye them right back and warn them off if needs be. Trey pulls herself up to sit on the hood next to him. She seems unperturbed by the idea of waiting around for the Guards; apparently, and reassuringly, there's nothing else she feels the need to be doing.

Cal has no problem with waiting around, either; he welcomes the opportunity to sit and evaluate. He can't see much downside to Rushborough's death, in itself. As far as he can tell, the guy contributed nothing but a heap of trouble to anyone. More to the point, with Rushborough off his back, Johnny is likely to waltz his scrawny ass straight out of this townland, to someplace that has more to offer a sophisticated guy like him. From Cal's standpoint, that looks like a win-win.

He's aware that the Guards don't have the licence to see it that way, though, which is where the potential downside kicks in. Depending on who killed this fuckball, and how hard they are to identify, that downside could be considerable. In a perfect world, Johnny would have knocked off Rushborough, and done it incompetently enough to land himself in cuffs by this evening. Cal doesn't dare to hope for that level of luck. There are too many other, less welcome possibilities.

Among them is the possibility that whoever killed Rushborough doesn't consider the job to be finished. There are plenty of people around who have reason to be seriously pissed with Rushborough, and who might extend that emotion beyond him. Mart said Trey wouldn't get any blowback, and Mart's say-so holds weight in this townland, but Mart isn't God, regardless of what he might think, and he can't make guarantees.

'Where's that road go after your place?' Cal asks, nodding to the lower path. 'Alongside some bog and into trees, and then what?'

'Nothing for a good way,' Trey says, 'and then Gimpy Duignan's. After that there was the Murtagh brothers, only Christy died and Vincent went into a home. Then it's just bog.'

'What about up that way?' Cal tilts his chin to the upper fork. 'Malachy Dwyer, and then who?'

'Seán Pól Dwyer, about half a mile on. After that it's grazing and forest till it turns down the mountain again, over towards Knockfarraney. There's aul' Mary Frances Murtagh on the way down.'

'Knockfarraney's where Rushborough was staying. Right?'

Trey nods. She slides off the hood and goes around to the side of the car. 'At the bottom of the mountain. In that aul' cottage that Rory Dunne rents to tourists.'

'I know it,' Cal says. So Rushborough could have been headed to or from his place, the Reddy place, or Ardnakelty, got jumped along the way, and then been dumped in this spot to widen the suspect pool. Alternatively, he could have been killed somewhere unrelated, and left here to point things in the wrong direction. 'You see him yesterday?'

Trey is digging in Cal's glove compartment, presumably for the water bottle he keeps there in this weather. 'Nah. I was home all day, he didn't call in. You sound like a cop again.'

'Nope,' Cal says. 'I just sound like a regular guy who'd like to know what went down here. What, you wouldn't?'

Trey has found the water bottle. She shuts the car door. 'Nah,' she says. 'Don't give a shite.'

She leans against the car door, downs half the water, and passes the bottle to Cal. She's hardly glanced at Rushborough's body since Cal stepped back from it. It would be natural enough for her to flinch from the sight, but Cal doesn't think that's what's going on. The kid seems at ease, like the dead man is barely even there, too faint a presence to contaminate her home territory. Whatever terms she needed to make with him, she made them before she came to find Cal.

He's still baffled by her mood, and disturbed by being baffled. Over the past two years he's got pretty good at interpreting Trey, but today she's a mystery to him, and she's not old enough, or solid enough, that he can afford to let her be a mystery in a situation like this one. He wonders if she's given a thought to any of the implications and ramifications Rushborough's death could hold.

There are three or four black-faced sheep meandering across the path and among the trees, cropping at weeds. 'You know whose sheep those are?' Cal asks.

'Malachy Dwyer's. There was more of 'em in our yard. I was gonna go tell him they were loose, only . . .' Trey motions with her head at the body.

'That'd take your mind off sheep, all right,' Cal says, handing her back the water bottle. So Malachy's sheep have been out since before dawn, trampling all over any footprints or tyre tracks that a killer might have left behind, and covering up any scent that a K-9 could have followed. Sheep do get loose on a regular basis around here, what with most of the mountain fields being bounded by ancient, patched-up stone walls; nobody much cares, and they all end up back where they belong in the long run. But this escape came in pretty handy for someone.

The crows have transferred themselves by degrees to lower branches, testing the waters. They're a dirty ash-grey, with a sheen like a bluebottle's on their black wings. Their heads twitch back and forth so they can keep tabs on Cal and Trey while evaluating Rushborough possessively. Cal leans over to find a good-sized rock and throws it at them, and they flap lazily up a few branches, unimpressed, prepared to bide their time.

'When you talk to the cops,' he says, 'they'll likely let you have an adult there. I can do it if you want. Or you could have your mama. Or your dad.'

'You,' Trey says promptly.

'OK,' Cal says. And she came to him rather than to Johnny when she found Rushborough, even though Johnny's interest in this development would be considerably more intense than his. Something has changed for her. Cal would very much like to know what, and whether it's something to do with the body lying on the stained dirt. He believes the kid that she had nothing to do with it getting there, but the question of what she might know or suspect is smudgier. 'Once the Guards get here, we'll head back to my place. They can come talk to you there, when they're ready. We'll make them tea and everything.'

The sheep have stopped cropping and raised their heads, looking up the road towards Trey's house. Cal straightens up off the car. There's the crunch of feet on pebbles, and a flash of white between the trees.

It's Johnny Reddy himself, freshly shaved and shiny, hurrying down the road like a man with important places to be. He sees Cal's red Pajero first, and stops.

Cal says nothing. Neither does Trey.

'Well, and good morning to the pair of ye, too,' Johnny says, with a whimsical cock of his head, but Cal can see the wariness in his eye. 'What's the story here? Is it me ye're waiting for?'

'Nope,' Cal says. 'We're waiting with your buddy Rushborough over there.'

Johnny looks. His whole body goes still, and his mouth opens. The shock looks genuine, but Cal doesn't take anything out of Johnny at face value. Even if it's real, it could just mean he didn't expect the body to be where it is, not that he didn't expect it at all.

'What the fuck,' Johnny says, when the breath goes back into him. He makes an instinctive move towards Rushborough.

'I'm gonna have to ask you to stay where you are, Johnny,' Cal says, in his cop voice. 'We don't want to compromise a crime scene.'

Johnny stays put. 'Is he dead?'

'Oh yeah. Someone made good and sure of that.'

'How?'

'I look like a doctor to you?'

Johnny makes an effort to get himself together. He eyes Cal and gauges his chances of convincing him to dump Rushborough in a bog and forget the whole thing. Cal doesn't feel inclined to help him reach a decision. He gazes blandly back.

Eventually Johnny, genius that he is, concludes that Cal is unlikely to play along. 'Go home,' he says sharply to Trey. 'Go on. Get home to your mammy and stay there. Say nothing about this to anyone.'

'Trey here's the one that found the body,' Cal explains, nice and reasonable. 'She's gonna have to give a statement. The police are on their way.'

Johnny looks at him with pure hatred. Cal, after weeks of feeling that way about Johnny and being powerless to do a thing about it, looks back and savours every second.

'You say nothing to the Guards about that gold,' Johnny tells Trey. Trey may not be taking on board the implications here, but Johnny sure is; Cal can practically see his brain cells ricocheting among them all. 'D'you hear me? Not a fucking word.'

'Language,' Cal reminds him.

Johnny bares his teeth in what's supposed to be a smile but lands closer to a grimace. 'I don't need to tell you, sure,' he says to Cal. 'You don't want that hassle either.'

'Gee whiz,' Cal says, scratching his beard. 'I hadn't thought of that. I'll take it under advisement.'

Johnny's grimace tightens. 'I've somewhere to be. Am I allowed head over that way, am I? Guard?'

'Be my guest,' Cal says. 'I'm sure the police'll find you when they need you. Don't you worry about us; we're just fine here.'

Johnny throws him one more vicious look, then cuts through the trees to give the body a wide berth and heads up the higher path, towards the Dwyers' places and incidentally towards Rushborough's holiday home, at a near-run. Cal allows himself the hope that the little fuck will trip and go head over heels into a ravine.

'Bet he's going to get your camera,' Trey says. 'Rushborough took it offa me. I was gonna rob it back, only I didn't get a chance.'

'Huh,' Cal says. That camera has been on his mind, along with the fact that it stopped being mentioned right around the time Trey got that fat lip. He was blaming Johnny. 'What's on there that Rushborough wanted?'

'You and them lads putting the gold in the river.'

There's a moment of silence.

'Didja know I was there?'

'Nope,' Cal says, carefully. She's not looking at him; she's watching the path where her father vanished, eyes narrowed against the sun. 'I half wondered, but nope, I didn't know. How come you filmed it?'

'To show Rushborough. So's he'd fuck off.'

'Right,' Cal says. He adjusts his ideas. Trey wasn't just doing her filming behind Johnny's back; she was doing it, with preparation and care, to fuck him over. This leaves Cal even more baffled about what she was doing waving Johnny's cute little gold nugget around the pub.

'I didn't know you'd be there,' Trey says. 'At the river. You never told me.'

She's turning the water bottle between her knees, head bent over it. If she's watching Cal out of the corner of her eye, he can't tell.

'You figure I should've,' he says.

'Yeah.'

'I was planning to. The day before, when I lent you that camera. Only then your dad showed up and took you off home, and I didn't get a chance.'

'How come you went with them? To the river?'

Cal is moved by the fact that she's asking: she knows him well enough to take for granted that he wasn't there to rip off some damn fool tourist. 'I wanted to keep an eye on things,' he says. 'Rushborough always looked squirrelly to me, and the situation seemed like it could get messy. I like having a handle on what's going on around me.'

'You shoulda said it to me from the start. I'm not a fuckin' kid. I keep telling you.'

'I know that,' Cal says. He's still picking his way with every bit of care and delicacy he has. He knows better than to lie to her, but he also knows better than to tell her he needs to look out for her. 'I wasn't thinking you were too little to understand, or anything. All's I was thinking is that Johnny's your dad.'

'He's a fuckin' tosspot.'

'I'm not denying that,' Cal says. 'But I didn't want to put you in the middle of anything by sounding like I was bad-mouthing him or his big idea, and I didn't want to go pumping you for information. I figured I oughta leave you to make your own calls. I just wanted to stay clear on what was going on.'

Trey thinks that over, turning the bottle. Cal wonders whether to bring up the fact, while they're on the subject, that there's plenty she hasn't been telling him. He decides against it. He knows, by everything about her, that she's not done keeping things to herself yet. She still feels unreachable. If he tries to reach her now, and she lies, she'll be even farther away. He waits.

In the end she looks up at Cal and nods. 'Sorry I got your camera took,' she says. 'I'll pay you back.'

'Don't worry about it,' Cal says. All his muscles loosen a notch. He may not have fixed things, but this time, apparently, he's at least managed not to make them worse. 'Your dad might have you give it back to me. Once he's wiped some stuff off the memory card.'

Trey blows air out of the side of her mouth. 'Throw it in the bog, more like.'

'Nah,' Cal says. 'He won't want me kicking up a fuss, drawing attention to it. He'll delete that footage, send back the rest. It'll be fine.'

Trey turns her head at the sound of a car behind them. Through the trees and the road-twists they can see flashes of it: chunky, white and blue, a marked car.

'Guards,' she says.

'Yep,' Cal says. 'They were pretty quick.'

He turns to take one last look at the silent thing under the stripes of shadow. It looks skimpy and easily dismissed, something that's in the way for now but that'll be blown to nowhere by the next good wind. Cal understands what Trey doesn't: the magnitude of the change, far-reaching and unstoppable, that the car is bringing.

15

The two uniforms could be brothers: young, beefy, healthy, with identical neat haircuts and identical raw sunburns. Both of them look like this moment is unprecedented in their careers, and they're being extra official to show each other they can handle it. They take names and details from Cal and Trey, ask Trey what time she found the body – which gets them a blank shrug and 'Early' – and whether she touched it. They take Rushborough's name, too – Cal has his doubts on this, but he keeps them to himself – and where he was staying. Cal figures, with mixed feelings, that by the time they get there Johnny will be long gone.

The uniforms start stringing crime-scene tape between trees. One of them shoos away a couple of sheep that have drifted closer to investigate. 'Is it OK if we head back to my place, Officer?' Cal asks the other one. 'Trey here helps me out with some carpentry, and we've got a job to finish.'

'That's grand,' the uniform says, with a formal nod. 'The detectives'll need to take statements. They'll be able to reach ye both at that number, will they?'

'That's right,' Cal says. 'We'll be at my place most of the day.' He glances at Trey, who nods. The crows, single-minded and in no hurry, have started to work their way down the branches again.

On the way down the mountain, Trey asks, 'What'll they do?'

'Who?'

'The detectives. How'll they find out who kilt him?'

'Well,' Cal says. He shifts the car down a gear and taps the brake. He learned to drive in the hills of North Carolina, but the grade of this mountain still sometimes sets his teeth on edge. No one was taking cars into account when this road was made. 'They'll have a crime-scene team to collect forensic evidence. Like take whatever random hairs and fibres they find on the body, so they can try and match them to a suspect or his house or his car. Take Rushborough's hair and fibres, in case some got on the suspect; samples of his blood, 'cause there's gonna be plenty of that wherever he was killed. Scrape under his fingernails and take samples of the bloodstains, in case he fought his attacker and got some DNA on him. Look for any tracks to tell them how he got there, and from what direction. And they'll have technical guys go through his phone, see who he was talking to, if he had any hassle with anyone.'

'What about the detectives? What do they do?'

'Talk to people, mostly. Ask around here to find out who saw him last, where he was headed, if he pissed anyone off. Get in touch with his family, his friends, his associates, look for any problems – love life, money, business, whatever. Any enemies.'

Trey says, 'He seemed like he'd have enemies. Not just here.'

'Yeah,' Cal says. 'To me, too.' He edges his way past a side road, craning his neck to make sure no one's blithely speeding down it. He wishes he was sure Trey's interest in police procedure was purely academic. 'He give you that fat lip a few days back?'

'Yeah,' Trey says, like her mind is doing other things. She disappears into a silence that lasts her all the way back to Cal's.

———

While he's frying up a fresh batch of bacon and eggs, and Trey is setting the table, Cal texts Lena: *Someone killed Rushborough. Up on the mountain.*

He can see that she's read it, but it takes a minute before she texts back. *I'll be over after work.* Trey, done with the table and sitting on the floor abstractedly stroking the dogs, doesn't react to the phone's beep. Cal sends Lena a thumbs-up and goes back to his frying pan.

They eat in more silence. By the time they move into the workshop, Cal has made the decision that he's not going to tell the detectives anything about gold, at least not yet. He wants to keep himself clear of this tangle, leaving himself free to step into any role Trey needs him to play, once he figures out what that might be.

This should be doable. The Guards are bound to find out at least the surface layer or two of the gold story, but when it comes to details, they're going to run into trouble. Cal has experience of the impressive thoroughness with which Ardnakelty, when it's motivated, can generate confusion. The detectives will be lucky if they ever get a solid sense of what the fuck was going on, let alone who was involved. And Cal, as an outsider, has every right to be oblivious to local business. In the ordinary run of things, he would have heard some vague bullshit story about gold, mixed in with Mossie's fairy hill and what-have-you, and paid it no particular heed. He misses the ordinary run of things.

It's almost lunchtime, and they're drilling dowel holes, when Banjo's ears prick up, Rip lets out a furious cascade of howls, and both dogs head for the door. 'Cops,' Trey says, her head going straight up like she's been waiting for this. She gets up off the floor and takes a breath and a quick shake, like a boxer going into the ring.

Cal is hit by the sudden, urgent sense that he's missed something. He wants to stop her, call her back, but it's too late. All he can do is dust himself down and follow her.

Sure enough, when they reach the front door, there's an obtrusively discreet unmarked car aligning itself tidily next to the Pajero. Two men are sitting up front.

'They're just gonna want to hear how you found him,' Cal says, blocking the dogs' exit with a foot. 'For now. Talk clearly, take your time if you need to think back. If you don't remember something or you're not sure, just say so. That's all. Nothing to worry about.'

'I'm not worried,' Trey says. 'It's grand.'

Cal doesn't know whether, or how, to tell her that that's not necessarily true. 'This guy's gonna be from Homicide,' he says, 'or whatever they call it here. He's not gonna be like that uniform from town who gives you shit when you play hooky too often.'

'Good,' Trey says, with feeling. 'Your man's a fuckin' dildo.'

'Language,' Cal says, but he's saying it automatically. His eyes are on the man getting out of the passenger door. The guy is around Cal's age, squat and short-legged enough that he must have to get his suit pants taken up, with a bouncy, cheerful walk. He's brought along one of the beefcake twins, presumably to take notes and leave his full attention free.

'I'll be mannerly,' Trey assures him. 'Just watch.' Cal doesn't feel reassured.

The detective is called Nealon. He's got scrubby greying hair and a lumpy, humorous face, and he looks like a guy who would run a prosperous mom-and-pop business, maybe a hardware store. Cal has no doubt that he knows how to use that look: the guy is no dummy. He makes nice with Rip and Banjo till they settle down, and then accepts a cup of tea so he can take a seat at the kitchen table and make small talk with Cal and Trey while they prepare it, giving himself a chance to place them. Cal sees his glance skim Trey's outgrown jeans and non-haircut, and slaps down the urge to tell Nealon straight out that this is no neglected delinquent, this is a good kid on a good path, with respectable people at her back to make sure no one fucks with her.

Trey is doing a fine job of establishing her respectability all by herself. She's being what Cal considers suspiciously polite: asking Nealon and the uniform whether they take milk, laying out cook-ies on a plate, giving full-sentence answers to the bullshit questions about school and weather. Cal would give a lot to know what she's playing at.

He himself, he knows, is harder to place, and the bruises won't help. Nealon asks where he's from and how he likes Ireland, and he gives the practised, pleasant answers that he gives everyone. He's leaving his occupation unmentioned for a while, so he can see how this guy operates in its absence.

'Now,' Nealon says, once they've all got acquainted with their tea and cookies. 'You've had some day already, yeah? And it's not even lunchtime. I'll try and make this quick enough.' He smiles at Trey, sitting across from him. The uniform has faded off to the sofa and taken out a notebook and pen. 'D'you know who that fella was, that you found?'

'Mr Rushborough,' Trey says readily. She's even sitting up straight. 'Cillian Rushborough. My dad knew him from London.'

'So he's over here visiting your daddy?'

'Not really. They're not mates, not properly. Your man's family was from round here. I think he mostly came 'cause of that.'

'Ah, yeah, one of those,' Nealon says tolerantly. Cal can't place his accent. It's faster than he's used to, and flatter, with a snap that gives ordinary sentences an edge of challenge; it has a city ring. 'What's he like? Nice fella?'

Trey shrugs. 'I only met him a coupla times. Didn't take much notice. He was OK. Bit posh.'

'Will we see can we work out what time you found him?'

'Haven't got a phone,' Trey explains. 'Or a watch.'

'No worries,' Nealon says cheerfully. 'We'll do a bitta the aul' maths instead. Let's see do I have this right: you found the body, you walked straight down here to Mr Hooper, and the pair of yous drove back up to the scene. Is that it?'

'Yeah.'

'Mr Hooper rang us at nineteen minutes past six. How long before that did yous reach the scene?'

'Coupla minutes, only.'

'We'll say quarter past, will we? Keep our lives simple. How long would you take driving up there?'

'Ten minutes. Maybe fifteen. The road's not great.'

'D'you see what I'm doing, now?' Nealon asks, smiling at Trey like a favourite uncle.

'Yeah. Counting backwards.'

Trey is playing it well: attentive, serious, cooperative but not over-helpful. It's taken Cal a minute to realise that that's what she's doing, and why she seems suddenly unfamiliar. He's never seen the kid play anything any way before. He didn't know she had the capacity. He wonders if this is something she learned by watching Johnny, or if it was in there all along, waiting for the need to arise.

'That's it,' Nealon says. 'So we're at around six o'clock when you left this place. How long were you here?'

'Like a minute. I told Cal and we went.'

260

'Still around six, so. How long would it take you to walk down here?'

'Half an hour, about. Maybe a bit more. I was walking quick. So I musta started just before half-five.'

Cal's need to know what Trey is doing has intensified. In normal circumstances, the kid would no more volunteer an unnecessary word to a cop than she would gnaw off her own fingers.

'Now you're sucking diesel,' Nealon says approvingly. 'How long were you up by the body, before you headed here?'

Trey shrugs, reaching for her mug. For the first time, there's a hitch in her rhythm. 'Dunno. A bit.'

'A long bit?'

'Fifteen minutes, maybe. Coulda been twenty. Haven't got a watch.'

'No problem,' Nealon says easily. Cal knows he caught the reluctance, and that he'll come back to this once Trey thinks he's forgotten about it. Cal has played out this scene so many times before that it feels like he's seeing it double: once from his accustomed seat in Nealon's chair, calibrating and recalibrating his balance of amiability and insistence as his assessment develops in more detail; once from his actual perspective, an entirely different place where the balance is a defensive one and the stakes are suddenly sky-high and visceral. He doesn't like either position one little bit.

'So,' Nealon says, 'what time's that we're at now? When you first found him?'

Trey thinks. She's back on track, now that they've moved away from that gap by the body. 'Like just after five, musta been.'

'There you go,' Nealon says, pleased. 'We got there in the end. Didn't I tell you?'

'Yeah. We got there.'

'Just after five,' Nealon says, tilting his head at a friendly angle, like a bushy dog's. 'That's awful early to be up and about. Had you got plans?'

'Nah. I just . . .' Trey moves one shoulder in a half-shrug. 'I heard noises, during the night. Wanted to see what was the story, had anything happened.'

That has to prick up Nealon's ears, but he doesn't show it. The guy knows what he's doing. 'Yeah? What kind of noises?'

'People talking. And a car.'

'Just before you got up? Or earlier in the night?'

'Earlier. I wasn't sleeping right; too hot. Woke up and heard something outside.'

'Would you know what time?'

Trey shakes her head. 'Late enough that my mam and my dad were asleep.'

'Did you call them?'

'Nah. I knew it wasn't on our land, too far away, so I wasn't worried, like. I went out to the gate, but, to see what was the story. There was lights down the road, like headlights. And men talking.'

Nealon is still at ease in his chair, drinking his tea, but Cal can feel the attention humming from him. 'Down the road where?'

'Towards where your man was, at the fork. Coulda been there, coulda been a bit closer.'

'Did you not go check, no?'

'Went a little way down the road, but I stopped. I thought maybe they wouldn't want anyone seeing them.'

This is plausible enough. Stuff goes on, up the mountain: moonshining, dumping, diesel-running from across the border, probably more hard-core stuff. Any mountain kid would know to stay clear. But Trey mentioned none of this to Cal.

'Looks like you might've been right,' Nealon says. 'Did you see them?'

'Sorta. Men moving around, just. The car lights were in my eyes, and they were outside the light. Couldn't tell what they were doing.'

'How many of them?'

'A few. Not a crowd, like; maybe four or five.'

'Did you recognise any of them?'

Trey thinks back. 'Nah. Don't think so.'

'Fair enough,' Nealon says easily, but Cal hears the unspoken *for now*: if Nealon comes up with a suspect, he'll be back. 'Did you hear any of what they were saying?'

Trey shrugs. 'Small bits, only. Like one fella said, "Over that way," and another one said, "Jesus, take it easy." And someone said, "Come on ta fuck" – sorry for cursing.'

'I've heard worse,' Nealon says, with a grin. 'Anything else?'

'The odd word, just. Nothing that made sense. They were moving around, like, so that made it harder to hear.'

'Did you recognise any of the voices?' Nealon asks. 'Take your time, now, and think back.'

Trey thinks, or else gives a good impression of it, frowning into her mug. 'Nah,' she says in the end. 'Sorry. It was all men, but. Like, not my age. Grown men.'

'What about the accents? Could you tell were they Irish, were they local, anything at all?'

'Irish,' Trey says, without a pause. 'From round here.' Cal's head goes up at the note in her voice, clean and final as an arrow slicing straight to the heart of the target, and he knows.

Nealon says, 'Round here like what? This county, this townland, the West?'

'Ardnakelty. Even just over the other side of the mountain, or across the river, they talk different. These were from round here.'

'You're certain, now, yeah?'

'Definite.'

The whole story is bullshit. Cal understands at last that Trey has never been her father's minion in this; she's playing a lone game, and has been all along. When the opportunity came her way, she aimed Ardnakelty down a phantom path after imaginary gold. Now that things have shifted, she's aiming Nealon, meticulously as a sniper, at the men who killed her brother.

She gave Cal her word never to do anything about Brendan, but all this is just distant enough from Brendan that she can convince herself it doesn't count. She saw clearly that she would never get a chance like this again, so she took it. Cal's heart is a heavy relentless force in his chest, making it hard to breathe. When he worried that Trey's childhood had left cracks in her, he had it wrong. Those aren't cracks; those are fault lines.

Nealon's expression hasn't changed. 'How long would you say you were out there?'

Trey considers this. 'Coupla minutes, maybe. Then the car engine started up, and I went back in the house. Didn't want them seeing me if they came our way.'

'Did they?'

'Don't think so. By the time they drove off I was in my room, it's at the back; I wouldn'ta seen their lights go past. But the car sounded like it was going the other way. I wouldn't swear, but. Sound echoes funny, up there.'

'True enough,' Nealon agrees. 'What'd you do after that?'

'Went back to bed. It was nothing to do with us, whatever they were at. And everything had gone quiet anyway.'

'But when you woke up early, you went to have a look.'

'Yeah. Couldn't get back to sleep; too hot, and my sister, that I share the room with, she was snoring. And I wanted to see what they'd been at.'

Cal knows now why Trey brought her find to him instead of to Johnny. There was nothing sentimental about it; she didn't trust him more in a pinch, or turn to him from the shock. She wanted the chance to tell this story. Johnny would have tossed Rushborough down that ravine and made damn sure Trey had seen nothing, heard nothing, and never got near a detective. Cal is better behaved.

'And that's when you found him,' Nealon says.

'My dog found him first.' Trey points at Banjo, sprawled with Rip in the shadiest corner by the fireplace, his side rising as he pants in the heat. 'The big fella there. He was up ahead, and he howled. Then I got there and saw.'

'It's a shock,' Nealon says, just sympathetically enough and not too sympathetically. The guy is good. 'Did you get up close to him?'

'Yeah. Up next to him. Went to see who it was, what was the story.'

'Did you touch him? Move him? Check was he dead?'

Trey shakes her head. 'Didn't need to. You could tell by him.'

'You were there about twenty minutes, you said,' Nealon reminds her, without any particular emphasis. His little blue eyes are mild and interested. 'What were you doing all that time?'

'Just kneeling down there. I felt sick. Hadta stay put for a bit.'

Trey's answering readily this time, now she's had a chance to plan, but Cal knows better. He's seen Trey taken apart by an animal's suffering, but never by a dead creature. Whatever she was doing by Rushborough's body, she wasn't waiting for her stomach to settle. The thought of her screwing around with evidence makes him flinch.

'Sure, that's only natural,' Nealon says soothingly. 'It takes all of us like that, the first few times. I know one Garda that's been on the job twenty years, great big lump of a fella, the size of Mr Hooper here, and he'd still get the head-staggers when he sees a dead body. Did you get sick, in the end?'

'Nah. I was grand in a bit.'

'Did you not want to get away from your man?'

'Yeah. Thought if I stood up I might puke, but, or get dizzy. So I stayed put. Kept my eyes shut.'

'Did you touch the man at all?'

He asked that already, but if Trey notices, she doesn't show it. 'Nah. Fuc— Sorry. No way.'

'I don't blame you. I wouldn't fancy touching him myself.' Nealon gives Trey another smile. She manages a half-smile back. 'So you took a little break to get your head together, and once you were all right, you came straight here.'

'Yeah.'

Nealon takes another cookie and mulls that over. 'That fella Rushborough,' he says, 'he was only, what is it, a few minutes from your own gate. Why didn't you go tell your mammy and daddy?'

'He usedta be a detective,' Trey says, nodding at Cal. 'I reckoned he'd know what to do, better'n they would.'

It only takes Nealon a fraction of a second to come back from that and change the surprise to a big grin. 'Jaysus,' he says. 'They say it takes one to know one, but I hadn't a notion. A colleague, hah?'

'Chicago PD,' Cal says. His heart is still slamming, but he keeps his voice easy. 'Back in the day. I'm retired.'

Nealon laughs. 'My God, what are the odds? You come halfway across the world to get away from the job, and you trip over a murder case.' He glances over his shoulder at the uniform, who has stopped scribbling and is looking up at them open-mouthed, unsure what to make of this development. 'We got lucky today, hah? A detective for a witness; Jaysus, you couldn't ask for better.'

'I'm no detective here,' Cal says. He can't tell whether there was a fine needle under the words – he's still waiting to find out how long you have to live in Ireland before you can reliably identify when people are giving you shit – but he's seen enough turf wars to make this much clear straightaway. 'And I never worked Homicide anyway. About all's I know is to secure the scene and wait for the experts to get there, so that's what I did.'

'And I appreciate it, man,' Nealon says heartily. 'Go on, give us the rundown: what'd you do?' He leans back in his chair to leave Cal the floor, and gets to work on his cookie.

'When I got to the scene I recognised the man as Cillian Rushborough, I've met him a couple of times. I gloved up' – Cal pulls the gloves out of his pocket and lays them on the table – 'and I confirmed that he was dead. His cheek was cold. His jaw and his elbow were in rigor, but his fingers still moved, so did his knee. I didn't touch him anywhere else. I backed off and called you guys.'

He figures he got a decent balance between subordinate and civilian. He also figures Nealon is noting and analysing that.

'Great,' Nealon says, giving him a colleague's nod. 'Fair play. And then you stayed on the scene till the uniforms got there?'

'Yeah. Stayed a few yards back, at my car.'

'Did you see anyone else while yous were up there?'

'Trey's dad came past. Johnny Reddy.'

Nealon raises his eyebrows. 'Ah, man, that's some way to find out your friend's dead. Was he all right?'

'He looked pretty shocked,' Cal says. Trey nods.

'He didn't hang on with yous?'

'He headed off up the mountain.'

266

'We'll be needing to talk to him,' Nealon says. 'Did he say where he was off to?'

'He didn't mention it,' Cal says.

'Ah, sure, in a place this size, we'll run into him one way or t'other,' Nealon says comfortably. He drains the last of his tea and pushes his chair back from the table, glancing at the uniform to signal that they're done. 'Right; we might have a few more questions down the line, and you'll need to come into the station in town and sign statements for me, but I'd say that'll keep us going for now. Thanks for the tea, and for your time.' He hitches his suit trousers to a comfortable arc under his belly. 'Would you walk out to the car with me, Mr Hooper, just in case I think of anything else I meant to ask you?'

Cal doesn't want a one-on-one with Nealon right now, before he's had a chance to rearrange his thoughts. 'Pleasure,' he says, getting up. Trey starts clearing the cups, prompt and deft as a waitress.

Outside, the heat has thickened. 'Go on up to the car,' Nealon tells the uniform. 'I'm gasping for a smoke.' The uniform strides off. His back looks self-conscious.

Nealon pulls out a packet of Marlboros and tilts it at Cal, who shakes his head. 'Good man,' Nealon says. 'I oughta quit, the missus is always on at me, but you know yourself.' He lights up and takes a deep grateful drag. 'D'you know that young one well?'

'Pretty well,' Cal says. 'I've been here two years last spring; I do some carpentering, and she's been helping me out most of that time, when school allows. Kid's got a knack for it, figures she might go into it full-time when she finishes school.'

'Would you say she's reliable?'

'I've always found her to be,' Cal says, considering this. 'She's a good kid. Steady-like, works hard, good head on her shoulders.'

He would love to say that Trey lies like a rug, but he doesn't have that option. Regardless of what else Nealon does or doesn't find, he now has one person who's straight out admitted to being on the mountainside when and where Rushborough was dumped.

If her story is made up, then from Nealon's perspective – since he's fortunate enough never to have heard of Brendan Reddy – she's either shielding someone else, or shielding herself. Cal can't tell whether Trey hasn't thought through the implications of what she's doing, or whether she understands them just fine and doesn't give a shit.

'Would she be the type, let's say, to imagine things?' Nealon asks. 'Or make up a story for the drama, maybe? Or even do a bitta embroidering round the edges?'

Cal doesn't have to put on the laugh. 'Hell no. Kid's got no time for that stuff. The most exciting story I've ever heard outa her is one time her math teacher threw a book at someone. That's all the detail I got, too: "Mr Whatsisname threw a book at this kid 'cause the kid was driving him mental, only he missed." Drama's not her thing.'

'Well, that's great,' Nealon says, smiling up at him. 'That's the witness you want, isn't it? I'm blessed with her. Mostly in places like this, the back of beyond, they wouldn't talk to the Guards if their lives depended on it.'

'The kid's used to me,' Cal says. 'That might have something to do with it.'

Nealon nods, apparently satisfied with this. 'And tell us: will she stick to the story, wouldja say? Or will she get cold feet if it comes to going on the stand?'

'She'll stick to it,' Cal says.

'Even if we land on one of her neighbours?'

'Yeah,' Cal says. 'Even if.'

Nealon's eyebrows jump. 'Fair play to her.' He tilts his head to blow smoke up at the sky, away from Cal. 'What about the accents? Is she right that you could tell this townland from the next one over?'

'So I'm told,' Cal says. 'I can't hear the difference, but my neighbour says the people across the river sound like a herd of donkeys, so he's hearing something.'

'You'd still get that in places like this, I suppose,' Nealon says. 'With the older people, anyway. Where I'm from, fuck me, half the kids talk like they're straight off a plane from LA. At least that young one sounds Irish.' He nods backwards at the house and Trey. 'Her da, what's his name, Johnny? What's the story on him?'

'I've only met him a few times,' Cal says. 'He's been in London since before I got here, just came back a couple of weeks ago. You'd get more outa the locals who knew him before.'

'Ah, yeah, I'll be asking them. I'd value a professional opinion, but. He's the only known associate the dead man had around here; I have to take an interest. What kind of fella is he?'

Nealon has decided that, for now anyway, Cal gets to be the local beat cop who helps out the investigation with his down-home on the ground knowledge. Cal is happy to play along with that. 'Friendly enough guy,' he says, shrugging. 'Sorta what you'd call a waster, though. Lotta talk, lotta smiles, no job.'

'I know the type well,' Nealon says, with feeling. 'I'll make sure I've a comfortable chair when I talk to him; that kind'd go on about himself till the cows come home. What about your man Rushborough? Was he the same?'

'I only met him a couple of times, too. He didn't give me that good-for-nothing vibe; I heard he was some kinda rich business-man, but I don't know if that's true. Mostly he just seemed pretty jazzed about being here. He had a ton of stories from his gramma, he wanted to go see the places she talked about, he got all excited 'cause one guy turned out to be a third cousin.'

'I know that type, too,' Nealon says, grinning. 'Mostly they're Yanks like yourself; we wouldn't get many Brits going all romantic about the Emerald Isle, but sure, there's always exceptions. Were your people from round here as well, were they?'

'Nope,' Cal says. 'No connection. Just liked the looks of Ireland and found a place I could afford.'

'How're the locals treating you? They wouldn't have a reputa-tion for being what you'd call welcoming.'

'Huh,' Cal says. 'They've been pretty neighbourly to me. Not saying we're bosom buddies or anything, but we've always got along fine.'

'That's great to hear. We wouldn't want them wrecking our

good name altogether; as if murdering a tourist wasn't bad enough.' Nealon has smoked his cigarette right down to the butt. He looks at the remains wistfully, and puts it out on the bottom of his shoe. 'If this was your case,' he says. 'Is there anyone in particular you'd have your eye on?'

Cal takes his time on that one. The uniform is sitting up very straight in the driver's seat with his hands ready on the wheel, resolutely ignoring the rooks, who, delighted to have a fresh target, are jeering down at him and dropping acorns on the car.

'I'd be taking a look at Johnny Reddy,' he says. He doesn't have much choice: Johnny is the right answer, and if this is a test, Cal needs to pass it.

'Yeah? Were there problems between himself and Rushborough?'

'Not that I saw. But, like you said, he's the only known associate Rushborough had around here. I don't know what kinda history they might've had over in London. I mean . . .' Cal shrugs. 'I guess Rushborough could've pissed off someone else that bad in less'n a week here. Hooked up with someone's girl, maybe, though he didn't seem like the type. Like I told you, I was never Homicide; I've got no experience here. But I'd start with Johnny.'

'Ah, yeah, him o' course,' Nealon says, waving his cigarette butt in dismissal, like he knows Cal can do better than that. 'But apart from him. Anyone that's a bit odd, we'll say, anyone you wouldn't want to meet on a dark road? The local mentaller, to make no bones about it. I know the young one said she heard four or five men, but even a mentaller might have friends, family, people that'd help him out when the shite hit the fan.'

'We don't really have one to speak of,' Cal says. 'Plenty of guys are a little bit odd around the edges, just from living alone too long, but I don't think any of 'em are odd enough to whack a random tourist just 'cause they don't like his looks.'

'An English tourist, but,' Nealon says, like the thought just struck him. 'There's always people that'd have strong feelings about the Brits, specially up here near the border. Anyone like that around the townland?'

Cal thinks that over. 'Nope,' he says. 'Everyone sings the

occasional pub song that might not be too friendly about the English, I guess. I sing 'em myself, now that I've picked up some of the words.'

'Don't we all, sure,' Nealon says, chuckling. 'No, I'm talking about someone that'd be a lot more hard-core than that. Someone that's giving out yards whenever the North comes on the news in the pub, or ranting on about what oughta be done to the royals, that kind of thing.'

Cal shakes his head. 'Nah.'

'Ah, well. It was worth asking.' Nealon watches the rooks, who have worked their way up to jumping up and down on the roof of his car. Cal finds himself kind of flattered: the rooks may give him shit, but they won't permit anyone else to take liberties. The uniform bangs on the roof, and they scatter. 'Anything else I oughta know? Did your man Rushborough spend a lot of time with anyone in particular? Any problems over family history, maybe? An old feud, or a piece of land that went where it shouldn't have?'

'Nope,' Cal says. 'Not that I know of.' He has never outright obstructed an investigation before. There were times when no one put much effort into establishing who did what to some high-carat asshole who clearly deserved it, but that was by unspoken agreement; this is the first time he's deliberately blocked another detective's way. That sense of double vision has faded. He wonders how long it'll take Nealon to spot that.

'Everything in the garden was rosy,' Nealon says. 'If anything comes to you, let me know. Anything at all, even if it seems like it'd have no bearing – sure, you know yourself. Here's my card. What happened there?' he inquires pleasantly and out of nowhere, pointing to his forehead.

'Slipped in the shower,' Cal says, tucking the card away in his pocket. He reckons there's a solid chance that Johnny will explain his own face by painting Cal as a rabid psycho who probably murders innocent tourists for kicks, but he also reckons Nealon has been a cop too long to take some waster's word about another cop, even when the waster's story happens to have a grain of truth mixed in.

Nealon, field-stripping his cigarette onto the dirt, nods like he believes this, which maybe he does. 'That's when you need the good neighbours, man,' he says. 'When there's trouble; when things get that bit dicey. You could've knocked yourself out cold and laid there for days, wasting away, unless you had neighbours that'd look out for you. They're a great thing to have.'

'One of the bonuses of being a carpenter,' Cal says. 'Sooner or later, someone's gonna come looking for their chair or what-have-you.'

'I'd better let you get back to your carpentry, so,' Nealon says, tucking his cigarette filter back in the packet, 'before they come looking.' He holds out his hand. Cal has no choice but to shake, and sees Nealon's glance flick to his battered knuckles. 'We'll keep you updated. Thanks again.'

He nods to Cal and stumps off towards the car. One of the rooks lands on the hood, looks the uniform in the eye, and takes a shit.

———————

Trey has washed out the cups and gone back to the workshop, where she's sitting cross-legged on the floor amid the carefully laid out pieces of chair, mixing stain colours and testing them on a leftover piece of the oak sleeper. 'That went grand,' she says, glancing up at Cal.

'Yeah,' Cal says. 'Told you.'

'Did he ask you anything else?'

'Just whether you were reliable. I said yeah.'

Trey goes back to her stain mixes. 'Thanks,' she says gruffly.

Sometimes when Trey has Cal stymied, he asks Alyssa, who works with at-risk youths, for advice. She's pointed him in the right direction plenty of times. This time he can't even imagine where he would start.

'Where's the guy from?' he asks. 'I couldn't place the accent.'

'Dublin. They think they're great.'

'Are they?'

'Dunno. Never knew anyone from Dublin. He didn't seem that great.'

'Don't make that mistake,' Cal says. 'He knows what he's doing.'

Trey shrugs, carefully brushing wood stain onto the sleeper.

Cal says, 'Kid.' He has no idea what should come next. What he wants to do is slam the door so hard she jumps out of her skin, rip the paintbrush out of her hand, and roar in her face till he gets it into her damn head what she's done to the safe place he busted his ass to build for her.

Trey lifts her head and looks at him. Cal reads her unblinking stare and the set of her chin, and knows he'll get nowhere. He doesn't want to hear her lie to him, not about this.

'I done a load of these,' she says. 'Look.'

She's gone all out: nine or ten perfect stripes of subtly different shades. Cal takes a breath. 'Yeah,' he says. 'Good work. This one and this one here, they look like pretty close matches. We'll take another look once they dry. You want some lunch?'

'I oughta go home,' Trey says. She presses the lid back onto the wood-stain tin. 'My mam'll be worrying. She'll know about Rushborough by now.'

'You can phone her.'

'Nah.'

She's turned unreachable again. Her ease with Cal up on the mountainside was just a brief respite she allowed herself, before she bent her back to the task she's chosen. That, or else it was her making sure she could stay with him until she'd told her story to Nealon unhindered. He can't be sure, any more, what she's capable of. When he thought she had none of the artifice other teenagers develop, he was wrong again. She's just been saving it, and tailoring it, for when it matters.

'OK,' he says. He wants to lock the doors, board up the windows, barricade the two of them in here until he can make the kid grow a working brain or at least until all this is done and gone. 'We'll clean up here, and I'll drive you.'

'I'm grand walking.'

'No,' Cal says. He welcomes finding a spot where he can finally put his foot down. 'I'm taking you. And you be careful out there. Anything happens to worry you, or you just feel like coming back here, you call me. I'll be right there.'

He expects Trey to roll her eyes, but she just nods, wiping her brush on a rag. 'Yeah,' she says. 'OK.'

'OK,' Cal says. 'There's more turps on the shelf, if you need it.'

'I wrote out how I mixed those,' Trey says, tilting her chin at the sleeper. 'Next to them.'

'Good. Make our lives easier when we come back to 'em.'

Trey nods, but doesn't reply. There was a note of ending in her voice, like she doesn't expect to be here for that. Cal wants to say something, but he can't find the right thing to say.

Sitting there on the floor in an unselfconscious tangle of legs and sneaker laces, with her hair all rucked up on one side, she looks like a little kid again, the way he first remembers her. He doesn't know how to stop her heading down the path she's created, so he has no choice but to follow her, in case she should need him, somewhere up ahead. She's calling the shots now, whether she ever intended that or not. He wishes he could find a way to tell her that, and to ask her to do it with care.

16

The mountainside is sticky-hot; Banjo spent the whole time in the car moaning loudly, to make the point that this weather is animal cruelty. Cal brought them the long way round, up the far side of the mountain and over, to stay clear of the crime scene.

As his car disappears in a cloud of dust, Trey pauses at her gate to listen, ignoring Banjo's dramatic gasping. The sounds rising up the road from the fork seem ordinary: unworried birds and deft minor rustles, no voices or clumsy human movement. Trey reckons the Guards must have finished up and taken Rushborough away, to scrape under his fingernails and pick threads off his clothes. She wishes she had known about all that stuff earlier, when she had a chance to do something about it.

She turns her head at the crunch of a footstep. Her dad appears out of the trees at the edge of the yard and heads towards her, waving like it's urgent.

'Well, there's my sweetheart at last,' he says, giving her a reproachful look. He has a twig in his hair. 'About time. I was keeping a lookout for you.'

Banjo, ignoring him, squeezes his belly through the bars of the gate and heads for the house and his water bowl. ''S only lunchtime,' Trey says.

'I know that, but you can't be going off without telling your mammy, not on a day like this. You had us worried there. Where were you, at all?'

'Cal's,' Trey says. 'Hadta wait for the detective.' Her dad gives no explanation of what he was doing among the trees, but Trey knows. He's been waiting for her out here, because he wants to find out all about the detective before he faces him. When he heard the car coming, he hid like a kid who broke a window.

'Ah, God, that's right,' Johnny says, slapping his forehead. Trey is under no illusion that he was worried about her, but he's worried all the same: his feet are jittering like a fighter's. 'Your man Hooper said they'd need to talk to ye, didn't he? What with everything else, it went straight outa my head. How'd it go? Did they treat you all right?'

He's in luck: Trey wants to talk to him, too. 'Yeah,' she says. 'It was just the one detective, and a fella taking notes. They were grand.'

'Good. They'd want to be nice to my wee girl,' Johnny says, wagging a finger, 'or they'll have me to deal with. What did they ask you?'

'Just wanted to know about me finding your man. What time it was when I first saw him. Did I touch him, what did I do, did I see anyone.'

'Didja tell them I came by?'

'Cal did.'

Behind Johnny, there's a movement in the sitting-room window. The light on the glass blurs the figure so that it takes Trey a second to identify it: Sheila, watching them, her arms folded at her waist.

Johnny rubs the corner of his mouth with a knuckle. 'Right,' he says. 'Grand; no panic. I can sort that. What about the gold? Didja say anything about that? Even a mention?'

'Nah.'

'Did they ask?'

'Nah.'

'What about your man Hooper, do you know did he say anything?'

'Nah. They just asked him the same as me. What he did with Rushborough, did he touch him. He said nothing about gold.'

Johnny lets out a quick, vicious laugh, up into the sky. 'Thought so. That's the fuckin' pigs for you. Hooper'd beat the shite outa any poor bastard that kept anything from him, I'd say he's done it many a time, but he's got no problem staying quiet when it's his own neck on the line.'

Trey says, 'Thought you didn't want them knowing.'

That gets his attention back on her. 'Jesus, no. You done great.

Even if they come back asking about it, you never heard of any gold, d'you get me?'

'Yeah,' Trey says. She hasn't decided yet what she's going to do about the gold.

'I'm not complaining about Hooper, now,' Johnny reassures her. 'I'm delighted he kept his mouth shut. I'm only saying: there's one rule for them, one for everyone else. You remember that.'

Trey shrugs. He looks like shite: older and white, except where the bruises are fading to a dirty green that makes her think of Cal's scarecrow.

'What'd you say about me and your man Rushborough? Did you say we were mates, or what?'

'Said you knew him a bit from London, but he wasn't over to see you or anything. He was just here 'cause it's where his family was from.'

'Good,' Johnny says. He blows out a long breath. His eyes are skittering to every rustle in the trees. 'Good good good. That's what I like to hear. Good girl yourself.'

Trey says, 'I told the detective I heard people talking down the road, late last night. So I went out, and there was fellas down at the fork, where I found your man. Didn't get close enough to see them, but fellas with local accents.'

That finally stops Johnny moving. He's staring at her. 'Didja?'

Trey shrugs.

After a second Johnny slaps the top bar of the gate so hard it shakes, throws back his head and bursts out laughing. 'Holy God almighty,' he says, 'where did I get you from, at all? That's my girl. That's my wee chip off the old block. Jesus, the brains on you, if brains was money we wouldn't need to be feckin' about with any aul' gold, we'd be billionaires—' He flings the gate open and reaches to catch Trey in a hug, but she steps back. Johnny doesn't register that, or doesn't care. 'You saw where them Garda fuckers were headed, didn't you? You were miles ahead of them. You weren't going to let them pin a murder on your poor daddy. That's my girl.'

'You oughta tell them the same thing,' Trey says. 'In case they think I made it up for notice.'

Johnny stops laughing to run that through his mind. 'That's some great thinking,' he says after a second, 'but no. If I say the same as you, they'll think I put you up to it. I'll tell you what we'll do: I'll say I heard you going out, sometime in the night. And maybe I oughta have gone after you' – he's pacing in zigzags, thinking it out as he goes – 'but I was half asleep. And I thought I heard voices somewhere, so I reckoned you were off to meet your pals for a bitta mischief, maybe someone had a naggin – I wasn't going to spoil your fun, sure haven't we all done the same at your age, and worse? So I left you to it. But I didn't hear you coming back in, so when I woke up this morning and you weren't in the house, I was a wee bit worried about my girl. So I went looking for you, and that's why I was out and about bright and early. Now.' He stops moving and spreads his arms, smiling at Trey. 'Doesn't that all hang together lovely?'

'Yeah.'

'There we go. Sorted and ready for the detectives; they can come whenever they like, now. Aren't you great, coming straight back to tell me?'

'Prob'ly,' Trey says. She knows he'll be grand talking to the detectives. Her dad isn't a fool; he's well able to do a good job, as long as there's someone with more focus to keep him moving along the right track. Trey has focus.

'One more thing,' Johnny says. 'While we're at it. D'you remember I went out for a walk, last night after the dinner? Just to clear the head?'

'Yeah.'

Johnny wags a finger at her. 'No I didn't. We don't know what time Mr Rushborough died, do we? For all we know, it coulda been while I was out and about, with no one to vouch for me but the birds. And we don't want that detective fella taking any notions into his head, wasting his time and letting a murderer get away. So I was home all evening, clearing up after the dinner and watching the telly. Have you got that?'

'Yeah,' Trey says. She approves of this. Her dad being suspected would get in her way. 'Didja say it to Mam and the little ones?'

'I did. That's all done and dusted and ready for action. It'll be no bother to you; the whole lot of ye are as sharp as a handful of brand-new shiny tacks, isn't that right?'

'Alanna might get mixed up,' Trey says. 'I'll tell her not to go talking to the detective. Just act scared of him.'

Her dad winks at her. 'Brilliant. She can hide away in her mammy's skirts and not say a word. Much easier for the child than trying to remember this, that, and t'other. Oh, and come here till I tell you,' he says, snapping his fingers as he remembers. 'I've your man Hooper's camera for you; I put it inside, in your room. That's where I went this morning, after I saw you. I knew you wouldn't want Hooper mixed up in this, so I went and got that camera before the Guards could find it. You hang on to it for a few days and then give it back to him, nice and casual-like, tell him you finished your school yoke. Don't be worrying; I deleted everything from the river.'

'Right,' Trey says. 'Thanks.'

'So everything's tickety-boo,' Johnny says merrily. 'Not for poor Mr Rushborough, o' course, God rest his soul,' he adds as an afterthought, crossing himself. 'But we're right as rain. The detective'll have his wee chats, he'll hear nothing interesting, and away he'll go to annoy some other poor feckers. And them lads that called round the other night won't be bothering us any more. All sorted: we'll live happy ever after.'

His plan to keep the family in luxury appears to have conveniently erased itself from his mind, overwritten by this new set of circumstances and their demands. Trey, who took it for granted that this would happen one way or another, is still impressed by the thoroughness of it. She's shifted goals herself a few times in the past couple of weeks, but she still remembers the old ones existed.

The thought reminds her. 'Do you still have to pay back that money?' she asks.

'Rushborough's few bob?' Johnny laughs. 'That's gone. Dust in the wind. I'm free as a bird.'

'His mates won't come looking?'

'Jesus, no. They'll have enough on their plates. More than enough.' He gives her a big reassuring smile. 'Don't you worry your little head about that.'

Trey says, 'So are you gonna leave?'

Johnny rears back reproachfully. 'What are you on about?'

'Now that you don't need to pay Rushborough back. And no one's gonna put their money into the gold, with him gone.'

Johnny comes closer and crouches, hands on her shoulders, to be face-to-face with her. 'Ah, sweetheart,' he says. 'Would I leave you and your mammy to deal with the big bold detectives all by yourselves? God, no. I'm staying right here, as long as ye need me.'

Trey translates this without effort: if he does a runner now, it'll look suspicious. She's stuck with him until the detectives have done their work. This doesn't bother her as much as it would have a few days ago. At least now, for once in his life, the fucker looks like coming in useful. 'Right,' she says. 'Grand.'

He's looking at her like the conversation isn't over. It occurs to Trey that he's waiting for her to ask if he killed Rushborough. She reckons he might have – he was afraid for his life of that fella, but it didn't take any guts to hit the man from behind – but she assumes he would lie if she asked, and it makes no difference to her either way. She just hopes that, if he did it, he had the brains not to leave anything for the detective to find. She looks back at him.

'Ah, sweetheart, you look wrecked,' Johnny says, tilting his head sympathetically. 'You musta got an awful shock, finding him like that. D'you know what you need? You need a good sleep. Go inside and get your mammy to make you a nice bitta lunch and tuck you into bed.'

Out of nowhere, Trey finds herself browned off right down to her bones. She should be over the moon with herself, everything is going great guns, but she hates her dad's guts and she misses Cal so hard she wants to throw back her head and howl at the sky like Banjo. This is idiotic, when she spent half the day with him, but she feels like he's a million miles away. She's grown accustomed to the sense that she could tell Cal anything; not that she does, but she could if she wanted to. What she's doing now is something she can never tell him. Trey is pretty sure Cal's code doesn't allow for straight-out lying to detectives about a murder to dump innocent men in the shite. When it comes to his code, Cal is inflexible. He's equally inflexible about keeping his word, which he takes as seriously as Trey does, and if he doesn't see this the same way as her, he'll think she's breaking her word about Brendan. Cal would forgive her many things, but not this.

She can't remember how any of this is worth it. In practical terms, this makes no difference: she isn't doing this because it's worth it, but because it needs to be done. But it lowers her spirits even further.

All she wants is in fact to go to sleep, but at this moment she despises her dad too much to stay that near him, now that she's done what she needed with him. 'Going to meet my mates,' she says. 'Just came back to leave Banjo. Too hot for him out here.'

It might as well be true; she can go over the mountain and find a couple of her mates, and start putting out her story. Once it takes root, it'll spread, change shape, shake off her mark, and find its way back to Nealon.

'Don't forget to talk to Alanna,' Johnny reminds her, as she turns away. 'You're great with her altogether; she'll do anything you say.'

'Do it when I get back,' Trey says, over her shoulder. Sheila is still standing in the window, watching them.

————

The minute Cal is wrist-deep in harvesting carrots, Mart appears, stumping across the defeated grass with the brim of his donkey hat flapping. Rip bounces up and tries to get Kojak to go for a run, but Kojak is having none of it; he flops down in the raggedy shadow of the tomato plants and lies there, panting. The heat is thick as soup. Cal has already sweated right through the back of his T-shirt.

'The size of them carrots,' Mart says, stirring Cal's bucket with his crook. 'Someone'll rob one of them and give your scarecrow a fine big mickey.'

'I got plenty to spare,' Cal says. 'Help yourself.'

'I might take you up on that. I got a recipe offa the internet for some Moroccan lamb yoke; a few carrots'd liven it up. Do they have the aul' carrots in Morocco?'

'Dunno,' Cal says. He knows why Mart's here, but he's not in the mood to do the work for him. 'You can go ahead and introduce them.'

'I won't get the chance. There's not a lot of Moroccans around these parts.' Mart watches while Cal pulls up another carrot and brushes the dirt away. 'So,' he says. 'Paddy Englishman, Paddy Irishman, and Paddy American walked into a gold rush, and Paddy Englishman never walked out. Is it true 'twas your Theresa that found him?'

'Yep,' Cal says. 'Took the dog out for a walk, and there he was.' He has no idea how Mart came by that information. He wonders if some mountainy man was watching from the trees, the whole time they were by the body.

Mart pulls out his tobacco pouch and starts rolling himself a cigarette. 'I saw the Guards calling in to you earlier,' he says, 'doing their aul' detectivating and investimagating. That car won't stay shiny for long, on these roads. What kinda men were they?'

'The uniform didn't say much,' Cal says, yanking up another carrot. 'The detective seems like he knows his job.'

'And you'd be the man to spot that. Wouldja look at that, Sunny Jim: after all this time, you're finally coming in useful.' Mart licks the rolling paper in one neat sweep. 'I'm looking forward to having the chats with them. I never talked to a detective before, and you say we've got ourselves a fine specimen. Is he a countryman?'

'Dublin. According to the kid.'

'Ah, fuck's sake,' Mart says in disgust. 'I won't be able to enjoy myself talking to him, if I've to listen to that noise the whole time. I'd rather have a tooth drilled.' His lighter isn't working; he gives it a pained look, shakes it, and tries again, with more success. 'Didja get any idea of what way he's thinking?'

'This early on, probably he's not thinking anything. And if he was, he wouldn't tell me.'

Mart's eyebrow lifts. 'Would he not? And you a colleague?'

'I'm not a colleague,' Cal says. 'I'm just another guy who could've done it. And I sure as hell won't be a colleague once he hears about us fooling around in that river.'

Mart shoots him an amused glance. 'Musha, God love you. Are you after getting yourself all in a tither about that bitta nonsense?'

'Mart,' Cal says, sitting back on his haunches. 'They're gonna find out.'

'Did you mention it to him, didja?'

'It didn't come up,' Cal says. Mart's grin widens. 'But someone will, sooner or later.'

'D'you reckon?'

'Come on, man. This whole county knows Rushborough was looking for gold. Half of them have to know about us salting the river. Someone's gonna say something.'

Mart smiles at him. 'D'you know something,' he says, 'you're after settling in so well around here, sometimes I do forget you're a blow-in. Sure, it feels like you've always been here.' He lets out a thin ribbon of smoke between his teeth. The air is so still that it hangs in front of him, slowly dissipating. 'No one'll say nothing about that, Sunny Jim. Not to the Guards. And if someone did . . .' He shrugs. 'This townland's a terrible place for the rumours. Everyone passing on what their auntie's cousin's missus said, adding a wee bitta decoration here and there to make it interesting . . . Stories do get terrible twisted up, along the way. Someone musta got the wrong end of the stick.'

'What if they check the story out, look for online purchases of gold delivered to this area in the last couple of weeks? You're gonna pop right up.'

'I don't trust them banks up in the Big Smoke,' Mart explains. 'Sure, what with the Brexit and all, they could collapse any day. Any man of sense'd feel safer with some of his savings where he can put his hand on them. I'd recommend the same financial strategy to you, sunshine. The gold standard: you can't beat it.'

'They're gonna go through Rushborough's phone. And Johnny's.'

'God, 'tis great having the inside scoop,' Mart says admiringly.

'I knew there was a reason we kept you around. I'll tell you why I'm not worried about what might be on them phones. It's 'cause them two fine examples of manhood weren't just a pair of messers chancing their arm, like myself and the lads. Them two are professionals. They went about this the right way. Thorough-like.'

'Johnny never went about anything thorough-like in his life,' Cal says.

'Maybe not,' Mart agrees. 'But your man Rushborough'd keep him up to the mark, all right. Johnny wouldn't put a toe outa line around that gazebo. There's nothing on them phones.'

His voice has a flat, gentle finality. 'OK,' Cal says. 'Maybe the Guards'll never prove anything about the gold. But they're gonna hear about it. Maybe not what Rushborough and Johnny were trying to pull, but what you and the guys were.'

'And yourself,' Mart reminds him. 'Credit where credit's due.'

'Whatever. Point is, either way, that's motive for someone. Rushborough found out about the river, he was going to go to the cops, someone got scared and shut his mouth. Or someone found out about Rushborough's scam and didn't appreciate it.'

'Is that what you reckon happened?' Mart inquires.

'I didn't say that. I said Nealon, the detective, he's gonna be looking at that possibility.'

'The man's welcome to look all he likes,' Mart says, with a magnanimous wave of his smoke, 'and good luck to him. I wouldn't wanta be in his shoes, but. He can have all the motive in the world, but it's no good to him without a man on the other end. Let's say, for argument's sake, someone lets slip something about gold. Paddy Joe says he heard it from Michael Mór, and Michael Mór says it was Michael Beag that told him, and Michael Beag says it mighta been Pateen Mike that said it but he was six pints in so he couldn't swear to it, and Pateen Mike says he got it from Paddy Joe. I'll tell you one thing for certain: there won't be a soul saying he was at that river, or can name a single man that was. If the gold is anything at all, it'll be just one of them mad rumours that do spring up in a backward wee community the likes of this one.

Morning mist, Sunny Jim, if you're feeling poetical. The minute you try to nail it down, it turns to nothing.'

He mimes it, catching air and holding up an empty hand.

'Someone might have a motive, all right, but who would it be? Here we go round the mulberry bush, bucko, all on a sunny morning.'

Cal goes back to his carrots. 'Maybe,' he says.

'Don't be worrying your head,' Mart says. 'Not about that, anyhow.' He drops his cigarette butt and grinds it out with the end of his crook. 'Tell me something, Sunny Jim,' he says. 'Just to satisfy the aul' curiosity. Was it you that done it?'

'Nope,' Cal says, working his hand fork around a stubborn carrot. 'If I was gonna whack anyone, it woulda been Johnny.'

'Fair enough,' Mart acknowledges. 'To be honest with you, I'm amazed no one's done that long ago. You never know your luck, but; it could happen yet. Was it the child?'

'No,' Cal says. 'Don't even go there.'

'I'll admit I can't see any reason why she woulda bothered her arse,' Mart says agreeably, ignoring his tone, 'but you'd never know with people. I'll take your word for it.'

'I oughta be asking you the same thing,' Cal says. 'You said you were aiming to do something about Rushborough and Johnny and their con. Did you?'

Mart shakes his head. 'You oughta know me better than that by now, bucko,' he says. ''Twouldn't be my style at all, at all. I'm a man of diplomacy, so I am. Communication. There's seldom any need for anything extreme, if you've the knack of getting your message across.'

'You oughta be a politician,' Cal says. He was just making a point; he doesn't in fact suspect Mart. He can see Mart killing someone, but not until all the more economical options had been exhausted.

'D'you know,' Mart says, pleased, 'I've often thought that myself. If 'twasn't for the farm, I'd love to head for Leinster House and pit my wits against that shower. I'd back myself against that eejit outa the Greens with the prissy aul' Mother Superior head on him, any day. That fucker hasn't a clue.'

He bends over in instalments, favouring his worse hip, to make a careful selection from the bucket. 'I'd love for it to be Johnny,' he says. 'Wouldn't that be nice and tidy altogether? We could be rid of the two of them rapscallions, all in one go. No question about it: if I'd my pick, I'd go for Johnny.'

He straightens up, holding his handful of carrots. 'At the end of the day,' he says, 'it doesn't matter a tap what I think, or what you think. All that matters is what the pride of Dublin City thinks, and for that we'll have to wait and see what way the wind blows him.' He waves the carrots at Cal. 'I'll enjoy these, now. If you spot any Moroccans, send them my way for the dinner.'

––––––––––

After letting it sit in her mind all day, Lena still isn't sure what she thinks about Rushborough being killed. She's hoping Cal, with his experience in this field, will help to clarify it for her. When she arrives at his place, she finds him working his way through a vast heap of carrots on the kitchen table, peeling them, chopping them, and packing them into freezer bags. Lena, who knows Cal's ways, doesn't take this as a good sign. He's like a man buckling down to face a hard winter, or a siege.

She's brought a new bottle of bourbon. While Cal tells her about his morning, she pours them each a drink, heavy on the ice, and settles herself opposite him at the table, to take over the chopping. Cal is peeling carrots like they threatened his family.

'I'd bet on the guy being good,' he says. 'Nealon; the detective. He's easy with the job, got a light hand, knows how to take his time, but you can tell he can pull out the hard-core stuff when it's needed. If I'da been partnered with him, back in the day, I wouldn't've complained.'

'You reckon he'll get his man,' Lena says, cutting herself a bit of carrot to eat.

Cal shrugs. 'Too early to say. He's the type that does. That's all I'm saying.'

'Well,' Lena says, testing, 'the sooner he gets him, the sooner he'll be outa our hair.'

Cal nods. There's a silence: only the soft monotonous snicks of the peeler and the knife, and the dogs sighing in their sleep, and the buzz of a faraway tractor.

Lena knows Cal is waiting for her to ask whether he killed Rushborough, and she's not going to do it. Instead she takes a sip of her drink and informs him, 'I never laid a finger on your man. Just so you know.'

Cal's taken-aback face makes her laugh, and after a second he grins too. 'Well, it woulda been indelicate to ask,' he says, 'but I guess that's good to know.'

'I didn't want you too scared to go to sleep tonight,' Lena explains. 'I couldn't be doing with you tossing and turning in the bed, wondering were you in with a homicidal maniac.'

'Well,' Cal says, 'neither are you. I'm not mourning the guy, but I didn't touch him either.'

Lena reckoned that anyway. She doesn't consider Cal to be incapable of killing, but if he did, she doesn't believe this is who or how it would be. Trey needs him around; that ties his hands.

She says, 'So who's your money on?'

Cal, turning back to his carrots, tilts his head noncommittally. 'Nealon asked me that too. I said Johnny. I don't know if I believe that, but he's the one that makes the most sense.'

Lena says, 'He showed up at my house last night.'

Cal looks up fast. 'Johnny did?'

'The man himself.'

'What'd he want?'

'He wanted rescuing from his own eejitry, is what. It's after getting out that his gold is a loada shite.'

'Yeah,' Cal says. 'I told Mart.'

From the moment she drove off and left Mart waving by Cal's gate, Lena suspected that would happen. Hearing it confirmed still makes her shoulders brace. Lena, who has been called cold plenty of times and acknowledges some truth in that, recognises it when she sees it: under all the chat and the mischief, which are real enough, Mart is cold as stone. She understands why Cal did what he did. She just hopes he turns out to be right.

'Well,' she says, 'Mart listened. Johnny had a warning, he said. He wasn't sure from who, but it was clear enough: get out or we'll burn you out.'

'What the *fuck*,' Cal says, putting down what's in his hands.

'What'd you expect?'

'Mart'd tell Johnny his big idea was tanked and there was no point sticking around. Maybe a few of them would give him a beat-down, I dunno. I was just trying to get the kid out of this mess. Not get her set on *fire*.'

He's ready to speed up the mountain and rip Trey away from that house, by force if needed. 'They won't be burned out,' Lena says. 'Not when they're at home, anyhow. The lads'd be careful about that.'

'Jesus Christ,' Cal says. 'The hell am I doing in this fucking place?'

'Johnny was panicking, last night,' Lena says. 'That's all. He didn't think this through, he got in deeper than he expected, and he lost the head. He could only ever handle things when they went his way.'

'Right,' Cal says. He shakes off the shot of fear and makes himself go back to his carrots. 'What'd he want you to do about it?'

'Talk to people. You. Noreen. Get the dogs called off.'

'What the hell,' Cal says. 'Why you?'

Lena raises an eyebrow at him. 'You don't reckon I've the diplomatic skills for it?'

She doesn't get a grin. 'You don't get mixed up in townland business. Johnny's not a moron, he has to know that. Why'd he go hassling you?'

Lena shrugs. 'I'd say that's why. He reckoned I wouldn't care what he was trying to put over on this place. He started off with old times' sake – you know I don't deserve this, I'm no angel but you know I'm not as bad as I'm painted, you're the only one that ever gave me a chance, all that jazz. He's awful charming when he wants to be, is Johnny, and he wanted to last night. He was scared, all right.'

'Gee,' Cal says. 'Sure sounds charming. "Hey, I got myself in trouble by being a shitheel and not even being smart about it, could you be a doll and pull me out?"'

'That's what I said to him, more or less: his poor misunderstood self wasn't my problem. He switched tack then: if I wouldn't help him for his own sake, I had to do it for Trey's.'

'Surprise,' Cal says. If Lena didn't know him so well, she wouldn't have caught the flash of anger.

'Yeah. He said he owed Rushborough money – did you know that?'

'Yeah.'

'And he had to make this work, or else Trey would end up either bet up or burnt, and did I want to see that happen. I'd had my fill of him by then. I told him if he gave a shite about Trey, he'd fuck off back to London and take his mess with him. We didn't part on the best of terms.'

Cal's eyebrows draw down. 'He give you any hassle?'

Lena blows out a contemptuous puff of air. 'God, no. He threw some kinda tantrum, but I don't know the details, 'cause I shut the door on him. In the end he flounced off.'

Cal goes silent, and Lena watches his face while he thinks. The knot between his eyebrows loosens, leaving him intent and closed. 'What time was he at your place?'

'Eight o'clock, maybe. Mighta been a bit after.'

'He stay long?'

'Half an hour, about. It took him a while to work round to what he was after; he had to go on about the view first, and a lovely wee pair of lambs he saw on his way over. That fella can't go at anything straight.'

Lena was wondering whether Cal would react like this, like a cop. He got there in the end, but it came last.

'A tantrum,' Cal says. 'What kind? Like sobbing and begging, or like yelling and banging on the door?'

'In between. I went in the kitchen and turned on a bitta music for myself, so I didn't catch the whole thing, but there was drama. Loads of shouting about how it'd be my fault if the lotta them ended up burnt to death, and would I be able to live with myself. I didn't pay him any notice.'

'You see which way he went?'

'I wasn't looking out the window. If that little fecker's face popped up, I didn't want to see it.'

'Anyone else he mighta gone to, asked them to call off the dogs?'

Lena considers this and shakes her head. 'No one I can think of. Most people had no time for him before this. And everyone got awful caught up in that gold: if they found out it was all a load of bollox, they'd reckon he deserved to be burnt out. There might be a woman somewhere that's got a soft spot left over for him, but if there was, he'da gone to her before he came to me.'

'He could've killed Rushborough,' Cal says. 'You said he was panicking. When he realised you weren't gonna pull him out of his mess, he could've been desperate. Had a few drinks to console himself, maybe, enough to get dumb. Then called Rushborough, gave him some reason why they had to meet.'

Lena watches him, seeing the detective still working in him, fitting together scenarios and turning them over for examination, giving them a tap to see if they hold.

'Would he do it?' Cal asks her. 'Best guess.'

Lena thinks over Johnny. She remembers him all the way back to a cheeky, angel-faced child sharing robbed sweets. The memories overlay themselves too easily on the man; he hasn't changed, not the way he should have. For a moment she sees the full strangeness of where she is now, sitting at a foreigner's table, considering whether he makes a suitable murderer.

'Drunk and desperate,' she says, 'he might. There's nothing in him that'd hold him back from it. I never knew him to be that kinda violent, but I never knew him backed into that kinda corner. He always had a way out, before.'

'That's what I figure,' Cal says. 'This time, he couldn't see any way out. I'd favour Johnny hands down, except for one thing: someone moved Rushborough after he died. They coulda left him anywhere, but they left him right in the middle of the road, where he'd be found inside a few hours. I can't see any reason why Johnny would want that. He'd just dump the guy in a bog, tell everyone Rushborough went off to London and he was gonna go bring him back, and never be seen in these parts again.'

'He would,' Lena agrees. 'Johnny was never one to deal with any hassle he could avoid.'

'I'd love it to be Johnny,' Cal says, 'but I can't get round that.' He passes another peeled carrot across the table to her.

Lena knows the signs of Cal not saying something. His shoulders are hunched too hard, and his eyes spend too little time on hers. Something, beyond the obvious, is at him.

'Did you tell Nealon about the gold?' she asks.

'Nope,' Cal says. 'And I told Trey to keep her mouth shut, too.'

Lena hides her surprise in a sip of her drink. She knew he wanted to leave his job behind, but she doubts he had this distance in mind, not till Trey needed shielding. His face tells her nothing about what this means to him.

'Well,' she says, 'she's good at that, anyhow.'

'According to Mart,' Cal says, 'everyone in the whole townland is gonna do the same.'

'He might be right,' Lena says. 'And without that, your man Nealon won't have a lot to go on. We'll have to wait and see what way the cat jumps.'

'He's not gonna tell me.'

'Not Nealon,' Lena says. 'This place.'

The surprise on Cal's face, as he looks up, tells her this hasn't even occurred to him. Just because he's seen more than enough of what this place is willing to do, he thought he knew its boundaries. She's caught by fear for him, so overwhelming that for a moment she can't move. After two years in Ardnakelty, he's still innocent, as innocent as the tourists who show up looking for leprechauns and redheaded colleens in shawls; as innocent as Rushborough, swanning in to rip off the gullible savages, and look where that got him.

'What are they saying?' he asks.

'I came here straight from work,' Lena says, 'in case you can't smell that. I've heard nothing, except from you. I'll go down to Noreen tomorrow and find out.' Her impulse is to get up and head straight for the shop, but there's no point. The whole of Ardnakelty will have headed for the shop this afternoon, to feed information and speculation into the formidable machine that is Noreen, and see what it pours out in exchange. Tomorrow, when Noreen's had a chance to sort through her harvest, Lena can find a way to catch her alone.

Cal says, 'Trey's giving Nealon the townland.'

Lena stops cutting, more at the note in his voice than at the words. 'Like what?'

'She told him she heard guys talking and moving around, middle of last night, right where the body was. Guys with local accents.'

Lena goes still again while she takes this in. 'Did she?'

'Nah.'

Lena finds her breath taken away by a rush of something that's half pride and half awe. Back when she was a teenager hating the bones of Ardnakelty, all she could think of to do was run as fast and as far as she could. It never occurred to her to stand her ground and blow the place sky-high.

She says, 'Does your man believe her?'

'So far. No reason he shouldn't. She was pretty convincing.'

'What'll he do about it?'

'Ask a whole lotta questions. See what he digs up. Take it from there.'

Lena has her breath back. Trey may be magnificent, but she's in dangerous territory. She's no innocent and no blow-in, but, like Lena, she's kept herself deliberately separate from this place. Lena is only starting to learn how much of the protective barrier this offers is an illusion.

She says, 'I feel like I shoulda seen that coming.'

'How?'

'I dunno. Somehow.' She's thinking of Trey asking her who did that to Brendan. She's glad she didn't share any guesses.

'Yeah,' Cal says. He gives up on his peeling and runs a hand down his face. 'Probably I should've too. It didn't occur to me 'cause she gave me her word not to do anything about Brendan, but I guess she figures she just got lucky and found a loophole.'

His voice is raw with too many things, anger and fear and hurt. Lena has never heard it like this before. 'How far would she take it?'

'Who knows. Nealon could line up half the guys around here and pull her in for a voice ID tomorrow, and I have no idea what she'd do. Identify someone, or what. Her head, these days, I don't have a clue what's going on in there. Every time I think I've figured it out, she pulls something new, and I find out I had the whole thing ass-backwards.'

Lena says, 'Should we do something?'

'Like what? If I tell her I know what she's doing and it's a dumb-ass, dangerous, shitty plan that actually could get her beat up or burned out or whatever people do around here, you think she's gonna listen? All that'll happen is she'll do a better job of hiding stuff from me. What the hell am I supposed to do?'

Lena stays silent. Cal is not, under normal circumstances, a man who lets his moods spill onto other people. She's not upset by it, but she's deeply unsettled by the implications. She finds she can't gauge him any more, what he's capable of once brought to this point.

Cal says, more quietly, 'You figure maybe she'd listen to you?'

'Probably not. I'd say she's got her mind set.'

'Yeah. Me too.' He slumps back in his chair and reaches for his glass. 'As far as I can see,' he says, 'there's not one single thing we could do. Not right now.'

Lena says, 'Is she coming here for dinner?'

'Who knows,' Cal says, rubbing his eyes. 'I doubt it. Which is probably a good thing, because what I feel like doing is giving the kid a good slap upside her head and telling her to smarten the hell up.'

Lena knows to leave it. 'Whatever we make,' she says, 'it'd better be something with carrots.'

Cal lowers his hands and blinks at the table like he'd forgotten what they were doing. 'Yeah,' he says. 'I didn't know if they'd take; I never grew them before. I think maybe I put in too many.'

Lena lifts an eyebrow. 'D'you reckon?'

'This is only half of 'em. The rest are still out there.'

'Jesus, Mary, and Joseph,' Lena says. 'This is what you get for going all back-to-nature. You'll be eating 'em till you turn orange. Carrot soup for lunch, carrot omelette for dinner—'

Cal comes up with a grin. 'You can teach me how to make carrot jam. For breakfast.'

'Come on,' Lena says, finishing her drink and getting up. She figures tonight is a good night for an exception to her no-cooking policy. 'Let's go make a carrot fricassee.'

In the end they settle on beef stir-fry, heavy on the carrots. Cal puts on Steve Earle while they cook. The dogs wake up at the smell and come hinting for scraps. Through the music and their talk and the sizzle of food, Lena can almost hear, all around them out in the warm golden air, the rising buzz and scurry of the townland, and the steady dark pulse of Nealon moving through it.

17

Forty-five minutes before the shop is even due to open, Lena finds Noreen on top of the stepladder with her sleeves rolled up, in a frenzy of whipping things off the shelves and checking their best-by dates, a task that Lena knows usually gets done on Fridays. 'Morning,' she says, poking her head in from the tiny back room where Noreen keeps files, problems, and the kettle.

'If you're here to tell me who kilt that English fella,' Noreen snaps, pointing a tin of tuna at her threateningly, 'you can turn yourself around and walk straight back out that door. My head's feckin' lifting with ideas and theories and – what's that Bobby Feeney had? – hypothesises, what the feck is that?'

'I'd a hypothesis once,' Lena says. 'Wore it to a wedding. Will I make us a cuppa tea?'

'What're you on about? Whose wedding?'

'I'm only codding you,' Lena says. 'I wouldn't have a clue what Bobby'd be on about. Was there aliens in it?'

'What d'you feckin' think? Your man Rushborough was a government investigator, that's what Bobby's got into his head. Sent down here to catch an alien and bring it up to Dublin. All that about the gold, that was just to give him an excuse for wandering about the mountains. Did you ever hear the like?'

'I'd say it's no madder than some of the other ideas going around,' Lena says. 'D'you want that tea?'

Noreen climbs with difficulty down the ladder and plumps down on a low step. 'I couldn't face a cuppa tea. Didja ever think you'd hear me say that? The state of me, look at me, I'm wringing; you'd think I'd been in swimming. And it not even half-eight in the morning.' She plucks at her blouse to fan her chest. 'I'm fed up to my back teeth with this heat. I'm telling you, I'll close up this place and move to Spain, so I will. At least they've the air-conditioning.'

Lena pulls herself up to sit on the counter. 'Cal makes iced tea. I shoulda brought some of that.'

'That stuff'd wreck your insides, no milk in it or anything. And don't be getting your arse on my counter.'

'I'll get down before you open up,' Lena says. 'D'you want a hand with that?'

Noreen gives the tin of tuna, which she's still holding, a look of loathing. 'D'you know what, feck it. I'll do it another day. If some eejit walks outa here with stale custard, it'll serve him right. Coming in here nosing for gossip.'

Lena has never known Noreen to complain about people hunting for gossip before. 'Was the whole place in yesterday?'

'Every man, woman, and child for miles. Crona Nagle, d'you remember her? She's ninety-two years of age, hasn't left the house since God was a child, but she got the grandson to drive her down yesterday. And she'd a feckin' hypothesis of her own, o' course. She reckons it was Johnny Reddy that done it, 'cause one time Melanie O'Halloran snuck outa the house to meet him and came home smelling of drink and aftershave. I didn't even remember Crona was Melanie's granny. Not that I'd blame her for keeping it quiet. Melanie, like.'

'I'd say Crona's not the only one betting on Johnny,' Lena says, stretching to take an apple from the fruit shelf.

Noreen gives her an odd sideways glance. 'There's a couple, all right. The only thing is, why would Johnny want your man dead? That fella was Johnny Reddy's whatd'youcallit, the goose with the golden eggs. With him gone, Johnny's got no fortune coming in, and he's not the big man in town any more, no one'll be buying him drink now and laughing at his jokes; he's the same aul' wee scutter that you wouldn't trust with tenpence. And besides . . .' She stares at the tin of tuna like she'd forgotten its existence, and shoves it onto a random shelf among the dish scrubbers. 'Dessie, now,' she says, 'he says he wouldn't wanta see Johnny arrested. Johnny's weak as water; if that detective fella went after him, he'd spill the beans about all that nonsense with the gold. Trying to get the lads in hot water, like, to take suspicion offa himself. He wouldn't mind what that'd mean for Sheila and the kids; he'd only care about saving his own skin. And Dessie's not the only one. People don't want it to be Johnny.'

Lena finds some change in her pocket, waves fifty cents at Noreen, and leaves it on top of the till to cover the apple. 'Then what do they reckon?'

Noreen blows out air. 'You name it, I've had someone in here saying it. And then they get their ideas mixed in together, till you wouldn't know who thought what— There's Ciaran Maloney came in saying it musta been just some roola-boola with drink taken all round, but then didn't he get talking to Bobby, and he's not fool enough to believe Bobby's blather, but he ended up wondering was Rushborough maybe some kinda inspector sent down to look for people claiming grants they oughtn't to be getting . . .' She shakes her head, exasperated. 'There's a few that think 'twas over land. They reckon the gold was only a whatd'youcallit, a cover story; your man Rushborough had a claim on some land, through his granny, and he was over here sussing it out, and someone didn't take well to that. I know the Feeneys do be awful pushovers, but they wouldn't hand over their land to some blow-in without a fight. Give me one of them apples, go on; maybe it'll cool me down.'

Lena tosses her an apple and puts another fifty cents on the till. Noreen rubs the apple clean on the side of her slacks. 'Clodagh Moynihan's convinced – dead certain, now – that Rushborough stumbled on young people doing drugs, and they put him outa the way. I don't know what kinda notion Clodagh has of drugs, at all. I said to her, why would anyone be at that carry-on in the middle of the night on a mountain road, and would they not just do a runner when they heard him coming, but there's no talking to her. If she hadn'ta been such an awful Holy Mary in school, she'd have more of a clue.'

It occurs to Lena that she, apparently alone in the county, has no hypothesis about who killed Rushborough. She doesn't particularly care. From her perspective, there are a number of other questions that are considerably more pressing.

'Ah well,' she says, biting off another piece of apple, ''tisn't our problem to solve, lucky for us. That detective fella – Nealon, Cal says his name is – he's stuck with it. Didja meet him yet?'

'I did. He came in at lunchtime looking for sandwiches, if you don't mind. I nearly asked him does this place look like a feckin' deli, but in the end I sent him next door to Barty for a toastie.'

Noreen does in fact make sandwiches on occasion, for people she likes. Apparently Nealon doesn't fall into this category, which strikes Lena as odd: she would have expected Noreen, as a gifted amateur, to jump on the chance of cosy chats with a professional. 'What's he like?' she asks. 'I haven't met him yet.'

'Big smiley feckin' head on him,' Noreen says darkly. 'Coming in here, hail-fellow-well-met, joking about the weather, practically taking off his hat to Tom Pat Malone, if he'd had a hat. Doireann Cunniffe nearly wet her knickers for him, so she did. I'd never trust a charmer.' She cracks off a bite of apple with vindictive force.

'Cal says the man knows what he's at,' Lena says.

She catches that odd sideways look from Noreen again. 'What?' she asks.

'Nothing. Who does Cal reckon done it?'

'Cal's retired. He reckons it's not his problem.'

'Well,' Noreen says. 'Let's hope he's right.'

'Go on,' Lena says. 'Spit it out.'

Noreen sighs, wiping sweat off her forehead with the back of her hand. 'Here was me telling you that you oughta quit your foostering about and marry him, d'you remember? And you got up on your high horse. I nearly gave you a clatter. But now I reckon you were right to ignore me, for once.'

Lena knows she's not going to like this. She doesn't like the way Noreen is mincing around it, either. She flattens the urge to whip her apple at Noreen's permed head.

'Why's that, now?' she inquires.

Sitting there on the stepladder with her elbows on her knees, twisting her apple stem, Noreen looks tired. Lena feels like everyone she's seen in days looks tired. Johnny has worn out the lot of them.

'Everyone likes your Cal, now,' Noreen says. 'You know that. He's a lovely fella, a gentleman, and everyone knows it. But if that Nealon goes giving people hassle . . .'

Lena gets it. 'If the wolves get close,' she says, 'they'll have to pick someone to push off the wagon.'

'Ah, for God's sake, don't be feckin' dramatic. No one's pushing anyone. Just . . . sure, no one wants to see their cousin or their brother-in-law locked up for murder.'

'They'd rather see a blow-in.'

'Wouldn't you? If 'twasn't Cal.'

'There's plenty of people from here that I'd only love to see locked up,' Lena says. 'Is there anyone thick enough that they actually believe he done it? Or arc they only saying it outa convenience?'

'What's it matter? They're saying it, either way.'

'How many of them?'

Noreen doesn't look up. She says, 'Enough.'

Lena says, 'And if Nealon makes a pain in the arse of himself, they'll say it to him.'

'Not straight out. No one's going to go accusing Cal of anything. Just . . . you know yourself.'

Lena does. 'Tell us,' she says. 'I'm only dying of curiosity. Why did he do it? For the laugh, is it? Or did he think I was after being swept off my feet by Rushborough's fancy city ways?'

'Ah, Helena, for feck's sake, don't be like that. I'm not the one saying it. I said to them, are ye mad, I said, Cal's no more behind this than I am. I'm only telling you, so you'll know what you've to deal with.'

'And I'm only asking you. Why would Cal go killing Rushborough?'

'I never said he would. But everyone knows he'd do anything for Trey. If Rushborough was one of them perverts, and he laid a finger on her—'

'He didn't. The man was trouble, all right, but not that kind. Do people not have enough drama on their plates, without adding in more?'

'Maybe you know the man did nothing on her. But the detective doesn't.'

Lena knows, without having to think about it, exactly how this will unroll. The talk curling its way around the townland will be gradual, aimless, nonspecific; no one will ever say, or even hint, that it would be simplest if Rushborough had been killed by that Yank over in O'Shea's place, but slowly the thought will thicken and take shape in the air. And down the line, someone will mention to Nealon that she didn't like the way Rushborough looked at her teenage niece; someone else will drop a bit of praise about how Cal is like a father to Theresa Reddy, fierce protective; someone else will point out that Rushborough, as Johnny's friend, must have spent time over at the Reddy house; someone else will mention in passing that Sheila, no harm to her, doesn't look out for that child the way she should. Unlike Johnny, Cal is safe to hand over. He's lived here long enough to understand that, if he squeals to Nealon about the gold, Trey will be in the townland's bad books right alongside him.

'I know you don't like getting mixed up in things,' Noreen says. 'You think I'm blind, or thick, or I don't know what, but I'm not. Why d'you think I was so set on you meeting Cal to begin with? I hated seeing you lonely, and I knew you'd never go near a local lad, for fear of getting dragged into all this place's doings. And now, if people start talking . . . you know what it'll be like. You'd hate to be dragged into that.'

'Well,' Lena says, 'too late. Me and Cal took your advice; sure, doesn't everyone around here know you're always right. We're going to get married.'

Noreen's head pops up and she stares. 'Are you serious?'

'I am, yeah. That's what I came down to tell you. D'you reckon I look better in blue or green?'

'You can't get married in green, it's unlucky— Mother a God, Helena! I don't know whether to congratulate you or— When?'

'We haven't set a date yet,' Lena says. She throws her apple core in the bin and slides down off the counter. She needs to get back to Cal's and inform him of the news, before someone calls round to congratulate him. 'But you can tell all them wee shite-talkers: he's no blow-in now. Anyone who wants to throw Cal to the wolves will have to throw me as well, and I'm not easy thrown. You tell them that, and make sure they hear you.'

———————

Cal is in his workshop, painting stain onto a turned piece of wood. Lena isn't used to finding him there alone. He hasn't put on music; he's just sitting at the worktable, head bent, his brush moving steadily and carefully. For the first time, the workshop, with its neatness and its carefully ordered array of tools, looks like a retired man's brave attempt to keep busy.

'Hey,' he says, looking up as her shadow falls through the window. 'Everything OK?'

'Never better,' Lena says. 'I just came to warn you: I told Noreen we're after getting engaged. I reckoned you oughta know.'

The look on Cal's face makes her burst out laughing. 'Put your head down between your knees,' she advises him. 'Before you go fainting on me. Don't be worrying: I've no intention of marrying anyone.'

'Then what . . . ?' Cal clearly wants to say *what the fuck*, but feels it might come across as impolite.

The laugh has done Lena good. 'There's forty shades of shite going around about Rushborough,' she says. 'One of 'em involves you. I reckoned I might as well stamp that one out before it had a chance to take hold. People'll think twice before they spread talk about a man that's about to be Noreen's brother-in-law.'

'OK,' Cal says. He still looks stunned enough to keep Lena grinning. 'OK. If you . . . OK. I mean, I've got no objection, I just . . . What are people saying?'

'Not a lot,' Lena says, shrugging. 'They're only throwing rumours around, trying them on for size; you know the way. I just don't want them deciding this one fits.'

Cal looks at her, but he doesn't press her. He understands some, at least, of what Ardnakelty is capable of weaving around him, if it should choose to.

The man came here asking for nothing but green fields and peace. Lena knows there was a time when he considered turning around and walking right back out the door. A part of her wishes, for his sake, that he had done it.

'Shit,' Cal says suddenly, realising. 'The damn *pub*. Next time I go in there, I'm gonna get roasted harder'n a Thanksgiving turkey. What are you getting me into, woman?'

'Listen to me, you,' Lena tells him severely. 'You haven't a notion of the slaggings I've put up with, going out with a blow-in and a Guard, and a beardy one at that. You can take your turn and like it.'

'I already get enough crap for coming over here and taking their women. If I actually get engaged to you, they'll probably get me blackout drunk on poteen and dump me on your doorstep in a wedding dress.'

'You'll be only gorgeous,' Lena says. 'Don't let them forget the veil.'

She knows he's wondering what Trey will make of this. She almost points out that they can tell Trey the real story – God knows the child can keep her mouth shut – but she stops herself. Something is going on between Cal and Trey; things are shifting and fragile. Lena shoving her oar in could easily do more harm than good.

'Come here,' she says, leaning in at the window and holding out her hands to him. 'If I was going to get engaged to anyone, I could do a lot worse than you.' When he comes to the window, she gives him a kiss that aims to make him forget everyone else in Ardnakelty, at least for a minute or two.

————

Ardnakelty, as Cal predicted, pounces joyfully on the opportunity to give him copious amounts of shit. Mart shows up on his doorstep right after dinnertime, with his fluff of grey hair slicked down and his donkey hat tilted at a jaunty angle. 'Put on your best shirt, bucko,' he orders. 'I've a pint to buy you.'

'Oh, man,' Cal says sheepishly. 'You heard, huh?'

'Course I heard. This requires a celebration.'

'Aw, Mart. Come on. It's not a big deal. I just figured, we've been together long enough that—'

'It's a big deal whether you like it or not. You've got friends around here that wanta congratulate you properly, and we need something to celebrate, after the few weeks we've had. We didn't win the hurling, so the next best thing is young love. You can't begrudge us that. Go take off that sawdusty aul' rag and put on something dacent, and we'll be off.' He flaps his hands at Cal like he's herding a sheep. 'Don't keep me hanging about. I've a mouth on me like Gandhi's flip-flop.'

Cal yields to the inevitable and heads inside to put on a shirt. He knows that, regardless of engagements, he needs an evening in Seán Óg's. He needs to find out how Trey's story has landed, and what ripples it's sending out.

At least, as it turns out, Mart has restrained himself from extending the festivities to the whole townland. Seán Óg's alcove is occupied by the guys Cal sees most often, Senan and Bobby and PJ and Francie – and, ominously, Malachy Dwyer, although Cal is relieved that no poteen bottles are in evidence so far – but the rest of the pub is its usual sparse weekday self. There are four spindly old guys playing cards in a corner, and two more at the bar exchanging the occasional grunt; they glance up and nod when Cal and Mart come in, but none of them show any inclination towards conversation. Rushborough alive brought everyone out to assess and discuss him; Rushborough dead is something to be talked about in private, or not talked about at all.

Cal is greeted with a collective roar – 'Here comes the bride!' 'Dead man walking!' 'Get this fella a pint, Barty, to drown his sorrows!'

'Jeez, guys,' Cal says, embarrassed and sliding into the banquette as fast as he can.

'We're just pleased to see you,' Bobby explains. 'We don't know when we'll get another chance, sure.'

'This,' Malachy says, tapping the table, 'this is a wake. For your social life, may it rest in peace. Lena won't let you out on the tear with the likes of us reprobates.'

'She will,' Francie says. 'Would you want to look at that big beardy head every evening?'

'I wouldn't wanta look at it any evening,' Senan says, settling himself better on his banquette to get down to business. 'What's Lena at? I thought that one had some sense.'

'I'd say the sun got to her,' PJ says. 'She'd want to get looked at.'

'Ah, now, love's a mysterious thing,' Mart says reproachfully. 'She sees sides of him that we don't.'

'Or else she's up the duff,' Malachy says. 'Is she?'

'Lena's a bit long in the tooth for that,' Senan says. 'So's himself, mind you. Is there any mojo left in the yoyo at this stage, man?'

'Is there *what*?' Cal says, starting to laugh.

'Any fizz in the firecracker. Any spin on the googlies. Fuck's sake, man, don't make me spell it out for you. D'you do the do?'

'He's no chicken,' Mart agrees, eyeing Cal with interest, 'but then again, he's a Yank. With all the hormones and chemicals they'd eat, they could have mad super-sperm on them. D'you have super-sperm, Sunny Jim?'

'What difference does it make?' Malachy says. 'Once he's married, he won't be getting the ride anyway. Enjoy it while you can, man.' He tilts his glass at Cal.

'If he can,' Senan points out. 'He hasn't answered me yet.'

'Fuck all y'all,' Cal says, red and grinning. In spite of everything, he can't help enjoying this.

'And me just after shouting you a pint,' Mart says reproachfully. 'There's gratitude for you. I oughta drink it myself.'

'Tell us, bucko,' Senan says. 'Solve the mystery. What the hell were you thinking, at all? The two of ye looked like ye were getting on great guns. Why would you wanta go wrecking a good thing?'

'I'd say he got religion,' Bobby says. 'The Yanks are always getting religion. Then they're not allowed do the business unless they're married.'

'Where would he get any religion round here?' Senan demands. 'Everyone's Catholic. You don't get that; it's not the fuckin' chickenpox. You're either born with it or you're not.'

''Twasn't the religion,' Mart says. ''Tis the uncertain times that's done it. Some people get awful edgy about that class of carry-on, and they go looking for something to make them feel settled. Wait and see: there'll be an epidemic of weddings around here now. Weddings and babas. So watch yourselves.'

The pints arrive, and the guys toast Cal's marriage loudly enough to draw a few ragged cheers from the main bar. 'Many happy years to you,' Francie tells him, wiping foam off his lip. 'And may there be never a cross word between you.' Francie missed out on the woman he loved, decades ago, and is easily moved by romance of any kind.

'While we're at it,' Mart says, raising his pint again, 'here's to us. You're stuck with us now, Sunny Jim. I wouldn't say that occurred to you, before you went down on one knee. Didja go down on one knee?'

'Sure,' Cal says. 'When I do a thing, I do it right.'

'Good thinking,' Malachy says. 'Get the job done before the aul' joints give out and she has to help you back up again.'

'Till death do us part,' Mart says, clinking his glass against Cal's. 'You're going nowhere now.'

'I wasn't planning on going anywhere anyway,' Cal says.

'I know that. But you coulda, if you'd wanted to. You were a free agent. We're on different terms now, psychologically speaking.'

'We've the divorce, these days,' Senan says. 'If he has enough of our bolloxology, he can divorce Lena and the lot of us, and ride off into the sunset.'

'Ah, no,' Mart says, smiling, his eyes resting thoughtfully on Cal's face. 'I wouldn't say Sunny Jim here is the divorcing type. Once he's given his word, he'd stand by it, come hell or high water.'

'I already got one divorce that disagrees with you,' Cal points out.

'I know you have. I'd bet my life she was the one that ditched you, but, not the other way round. If she hadn'ta kicked you out the door, you'd be there still. Am I right?'

'What are you, my therapist?' Cal demands. He's aware that tonight isn't only, or even primarily, about his engagement. Every-one here has stuff to tell him and ask him, and stuff they want to tell each other about him. Not a one of these things will be said in so many words; lack of clarity is this place's go-to, a kind of all-purpose multi-tool comprising both offensive and defensive weapons as well as broad-spectrum precautionary measures. The only smart thing Cal can do is keep his mouth shut as much as possible and pay attention. The booze won't help. If Malachy has a bottle of poteen under the table, he's screwed.

'I'd make a fine therapist,' Mart says, diverted by this intriguing new possibility. 'There'd be none of this "Tell me about your childhood" blather that's only meant to keep you coming back till your bank account runs dry. Practical solutions, that's what I'd offer.'

'You'd be fuckin' woeful,' Senan says. 'Some poor bastard would come in to you looking for help with the depression, and you'd tell him all he needed was to get a hobby and buy himself a hat with fuckin' – earflaps, or sequins, or some shite. Half the place would kill themselves before the year was out. The hills'd be alive with the sound of shotguns.'

'They would not,' Mart says with dignity. 'They'd be alive with the sound of contented men in elegant headgear learning to play the trombone, or reading up on Galileo. You'll come to me when yourself and Lena hit the rough patches, won't you, Sunny Jim?'

'Sure,' Cal says. 'You can get me a top hat.'

'You'd do better in one of them raccoon ones. With the tail left on.'

'You'll haveta do the Marriage Mile now,' Malachy tells Cal, settling back on his banquette.

'Yeah?' Cal asks. 'What's that?' He sinks a couple more inches of his pint. Each of the guys is going to buy him one to congratulate him, and then he'll have to buy a round to show his appreciation; and, while he's the biggest guy there, the rest have put in a lot more dedicated training. He made himself a hamburger the size of his own head for dinner, as what Mart calls soakage, but he still has a tough evening's work ahead.

'Have you never seen it done?'

'How would he have seen it done?' Senan asks. 'There's been fuck-all marriages here the last coupla years, and all the lads were from outside the parish. Other townlands wouldn't do it,' he explains to Cal.

'Ah, no,' Malachy says. ''Tis an old Ardnakelty tradition. My granddad said it was old when his granddad was young; you wouldn't know how far back it'd go. Thousands of years, maybe.'

'What've I gotta do?' Cal asks.

'You've to get a torch,' Malachy explains, 'and you light it from your hearth fire. Have you a fireplace?'

'What's that matter?' Senan demands. 'I lit mine with a fuckin' Zippo. No one gave a shite.'

'I got a fireplace,' Cal says. 'I'd rather not light it in this weather, though.'

'I'll lend you my Zippo,' Senan says. To Malachy: 'Go on there.'

'You run with the torch through the village,' Malachy says, 'and then up to your woman's house and all round it, and then back to yours. To show the place that you're bringing the two hearth fires together.'

'And you do it in your jocks,' Francie says. 'To prove that you're hale and hearty, and fit to be the head of a family. I heard back in the day the lads ran it naked, but then the priests put the kibosh on that.'

'Huh,' Cal says. 'I better buy myself some fancy new boxers.'

'That's the real reason the lads around here get married young,' Malachy explains to Cal. 'While they can still put on a good show. No one wants to see a big aul' dad bod puffing down the street.'

'I looked like Jason Momoa,' Senan tells him. 'Back when he was on *Baywatch*.'

'You did in your hole,' Francie said. 'The pasty fuckin' legs on you, glowing in the dark all the way—'

'The *muscles* on me. I was a fuckin' ride back then.'

'Well, shit,' Cal says, giving his belly a rueful look. 'Sounds like I better start working out, too.'

'At least you got engaged in summer,' Francie points out

consolingly. 'This fella' – Senan – 'got engaged on New Year's Eve, and he froze his bollox so bad he thought he'd have to call off the wedding.'

'Damn,' Cal says. 'I'm gonna be a busy man. We got traditions where I come from, too, and I gotta cover all those.'

'Have you to wave a flag?' Mart inquires. 'The Yanks'd wave a flag at the drop of a hat. We're different here; we reckon most people probably already noticed we're Irish.'

'No flags,' Cal says, 'but I'm supposed to bring her daddy an animal I shot myself, to show I'm a good provider. Lena's daddy's gone, though, so probably I should bring it to her oldest brother.'

'Mike'd eat a rabbit,' PJ says helpfully. 'He's a great man for the meat, is Mike.'

'Well, that's a relief,' Cal says. 'I don't know what I'da done if he was a vegetarian.'

'Some of them carrots,' Mart advises him. 'They were fierce flavoursome, so they were.'

'I might throw in some of those either way,' Cal agrees. 'And I've gotta build us a bed, too. Most guys just hire a carpenter to do it, these days, but I'm lucky that way.'

'Jesus, man,' Malachy says, eyebrows up. 'You weren't joking about being busy.'

'Nope,' Cal says, smiling at him. 'And somewhere in there, I gotta find time for the ancient tradition of looking a guy in the eye and calling bullshit.'

That gets a roar of laughter, and Malachy takes a couple of arm-punches. 'Didn't I tell you?' Mart says, delighted. 'I told you this lad wasn't some fool of a tourist that'd fall for your guff. I shoulda made you put money on it.'

'Get off me,' Malachy says, grinning. 'It was worth a go. He'da been only gorgeous jogging down the road in his boxers.'

'I'da bought Jason Momoa ones,' Cal says. 'In honour of Senan.'

'He had you there with the rabbit,' Mart says, jabbing Malachy gleefully in the shoulder. 'Admit it.'

'He did not. I was only—'

'Have you really got to bring Mike a rabbit?' PJ asks Cal, trying to get matters straight.

'Nah,' Cal says. 'Probably I oughta buy him a beer, though, just to get on his good side.'

'My round,' Senan says, reminded by this. 'Barty! Same again!'

Cal finishes off his pint to make room for the new one. After all this time, the guys still have the power to impress him by the flawless, impregnable unity with which they come together in a common cause. He passed this test, at least, but he's under no illusion that it'll be the last.

Mart is still gloating at Malachy and Senan, who are defending themselves vehemently. 'I asked Lena to marry me, one time,' Bobby confides in Cal, under cover of the argument. 'I kinda reckoned she'd say no, but I hadta give it a go. I knew she wouldn't give me shite over it either way, d'you see. There's some ones around here, if you proposed to them, you'd never hear the end of it.'

'Well,' Cal says, 'I gotta admit, I'm glad she turned you down.'

'True enough,' Bobby says, struck by this. 'Every cloud has a silver lining, isn't that what they say? Only now there's no one left around here that I can ask.' He sighs, down at his glass. 'That's what I liked about all that carry-on with the gold,' he says. 'I thought I'd a chance.'

'You just liked having a posh cousin,' Senan tells him.

'No,' Bobby says mournfully. 'I liked having a chance. Only I never did. And now he's gone and got himself murdered, and even if I hadda had a chance, I don't now.'

The drink is starting to get to Bobby. 'I never once expected him to get murdered,' he tells Cal. 'That's not the kinda thing anyone could see coming. And now there's detectives knocking on doors, disturbing everyone's dinner. My mammy's digestion was ruint for the whole night.'

At the mention of detectives, the other conversations fall away. The men's feet shift under the table, and then are still.

'I didn't like that fucker,' Francie says. 'The detective. Nealon.'

'He's smooth,' PJ says, 'so he is. Sly. And pretending he's not.'

'I nearly decked the little prick,' Senan says. 'Sitting in my

309

kitchen complimenting my missus's tea, hearty as Santy, like he's an old pal of mine, and then outa the blue he said to me, "I'm working on a list of everyone that had any problems with Rushborough. Is there anyone else that you can think of?" I don't mind him asking questions, it's his fuckin' job, but I mind him thinking I'm thick enough to fall for that.'

'He's a Dub, sure,' Malachy says, the corner of his mouth lifting ironically. 'They'd always reckon we'll fall for their guff.'

'He said to me,' Bobby says, worried, to Cal, 'he said, "No need to come into the station yet, we'll chat here for now." What did he mean by that? "For now"?' He has his glass clutched in both hands.

'If you weren't fuckin' wojous at cards,' Senan says, 'you'd know a bluff when you hear one. He was trying to shake you up, so's you'd give something away. That's how they work. Don't they?' he shoots at Cal.

'Sometimes,' Cal says. The air in the alcove has tightened. They're coming closer to the evening's business.

'I still haven't met the man,' Mart says, put out. 'He called round, but I was away to town. I came home to a pretty wee card through the door, saying he'd try me again. Here's me only dying to make his acquaintance, and he's off bothering the likes of ye who don't appreciate him at all.'

'Tell us, so,' Senan says to Cal. 'What does he reckon?'

'What are you asking him for?' Mart demands. 'Sure, how would he know?'

'He's a fuckin' detective. They talk shop, same as anyone else.'

'He's not a fuckin' detective as far as your man's concerned. He's a suspect, the same as yourself and myself.'

'Are you?' Senan asks Cal. 'A suspect?'

'Nealon wouldn't tell me if I was,' Cal says. 'But yeah, probably, as much as anyone else. I was here. I knew Rushborough. I can't be ruled out.'

'Ah, you wouldn't hurt a fly,' Mart tells him. 'Not without a good reason. I'll be sure Detective Nealon knows that.'

'How does it feel?' Malachy inquires, giving Cal a grin that has a slip of malice in it. 'Being on the wrong side, for a change?'

'Doesn't feel like much of anything,' Cal says, shrugging and reaching for his pint. 'It's just where I happened to land.' In truth, it feels deeply, turbulently strange. It has the ominous savagery of a tornado siren: all bets are off.

'Did your man Nealon interrogate you?'

'He wanted to hear about finding the body,' Cal says. 'That was pretty much it.'

'My God,' Bobby says, struck by this, 'and I never asked you. How was it? Were you awful shook up?'

'He's a *detective*,' Senan tells him. 'You *amadán*. He's seen dead bodies before.'

'I'm OK,' Cal tells Bobby. 'Thanks.'

'Was he in a terrible state? Rushborough, like. Not Nealon.'

'The man was dead,' Francie says. 'It doesn't get much worse than that.'

'I heard his guts was spilling out,' Bobby says. His eyes are round. Cal knows that Bobby is capable of being genuinely shaken, and genuinely concerned for his state of mind, and at the same time probing for information that might come in useful.

'His guts looked fine to me,' he says.

'I know where you got that,' Mart tells Bobby. 'Your mammy heard it off Clodagh Moynihan. I know 'cause I was the one that said it to her. I can't stomach that bitch; I wanted her outa Noreen's so I could do my shopping in peace, and I knew that'd send her running off to tell the world before Noreen could get in there first.'

'So what does Nealon reckon?' Senan asks Cal.

'You tell me,' Cal says. 'You probably know more'n I do. What does Nealon think?'

'He thinks it was someone from around here that done it,' Francie says, 'is what he thinks.'

His voice leaves a small silence in its wake. PJ scrapes at something on the table; Mart picks a midge out of his pint.

'Huh,' Cal says, feeling a response is expected from him. 'How do you know?'

''Cause he's got his posse going all around the place asking who was up the mountain, night before last,' Senan says. 'They're not asking that in Knockfarraney, or Lisnacarragh, or across the river. Just here.'

'The way he went about it was awful confusing,' PJ says, rubbing his head as he remembers. 'He didn't go asking, "Were you up the mountain? D'you know anyone that was?" I'da known how to answer that. 'Twas all like, "What would you be doing up there in the middle of the night? Would you have a good reason for being up there? What about your neighbours, what reason would they have?" I didn't know how to answer him at all, at all.'

'He was aiming to confuse you,' Francie says. 'He's a cute hoor, that fella.'

'Sure, I'm up the mountain anyhow,' Malachy says, 'no excuse needed. They came asking me what cars passed by my house that night, coming from this side or going back down. They've got no interest in the other side; themens coulda been drag racing up and down the mountain, for all Nealon cares. He's got his eye on this place.'

All of them are watching Cal. He looks back at them and keeps his mouth shut. Trey's story has taken root and is spreading, underground, sending out tendrils.

'Now, d'you see,' Mart says, leaning back in his seat to gaze up at the damp stains on the ceiling, 'that's the part that came as a surprise to me. Detective Nealon's feeling awful specific, and I can't see any reason why. He hasn't brought up the subject of gold, that I've heard of; if anyone's mentioned it to him, he's keeping it awful quiet. So what's got him narrowing things down to our wee neck of the woods?' He cocks an inquisitive eye at Cal.

'Could be anything,' Cal says. 'Maybe he tracked Rushborough's phone, and it says he was round here all night. Or maybe it's just 'cause here's where he mostly hung out.'

'Or he could have a witness,' Mart says, with a musing twist to his voice, like the word is foreign and interesting. 'What would that mean, now, Sunny Jim? What would a witness have witnessed?'

Cal has been drinking too fast, aiming to be mannerly and show his appreciation. Regardless of the hamburger, the booze is start-ing to reach him. He feels suddenly and vividly, as he's no doubt intended to, the lonesomeness of his position. He's got Nealon side-eyeing him because he thinks Cal is a local, and the locals side-eyeing him because they think he's a cop, while the truth is that he's neither one and has neither to take refuge in. No matter which set of wagons is circling, he's outside, in the darkness with the pacing predators. He's not frightened by this – Cal has always been practical about fear, saving it for when the danger is solid and close at hand – but the lonesomeness sits as deep as fear. He knows the country outside the window is small and busy with men and their doings, but today something in the hot sunset light hitting the stained glass implies a vast, featureless emptiness, as though he could go out the door and walk himself to death without seeing a human face, or a place to give him shelter.

'I got no idea,' he says. 'I don't read minds. If anyone said Neal-on's got a witness, ask them.'

'There's a terrible loada possibilities,' Mart says with a sigh, 'when you're dealing with the likes of Paddy Englishman. Even dead, you couldn't watch the fucker. The man struck me as being that many shades of dodgy, you wouldn't know which one to keep your eye on.' He glances sideways at Cal. 'Tell us, Sunny Jim: what did your Theresa think of him? Sure, she saw more of him than any of us, what with him being a friend of her daddy's. Did she say he was dodgy?'

'Course she didn't,' Malachy tells him. 'If she was uneasy around him, this fella wouldn'ta let the man near her. Wouldja?'

Cal feels danger rise in the air like heat-shimmer off a road. 'I didn't need any kid to tell me that guy was squirrelly,' he says. 'I got that far all by myself.'

'You did,' Mart concedes. 'You said to me, right up at that bar, you didn't like the cut of him.'

'I've a pain in my hole with Rushborough,' PJ declares suddenly and with force. 'I'd had enough of him even before this, and 'tis only after getting worse. I've my hands full, with this drought. I'm feeding out winter rations; I'll have to sell stock if this keeps up.

I can't afford to be thinking about anything else. He came in here distracting me, getting my hopes up. He's dead now, and he's still distracting me. I want the fella gone.'

PJ mostly doesn't get listened to, but this draws a ripple of nods and low noises of agreement. 'You and all the rest of us,' Senan says, raising his glass. 'We shoulda run the fucker outa town the day he walked in.'

'Young Con McHugh's only devastated,' PJ tells Cal, his long face creased with concern, 'so he is. With the weather the way it is,' he says, 'it'd take a miracle for him to come outa this year OK. He thought your man Rushborough was the miracle, like.'

'More fool him,' Senan says, knocking back the last of his pint.

'We all thought it,' Bobby says quietly. 'You can't be blaming Con.'

'Then more fool all of us.'

'Con's grand,' Francie says. 'He'll have a kiss and a cuddle with the missus and he'll get over it. 'Tis Sonny who's not great. Sonny talks big, but he gets the moods something fierce.'

'That's why he's not here to congratulate you,' PJ explains to Cal. 'He woulda been, only he hadn't the heart.'

'Sonny wishes he'da been the one that kilt Rushborough,' Francie says. 'He never touched him, but he wishes he'd taken his shotgun and blown your man clean away.'

'We all do,' Senan says. 'Your man came swanning in here, making believe he was our salvation. All the while he was fucking us right up the arse.'

Mart, who's been watching in silence from his corner, moves. 'Paddy Englishman was nothing,' he says. 'Forget about him. He was no more than vermin that wandered onto our land and got itself shot, and good riddance.'

'He was no cousin of mine,' Bobby says, simply and a little sorrowfully. 'I shoulda known. I did know, underneath; I just didn't wanta. Like when I asked Lena to marry me. All the things that disappoint me worst, I knew them all along.'

'He was no cousin or neighbour or nothing to any of us,' Mart says. 'There was no reason he shouldn't try to con us outa our money, the same as he woulda conned anyone else he ran across. That's what vermin does: scavenges what it finds. Johnny Reddy's a different matter.'

'Wee Johnny sold out his own people,' Francie says. His deep, slow voice feels like a dark tremor running in the floor, up through the banquettes and the table. 'That's dirty. A dirty thing to do.'

'Sold us to an Englishman, no less,' Malachy says. The men stir at the word. Cal feels something old in the air, stories too long ago to tell, but built into these men's bones. 'Rounded us up and handed us over to him like livestock.'

'Not only us,' Mart says. 'He handed over our parents and our grandparents and all. Fed Paddy Englishman fulla their stories, fattened him up on those till he could talk like he had genuine Grade-A Ardnakelty blood, and then let him loose here. He did a good job, did wee Johnny; I'll say that for him. Once your man gave us a round of "Black Velvet Band", I fell for it, hook, line, and sinker.'

'Your man knew about my great-granddad falling down the well,' Francie says. 'That story was none of his fuckin' business. The man nearly died; the whole townland worked their arses off, getting him out. They didn't do it for some fuckin' gombeen in poncy shoes to try and con me outa what's mine.'

'I'll tell you what else of ours Johnny sold to Rushborough,' Mart says to Cal. 'He sold him our bad luck. It's been a hard year for us, boyo, and getting harder every day without rain. Other years, we mighta laughed in Paddy Englishman's face, but this summer we were ripe and ready for any flimflam merchant that'd offer us some hope to think about when we were low. Johnny knew that, and he handed it over.'

The men are still shifting, slow and heavy, turning their necks and rolling their shoulders like men readying for a fight.

'D'ye know the word "outlaw"?' Mart asks the table in general. 'D'ye know where that comes from? Back in the day, a man that done the dirt on his people was put outside the law. If you could catch him, you could do whatever you chose to him. You could tie him up hand and foot and hand him over to the authorities, if you wanted. Or you could beat the shite outa him, or hang him from a tree. The law didn't protect him any more.'

'You're the law,' Francie says to Cal. 'Would you be in favour of that? It'd be awful convenient. Some wee shitehawk, that you probably didn't like anyhow, wouldn't be your responsibility any more.'

'He wouldn't be my responsibility anyway,' Cal says. 'I'm no kinda law around here.'

'Exactly,' Mart says to Francie. 'Isn't that what I'm after telling you? Shut your trap and listen to me, and you might learn something by accident. The only sensible thing an outlaw could do was leg it. Head for the hills, get himself a safe distance away, and start over somewhere no one knew him. And I'd say Johnny's been giving that option plenty of consideration, the last coupla days.'

'I'd be giving it more than consideration,' Malachy says, one corner of his mouth lifting in a sweet smile, 'if I was in his shoes. I'd run like a rabbit. Johnny must be a braver man than I am.'

'Ah, not braver,' Mart says, waving a finger at him. 'Wiser, maybe. Tell us, Sunny Jim: let's say the bold Johnny ran. What would Detective Nealon make of that?'

'I only met the guy one time,' Cal says. 'Your guess is as good as mine.'

'Don't be acting the maggot,' Mart says. 'You know what I'm getting at. If that was you investigating, you'd think Johnny legged it because 'twas him that kilt Paddy Englishman. Amn't I right?'

'I'd wonder,' Cal says.

'And you'd go looking for him. Not just yourself; you'd have people watching out for him, here and over the water. Red flags on his name on the aul' computers.'

'I'd want to find him,' Cal says.

'Johnny knows that,' Mart says. 'That's why he's still hanging about. He's keeping the head down, he's not strolling into Noreen's to sprinkle his charm over any poor soul that happens to stop in, but he's there.' He nods to the window. Outside, the light is fading;

it puddles sullenly in the stained glass. Cal thinks of Johnny, trapped and humming with tension somewhere on the darkening mountainside, and of Trey methodically going about the business she's set in motion.

'And he'll keep hanging about,' Mart says, 'being a blot on the landscape, till one of three things happens.' He holds up a finger. 'Nealon hauls him away in handcuffs. And then he'll sing like a wee birdie.' A second finger. 'Or Johnny gets frightened enough – of Nealon, or of someone else – that he makes a run for it.' A third. 'Or else Nealon hauls someone else away, and Johnny feels safe to jog on.'

'If Nealon went after him hard,' Francie says, 'he'd jog on all right.'

'Life's a balance, Sunny Jim,' Mart says, to Cal. 'We're always weighing up the things we're most afraid of, and seeing which one weighs heaviest. That's what Johnny Reddy's doing this minute. I'd like to see his personal balance tilt the right way. Wouldn't you?'

Cal can think of few things he would like better than setting Nealon on Johnny's trail. He has no doubt that the guys have an excellent strategy all ready to roll, and that having him on board would help it go down smoothly with Nealon. He finds he doesn't give a shit about the prospect of lying to a detective, as long as it would get rid of that little asswipe Johnny once and for all, shut down this Rushborough business before it gets out of control, and whip Trey's plan out of her hands before it can detonate.

Trey has made it crystal clear that this isn't Cal's territory, and he has no right to trespass on it. It's her place, not his; her family, and her quarrel. Regardless of what level of shit she's pulled, he can't bring himself to go up against her. She isn't a little kid any more, for him to take decisions away from her and make them himself in the name of her own good. She has her plan; all he can do is keep following along behind her, in the hope that, if things go wrong, he'll be close enough.

'One reason I retired,' he says, 'was so I could stop having to deal with people I don't like. Johnny Reddy's a shitbird and I don't like him. That means I don't plan on having any dealings with him ever again. As far as I can, I plan on ignoring that he ever walked into this town.'

None of the men answer that. They drink, and watch Cal. Dull patches of colour from the window slide along their sleeves and their faces as they move.

Mart sips his pint and regards Cal meditatively. 'D'you know something, bucko,' he says, 'I've a bone to pick with you. You're here, what, two year now?'

'Two and a half,' Cal says. 'Near enough.'

'And you're still refusing to play Fifty-Five. I was willing to cut you a bitta slack while you settled in, but at this stage you're only taking up space, and plenty of it. It's time you started earning your keep.' He shifts on the banquette, with difficulty, and fishes a battered pack of cards out of his pocket. 'Now,' he says, slapping it down on the table. 'Whatever money Johnny left you, get ready to lose it.'

'D'you know what goes well with Fifty-Five?' Malachy says, leaning to reach under the table.

'Oh, shit,' Cal says.

'Quit your whinging,' Malachy says, coming up with a two-litre Lucozade bottle half full of innocent-looking clear liquid. 'This stuff's great for sharpening the mind; you'll learn twice as fast.'

'And you can't get engaged without it,' Mart says. ''Twouldn't be legal. Barty! Give us a few shot glasses there.'

Cal resigns himself to the ruin of everything he had planned for tomorrow, which luckily wasn't much. The night's business was serious enough that Malachy saved the poteen for afterwards, to make sure everyone kept a relatively clear head, but it's over and put aside, at least for now. Mart is shuffling the cards, more deftly than anyone could expect from his swollen fingers; Senan is holding the poteen bottle up to the light and squinting at it to assess its probable quality. 'You asked Lena to marry you?' PJ asks Bobby, his head suddenly popping up as he chews over the conversation. 'Lena Dunne, like?'

Everyone starts ribbing Bobby about his proposal, and PJ about his slowness on the uptake, and giving Cal another round of shit just for the sake of thoroughness. The warmth has flowed back into the air, stronger than ever. What gets to Cal is that, just like everything else that's passed in the alcove that evening, it's real.

18

Johnny won't go beyond the boundaries of the yard. During the day he sleeps, fitfully, surfacing every couple of hours to demand a cup of coffee or a sandwich, most of which he leaves uneaten, and to pace around the edges of the yard, smoking, peering into the trees and twitching at the strident buzzes of grasshoppers. Sometimes he watches telly with the little ones on the sofa, and does Peppa Pig noises to make Alanna laugh. Once he kicks a football around the yard with Liam for a while, till the rustles among the trees make him edgy and he heads inside again.

At night he's awake: Trey hears the faint insistent yammer of the telly, the creak of the floorboards as he moves around, the front door opening as he looks out and then closing again. She can't tell who he's afraid of. It could be Cal, or the men of the townland. In her opinion, he'd be right to be afraid of either, or both.

He's still afraid of Nealon, even though the interviews went smooth as silk. Sheila dredged up some reserve of energy and became suddenly more ordinary than Trey has ever seen her, politely offering tea and glasses of water, laughing at the detective's jokes about the weather and the roads. Maeve and Liam, both of whom have known the Guards for the enemy since the first time Noreen threatened them for robbing sweets, explained to Nealon without a blink that Johnny never left the house on Sunday; Alanna peeped out shyly from under Trey's arm, and dived back into hiding whenever Nealon looked at her. Every one of them was perfect, like they were born and bred to it. When the sound of the detective's car faded down the mountainside, Johnny was cock-a-hoop, hugging everyone he could catch, praising them for their brains and their bravery, and assuring them that they're out of the woods with not a thing to worry about in the world. He still jumps every time he hears an engine.

Trey doesn't stay within the yard. She's as restless as her dad, not from fear, but from waiting. She has no way of knowing whether the detective believed her story, whether he's following it up, whether he's getting anywhere, or whether he ignored it completely. She has no idea how long it should take for the story to work, if it's going to. Cal could tell her, but she doesn't have Cal.

She goes out; not down to the village and not to Cal's, but to meet up with her mates, in the evening. They climb walls in a ruined cottage and sit there, sharing a packet of robbed cigarettes and a few bottles of cider that Aidan's brother bought for him. Below them, the sun sits heavily on the horizon, turning the west a sullen red.

Her mates, none of whom are from Ardnakelty, haven't heard anything useful. They don't really give a shite about the detective; mainly they want to talk about Rushborough's ghost, which apparently is already haunting the mountain. Callum Bailey claims a see-through grey man came at him through the trees, snapping its jaws and ripping down branches. He's only saying it to scare Chelsea Moylan so he can walk her home and maybe shift her, but of course after that Lauren O'Farrell saw the ghost too. Lauren will believe anything and has to be part of everything, so Trey tells her there were men in a car hanging around the mountain the night Rushborough got killed. Straightaway, easy as that, Lauren was looking out her window that night and saw car headlights going up the mountain and stopping halfway. She'll tell everyone who'll listen, and sooner or later someone will tell the detective.

Hanging out with the lads has changed. Trey feels older than them, and separate. They're having a laugh like always, while she's watching and measuring everything she says; she feels the heft and ripple of every word, where they hold everything lightly. Before the cider is finished, she heads home. She never gets drunk, but she's tipsy enough that the dark mountainside feels loosely bounded and hard to gauge, as if the spaces outside her line of vision could be closing in on her or expanding faster than she can picture. When she gets in, her dad smells her breath and laughs, and then gives her a slap across the head.

Maeve goes out too. Maeve has mates down the village, or about half the time she does; the rest of the time they've had some massive complicated fight and aren't speaking. 'Where you going?' Trey asks, when she catches Maeve doing something stupid with her hair and checking different angles in the bathroom mirror.

'None of your business,' Maeve says. She tries to kick the door closed, but Trey catches it.

'You keep your mouth fuckin' shut,' Trey says. 'About everything.'

'You're not the boss of me,' Maeve says.

Trey doesn't have the energy to get into it with Maeve. Sometimes these days she feels like her mam, scraped so empty she could fold in half. 'Just keep your mouth shut,' she says.

'You're just jealous,' Maeve says. 'Because you made a balls of helping Daddy, and now he's sending me to find stuff out instead of you.' She smirks at Trey in the mirror, rearranges a strand of hair, and checks her profile again.

'What stuff?'

'I'm not telling *you.*'

'Go on outa that bathroom,' Johnny says, appearing behind Trey in T-shirt and boxers, rubbing his face.

'I'm going out now, Daddy,' Maeve says, giving him a big smile.

'Good girl,' Johnny says mechanically. 'Aren't you Daddy's great helper?' He aims a vague pat at her head as she nudges for a hug, and guides her past him into the hall.

'What's she finding out for you?' Trey asks.

'Ah, sweetheart,' Johnny says, scratching his ribs and pulling out a half-arsed laugh. He hasn't shaved, and his fancy haircut lies lank on his forehead. He looks like shite. 'You're still my number-one right-hand woman. But our Maeveen needs something to do as well, doesn't she? The poor wee girl's been feeling left out.'

'What's she finding out?' Trey asks again.

'Ah,' Johnny says, waving a hand. 'I like to keep an ear out for what way the wind's blowing, is all. What the place is saying, what the detective's asking, who knows about what. Just keeping myself well-informed, like a sensible man – information is power, sure, that's what—' Trey has already tuned out his babble by the time the bathroom door shuts behind him.

Maeve comes back that evening looking smug. 'Daddy,' she

says, shoving herself under his arm on the sofa, where he's staring at the telly. 'Daddy, guess what.'

'Now,' Johnny says, snapping out of his daze and smiling down at her. 'There's Daddy's little secret agent. Tell us everything. How'd you get on?'

Trey is in the armchair. She's been putting up with her dad's smoke and his channel-flipping because she wanted to be there when Maeve got back. She leans over for the remote and switches the telly off.

'It's all totally grand,' Maeve says triumphantly. 'Everyone says their dads are going *mental* 'cause there's detectives calling round talking like they killed your man. And Bernard O'Boyle punched Baggy McGrath in the head 'cause the detective said Baggy said Bernard was up here that night, and Sarah-Kate isn't allowed to hang out with Emma any more 'cause the detective asked Sarah-Kate's dad does he hate the Brits and Sarah-Kate's mam thinks Emma's mam said it to them. See? That detective doesn't think it's you.'

Trey stays still. She can feel victory rocketing like whiskey through every vein of her; she's afraid to move in case her dad and Maeve see it. Nealon is doing the work she set him to, plodding obediently along the path she laid out for him. Down at the bottom of the mountain, among the pretty little fields and the neat smug bungalows, Ardnakelty is ripping itself to pieces.

'Well, God almighty, wouldja look at that,' Johnny says, rubbing Maeve's shoulder automatically. He's gazing at nothing and blinking fast, thinking. 'That's great news, isn't it?'

'Serves them right,' Maeve says. 'For being a shower of bastards to you. Doesn't it?'

'That's right,' Johnny says. 'You done a great job, sweetheart. Daddy's proud of you.'

'So you don't need to worry,' Maeve says, wriggling closer to Johnny. She gives Trey a smirk and the finger, close to her chest so he won't see. 'Everything's grand.'

After that Johnny doesn't leave the house any more. When Maeve presses up against him and asks stupid questions, or Liam tries to get him to come play football, he pats them and moves away without seeing them. He smells of whiskey and stale sweat.

Trey goes back to waiting. She does what she's told, which is mostly housework and making her dad's sandwiches, and when there's nothing to do she goes out some more. She walks the mountains for hours, taking breaks to sit under a tree when Banjo ups his panting to melodramatic groans. Cal told her to be careful out and about, but she's not. She reckons most likely her dad killed Rushborough, and he's not going to kill her. Even if she's wrong, no one else is going to do anything either, not with Nealon buzzing all through the air.

The drought has stripped back undergrowth and heather on the mountainside, revealing strange dents and formations here and there among the fields and bogs. Trey, scanning every dip, feels for the first time a chance she might spot the marks of where Brendan's buried. The bared mountainside seems like a signal aimed straight at her. When something laid Rushborough in her path, she accepted; this is its response. She starts leaving Banjo at home, so she can walk herself to exhaustion without having to take him into consideration. She finds sheep's bones, broken turf-cutting tools, the ghosts of ditches and foundation walls, but nothing of Brendan. Something more is required of her.

She feels like she's somewhere other than her own life; like she's been coming loose from it ever since the morning her dad strolled back into town, and now the last thread has snapped and she's drifting outside of it altogether. Her hands, cutting potatoes or folding clothes, look like they belong to someone else.

She doesn't think about missing Cal; she just walks on it all day long, like walking on a broken ankle, and lies down with it at night. The feeling is familiar. After a day or two it comes to her that this is how she felt after Brendan went.

Back then she couldn't live with it. It ate her mind whole; there was no room left for anything else. She's older now, and this is something she chose for herself. She has no right to complain.

––––––––––

Cal waits for Trey. He has a fridge full of pizza toppings, and a tin of the best wood stain mixed and ready to go, like she'll somehow sense them and come to their call. He imagines by now she must have heard about him and Lena, although he can't begin to guess what she'll make of it. He wants to tell her the truth, but in order to do that, he'd have to see her.

What he gets instead is Nealon, tramping up the drive with his suit jacket over his arm and his sleeves rolled up, blowing and puffing. Cal, with Rip to warn him, is waiting on the step.

'Afternoon,' he says. He can't help resenting Nealon, for the painful surge of hope when Rip jumped up and went for the door. 'You on foot in this heat?'

'Jaysus, no,' Nealon says, wiping his forehead. 'I'd be melted. I left the aul' motor out on the road, where your birds won't shite on it again. You've got more patience than I do; I'd've shot the little bolloxes by now.'

'They were here first,' Cal says. 'I just try to stay on their good side. Can I get you a glass of water? Iced tea? Beer?'

'D'you know something,' Nealon says, rocking on his heels, with a mischievous grin breaking across his face, 'I'd only murder a can of beer. The lads can get along without me for a bit. They'll never know the difference.'

Cal puts Nealon in Lena's porch rocker and goes inside for a couple of glasses and two cans of Bud. He knows damn well Nealon isn't taking time off from this kind of investigation just to chug a cold one and shoot the shit on his porch, and Nealon has to know he knows. The guy wants something.

'Cheers,' Nealon says, clinking his glass against Cal's. He raises it to the view, swallows curvetting back and forth between golden cut fields and a blazing blue sky. 'God, this is great, all the same. I know you're used to it, but I feel like I'm on me holidays.'

'It's a pretty place,' Cal says.

Nealon wipes foam off his lip and relaxes back into the rocking chair. He's grown a touch of salt-and-pepper stubble since Cal saw him last, just enough to look rumpled and non-threatening. 'Jaysus, this yoke's comfortable. I'll be going asleep if I don't watch out.'

'I'll take that as a compliment,' Cal says. 'Made it myself.'

Nealon raises his eyebrows. 'That's right, you said something about the carpentry. Fair play to you.' He gives the arm of the chair an indulgent pat that dismisses it as cute but unimportant. 'Listen, I'm not being as lazy as I make out. I'm here on business. I reckoned you wouldn't say no to an update on the case. And I'll be honest with you, I wouldn't mind a second opinion from someone who's got the inside scoop. Local consultant, like.'

'Happy to help,' Cal says. He rubs Rip's head, nudging him to settle down, but Rip is still bouncy from the thrill of a visitor; he takes off, down the yard and through the gate into the back field, to hassle the swallows. 'Not sure how much use I'll be, though.'

Nealon flaps a hand like Cal's being self-deprecating, and takes another swig of his beer. 'Your man's name wasn't Rushborough,' he says. 'Didja guess that already?'

'I had my doubts,' Cal says.

Nealon grins at him. 'I know you did. You caught the smell off him, yeah?'

'I wasn't sure,' Cal says. 'Who was he?'

'Fella called Terence Blake. Not a nice fella. He was from London, like he said; the Met have had their eye on him for a while now. He had a bit of a line in money laundering, bit of a line in drugs, bit of a line in brassers – he liked to keep his portfolio diversified, Terry did. He was no Mr Big, but he'd built up a solid little organisation for himself.'

'Huh,' Cal says. He's getting warier by the minute. Nealon shouldn't be telling him this. 'Was Johnny Reddy one of his boys?'

Nealon shrugs. 'He's not on the Met's radar, but that doesn't say; if he was only hanging round the edges, they could've missed him. Johnny says he hadn't a clue about any of it. As far as he knew, a lovely fella called Cillian Rushborough got talking to him in the pub, Johnny mentioned he was heading home to Ardnakelty soon, and Rushborough was only dying to see the place. Johnny's shocked, so he is, to find out that wasn't the truth. Shocked.'

Cal doesn't ask whether Nealon believes any or all of it. He understands the parameters of this conversation. He has licence to ask about facts, although he may not get answers, or true ones. Inquiring about Nealon's thoughts would be overstepping.

'Blake have any connections here?' he asks.

'Great minds,' Nealon says approvingly. 'I asked myself the same thing. Not a one, as far as we've found. All that about his granny being from round here, that was bollox: he was English straight through. Never set foot in the country before, that we know of.'

Nealon's rhythms, in their familiarity, are distracting Cal so that he has to snap himself back to listen to the words. If he had thought about it, he would have expected an Irish detective to sound different from the ones he used to know. The accent is different, the slang and the sentence shapes, but under all that, the blunt, driving rhythms are the same.

'That could've been what brought him here,' Nealon says, tilting his head to consider his beer glass. 'These small-time setups, they've always got some kinda beef going on. They use amateurs, stupid young fellas, and those lads fuck up or start in throwing shapes at each other: next thing you know, you've got a feud on your hands. Blake could've needed to get outa town for a while. He ran into Johnny, just like Johnny says, and reckoned Ardnakelty was as good as anywhere. From what I've been told, it'd be his style. He was unpredictable, did things on a whim. Not a bad way to live, if you're in his line of business. If there's no logic to what you do, no one can be one step ahead of you.'

Cal says, 'So someone could've followed him over here.' If Nealon is working along those lines, it means he's not hanging his hat on Trey's story. Cal would love to hear that he's found a reason to dismiss it as irrelevant, but he can't afford to let Nealon know he has any feelings on the subject. As far as Nealon is concerned, Trey's story needs to stay a straightforward thing.

'They could, yeah,' Nealon agrees. 'I'm not ruling it out. All I'm saying is, if they followed him over here from London and then found their way all round that mountain in the dead of night, fair play to them.'

'There's that,' Cal says. 'Anything on his phone?' He's had this conversation so many times that it comes to him with the effortlessness of muscle memory. Whether he likes it or not, it feels good to be doing something that comes easily and well. This is why Nealon is telling him too much: to shape him back into a cop, or remind him that he was one all along. Nealon, just like the guys in the pub, is aiming to put Cal to use.

Nealon shrugs. 'Not a lot. It's a burner, only a few weeks old – I'd say Blake started fresh every coupla months. And he didn't use texts, or WhatsApp; he was too cute to put anything in writing. Plenty of calls back and forth with the London lads, and plenty with Johnny Reddy, including a couple of long ones the day before he died – according to Johnny, they were having a chitchat about what sights to go see.' The wry twitch of his mouth says he's not convinced. 'And two missed calls from Johnny the morning you found him. When he was already dead.'

'Johnny's no dummy,' Cal says. 'If he killed someone, he'd have the sense to leave missed calls on their phone.'

Nealon cocks an eyebrow at him. 'Your money's still on Johnny?'

'I don't have money in this game,' Cal says. 'All I'm saying is, for me, those calls wouldn't rule Johnny out.'

'Ah, God, no. He's in the mix, all right. So are a lot of people, but.'

Cal has no intention of asking. His best guess, if he had to make one, is that Trey was accidentally sort of right: one or more of the guys killed Blake and dumped him on the mountain road for Johnny to find, assuming that Johnny would dispose of him in the nearest convenient bog or ravine and then take off running. Only, before he could do that, Trey came along.

They sit watching Rip streak zigzags across the back field, leaping and snapping for the swallows. Nealon sways the rocking chair in easy, unhurried arcs.

'He ever catch one?' he asks.

'He's caught a few rats,' Cal says. 'He'd give a lot to catch a rook, with all the shit they give him, but I don't think much of his chances.'

'You never know, man,' Nealon says, wagging a finger. 'Don't write him off. He's got the persistence, anyhow. I'm a big believer in the aul' persistence.'

The swallows, unworried by Rip's persistence, loop blithely above his head like he's been put there for their enjoyment. Cal would bet Nealon wants a smoke with his beer, but he hasn't asked permission; he's being the perfect guest, not presuming on Cal's hospitality. Cal doesn't offer. He isn't aiming to be the perfect host.

'We got the postmortem results back,' Nealon says. 'Your man Blake died somewhere between midnight and two in the morning, give or take. He took a fierce belt from a hammer, or something like it, to the back of his head. That would've probably done the job on its own, over an hour or two, only it didn't get the chance. Someone stabbed him three times in the chest. Got the heart, boom, finished him off inside a minute.'

'That woulda taken some strength,' Cal says.

Nealon shrugs. 'A bit, yeah. A little kid couldn't've done it. But Blake was out cold, remember. Our fella had plenty of time to pick his spot, lean on the knife to get it through the muscle. You wouldn't need to be a great big bodybuilder.' He takes another swig of beer and grins. 'Imagine that: a bad bastard like Blake, getting taken out by some scrawny little bollox from the arse-end of nowhere. You'd be scarlet for him.'

'I bet he never saw that coming,' Cal agrees. He thinks of Blake in the pub, the arrogant sweep of his eyes around the alcove, faintly amused by the halfwit peasants who believed they had the reins. It strikes him that he's hardly thought about Blake once since he walked away from the body. Alive, the guy spread through the whole townland like poison through water. Now it feels like he barely even existed; all that's left of him is hassle.

'So that does fuck-all to narrow things down,' Nealon says. 'One thing that's going to help, but: the man was a bleedin' mess. Covered in trace evidence: dirt, fibres, bits of plants, bits of insect, cobwebs, rust flakes, coal dust. Some of it was stuck to the blood, so it got there after he was kilt. And not all of it came from the place where you found him.'

'I figured he was moved,' Cal says. And, when Nealon raises an inquiring eyebrow: 'It didn't look like there was enough blood.'

'Once a cop,' Nealon says, giving him a nod. 'You were bang on.'

'Well,' Cal says, 'that fits with what the kid saw.'

Nealon doesn't bite on that. 'And,' he says, 'you know what all that trace means, yeah? When we find the place where he was killed, or the car he was moved in, we should have no trouble showing a match.' His eyes skim leisurely across Cal's back yard, pausing for a second with mild interest on the shed. 'The problem's pinning them down. Sure, you know yourself, I can't just get a warrant to search every building and every car in the townland. I need a nice little bitta probable cause.'

'Damn,' Cal says. 'Long time since I heard those two words. I don't miss 'em one bit.'

Nealon laughs. He stretches out his legs and lets out something between a sigh and a groan. 'Jaysus, this is great. I needed a break. This place is doing my head in.'

'They take some getting used to,' Cal says.

'I'm not talking about the people, man. I'm well used to bog-monsters. I'm talking about the actual place. If this fella had got himself killed in a city, or even a half-decent town, I could've tracked his every move, and yours, and everyone else's, off your phones. Sure, you've done it yourself. Easy as watching a game of Pac-Man, these days.' Nealon mimes with his fingers in the air. 'Beep-beep-beep, here comes Blake, beep-beep-beep, here comes one of them ghost yokes to eat him all up; beep-beep-beep, here comes me with my handcuffs to take the ghost yoke away. In this place, but . . .' He casts his eyes up to heaven. 'Christ al-bleedin'-mighty. There's fuck-all reception. There's fuck-all wi-fi. The GPS works grand until you get too close to the mountain, or in among trees, and then it loses the plot altogether. I know Blake was somewhere near his cottage till around midnight, and after that, fuck me. He's halfway up this side of the mountain, a minute later he's on the other side, then he's back, then he's halfway to Boyle . . . That goes on all fuckin' night long.'

He shakes his head and consoles himself with a swig of his beer. 'Once I get a decent line on a suspect,' he says, 'I can try tracking him, but it'll be no better. And that's if the fella even brought his phone along. Nowadays, with all the CSI, they know more about forensics than I do.'

'One time I pulled in this guy that broke into a house,' Cal

330

says. 'Kid had watched way too many cop shows. Started giving me a hard time about whether I had his DNA, fibres, I don't know what-all. I showed him his dumb ass on CCTV running away. He said that's from the back, you can't prove it was me. I said yeah, but see that bystander watching you run? You're reflected in his cornea. We enhanced the image and matched it to the biometric data from your mug shot. Dumb shit folded like origami.'

That gets a great big laugh out of Nealon. 'Jaysus, that's beautiful. It'd be great if this one turned out to be that thick, but . . .' He's stopped laughing. Instead he sighs. 'If he was, I'd have a line on him by now. But we've talked to every man in this townland, and not one of 'em jumps out at me.'

Cal says, knowing he's taking the bait, 'You're sticking to this townland?'

Nealon's eyes flick to him for a second, intrigued and assessing. 'Theresa Reddy's story checks out,' he says. 'As far as I can check it, anyway. Her da says he heard voices and heard her going out that night, but he thought she just snuck out meeting some pals, so he left her to it. The ma says she heard nothing, but she remembers Johnny sitting up in bed like he was listening to something, and then lying back down again. And my lads found another kid, round by Kilhone, who says she saw headlights going up the mountain and stopping halfway.'

'Well,' Cal says. 'That should help narrow things down.'

'You could still be right about Johnny,' Nealon reassures him. 'He could have pals that'd be willing to come help him move a body, if the shit hit the fan. And himself and the missus could be lying their arses off. Theresa didn't check if her daddy was in his bed before she went out.'

'You get any tyre tracks?' Cal asks. 'Footprints?'

'Ah, yeah. Both, all round where the body was found. Only little bits of them here and there, but; not enough to get a match. Those bleedin' sheep got rid of the rest. And with the weather the way it's been, we can't tell which tracks were fresh and which were there for days. Weeks, even.' He reaches down for his glass. 'Dublin may not be this good-looking, but at least there I don't have to worry about sheep trampling my evidence.'

He laughs, and Cal laughs along.

'So Theresa's story holds,' Nealon says, 'so far. And it's great to have things narrowed down to Ardnakelty. But not one man in the place admits to being up that mountain.'

'I'd be more surprised if they did,' Cal says. 'Guilty or innocent.'

Nealon snorts. 'True enough. And sure, it's early days. I'm only after doing the preliminary stuff. I haven't gone at anyone hard; it's all been the tippy-toes and the nice light touch.' He smiles at Cal. 'Time to start rattling the cages.'

He'll do it well, and thoroughly. Cal can't tell whether he likes the guy or not – he can't see him straight, through all the layers of things going on between them – but he would have liked working with him.

'It'd be great if Theresa could have another think,' Nealon says, 'see if she can put a name to any of the voices. Maybe you could ask her. I got the sense she'd listen to you.'

'I'll ask her next time I see her,' Cal says. The last thing he wants is for Trey to get specific. 'Not sure when that'll be, though. We don't have a regular schedule.'

'What about yourself?' Nealon asks, cocking an eye at him over the glass. 'Would you have any new ideas? Anything you've heard around the place, maybe?'

'Man,' Cal says, giving him a look of disbelief. 'Come on, now. You think anyone's gonna tell me something like that?'

Nealon laughs. 'Ah, I know what you mean. Places like this, they wouldn't give you the steam off their piss, in case you'd find a way to use it against them. But you could've picked something up. I'd say they might underrate you, round here, and that'd be a mistake.'

'Mostly,' Cal says, 'people just want to pick my brains for what I might have heard from you. They don't have much to offer in exchange.'

'You could ask,' Nealon says.

They look at each other. Over the field, the swallows' twitters and chirrs swirl in the warm air.

'I could ask,' Cal says. 'I doubt anyone would answer.'

'You won't know till you try.'

'This place already thinks I'm buddy-buddy with you. If I start sticking my nose in, asking questions, I'm gonna get nothing but a fuckton of disinformation.'

'I don't mind that, sure. You know how it works, man. A few answers would be great, but just asking the right questions could do a lot to get things moving.'

'I live here,' Cal says. 'That's what I do now. Once you've packed up and gone, I still gotta live here.'

He never considered doing differently, but saying the words hits home in a way he wasn't expecting. It's not that he wants his cop life back; that's gone and done with, and he doesn't regret it. But somehow he seems to have spent the last while cutting himself off from everyone round him. If this goes on, he'll wind up a hermit, holed up in this house with no one to talk to but Rip and the rooks.

'No problem,' Nealon says easily. He's too experienced to keep pushing when he'll get nowhere. 'Had to give it a shot.' He settles back in the rocking chair, shifting it to turn his other cheek to the sun. 'Jaysus, the heat. If I don't watch myself, I'll go home looking like a lobster. The missus won't know me.'

'It's some sun,' Cal agrees. He doesn't believe in Nealon's missus. 'I was thinking about shaving off my beard, till everyone pointed out I'd be two-toned.'

'You would, all right.' Nealon examines Cal's face, letting his eyes move leisurely over the bruises, which have faded to faint yellow-green shadows. 'Why'd you fight Johnny Reddy?' he inquires.

Cal recognises the shift as the conversation switches track. He's felt it plenty of times before, but then he was always the one pulling the lever. Nealon's making a point: Cal can be a cop, or he can be a suspect. Just like the guy said, he's rattling cages.

'I didn't fight anyone,' he says. 'I'm a guest in this country. I mind my manners.'

'Johnny says different. So does his face.'

Cal has pulled this one too often to fall for it. 'Well,' he says, lifting an eyebrow, 'then you best ask him the reason.'

Nealon grins, unabashed. 'Nah. Johnny says he fell down the mountain drunk.'

'Then he probably did.'

'I saw your knuckles, the other day. They've healed now.'

Cal glances down at his knuckles, bemused. 'They might've been scraped up,' he agrees. 'My hands mostly are. Goes with the job.'

'It would, yeah,' Nealon acknowledges. 'How's Johnny treat Theresa?'

'He treats her OK,' Cal says. He expected this, and he's a long way from feeling any need to worry. He's on guard, but he was that anyway. 'He's not gonna win any Father of the Year awards, but I've seen a lot worse.'

Nealon nods like he's giving this some deep thought. 'What about Blake?' he asks. 'How'd he treat her?'

Cal shrugs. 'Far as I know, he never said two words to her.'

'As far as you know.'

'If she had any hassle with him, she'd've told me.'

'Maybe, maybe not. You'd never know with teenagers. Blake seem like the type that might take an interest in teenage girls?'

'He didn't run around wearing a badge that said PERVERT,' Cal says. 'That's as much as I can tell you. I hardly saw the guy.'

'You saw enough of him to spot he was dodgy,' Nealon points out.

'Yep. That wasn't hard.'

'No? Anyone else spot it?'

'No one mentioned anything,' Cal says. 'But I doubt I was the only one. When I moved here, I didn't bring up what I used to do, but people made me for a cop inside a week. I'd bet good money that some of 'em, at least, made Blake.'

Nealon considers that. 'They might've,' he agrees. 'No one's said a bad word about the man, but like we said, they're slippery, down here – or careful, if you want to put it that way. Even if they made him, though, why would they want to kill him? They'd just stay outa the dodgy fucker's way.'

Nealon could be testing, but Cal doesn't think he is. Just like Mart predicted, no one has said a word about any gold. 'Most likely,' he says. 'That's what I did.'

Nealon smiles at Cal. 'GPS works grand down here on the flat,' he assures him, 'away from the trees. If I have to check out your phone, you'll have nothing to worry about, as long as you stayed home that night.'

'I was here,' Cal says. 'All evening and all night, till Trey came round in the morning. But if I'd been out killing anyone, I'da left my phone at home.'

'You would, o' course,' Nealon agrees. He arranges his legs more comfortably and takes a pleasurable swig of his beer. 'I'll tell you one interesting thing I've got from the phone tracking,' he says. 'I managed to get a warrant for Johnny's records, seeing as he was the closest known associate. My man Johnny says he was at home all day and all night, before Blake was found. The whole family says the same. Johnny's phone says different, but. During the day, it did what phones do on the mountain, all right: bounced around from this side to that side to the bleedin' Arctic Circle. But in the evening, he was racking up the Fitbit steps big-time. He headed down off the mountain, he passed by here – didja see him?'

'Nope,' Cal says. 'We're not on dropping-in terms.'

'I got that, yeah.' Nealon's eyes flick to Cal's bruises one more time. 'Johnny spent a good while over at Mrs Lena Dunne's place. That's your fiancée, isn't that right?'

'Yep,' Cal says. 'Unless she smartens up.'

Nealon laughs. 'You've got nothing to worry about. I've met her other options. Did she see Johnny that evening?'

'She didn't mention it,' Cal says. 'Ask her.'

'I will,' Nealon assures him. 'Give me a chance, man; I'll get to her.'

'From what you say,' Cal points out, 'Blake didn't die in the evening.'

'Ah, no. And Johnny never went near his place, anyway. But once

335

someone lies to me, I'm interested. And . . .' He points his glass at Cal. 'You mentioned Johnny passing by, while you were hanging on with the body for the uniforms to show up. Guess where he went after he left yous.'

Cal shakes his head.

'He says he went for a walk, to clear his head from the terrible shock. Musha, God love him.' Nealon raises his eyes to heaven. 'Where he went was down to Blake's Airbnb. He spent about fifteen minutes there, and then his phone started doing the mountainy dance again, so it looks like he legged it home. He's got no key to Blake's that we know of, but there's a spare under a rock by the door, right where anyone would look for it. So that's another lie.' He gives Cal a meaningful look.

'Doesn't mean he's your guy,' Cal says, not biting. He's not dumb enough to push Johnny on Nealon, even if he wanted to. 'Blake coulda had something Johnny didn't want you getting your hands on. Another phone, maybe.'

Nealon cocks his head at Cal, curious. 'I thought Johnny had your vote.'

'I don't have a vote,' Cal says.

'Well,' Nealon says, rocking peacefully, 'even if he's not my fella, I reckon he knows something. Maybe he saw someone while he was out wandering, or maybe Blake mentioned he was meeting someone, or had words with someone. Johnny's being smooth with me – saw nothing, heard nothing – but he's keeping something back, all right. I'll get him talking. He should be easy enough to shake up; he has to know he's in my sights.'

Cal nods agreeably. Nealon has moved on. If Cal's not interested in being a mole, and not fazed by being a suspect, he can still come in useful. Nealon is handing him the scraps of bait that he wants scattered around the townland, to get those cages rattling. He wants it out there that he'll be able to match Rushborough to a crime scene or a dump vehicle, that he's tracking phones, that Johnny knows something, and that he's going to spill it.

'Johnny likes talking,' he says. 'Good luck.'

'I'll take that. Well,' Nealon says, slapping his leg, 'I'm not getting paid to sit here enjoying myself. Time to go ruffle some feathers.' He drains his glass and stands up. 'I'll need you and the young one to come into the station and sign your statements. At your own convenience, o' course.'

'Sure,' Cal says. 'I'll find out when she's free over the next coupla days, get her in there.'

'Make sure she knows,' Nealon says. 'Once it's in writing, it's a different ball game. No going back.'

'She's no dummy,' Cal says.

'I got that, yeah.' Nealon tugs his shirt straight over his belly. 'If she was lying,' he says. 'To shield her da, say. Or whoever else. What would you do about it?'

'Jeez, man,' Cal says, grinning at him like it's a big joke. 'Do I need to get a lawyer down here?'

'That depends,' Nealon says, just like Cal has said it a thousand times, grinning right back. 'Is there a reason you'd need one?'

'I'm American, man,' Cal says, holding the grin. 'It's our national motto. When in doubt, lawyer up.'

'Thanks for the beer,' Nealon says. He swings his jacket over his arm and stands looking at Cal. 'I'd bet a few bob that you were a good detective,' he says. 'I'd've liked to have had the pleasure of working with you.'

'Likewise,' Cal says.

'We might still get the chance, one way or another. You never know your luck.' Nealon squints out into the field at Rip, who's zigzagged himself dizzy and is staggering in circles, still jumping for the swallows. 'Look at that,' he says. 'Persistence. He'll get one yet.'

———

'Tell me, Sunny Jim,' Mart says the next day, when he shows up at Cal's door with a lettuce to repay Cal for the carrots – Mart has never shown any inclination to repay Cal for anything before. 'What did the sheriff want with you?'

'He wanted to stir shit,' Cal says. He's had it with dancing around things. The level of subtlety around here is pretty near

337

bringing him out in hives, and if he's a foreigner, he has every right to act foreign. 'And he wanted me to help him. I'm not planning to oblige.'

'He'll do grand without you,' Mart informs him. 'He's stirring plenty of shite all by himself, not a bother on him. D'you know what he's after doing? He spent three hours this morning badgering poor Bobby Feeney. That's dirty, so 'tis. Dirty warfare. 'Tis one thing going after the likes of me, that can enjoy a bitta give-and-take; 'tis another leaving a great soft eejit like Bobby practically in tears, thinking he's about to be arrested for murder and no one to look after the mammy.'

'The guy's doing his job,' Cal says. 'He's gonna go after the weakest link.'

'Weakest link, me arse. There's nothing wrong with Bobby, once you let him go about his business and don't be wrecking his head. We'd take the almighty piss outa him ourselves, but that doesn't mean the likes of this fella has the right to swan in from the Big Smoke and upset him. Senan's bulling, so he is.'

'Senan better get used to it,' Cal says. 'Nealon's gonna keep right on hassling whoever he wants.'

''Tisn't only Senan,' Mart says. His eyes are level on Cal's. 'There's a loada people around here that aren't happy campers at all, at all.'

'Then they all better get used to it,' Cal says. He understands what he's being told. Mart said no one would hold this business against Trey, but that was before there was a dead body and a detective to be reckoned with. Cal knows, better than Mart does, how inexorably and tectonically a murder investigation shifts everything in its path. 'You can thank whoever went and killed Rushborough.'

'Foolish fuckin' thing to do,' Mart says with deep disapprobation. 'I can see why someone would want to bang that shitemonger over the head, mind you; I'm not faulting anyone for that. I wanted to myself. But 'twas fucking foolish to do it.'

His indignation has cooled; he stands mulling it over. 'This wee caper's after letting me down something fierce,' he informs Cal.

'I was expecting a nice bitta crack to while away the summer, and now look at the state of us.'

'You said it was gonna be interesting times,' Cal reminds him.

'I didn't bargain for this fuckin' level of interesting. 'Tis like ordering a nice curry and getting one of them ghost pepper yokes that'd blow the head clean off you.' Mart ruminates, squinting over at the rooks, who are huddled in their oak tree bitching raucously about the heat. 'And apparently the man still isn't stirring enough shite for his own liking,' he says, 'if he's trying to get you on board. What does that mean, now, Sunny Jim? Would it mean his investigation's going nowhere? Or would it mean he's on a trail, and he's looking for something to back him up?'

'I got no fucking idea what it means,' Cal says. 'Mostly I've only got half an idea what any of you guys mean, and I'm too worn out from getting that far to have any brainpower left over for this guy.'

Mart giggles like he thinks Cal's kidding. 'Tell me this much, anyhow,' he says. 'The sheriff doesn't seem like the kind that gives up easy. If he gets nowhere, I wouldn't bank on him scuttling back to Dublin with his tail between his legs. Am I right or am I right?'

'He's not going anywhere,' Cal says. 'Not till he gets what he's after.'

'Well,' Mart says, smiling at Cal, 'we'll have to give the poor man a hand, so. We can't have him cluttering up the place forever, upsetting the weak links left and right.'

'I'm not giving anybody a hand with anything,' Cal says. 'I'm out.'

'We'd all like to be that, Sunny Jim,' Mart says. 'Enjoy the lettuce. I do mix up a bitta mustard and vinegar and shake it all about, but that's not to everyone's taste.'

———

Johnny runs out of smokes and sends Trey down to Noreen's for more. This time she doesn't argue. Maeve exaggerates, and she'd say anything she thinks their dad wants to hear. Trey wants to test the feel of the village for herself.

From outside the shop she can already hear Long John Sharkey's voice, raised and belligerent: '. . . in my own fuckin' house . . .'

When she pushes the door open, he's at the counter with Noreen and Mrs Cunniffe, hunched close. At the ding of the bell, all three of them turn.

Trey nods at their blank faces. 'Hiya,' she says.

Long John straightens up off the counter and moves forward, blocking her way. 'There's nothing here for you,' he says.

Long John isn't long – he got the name because he has a stiff knee where a cow kicked him – but he's built like a bull, with the same bad, pop-eyed stare. People are intimidated by him, and he knows it. Trey used to be. Now she takes the look on him as a good sign.

'Need milk,' she says.

'Then get it somewhere else.'

Trey doesn't move.

'I'll decide who comes in my shop,' Noreen snaps.

Long John doesn't take his eyes off Trey. 'Your fuckin' father needs a few fuckin' skelps,' he says.

'She didn't pick her father,' Noreen tells him tartly. 'Go on home, before that butter melts on you.'

Long John snorts, but after a moment he shoulders past Trey and bangs out the door, setting the bell jangling.

'What's wrong with him?' Trey asks, gesturing after him with her chin.

Mrs Cunniffe sucks in her lips over her buckteeth and cuts her eyes sideways at Noreen. Noreen, swapping out the till roll with fast sharp jerks, looks like she's not going to answer. Trey waits.

Noreen can never resist a chance to share information. 'Them detectives are after giving him awful hassle,' she informs Trey curtly. 'Not just him, either. They've everyone in the place up to ninety. They got Long John flustered enough that he let slip that one time Lennie O'Connor bet up some lad from Kilcarrow for trying to chat up his missus, and now the detectives do be on at Lennie about what did Rushborough say to Sinéad, and Lennie says he won't let Long John lease his back field any more, so he'll have nowhere to put the calves.' She slams the till shut. Mrs Cunniffe jumps and hoots. 'And if your daddy hadn'ta brought that

340

feckin' gobdaw round here, none of this woulda happened. That's what's wrong with him.'

Trey feels the savage surge of triumph right through her. She turns away to the shelves, pulling out bread and biscuits at random, so they won't see it in her. The power of it feels like she could topple Noreen's counter with a single kick and set the walls on fire with a press of her hands.

Now all she needs to do is line up her sights. Lena said she could take a guess at who it was that got Brendan, and Trey trusts Lena's guesses. All she needs is a way to make her tell.

'And forty Marlboro,' she says, dumping her stuff on the counter.

'You're not eighteen,' Noreen says, starting to ring things up without looking at her.

'Not for me.'

Noreen's mouth tightens. She jabs the till keys harder.

'Ah, go on and give the child what she wants, Noreen,' Mrs Cunniffe says, flapping a hand at Noreen. 'You've to take good care of her, now ye'll be practically in-laws.' She bursts into a high, one-note *hee-hee-hee* that carries her out the door.

Trey looks at Noreen for an explanation, but Noreen has her mouth pinched up even tighter and is fussing under the counter among the cigarettes.

'What'd she mean?'

'With Cal and Lena,' Noreen says crisply. She slaps the Marlboros on the counter and rings them up with a neat *ding*. 'That'll be forty-eight sixty.'

Trey says, 'Cal and Lena what?'

Noreen glances up sharply, almost suspiciously. 'Getting married.'

Trey stares.

'Did you not know?'

Trey pulls a fifty out of her pocket and hands it over.

'I'da thought Lena woulda asked your permission,' Noreen says, part bitchy, part probing.

'None a my business,' Trey says. She fumbles her change and

has to pick it up off the floor. Noreen's speculative eyes follow her all the way out the door.

The three old guys sitting on the wall of the Virgin Mary grotto watch her pass without changing expression. 'Tell your daddy I was asking for him,' one of them says.

19

Lena is at the washing line when she sees Mart Lavin stumping towards her, across what used to be her and Sean's back field and is now Ciaran Maloney's. Her first instinct is to run him off her land. Instead she returns his wave and vows to buy a tumble dryer, since apparently nowadays this bloody place won't even leave her the pleasure of hanging out her wash in peace. Kojak, trotting ahead, comes to exchange sniffs with Nellie through the fence; Lena gives them a moment and then snaps her fingers, bringing Nellie back to heel.

'That'll be dry before you get it hung,' Mart says, when he gets close enough. 'This heat's something fierce.'

'No change there,' Lena says, stooping for another armful of clothes. Mart Lavin has never called round to her before, even when Sean was alive.

'Tell me, now,' Mart says, arranging himself comfortably on his crook and smiling at her. Kojak settles himself at Mart's feet and starts nipping through his fur for burrs. 'What's this I hear about you getting yourself engaged to the one and only Mr Hooper?'

'That's old news,' Lena says. 'I thought you'da heard it days ago.'

'Oh, I did, all right. And I congratulated your fiancé properly, although I'd say he's recovered by now. But I haven't seen you to felicitate you, and it came to me today that I oughta do that. Seeing as we'll be neighbours now.'

'We might be,' Lena says, 'or we might not. Myself and Cal haven't decided where we'll live yet.'

Mart gives her a shocked look. 'Sure, you couldn't ask the man to tear himself outa that house, and him only after putting in all that work getting it the way he wants it. Not to mention me putting in all the work getting him the way I want him, give or take. I couldn't be doing with starting all over again. Likely enough, with house prices the way they are, I'd be stuck with some fool of a hipster that'd live on flat white craft beer and commute to Galway every day. No: you'll haveta bite the bullet and move down our way. We're great neighbours to have, myself and PJ. Ask your fiancé; he'll vouch for us.'

'We might keep on both places,' Lena says. 'One for the winter, and one for a holiday home. We'll be sure and let you know.'

Mart giggles appreciatively at that. 'Sure, there's no rush,' he acknowledges. 'I wouldn't say you'd be in any hurry to the altar. Am I right?'

'When we set a date you'll get your invite. Fancy lettering and all.'

'Show us the ring, go on. Amn't I supposed to give it a twist on my own finger, to bring me luck in love?'

'It's in getting resized,' Lena says. She's had this conversation with every woman in the townland, and has decided that if she ever gets an impulse to make another snap decision, she'll have herself committed. She digs a few more clothespegs out of her bag.

Mart watches her. ''Twas a good move, the aul' engagement,' he says. 'A wise move.'

'Funny,' Lena says. 'That's what Noreen told me. The two of ye have a load in common.'

Mart raises an eyebrow. 'Did she, now? I wouldn'ta thought she'da been in favour. Not right now, anyhow.' He shifts his weight to pull a tobacco pouch out of his pocket. 'Have I your permission to smoke?'

'The air's not mine,' Lena says.

'Personally,' Mart says, propping his crook carefully against her fencepost, 'I'm all in favour of you putting a ring on that fella. Like I said, I'm after rubbing the corners off him, but he's got a little way left to go; he doesn't always heed me the way he oughta. It's been a worry to me, the last while. Now that he's your responsibility, we can discuss the problem together.'

Lena says, giving a T-shirt a neat flick to straighten it, 'I've got nothing to say about Cal to anyone.'

Mart laughs. 'God almighty, you're the same as you ever were.

I remember one morning – you were a wee bit of a thing, only this high – you came marching past my gate wearing your First Communion getup, veil and all, and a pair of welly boots. I asked you where were you off to, and you stuck your chin up just like you're doing now, and you said to me, "That's classified information." Where were you headed, at all?'

'Haven't a notion,' Lena says. 'That's forty years ago.'

'Well,' Mart says, sprinkling tobacco into his rollie paper, 'you're the same today, only now you're no wee bit of a thing. You're the woman of the house now, is what you are – whichever house ye settle on in the end. If there's trouble with the man or the child, you're where people will come. And you're where I'm coming.'

None of this is surprising to Lena; it's what she bargained for. She's having second thoughts all the same.

'Lucky for me,' she says, 'neither one of them's the type to make trouble. Unless they've no choice.'

Mart doesn't answer that. 'I like your fella,' he says. 'I'm not the sentimental type, so I don't know if I'd go as far as to say I've got fond of him, but I like the man. I've respect for him. I wouldn't want to see him come to any harm.'

' "Nice fiancé you've got there," ' Lena says. ' "Be a shame if anything was to happen to him." '

Mart, tilting his head to lick his cigarette paper, glances at her. 'I know you're not mad about the idea of yourself and myself being on the same side. But that's where we've landed. You'll haveta make the best of it.'

Lena has had enough of Mart's sidelong ways. She leaves her washing and turns to face him. 'How did you have in mind?'

'The fine Detective Nealon's been all round the townland,' Mart says. 'Interviewing people, like, although he's not calling it that. "Would you have time for a chat?" That's what he says, when he does show up at the door. Very civilised; as if you could say to him, "Go on outa that, young fella, I've the dinner burning on me," and off he'd trot, no problem. Has he been round to you?'

'Not yet. Or I missed him, maybe.'

'I'd say he's starting off with the men,' Mart says. 'And I'd say

I know why. He said to me – halfway through our wee chat, all casual like – "Were you up on the mountain at all, Sunday night?" I told him the farthest I went from home was the back garden, when my fella Kojak here had a bitta business with a fox. And Detective Nealon explained to me that he's been told there was a buncha lads messing about up the mountain, just about the time Rushborough died and just about the place he was found. And he needs to talk to them, 'cause they mighta seen or heard something valuable to the investigation. He can do a voice lineup with his witness, if he has to, but it'd be easier on everyone if the lads cut to the chase and come tell him all about it.' Mart examines his cigarette and nips away a loose thread of tobacco. 'That, now,' he says, 'that's what you might call problematic.'

'Cal said nothing like that to Nealon,' Lena says.

'He didn't, o' course. I never thought he did. Nor does anyone.'

'Then what's he got to do with it?'

'Not a sausage,' Mart says promptly. 'That's what I'm telling you: I'd like to see things stay that way. If I haveta have a blow-in living next door, I could do a lot worse.'

'He's no blow-in now,' Lena says. 'He's my man.'

Mart's eyes flick over her, not in the mindless way a man assesses a woman, but with thought behind them. It's the way he might assess a sheepdog, trying to prise out its capabilities and its temperament, whether it might turn vicious and how well it would come to heel.

''Twas a good move, getting engaged,' he says again. 'I haven't heard a whisper about your fella since you done that. But if Detective Nealon keeps on making a nuisance of himself, I will. I'll be honest with you: you haven't the same clout as, we'll say, Noreen, or Angela Maguire, or another woman that's coaching the camogie and helping out with the parish fundraiser and spreading gossip over the tea and custard creams. If Mr Hooper was Noreen's man, or Angela's, no one would touch him with a ten-foot pole. As it is, they'd prefer to leave him be, outa respect for you as well as for him. But if they haveta, they'll hand him over to Detective Nealon tied up in a bow. If I haveta, so will I.'

346

Lena knew all this already, but coming from him and like this, it reaches her in new terms. Cal is a foreigner, and she's spent the last thirty years trying to make herself into one. She only ever managed to get one foot outside the circle, but when the enemy is closing in, it's enough.

She says, 'You can hand over whatever you like. Nealon can't throw a man in jail with no evidence.'

Mart, unfazed, takes off his straw hat to wave it leisurely in front of his face. 'D'you know something that gives me a pain in the backside?' he asks. 'Shortsightedness. 'Tis a feckin' epidemic. I'll believe a man has good sense – or a woman, or a child – and then, outa the blue, they'll come out with some piece of nonsense that shows they haven't spent two minutes thinking it through. And bang goes another little bitta my faith in humanity. I haven't enough in stock that I can afford to go losing much more of it. Honest to God, I'm ready to start begging people on my knees to just take the two minutes and think things through.'

He blows smoke and watches its slow spread in the motionless air. 'I don't know who fed Nealon that loada flimflam about lads up on the mountain,' he says. 'It coulda been the bold Johnny, o' course, but somehow I don't reckon he'd go outa his way to stir up the townland against him just now, unless he had no choice. If Nealon arrests him it'll be a different story altogether, but for now, I'd say Johnny's got enough sense that he's keeping his mouth shut and his ears open. So let's say, just for argument's sake, that 'twas young Theresa Reddy that did the talking. Will you humour me on that for a moment?'

Lena says nothing.

'And in exchange, we'll say you're right, and there's not enough to tie Mr Hooper to the murder. Or we'll say he doesn't appeal to Detective Nealon as a suspect – sure, aren't the cops known for sticking together, the whole world over? And we'll say there's no evidence to put anyone else up the mountain that night, either. There's poor aul' Detective Nealon, empty-handed – except he's got one person, ready and waiting, in his sights.'

Lena's hands feel weak before she understands why. She stays still and watches him.

'There's one person that admits straight out they were at the scene of the crime. They say there was a few men there, but they've nothing to back that up. And they mighta had a good reason to want Paddy Englishman dead. We all know Rushborough had a hold on Johnny, and we all know Johnny Reddy'd sell his own flesh and blood to save his own skin, not a bother on him.'

He watches Lena from under his tangle of eyebrows, steadily fanning himself. Somewhere a sheep calls, a familiar undemanding sound, far away in the fields.

'Think it through,' Mart says. 'This isn't the time for shortsightedness. What'll happen next? And then what'll happen after that?'

Lena says, 'What is it you want off me?'

'It was wee Johnny Reddy that killed Rushborough,' Mart says, gently but with great finality. ''Tis a sad thing to say about a man we all knew from a baba, but let's be honest: Johnny was always a charmer, but he was never what you'd call a man of conscience. There's people saying Johnny wouldn'ta done it because Rushborough was more good to him alive than dead, but the fact is, the two of them brought over some unfinished business from London. Johnny owed your man a fair bitta cash, and your man wasn't the type that'd take well to being left outa pocket. That's why Johnny came home: he was hoping people here had enough fondness for one of their own that they'd dip into their savings to keep him from getting his legs broke, or worse. And that's why Rushborough came after him: he wasn't going to have Johnny giving him the slip. There might be a few people that heard some wild rumour about gold, but I'd say that's a story Johnny put about to explain what the two of them were doing here.'

He uses his hat to waft his smoke politely away from Lena, and cocks an eye at her. 'Are you with me so far?'

'I'm following you,' Lena says.

'A-one,' Mart says. 'Well, Johnny had a bitta success. There's plenty of people that'll testify, if they haveta, that he came asking them for a loan. Some of them even gave him a few bob, for old times' sake.' He smiles at Lena. 'I'm not ashamed to say I loaned him a coupla hundred quid myself. I knew I'd never see hide nor hair of it again, but I suppose I'm an aul' softie at heart. Maybe your Cal did the same, did he, for Theresa's sake? And maybe his bank statement'd show him withdrawing that few hundred quid, a few days after Johnny came home?'

Lena watches him.

'How and ever,' Mart says, 'Johnny couldn't scrape together the full whack, and Rushborough wouldn't be satisfied with any less than he was owed. There's a few people that'll say Johnny came back to them in the last coupla days before Rushborough died, begging for money again, saying 'twas life or death. Maybe you're one of them, sure. Maybe that's what Johnny was doing round here, the evening before it happened, banging on your door and bellowing outa him.'

He arches an inquiring eyebrow at Lena. She says nothing.

'Johnny was a frightened man,' Mart says. 'And no wonder. I was never a fan of Mr Rushborough; underneath the fancy shirts and the fancy talk, he always seemed like a right hard chaw to me. The Guards must be looking into him, and I don't know what they'll find, but I'd say 'twould frighten the life outa anyone, let alone a wee scutter like Johnny. He couldn't run: if Rushborough had followed him once, he'd do it again. And sure, Johnny wouldn'ta wanted to head for the hills, anyway, leaving his wife and childer unprotected with that fella out for blood. No dacent man'd do that.'

Lena doesn't bother to hide her dry look. 'I'm feeling charitable,' Mart explains. 'No harm in thinking the best of people. One way or t'other, Johnny couldn't see a way out. He arranged to meet Rushborough somewhere on the mountain. Maybe he said he had the money ready for him after all. Rushborough'd be an awful eejit to meet him somewhere lonely, but sure, anyone can get overconfident, specially when he's dealing with the likes of Johnny Reddy. Only instead of paying him, Johnny kilt him. I've heard he hit him over the head with a lump hammer, but then again, I've heard he stabbed him with a screwdriver, either right through the heart or right through the eye. Would you have any information on that?'

'No more than you have,' Lena says. 'Noreen heard he was hit with a rock. But then she heard he was knifed, or maybe his throat was cut. That's as much as I know.'

It sets her teeth on edge to give him even this much. It's a surrender.

'Detective Nealon said nothing to your fella?'

'Not that he's told me.'

'No matter,' Mart says peacefully, dropping his smoke to crush it out under his boot. ''Twoulda been useful to know, but we'll do grand without. Whichever or whatever hit him, that was the end of the bold Mr Rushborough. 'Tis an awful tragic story, and 'twon't be popular with the tourist board, but you can't please everyone. And most of the tourists that come here do be passing through to somewhere else anyway, or else they're lost, so 'twon't do much harm.'

Birds dive in the blue sky behind his head. The mountains are a slip of shadow in the corner of Lena's eye.

'It all hangs together beautiful,' Mart says. 'There's just one wee bitta mud in the waters: that story about a buncha local lads doing something nefarious on the mountain that night. As long as Nealon's got that to contend with, 'tis hard for him to settle comfortably on Johnny, or anyhow Johnny all on his ownio. And I'd like Detective Nealon to be comfortable.'

He arranges his hat back on his head. 'There was no one on the mountain that night,' he says. 'Only Rushborough and Johnny. Whoever's been saying different needs to go back to Detective Nealon and correct the record. I'm not saying they musta seen Johnny leaving the house late that night, not for definite, but 'twould be helpful.'

At his feet, Kojak flops over onto the other side and sighs gustily. Mart bends, painfully, to rub his neck.

'If that loada flimflam did happen to come from young Theresa,' he says, 'nobody'd blame her for making up a story to shield her daddy. Sure, it'd be only natural. Not even the detective himself could hold that against her. As long as she's got the sense to know when 'tis time to come clean.'

He straightens up and pats his pockets, making sure everything is in its proper place. 'If you think of it,' he says, ''tis no more than justice. Regardless of who kilt Rushborough, all this was Johnny Reddy's doing.'

Lena agrees with him on this. Mart sees it in her face, and that she refuses to admit it. He grins, enjoying that.

'Johnny won't go down easy,' she says. 'If he gets arrested, he'll tell the detective about the gold. Try and drop all of ye in the shite.'

'I'll handle Johnny,' Mart says. 'Don't you worry your head about him.' He snaps his fingers for Kojak and smiles at her. 'You just get your house in order, Missus Hooper. I've faith in you. No better woman.'

One of the deep pleasures woven through Lena's life is walking around Ardnakelty. She has a car, but she walks everywhere she can, and counts it among the main compensations of her decision to stay. Lena doesn't consider herself an expert on much, but she takes an expert's fine-tuned satisfaction in the fact that here she could distinguish March from April blindfolded, by the quality of the damp earth in its scent, or tell how the last few seasons have unfolded by watching the movement of sheep in their fields. No other place, however familiar, could provide her with a map that's built into her bones as well as her senses.

Today she drives up the mountain. She doesn't like doing it – not only because of losing the walk, but because right now she would rather be out on the mountainside, where she could catch its every nuance. The car insulates her; she could miss something. But she's hoping that, after she's talked to Trey, they'll need the car. She's left the dogs behind.

Johnny answers the door. For the first time since he came back to Ardnakelty, he has the face he's earned: old, pinched and stubbled, with a faint whiskey blur in his eyes. Even his vanity has gone. He barely seems to register Lena's second of shock.

'God almighty,' he says, with a smile like a tic, ''tis Lena Dunne. What brings you up here, at all? Have you news for me?'

Lena watches his mind zip between hope and wariness. 'No news,' she says. 'I'm looking for a word with Theresa, if she's about.'

'With Theresa? What would you want with Theresa, now?'

Lena says, 'This and that.'

'She's inside,' Sheila says, in the dark hallway behind Johnny. 'I'll get her for you now.' She disappears again.

'Thanks,' Lena calls after her. She says to Johnny, 'Sorry for your loss.'

'What . . . ?' It takes him a squinting moment to work out what she's on about. 'Ah, God, right. Himself. Ah, no, I'm grand – he'll be missed, o' course he will, but sure, we weren't close or anything. I hardly knew him, only from down the pub. I'm grand, so I am.'

Lena doesn't bother answering him. Johnny tries to lounge in the doorway, but his muscles are too tense for that; he just ends up looking like there's something wrong with him. 'So,' he says. 'What's the story from down in the valley-o?'

'You oughta come down and see for yourself, one of these days,' Lena says. 'Take a bitta pride in your work.'

'Ah, here, get away outa that,' Johnny protests. 'This has nothing to do with me. I done nothing on Rushborough. I'm just minding me own business up here, not saying a word to anyone, not saying a word to Nealon and his boyos. Everyone knows that. Amn't I right?'

'Haven't a clue,' Lena says. 'Go ask them yourself.' She doesn't blame him for getting panicky. Johnny's between a rock and a couple of hard places. If Nealon believes Trey's story, then the townland is going to come after Johnny; if Nealon doubts her, then Johnny's going to be top of his list. If Johnny runs, Nealon will hunt him down. For once in his life, Johnny has no easy out. She feels no sympathy for him.

Trey, with Banjo at her knee, appears in the hallway behind him. Lena knows from one look at her face that this won't be easy.

'Come out for a walk with me,' she says to Trey. 'Leave Banjo.'

'Now there's a great idea,' Johnny says. 'Get yourself a bitta sunshine, have a nice chat. Not for too long, now, your mammy'll need help with the dinner, but sure Maeve can—'

Trey gives Lena a quick wary look, but she doesn't argue. She steps out and closes the door on Banjo and Johnny both.

They head up the road, higher onto the mountain, moving themselves well away from the house. Trey doesn't talk, and Lena takes her time, getting her bearings. Like Cal, she's become adept at reading Trey's moods, but today Trey has a feel to her that Lena can't interpret, something unyielding and almost inimical. She's walking at a hard, fast lope, keeping the full width of the road between herself and Lena.

Gimpy Duignan, shirtless in his front yard washing the layers of dust off his car, turns at the crunch of their feet and lifts a hand to them; they nod back without slowing. The heat has shifted, turned denser and heavier. Between the tall spruces, the blue of the sky is thick and smeared like paint.

'I was gonna come see you anyway,' Trey says. She's not looking at Lena. 'Need to ask you something.'

Lena says, 'Go on.'

'Brendan,' Trey says. 'You said you had a guess who done that on him.'

Lena is rocked by the strength of her urge to give Trey everything she has. For generations, this townland has been begging for someone to come along and defy it wholesale, blow all its endless, unbreakable, unspoken rules to smithereens and let everyone choke on the dust. If Trey has the spine and the will to do it, she deserves the chance. Lena only wishes she had got there herself, back when she was young enough and wild enough to throw everything else away.

She's got too old. The risks she takes now are middle-aged risks, carefully gauged to gain the best results with the least damage. Cal and Trey, as well as her changed self, keep her in check. She might still be willing to risk herself; she won't risk them.

'I did,' she says. 'And I told you it's only a guess.'

'Don't care. You know themens around here. Whatever you guess, you're probably right. I need to know.'

353

Lena understands exactly what Trey is doing. In theory, she even approves. Trey could have decided to keep blasting away scatter-gun at a place that's never treated her anything but poorly; instead, she's taking deliberate, accurate aim, and Lena agrees with her that a matter this serious deserves accuracy. She has no idea how to communicate to Trey the chasm between theory and reality.

'I get what you're at,' she says. 'Just so you know.'

Trey glances swiftly across at her, but then she nods, unsurprised. 'I only wanta get the ones that done that on Brendan,' she says. 'Just them. I wanta leave the rest outa it.'

They pass the abandoned Murtagh house, slates coming off the roof and yellow-flowered ragweed growing waist-high up to the door. A bird, startled by something unseen, bursts up from the trees on the slope above them. Lena doesn't look around. If someone is watching, the fact that she's talking to Trey will do nothing but good. Mart will have spread the word, by now, that Lena's been brought to heel.

'That's why I need to know now,' Trey says. 'Before your man Nealon ends up getting set on the wrong people.'

'Right,' Lena says. 'Let's say I give you my guesses, that I pulled straight outa my arse, going on nothing except I don't like the cut of this fella, and that fella had a funny look to him around then. Are you going to stand up and say in court that you heard those lads dumping Rushborough?'

'Yeah. If I haveta.'

'What if I'm wrong?'

Trey shrugs. 'Best I can do.'

'What if some of 'em can prove they weren't there?'

'Then I'll only get the ones that can't. Better'n none. I already *thought* about all this.'

'And then what? You'll come back here and go back to mending furniture with Cal, is it? Like nothing ever happened?'

The mention of Cal makes Trey's jaw set. 'Work that out when I get to it. All I'm asking you for is names. Not advice.'

Lena spent the whole drive looking for the right way to go about this, but all she found was the looming, intractable sense that she's out of her depth. Someone else should be doing this, Noreen or Cal or someone who has a bull's notion of how to deal with teenagers; anyone but her. Trey's feet bite at the dirt and gravel with quick sharp crunches; the urgency thrums off her, barely kept in check.

'Listen to me,' Lena says. The sun comes at her like a physical force, pressing her down. She's doing what she swore she'd never do: bending a child to this townland's will. 'You're not going to like it, but hear me out all the same. I'm not going to give you any names, 'cause they'd do you no good. You'd have to be pure thick to send men to jail on nothing but someone else's half-made-up guesses, and you're no thick.'

She feels Trey's whole body stiffen, rejecting that. 'And now that you hate my guts,' she says, 'I've something I need from you. You need to go into town, to this Nealon fella, and tell him you never saw anyone on the mountain last Sunday night.'

Trey stops moving, balked like a mule. 'Not doing it,' she says flatly.

'I said you wouldn't like it. I wouldn't ask you if I didn't have to.'

'Don't give a shite. You can't make me.'

'Just listen to me for a minute, is all. Nealon has this townland like a hornet's nest; people are going mental. If you stick to that story—'

'I'm sticking to it. Serve them all right if they're—'

'Here's you saying you thought this through, and I'm telling you now, you haven't. Nowhere near enough. You think people are just going to sit on their arses and let you work away?'

'That's my business. Not yours.'

'That's children's talk. "You can't make me, you can't stop me, mind your own beeswax—"'

Trey says, straight into Lena's face, 'I'm *not a fuckin' child*.'

'Then don't be talking like one.'

They're squared off across the path; Trey is set like she's seconds from a fistfight. 'You don't tell me what to do. Tell me who done that on Brendan, and then leave me the fuck alone.'

Lena finds herself, suddenly and for the first time in a long time, losing her temper. Out of all the possibilities in the world, the last way she would have chosen to spend her summer was getting herself tangled neck-deep in a snarl of Ardnakelty drama, with Dymphna Duggan picking through her secret places and Mart Lavin calling round to discuss her relationship. She wouldn't have done it for anyone in the world but Trey and possibly Cal, and now the contrary little fucker is giving her shite for it. 'I'd only *love* to leave you alone. I've no wish to have anything to do with this bloody—'

'Then do it. Go home. Fuck off, if you're not gonna help me.'

'What do you think I'm doing here? I'm *trying* to help you, even if you're too—'

'I don't want that kinda help. Fuck off to Cal's, and the pair of ye can help each other. I don't want you.'

'Shut the fuck up and listen. If you keep on at what you're doing, this townland will tell Nealon it was Cal that kilt Rushborough.' Lena's voice is rising. She doesn't give a damn if everyone on the mountainside hears her. It'll do this place good to hear things said out loud for once.

'They can all go and shite,' Trey snaps back at her, just as loud. 'And Cal as well. Same as you, treating me like a kid, telling me fuckin' nothing—'

'He was trying to look out for you, is all. If he—'

'I never asked him to look out for me! I never asked for anything off either one of ye, only—'

'The hell are you on about? What difference does that make?'

'The *only* thing I asked you for was who kilt Brendan, and you told me to get fucked. I owe you nothing.'

Lena is on the edge of shaking her till some sense comes out. 'So you're grand with Cal going to jail, is it?'

'He won't go to fuckin' jail. Nealon can't do anything on him with no—'

'He can, yeah. If Cal confesses, he can.'

Trey opens her mouth. Lena doesn't give her a chance to get anything out of it. 'If Nealon's got no evidence against Cal or anyone, he'll go looking at the one person that was out on the mountain when Rushborough got kilt. This place'll be well on board with that. Everyone knows you're the one dropping them in the shite; they've the knives out for you already. They'll give Nealon a motive for you and all, tell him Rushborough was abusing you or the little ones—'

'I'm not fuckin' scared of them. They can say whatever they—'

'*Shut up* and listen to me for *one fucking second*. If Nealon starts going after you, what d'you reckon Cal will do?'

Trey shuts up.

Lena leaves her plenty of time before she says, 'He'll say it was him that done it.'

Trey punches straight for her face. Lena half-knew it was coming, but all the same she's barely in time to block the punch away. They stare at each other, breathing hard and balanced like fighters, ready.

'Kid stuff,' Lena says. 'Try it again if you want. It'll change nothing.'

Trey wheels and starts walking fast up the path, with her head jammed down. Lena keeps pace with her.

'You can throw all the tantrums you like, but that's what he'll do. Are you going to let him?'

Trey speeds up, but Lena's legs are longer. She's done talking, but she's not going to let Trey walk away.

They're high on the mountainside, out of the spruce groves and into the wide expanses of heathered bog. Whatever about earlier, no one is watching them now. A small, hot wind strays down from the mountaintop, pulling at the heather with a child's absent-minded destructiveness; the sky off to the west has a dingy haze.

Trey says, down to the path, 'Are you and Cal getting married?'

Lena wasn't expecting that, although she feels like she should have been. 'We are not,' she says. 'I thought you'd more sense than that. I already told you I'm done with marriage.'

Trey has stopped moving again. She's staring Lena out of it, unconvinced. 'Then why's everyone saying you are?'

'Because I told them so. I was trying to get the place off Cal's back. It woulda worked, only for you setting Nealon on them, getting them all stirred up.'

Trey shuts her mouth. She walks on more slowly, her eyes down, thinking. Insects buzz and zip in the heather around them.

'If we hadda been getting married,' Lena says, 'do you not think you'da heard about it before Noreen did?'

Trey glances up sharply at that. Then she goes back to trudging along, scuffing up dust with the toes of her runners. Her silence this time has lost its quality of stubborn resistance; all her mind is on working this through.

'I was an eejit,' she says gruffly, in the end. 'Thinking ye were getting married, like. Not the rest.'

'You're all right,' Lena says. 'Everyone's an eejit now and then. Now's not the moment for it, but.'

Trey goes back to her silence. Lena lets her have all she needs. Things are shifting in the layers of Trey's mind: plates grating across each other, crushing old things and heaving new ones to the surface, faster and more painfully than they should have. There's nothing Lena can do about that; it's a demand of the circumstances and the place, neither of which has any truck with mercy. All she can do is give Trey these few minutes to get her bearings amid her new landscape.

Trey asks, 'How'd you know it was me that said it to Nealon? About men on the mountain that night?'

'Cal. And he said it was a load of shite.'

'He knew I made it up?'

'He did, yeah.'

'Then how come he didn't say it to me? Or to Nealon?'

'He reckoned,' Lena says, 'God help us all, that it was your choice to make. Not his.'

Trey digests that for another while. 'He know you were coming here?'

'No,' Lena says. 'I don't know whether he'da argued with me or not. I'da come either way. You've a right to know what you're in.'

Trey nods. That much, at least, she agrees with.

'I don't blame you for wanting revenge,' Lena says. 'But you haveta take into account where it'll lead, whether you like it or

358

not. That's what I mean when I tell you not to act like a child. Children don't take things into account. Adults have no choice.'

'My dad doesn't,' Trey says. 'Take into account where things'll lead.'

'Right,' Lena says. 'Your dad's not what I'd call an adult.'

Trey turns her face upwards. This high on the mountainside, what's around them is mostly sky, with a wide rim of heather that gives the air a wild, expansive sweetness. A hawk, tilting on currents, is only a flick of black against the blue.

'I had every right,' she says. A deep note of sadness weighs down her voice. 'To get back at them. Whatever way I could.'

'Yeah,' Lena says. She understands that she's won. 'You did.'

'It was going great,' Trey says. 'I done everything right. It woulda been good. And then some fucker went and kilt Rushborough, and ruint it all.'

Something in the way her head falls back, the skid of her eyes across the sky, looks like she's worn too thin: she's done too much trying, come too long a road, she's relinquishing too much. Lena doesn't regret asking it of her, but she wishes with all her heart that she could drive Trey straight to Cal's and send the pair of them out to get a rabbit for dinner, instead of bringing her into town and aiming her into a detective's hands. She wishes, for the thousandth time, that Johnny Reddy had never come home.

'I know,' she says. 'I reckon you're better off this way, myself, but I can see where you'd be pure pissed off.'

'Yeah,' Trey says. 'Well.'

Lena finds herself grinning. 'What?' Trey demands, instantly prickly.

'Nothing. You sound like Cal, is all.'

'Huh,' Trey says, the way Cal says it, and the two of them actually laugh.

———

Trey – settled in the back office of the shabby little Garda station with a Coke and a packet of crisps, in front of a chewed-looking MDF desk with a discreet voice recorder in one corner – plays a blinder. Lena, tucked away on a lopsided chair beside a filing cabinet, is watching for missteps, ready to shift in her chair as a warning, but there's no need. She didn't really expect there to be. When she asked Trey to do this, she didn't overlook the fact that the undertaking would spook many a grown adult. She's also aware that Cal would never have asked such a thing of Trey, who he feels has already dealt with more than enough in her life. Lena thinks differently. In her view, Trey's hard-edged childhood has left her capable of more than the average kid her age. If she makes use of that when it's needed, then at least all she's been through has a point to it.

Nealon makes it easy for her. He putters about, boiling the kettle and keeping up the steady stream of talk, complaining cheerfully about the downsides of the job, staying in B&Bs and leaving the missus to mind the kids, spending his time annoying people who've all got better things to do than talk to the likes of him. Lena watches him and thinks of Cal, and how he must have done this a thousand times. He would have done it well; she can see him at it.

'And it's not like on the telly,' Nealon informs them, pouring tea for himself and Lena, 'where you have the one chat with someone and you're done. In real life, you have the chats with everyone, and then one fella comes back to you saying he needs to set a few things straight. And o' course you've been going off his statement when you talked to other people, so then you've to start all over again. D'you take milk? Sugar?'

'Just milk, thanks. D'you get that often?' Lena asks helpfully. 'People changing their stories?'

'Wouldja stop,' Nealon tells her, passing her a big stained mug that says DAD JOKE CHAMPION on the side. 'You wouldn't believe how often. People get caught on the hop, if you get me, the first time we talk. They feel like they're on the back foot, and they keep things to themselves, or they come out with some load of aul' rubbish. And then they go home and think, *What the hell was I at?* Then it takes them ages to come back in and put things right, 'cause they're afraid they'll get in trouble.'

Trey glances up at him, nervous, but she can't hold his eyes. 'Do they get in trouble?'

Nealon looks surprised. 'God, no. Why would they?'

'Wasting your time.'

Nealon, pulling up his chair behind the desk, laughs. 'Sure, that's most of this job: wasting my time. Filling in this form and that form, and I know no one'll ever look at the bleedin' things, but it has to be done anyway. Come here, can I have one of those crisps?'

Trey holds out the packet across the desk. 'Lovely,' Nealon says, selecting a crisp with care. 'Cheese-and-onion's your only man. Think about it this way: say some fella feeds me a load of rubbish, and then he's got the sense to come back and clear it up before I go making an eejit of myself. Now, if I give him hassle, word'll get around, and the next person who needs to set the record straight, they're going to keep their lip zipped, aren't they? But if I just shake his hand and thank him, nice and polite like, then the next person won't have any problem coming in to me. And everyone's happy. D'you get me?'

'Yeah.'

'When everyone's happy,' Nealon says comfortably, leaning back in his chair and balancing his mug on his belly, 'I'm happy.'

Trey glances over her shoulder at Lena. Lena nods encouragingly. She's trying to look like a respectable pillar of the community, but she's not in practice.

'What I told you that day,' Trey says, and dries up. Her face is pinched with tension. Nealon slurps his tea and waits.

'About hearing lads talking. The night your man died.'

Nealon cocks his head to one side. 'Yeah?'

'Made that up,' Trey says, to her Coke can.

Nealon gives her an indulgent grin and a finger-wag, like he just caught her mitching off school. 'I knew it.'

'You did?'

'Listen, young one, I've been doing this job since you were in nappies. If I couldn't spot someone giving me the runaround, I'd be banjaxed altogether.'

'Sorry,' Trey mumbles. She's got her head well down, picking at the skin around her thumbnail.

'You're grand,' Nealon tells her. 'Tell you what: you can fill out my expense claim for me, and we'll call it quits. How's that?'

Trey manages a small puff of a laugh. 'There you go,' Nealon says, smiling. 'So come here to me: was any of that story true?'

'Yeah. The morning stuff, how I found him. That part all happened like I said.'

'Ah, lovely,' Nealon says. 'That'll save us some hassle. How about the night before?'

Trey twists one shoulder.

'Did you go out at all?'

'Nah.'

'Don't be picking at your nails,' Nealon tells her. He's clearly come to the conclusion, after meeting Johnny, that Trey must be craving a father figure. 'You'll give yourself an infection. Did you hear voices outside?'

Trey obediently flattens her hands on her thighs. 'Nah. Made up that part.'

'See headlights? Hear a car?'

'Nah.'

'We'll start over, so,' Nealon says cheerfully. 'You just slept through the night, is it? Then woke up early and brought the dog for a walk?'

Trey shakes her head. 'Say it out loud,' Nealon reminds her, tapping the voice recorder. 'For this yoke here.'

Trey gives the recorder a nervy glance, but she takes a breath and keeps going. 'I did wake up in the night. Like I said. 'Cause I was hot. Just lay there for a while – I was thinking about getting up and watching the telly, only I couldn't be ars— bothered. After a bit . . .'

She stops and glances over at Lena. 'You're grand,' Lena reassures her. 'Just tell him the truth, is all.'

'Heard someone moving about,' Trey says. Her voice has turned jerky. 'In the house, like. Real quiet. And then the door opening, the front door, and then it shut again. So I went out to the sitting room to look out the window, see who it was.' She glances up at

Nealon. 'I wasn't being nosy. It coulda been my brother, he's only little, and sometimes he walks in his sleep—'

'Listen,' Nealon says, grinning, 'I've no problem with anyone being nosy. The nosier the better. Did you see someone?'

Trey takes a tight breath. 'Yeah,' she says. 'Saw my dad.'

'Doing what?'

'Not doing anything. Going out the gate, just.'

'Right,' Nealon says, very easily. 'You're sure it was him? In the dark?'

'Yeah. The moon was up. Full, like.'

'What did you reckon he was at?'

'At first . . .' Trey's head goes farther down, and she scrapes at something on the thigh of her jeans. 'I thought maybe he was leaving, like. Going off on us. 'Cause he did before. I was gonna go out to him, try and stop him. Only he didn't take the car, so . . .' One shoulder lifts. 'I reckoned it was grand. He was just going for a walk 'cause he couldn't sleep either.'

Her head comes up, and she looks at Nealon straight on. 'Only I knew if I said it to you, you'd think he kilt your man Rushborough. And he didn't. They got on, like. They had no row or anything. My dad, that same night he was talking about how he was gonna bring your man to see this aul' abbey up in Boyle, 'cause your man was into history – like, that's the way he talked about him, just a guy he knew that was in town, not like he was—'

'Jaysus, young one, breathe,' Nealon says, leaning back and holding up his hands. 'You'll give yourself the head-staggers. Cross my heart and hope to die, I've never thrown a fella in jail for going outside his own gate. Like you say, your da probably just needed some air. How long was he gone?'

Trey leaves a second of silence. 'Dunno. I went back to bed.'

'After how long?'

'A bit.'

'Go on, give us a guess. Ten minutes? Half an hour? An hour?'

'Half an hour, maybe? Coulda been less. Just felt long 'cause I was . . .' Trey twitches one shoulder.

'You were worrying he'd done a runner,' Nealon says

matter-of-factly. 'So would I have been. You didn't go after him, just to make sure?'

'Nah. I wasn't that worried, like. Just wanted to wait and see him come back. Only . . .'

'Only he didn't.'

'He musta done, only I got tired. Falling asleep. So I went to bed. Woke up early, but, and I kept wondering, so I went to check if he was in his room.'

'And he was?'

'He was, yeah. Sleeping. Only by then I was awake. And Banjo – my dog – he was looking for a walk, and I didn't want him waking everyone else. So I brought him out.'

'And that's when you found Rushborough.'

'Yeah. The rest was like I told you before.' Trey catches a quick breath, almost a sigh. Her face has loosened: the hard part is over. 'That's why I stayed there so long, before I headed to Cal's. I was trying to think what to do.'

Lena has stopped watching for her to put a foot wrong. She's sitting still, holding her mug and taking in the new subtleties unfurling in Trey, the intricacies that just a few months back she couldn't have fit into her mind, never mind put into skilled action. Trey may be doing Ardnakelty's bidding, but her aims and her reasons are all hers. She's not the townland's creature in this, or Lena's, or Cal's: she's rising up as no one's creature but her own. Lena knows probably she should be afraid for Trey, for where this indomitability might land her – Cal would be – but she can't find that in herself. All she finds is an explosion of pride, firing through her so fiercely she feels like Nealon will sense it and turn. She keeps her face prim.

'Tell us something,' Nealon says, tilting his chair on its back legs and sipping his tea. 'Makes no difference to the investigation, I'm just curious. What made you change your mind today?'

Trey shrugs uncomfortably. Nealon waits.

'I was stupid, before. Made a hames of it.'

'How's that?'

'I wasn't trying to get anyone in trouble. I just wanted you to leave my dad alone. I thought, if I didn't say any names, you couldn't go hassling anyone. Only . . .'

'Only instead,' Nealon says, with a grin, 'I went around hassling everyone. Is that it?'

'Yeah. It all went to shi— to bits. I didn't— I never expected that. I wasn't thinking.'

'Ah, you're fifteen, for Jaysus' sake,' Nealon says tolerantly. 'Teenagers never think ahead; that's their job. Was it something Missus Dunne here said to you that made you change your mind?'

'Nah. I mean, sorta, but not really. Lena came up to ours, to say she'd bring me in here to sign the statement yoke, 'cause my mam couldn't do it, with the little ones. So I told her what I said to you just now, 'cause it was wrecking my head, and I figured she'd know what to do. I was thinking maybe I'd just tell you I made the whole thing up. Not say about my dad going out, like. Only . . .' Trey glances over at Lena again. 'Lena said I oughta tell you the whole thing. She said if I left something out, you'd know, and then you wouldn't believe a word outa my mouth.'

'Missus Dunne's a wise lady,' Nealon says. 'You did the right thing, telling me. Your daddy could've seen something while he was out there – maybe something that he doesn't think was important, or else maybe his mate getting killed sent it right out of his head. But it could be something I need to know about.'

'I know he said he never went out,' Trey says. Her face is tightening again. 'But my dad, he doesn't . . . he's scared of the Guards. I was as well, till I got to know Cal – Mr Hooper. My dad was just worried, same as I was, if he told you he was out—'

'Listen to me, young one,' Nealon says. 'Just shush a moment and listen. I'll tell you something for nothing: you've done no harm to anyone except whoever killed that poor fella. And like you said, your da had no reason to do that.'

It's the soothing, rock-solid voice that Lena uses with spooked horses. Nealon is ready and itching to arrest Johnny, and leave Trey to live with the knowledge that she put her dad in prison. Lena is fiercely, protectively glad that Cal is out of this job.

'Yeah,' Trey says eagerly. 'I mean, no, he didn't. He *liked* your man Rushborough, he never said a bad word about him, and if there was any trouble he'da said it to me – I'm the oldest one that's still at home, see, so he trusts me, he talks to me—'

'Ah, here,' Nealon says, grinning and holding up a hand, 'don't start that again, for Jaysus' sake. You'll give the whole three of us the head-staggers. I'll tell you what' – he glances up at the clock on the wall – 'it's headed for dinnertime, and I don't know about yous two, but I'm starving. I can always come back to you for more details if I need them, but we'll leave it here for today, will we?'

Lena knows what he's at: he wants this signed and solid, before Trey has second thoughts. 'Yeah,' Trey says, catching a sudden shaky breath. 'That'd be good.'

'Listen to me, now,' Nealon says, suddenly serious. He taps the desk to get Trey's attention. 'I'm going to ask that nice fella out front to type up your statement, and then you'll need to sign it. Like I said before, the minute you sign that, things change. That's no joke; it'll be a legal document that's part of a murder investigation. If there's anything going in there that's not true, now's the time to clear it up, or you could land yourself in serious trouble. D'you hear me?'

He sounds like a stern daddy, and Trey responds like a good kid, nodding hard and looking him in the eye. 'I know. I get it. I swear.'

'No more surprises?'

'Nah. Promise.'

Her voice is steady, final. For a second Lena hears the deep note of that grief again, running underneath it.

Nealon only hears the certainty. 'That's great,' he says. 'Well done.' He pushes his chair back from the desk. 'Let's get this typed up, and you can have a read of it, make sure your man doesn't get anything wrong. How's that? D'you want another Coke while you wait?'

'Yeah,' Trey says. 'Yes please. And sorry.'

'You're all right,' Nealon says. 'Better late than never, wha'? Interview terminated at five-thirteen p.m.' He taps the recorder off and stands up, lifting his eyebrows at Lena. 'I'm dying for a smoke – don't you be following my example, young one, it's a filthy aul' habit. Missus Dunne, d'you fancy a breath of fresh air?'

'Might as well,' Lena says, taking the hint. She glances at Trey as she gets up, to make sure she's all right being left, but Trey isn't looking at her.

The Garda station is a small boxy building, painted a neat white and popped in among a cheerful line of macaron-coloured houses. A bunch of little kids are hauling scooters up the slope of the road and freewheeling back down, yelling; a few mammies in a front garden are keeping an eye on them and laughing about something and wiping babies' noses and stopping toddlers from eating dirt, all at once.

Nealon tilts his smoke packet at Lena, and grins when she shakes her head. 'I reckoned,' he says, 'if you smoked, you might not want the young one knowing. Thought fresh air was a safer offer.'

'I wouldn't try hiding that from her,' Lena says. 'She doesn't miss much.'

'I got that, all right.' Nealon tips his head back to examine Lena – she's taller than he is. 'Helena Dunne,' he says. 'Let's see: Noreen Duggan's your sister, and Cal Hooper's your fella. Have I got that right?'

'That's me,' Lena says. She leans back against the wall to shorten herself. 'For their sins.'

'Look at that,' Nealon says, pleased with himself. 'I'm getting the hang of this place. I called around to you there a couple of days ago, looking for a chat, but you were out.'

'Work, probably.'

'Must've been.' Nealon selects a cigarette and balances it between finger and thumb, apparently considering it. 'Your fella, Hooper,' he says, 'he was there when Theresa told me the original story. He said she was reliable.' He cocks an eyebrow: it's a question.

'She is, yeah,' Lena says. 'Or she always has been. But she's not at her best, these last few weeks. Her daddy coming home, that threw her for a loop. She was always mad about him.'

'Girls and their daddies,' Nealon says indulgently. 'It's great. One of mine's still little enough that she thinks the sun shines out of my arse. I'm making the most of it while it lasts: the other one's thirteen, God help me, so everything out of my mouth is so stupid she could just die. Does Theresa not hold it against her da that he done a legger?'

Lena gives that a bit of thought. 'Not that I ever saw. She's been too over the moon about having him back. And scared he'll take off again.'

Nealon nods along. 'Don't blame her. Will he?'

Lena glances behind her to make sure Trey hasn't come out, and lowers her voice. 'I'd say so, yeah.'

'The poor young one,' Nealon says. 'That wasn't easy for her, coming clean with me. Fair play to you, convincing her. I appreciate that.' He smiles at her. 'I'll be honest with you, I'm pleasantly surprised. Places like your townland, let's face it, mostly they wouldn't go out of their way for the likes of me.'

'My fiancé's a cop,' Lena points out. 'Or was. I'd see things a bit differently from most people round my way.'

'That'd do it, all right,' Nealon acknowledges. 'How'd you convince her?'

This is the loose joint in their story, and Lena knows better than to try and pretend it's not there. She takes her time considering. After the performance Trey put on in there, there's no way in hell Lena is going to let her down.

'D'you know,' she says, 'I didn't have to do as much convincing as I would've expected. She was halfway there already; she just needed the bitta encouragement. You've got the whole townland up to ninety – I wouldn't say you need me to tell you that, sure.' She throws Nealon a look that's half wry, half impressed. He dips his head mock-modestly.

'Trey should've seen that coming,' Lena says, 'but she didn't. She had herself all worked up, thinking you'd get the wrong men and it'd be all her fault. At first she wanted to leave out the bit about her daddy, but I told her there wasn't much point: you'd know there had to be a reason why she made up the first story, and you'd keep on at her till she came out with it. She got that. Mostly, but, I think she just couldn't handle telling any more lies. Like I said, she's not much of a liar. It stresses her out.'

'There's people like that,' Nealon agrees. He twirls his cigarette, still unlit, between two fingers. Lena, as she's intended to, gets the message: they were never out here for air, fresh or otherwise. 'What d'you think of her da?'

Lena shrugs and blows out a puff of air. 'Johnny's Johnny. He's a bit of an eejit, but I wouldn't've said there was much harm in him. You never know, but.'

'True enough,' Nealon says. He watches the scooter kids. One of them has fallen and is howling; a mammy checks for blood, gives the child a hug and sends it back to its game. 'Tell us something. The evening before Rushborough died, Johnny was round your place for a good half-hour. What was going on there?'

Lena takes in a breath and then stops. 'Ah, now,' Nealon says wryly, wagging a finger at her. 'Didn't I just tell you I've got daughters? I know when someone's deciding whether or not to tell me the truth.'

Lena lets out a shamefaced laugh. Nealon laughs with her. 'I've known Johnny all my life,' she explains. 'And I'm fond of Trey.'

'Jaysus, woman, I'm not going to drag the man away in chains if you say the wrong thing. It's not like on the telly. I'm just trying to find out what went on here. Unless Johnny told you he was off to bash Rushborough's head in, you're not going to land him in jail. Did he?'

Lena laughs again. 'Course not.'

'Well then. You've nothing to worry about. So would you ever give us the scoop, before you have my head melted?'

Lena sighs. 'Johnny was looking to borrow money,' she says. 'He said he owed it.'

'Did he say to who?'

Lena leaves half a second before she shakes her head. Nealon cocks his to one side. 'But . . . ?'

'But he said something like "Your man's followed me this far, he's not going to give up now." So I reckoned . . .'

'You reckoned Rushborough.'

'I did, yeah.'

'And you might've been right,' Nealon says. 'Did you give Johnny anything?'

'I did not,' Lena says with spirit. 'I'd never see it again. That fecker still owes me a fiver from when we were seventeen and I subbed him into the disco.'

'How'd he take it? Did he get upset? Narky? Threaten you?'

'Johnny? Jesus, no. He gave it a bitta sob stuff about old times' sake, and when he saw that was getting him nowhere, he cut his losses and headed off.'

'Where to?'

Lena shrugs. 'I'd the door shut on him by that time.'

'I don't blame you,' Nealon says, grinning. 'Come here, would you do us a favour? I don't want to keep the young one away from her dinner any longer than I have to, but would you come in to me tomorrow and get this on paper?'

Lena thinks of what Mart Lavin said about Nealon, how he makes things sound optional. 'No problem,' she says.

'Brilliant,' Nealon says, tucking his unlit cigarette back into the packet. The flash of a look Lena catches on him, as his head comes back up, is hot and driven as lust, the triumphant swell of a man after a woman he knows he can get. 'And don't worry,' he adds reassuringly, 'I won't be mentioning this to Johnny or anyone else. I'm not in the business of making anyone's life harder.'

'Ah, that's great,' Lena says, giving him a big relieved smile. 'Thanks a million.' One of the mammies, joggling her baby on her hip, is looking up the road at them. She moves closer to the others to say something, and they all turn to watch Nealon and Lena go back into the station.

———

As the car doors slam and Nealon raises a hand from the station step, Trey's well-behaved earnestness falls away. She vanishes into a silence so thick that Lena can feel it building up around her like snow.

It would take some brass neck for Lena to offer comfort or

words of wisdom. Instead she leaves the silence untouched till they're out of town, onto the main road. Then she says, 'You did a good job.'

Trey nods. 'He believed me,' she says.

'He did, yeah.'

Lena expects Trey to ask what will happen next, but she doesn't. Instead she says, 'What're you gonna tell Cal?'

'I'm not going to tell him anything,' Lena says. 'I reckon you should tell him the whole story, but it's your call.'

'He'll be raging.'

'Maybe. Maybe not.'

Trey doesn't answer. She leans her forehead against the windowpane and looks out at the countryside moving by. The road is busy with commuters zipping homewards. Beyond it, and unaffected by its frenetic rhythms, cattle nose at their leisure for bits of green among the yellowing fields.

Lena says, 'Where'll I drop you?'

Trey catches her breath like she'd forgotten Lena was there. 'Just home,' she says. 'Thanks.'

'Fair enough,' Lena says, flicking on her indicator. She's taking the long way, the twisting roads up the far side of the mountain and over, to minimise the number of Ardnakelty people who'll see them. Today will be general knowledge soon enough. Trey can at least have a bit of respite to grow accustomed to what she's done, before the townland gets its hands on it.

Trey goes back to gazing out the window. Lena glances sideways at her now and then, watching her eyes scan methodically back and forth across the mountainside, like she's searching for something that she knows she won't find.

20

Cal is doing the dinner dishes when the knock comes at the door. Mart is on the step, car keys jingling on his finger.

'Saddle up the prize pony, Sunny Jim,' he says. 'We've a job to do.'

Cal says, 'What kinda job?'

'Johnny Reddy's worn out his welcome,' Mart says. 'Leave the dog behind.'

Cal has had it up to the back teeth with being herded like a damn sheep by Mart and his plans and his sidelong dark warnings. 'Or what?' he asks.

Mart blinks at him. 'Or nothing,' he says gently. 'I'm not giving orders, man. We could do with you there, is all.'

'Like I told you,' Cal says. 'Johnny Reddy's not my problem.'

'Ah, for feck's sake,' Mart says, exasperated. 'You're marrying one of our women, bucko. You're raising one of our childer, God help you. You're growing tomatoes on a piece of our land. What else is there?'

Cal stands there in the doorway, with the dishcloth in his hand. Mart waits patiently, not hurrying him. Behind him, this year's young rooks, gaining confidence with their wings, tumble and play knock-down tag in the warm evening air.

'Lemme get my keys,' Cal says, and he turns back into the house to put the dishcloth away.

———

The low chatter of the telly is coming from the sitting room, but in spite of that the house feels silent, sunk deep under stillness. Trey can tell by the air that her dad is out, not just asleep. She doesn't know what to make of this. He hasn't left their land since the day Rushborough died.

She finds her mam in the kitchen. Sheila is sitting at the table, not peeling anything or mending anything, just sitting there eating toast thick with blackberry jam. Trey can't remember the last time she saw her mam doing no work.

'I fancied something sweet,' Sheila says. She doesn't ask where Trey went with Lena, all this time. 'D'you want a bit? The dinner's all eaten.'

Trey says, 'Where's my dad gone?'

'Men came for him. Senan Maguire and Bobby Feeney.'

'Where'd they take him?'

Sheila shrugs. 'They won't kill him, anyway,' she says. 'Not unless he's stubborn, maybe.'

With everything else on her mind, Trey hasn't looked at her mother properly in days. At first she can't tell what seems strange about her, until it comes to her that Sheila is the first person she's seen in weeks who looks peaceful. Her head is tilted back, to take the late warm light through the window full on her face. For the first time, in the high harsh sweeps of her cheekbones and the wide curves of her mouth, Trey sees the beauty that Johnny talked about.

Trey says, 'I went into town with Lena. To the Guards. I told them there was no one on the mountain that night, only my dad went out.'

Sheila takes another bite of toast and thinks that over. After a bit she nods. 'Did they believe you?' she asks.

'Yeah. Think so.'

'So they'll arrest him.'

'Dunno. They'll bring him in there and ask him questions, anyhow.'

'Will they come search this place?'

'Prob'ly. Yeah.'

Sheila nods again. 'They'll find what they're after,' she says. ''Tis all in the shed for them.'

In the long silence, the faint telly chatters busily on.

Sheila points with her chin at the chair opposite her. 'Sit down,' she says.

The chair's legs rake dully on the linoleum as Trey pulls it out. She sits down. Her mind can't move.

'I saw what you were at,' Sheila says. 'First you only wanted your father gone, same as I did. Isn't that right?'

Trey nods. The house feels like a place in a dream; the row of faded mugs hanging from hooks under the cupboard seem like they're floating in mid-air, the chipped enamel of the cooker has an impossible glow. She's not afraid that any of the little ones will burst in, or that Nealon will come knocking at the door. Everything will be motionless till she and her mother are done here.

''Twas no use,' Sheila says. 'I saw that early. He was going nowhere, as long as he had that Rushborough fella on his back. All he could think of was getting that money.'

Trey says, 'I know that.'

'I know you do. The night him and Cal had that fight, there was me cleaning the blood off him, and him acting like I wasn't there. He never did see me. But I was there. I heard what he was at. He was taking you to use.'

'He didn't *take* me. I wanted to help him.'

Sheila looks at her. 'This place has no mercy,' she says. 'Once you step foot over the line, they'd ate you alive. You'da been gone, one way or the other.'

'I don't give a shite,' Trey says. Her mind is starting to stir again. It hits her full force that her mother is a mystery to her. She could have anything folded away inside her silence.

Sheila shakes her head briefly. 'I lost one child to this place,' she says. 'I'm not losing another.'

Brendan is a swift slice through the air between them, bright as life.

Trey says, 'That's why I wanted to help my dad. To get back at them. He wasn't using me. I was using him.'

'I know that,' Sheila says. 'You're as bad as him, thinking I know nothing. I knew that all along. I wouldn't have it.'

'You shoulda left it,' Trey says. She finds her hands are shaking. It takes her a moment to realise it's from anger.

Sheila looks at her. 'You wanted your revenge on themens,' she says.

'I *had* it. Had it fuckin' sorted. I *had* 'em.'

'Quiet,' Sheila says. 'The children'll come in.'

Trey can barely hear her. 'They were walking straight into it. All you hadta do was leave me at it. The fuck did you go interfering for?' Fury has her on her feet, but once she's there she can't find what to do with it. When she was a kid she would have thrown something, smashed something. She wants that back. 'You wrecked fuckin' everything.'

In the sunlight Sheila's eyes are blue as flames. She doesn't blink against it. 'You're my revenge,' she says. 'I won't have you ruined.'

That stops Trey's breathing. The peeling cream paint of the walls is achingly radiant and the stained linoleum has a simmering, risky translucence, ready to boil up. She can't feel the floor under her feet.

'Sit,' Sheila says. 'I'm talking to you.'

After a moment Trey sits back down. Her hands on the table feel different, humming with strange new kinds of power.

'Cal knew what you were at, as well,' Sheila says. 'That's why he bet up your dad: he wanted him gone as much as I did. Only your dad wouldn't go. In the heel of the hunt, Cal woulda had to kill him. Or kill Rushborough, one or the other.'

She considers her piece of toast and reaches for the knife to add more jam. Sun catches in the jar, lighting it the rich purple of a jewel.

'He woulda done it,' she says. 'I knew by your dad, by how afraid he was: Cal almost done it that night. The next time, or the next, he'da done it.'

Trey knows it's true. Everyone around her is changing, layered with things barely held in check. The scrubbed grain of the table looks too sharp to be real.

'Cal's your chance,' Sheila says. 'At having more than this. I couldn't have him ending up in prison. You can do without me, if you haveta.' Her voice is matter-of-fact, like she's saying something they both know well. 'So I reckoned I'd haveta do the job instead.'

Trey says, 'Why Rushborough? Why not my dad?'

'I married your daddy. I made him promises. Rushborough was nothing to me.'

'You shoulda gone for my dad. He was the one that brought Rushborough.'

Sheila flicks her head, dismissing that. 'That woulda been a sin,' she says. 'I'da done it if I had to, but there was no need. Rushborough was good enough. I mighta done different if I'da known you were going to come up with that loada shite about men up the mountain, maybe. I don't know.'

She considers this for a moment, chewing, and shrugs. 'What stopped me at first,' she says, 'was the little ones. Cal would take you, if I went to prison, but he couldn't take the lotta ye; he wouldn't be let. I wasn't having them go into care, and I wasn't having your sister give up the life she's made in Dublin and come back here to look after them. I was stuck.'

Trey thinks of the last weeks, her mam cutting potatoes and ironing her dad's shirts and washing Alanna's hair, and all the time steadily working at this. The house was nothing like Trey thought.

'Only then,' Sheila says, 'Lena Dunne came here telling me she'd take us in. The lot of us. She's the last woman I'da expected that out of, but Lena was always a woman of her word. If I hadda been taken for this, she'da had the little ones till I could come back for them.'

Trey sees Cal solid beside her at his kitchen table, while she lied her arse off to the detective. The thought of him has such force that for a second she can smell him, wood shavings and beeswax. She says, 'And me. Cal wouldn't want me.'

Sheila says, with no sharpness but with finality, 'He'd do what needs doing. Same as I done.' She smiles across the table at Trey, just a small flicker and a nod of approval. 'No need now, anyhow. Not after what you said to the Guards. They'll take your da, if he comes back here. If he doesn't, they'll go after him.'

Trey says, 'They'll be able to tell it was you. Not him.'

'How?'

'Cal told me. They have people that look for evidence. Match things up.'

Sheila swipes a dab of jam off her plate and licks her finger. 'Then they'll take me,' she says. 'I thought they would anyhow.'

Trey's mind is moving again, gaining a steady, cold momentum that feels beyond her control, ticking through the things Cal said. If there's Sheila's hair and fibres from her clothes on Rushborough's body, those can be explained away; they could have come off Johnny. The wandering sheep trampled her footprints.

She says, 'How'd you do it?'

'I called the man,' Sheila says, 'and he came. Not a bother on him. He never saw me there, either.'

Cal said the Guards would check Rushborough's phone. 'Called him when? Offa your phone?'

Sheila is watching her. The look in her eyes is strange, almost like wonder; for a second Trey thinks she's smiling.

'The same night I done it,' she says. 'Once your daddy was asleep. Off your daddy's phone, in case your man wouldn't answer a number he didn't know. I told him I'd money saved, only I didn't wanta tell your daddy or he'd take it all off me. But your man Rushborough could have it, if he'd leave this place and take your daddy with him.'

She thinks back, biting a crust. 'He laughed at me,' she says. 'He said your daddy owed him twenty grand, and did I have that saved outa my dole? I told him I'd fifteen that my granny left me, and I'd been keeping it for you to go to college. He stopped laughing then. He said that'd do, it'd be worth leaving the other five to get outa this shitpit, and he'd take the rest outa your daddy one way or another. He talked different,' she adds. 'He didn't bother with the posh accent for me.'

Trey says, 'Where'd you meet him?'

'Out at the gate. I brought him up to the shed – I said the money was hid there. I'd the hammer in the pocket of my hoodie. I said the money was in that aul' toolbox on the shelf, and when he bent down to get it, I hit him. I done it in the shed in case he shouted or fought, but he went down easy as that. That big bad bastard that had your daddy terrified: not a peep outa him.'

If Rushborough didn't fight, then there's none of Sheila's blood on him, no trace of her skin under his nails. His body, somewhere beyond reach in Nealon's hands, is harmless.

'I'd put the kitchen knife ready in the shed,' Sheila says. 'That sharp one that we'd use for the meat. Once he was dead, I got him in the wheelbarrow and brought him down the road.' She examines the last crust of her toast, thinking. 'I felt like there was someone watching me,' she says. 'I'd say 'twas Malachy Dwyer, or Seán Pól maybe. Them sheep didn't let themselves out.'

'You coulda thrown your man down the ravine,' Trey says.

'What good would he have done there? I needed your daddy knowing he was dead, so he'd go. I woulda left him on the doorstep, only I didn't want ye seeing him.'

Sheila wipes the last of the jam off her plate with the crust. 'And that was the end of it,' she says. 'I done right by you then, even if I never did before. That time, I done what you needed.'

Trey says, 'Didja wear gloves?'

Sheila shakes her head. 'I wasn't bothered,' she says.

Trey sees the shed blazing up with evidence like marsh fire: fingerprints on the hammer, the wheelbarrow, on the door, the shelves, in blood, footprints tangled on the floor. Rushborough's body is nothing; the danger is here.

'The clothes you were wearing,' she says. 'D'you remember what ones?'

Sheila looks at her, the strange look in her eyes strengthening to a half-smile. 'I do,' she says.

'D'you still have 'em?'

'I do, o' course. I gave them a wash. They needed it.'

Trey sees her mother's familiar faded T-shirts and jeans alight with tiny incandescent trails, Rushborough's hairs, wisps of shirt cotton, spatters of blood, matted deep into the fabric. Once Sheila had set this in motion, she never even tried to move out of its way; she just stood still and waited for it to hit her or miss her. Trey can't tell whether this was exhaustion or a defiance deeper than any she's known before.

'Get 'em anyway,' she says. 'And the shoes.'

Sheila pushes her chair back and stands up. She's smiling full-on

378

at Trey, her head going up like a wild proud girl's. 'Now,' she says. 'Like I said: we do what needs doing.'

———————

The sun is sinking. Out in the fields, the light still turns the grass gold, but here at the foot of the mountains the shadow is deep as dusk. The heat is different, not the naked blaze from the sky, but the thick accumulated heat of the day seeping up from the earth. The men stand silent, waiting. Sonny and Con are shoulder to shoulder. PJ shifts from foot to foot, rustling the dry brush; Francie smokes; Dessie whistles a shapeless tune between his teeth, and then stops. Mart leans on a spade. Francie has a hurley tucked under his arm, and PJ is absently swinging a pickaxe handle. Cal watches them without seeming to, and tries to gauge what they've come here aiming or willing to do.

The sound of Senan's station wagon comes to them faintly from far around the bend. It pulls up away on the road next to the other cars, and Francie crushes out his smoke underfoot. Johnny gets out of the car and picks his way through the grass and weeds towards them, with Senan and Bobby at his back like guards.

When he gets close enough, Johnny glances from one face to another and half-laughs. 'What's all this, lads?' he asks. 'God almighty, ye're looking awful serious.'

Mart holds out the spade. 'Dig,' he says.

Johnny looks at it in disbelief, grinning. Cal can see his mind skittering for escape routes. 'Ah, now,' he says. 'I'm not dressed for—'

'You said there was gold,' Sonny says. 'Let's see it.'

'Jesus, lads, I never said 'twas on this spot. Your man Rushborough never pinned down the places that close. And sure, I told ye from the start, the whole thing coulda been—'

'Here'll do,' Francie says.

'Ah, lads,' Johnny says. 'Is this my penance, is it, for bringing Rushborough here? Sure, I've lost more than any of ye, but I'm not—'

Mart says, 'Dig.'

After a moment Johnny shakes his head like he's humouring

379

them, steps forward and takes the spade. For a second his eyes catch Cal's. Cal looks back at him.

He strikes the spade into the earth, with a small gritty scrape, and drives it home with his foot. The ground is dried hard; it sinks only a couple of inches. Johnny glances up wryly, inviting the other men to share the absurdity. 'We'll be here all night,' he says.

'Then you'd better get moving,' Con says.

Johnny looks around their faces again. None of them change. He bends back to the digging.

———————

Nobody wants to get in the car. Somehow they've all picked up something in the air, something they don't understand but don't like, and they all turn defiant against it. Liam shouts, demanding to know where they're going and why and where Daddy is, till Sheila shoves him, still yelling and kicking out at her, into the back seat. Alanna, sobbing piteously, attaches herself to Trey's legs and has to be peeled off, while Sheila retrieves Liam from halfway across the yard and throws him back into the car with a slap to keep him there. Even Banjo hides under Trey's bed; Trey has to drag him out, while he howls tragically and tries to burrow into the floor, and carry him to the car. The catch of the boot is broken; with so much stuff jammed into it, it keeps flying open, and every time it does, Banjo tries to make a break for it over the back seat.

Maeve gets into bed, pulls the sheet over her head, and refuses to move. Trey tries dragging her and tries hitting her, but she just kicks and stays put. Sheila, battling the others, can't help. Trey doesn't have time for this shit. Nealon could drive up any minute.

She kneels by Maeve's bed. She can tell by the shape under the sheet that Maeve has her hands over her ears, so she pinches a fold of arm and digs her nails in. Maeve squeals and kicks out.

'Listen to me,' Trey says.

'Fuck off.'

'Listen or I'll do it again.'

After a second Maeve takes her hands off her ears. 'I'm not going,' she informs Trey.

'That detective's coming for Daddy,' Trey says.

That puts a stop to Maeve's fussing. She pulls the sheet off her head and stares. 'Why? Did he kill your man?'

'Rushborough was dodgy,' Trey says. 'Daddy was only protecting us. Now we've to protect him. I'm gonna stop the detective getting him.'

'You are not. How?'

Outside, the car horn beeps. 'Don't have time to explain,' Trey says. 'The detective's coming. You haveta help Mammy get the little ones away, quick.'

Maeve is giving Trey a suspicious stare. Her hair is a mess from being under the covers. 'Daddy's not even here. He went out with some guys.'

'I know, yeah. They're gonna rat him out if we don't move quick.' Trey is sick to death of coming up with the stories people want to hear. All this talking feels unsafe and fake, like she's pretending to be someone else. She wants Maeve gone, all of them gone, so she can get on with things in quiet. 'Come *on*,' she says.

After a moment Maeve kicks off the sheet and gets up. 'You better not fuck up,' she tells Trey, as they head out.

Sheila has the car pointed at the gate and the engine running. 'Wait till you see the car,' she says to Trey, out the window. 'And then run like mad, after.'

'Yeah,' Trey says.

Maeve slams the car door. Sheila reaches a hand out the window and grips Trey's arm for a second. 'Jesus,' she says. That smile is back on her. 'I never reckoned on you.' Then she puts the car into gear and takes off, out the gate and down the road.

Trey watches the car's dust cloud wander lazily across the yard, golden in the last sunlight splitting through the pines, and then dissipate. The sound of the engine fades. The birds, unfazed by all the yelling and carry-on, are settling for evening, flipping back and forth between trees and bickering over perches. Under the dusky air, its windows shuttered by the reflections of trees in the glass, the house looks like it's been empty for weeks. For the first time Trey can remember in all her life, it feels peaceful.

She supposes she should walk through it one more time, but she has no impulse to do that. She's already taken Brendan's watch out of its slit in her mattress and strapped it on her wrist. She would have liked to take away the coffee table that she made at Cal's, but she has nowhere to take it. Apart from that, there's nothing she wants from here.

She picks up the spare petrol can from the dirt of the yard, where her mother left it, and heads for the shed.

———————

The shadow of the mountain has stretched far across the fields, and the sky has dimmed to a dull, filmed lilac. The hole in the dirt is growing, but slowly. Johnny is soft, a limp-muscled wisp next to the dense, unspared bodies around him; he's panting, and the gaps between spade strikes are getting longer. Cal barely notices him. Johnny, after weeks at the centre of Ardnakelty's universe, isn't important any more; nothing he does will make a difference now. Cal is watching the men watching him.

'Come on, lads,' Johnny says, raising his head and shoving hair out of his eyes with a forearm. 'We'll find fuck-all here. If it's gold ye want, at least let me take ye where Rushborough said it'd be. I'm not guaranteeing anything, I never did, but—'

'You're not deep enough,' Senan says. 'Keep going.'

Johnny leans on the spade. Sweat shines on his face and darkens the underarms of his shirt. 'If ye want your money, I'll pay ye back. All this drama, there's no need for—'

Con says, 'We don't want your money.'

'Lads,' Johnny says. 'Listen to me, lads. Give me a few weeks, just, and I'll be outa your hair for good. I swear to God. I'm only waiting till it won't bring that Nealon fella after me, is all. Then I'll be gone.'

'You're waiting for him to settle on some of us, instead,' Bobby says. Mostly Bobby is a funny little man, but the depth of his anger has burned that away; no one would make fun of him today. 'Get to fuck.'

'Ye don't want Nealon pulling me in. I'm telling ye. I'd never say a word about what went in the river, ye know I wouldn't, but there's stuff on my phone. If he starts looking into me, we'll all be in the shite together. If ye'll just hang on a few—'

'Hold your whisht,' Francie says. His voice comes down hard across Johnny's, flattening it. 'Keep digging.'

The mountain feels different. Trey stands balanced on the stone wall opposite her gate, watching the road far below for her mam's car. The fields should have the dreamy ease of evening, but instead they're swollen with a strange bruised glow, under a thickening haze of cloud. Closer around Trey, shadows flick silently among the underbrush, and branches twitch in no wind. The air simmers; she feels watched from every direction at once, by a hundred hidden, unblinking eyes. She remembers how she used to move about this mountain when she was a kid, feeling herself passed over as too light for notice, just another half-grown wild thing to be allowed free rein. She's worth watching now.

A gorse bush rattles with the sharpness of a deliberate taunt, and Trey barely keeps her footing on the wall. She understands for the first time what hunted her dad indoors and kept him penned there, these last few days.

She recognises this as an inevitable response to what she told Nealon. Something brought her the chance of revenge, the same way it brought her Cal, only this time she turned it down. Whatever's up here isn't on her side any more.

She marks out the route she'll take, cutting across fields and over walls, the quickest way down the mountain for anyone who knows it like she does. It's starting to get dark, but the summer dusk is still long; she'll have time. She'll be careful.

Her mam's silver Hyundai appears on the road, tiny with distance but still identifiable, going fast. Light flashes off it as it turns into Lena's gateway. Trey jumps down off the wall.

Lena is on her sofa, with a mug of tea and a book, but she's not reading. She's not thinking, either. Trey's face and Cal's are in her mind, oddly alike in the closed-off, determined set of their features, but she lets them be, not trying to work out what to do about either one of them. The air feels thick and restless, pressing in from all sides; at the window, the evening light has a sickly greenish-purple tinge, like something rotting. Lena stays still, conserving herself for whatever is going to happen.

In their corner, the dogs twitch and huff irritably, trying to doze and getting on each other's nerves. Lena drinks her tea and eats a couple of biscuits, not out of hunger but while she has the chance. When she hears the car coming up her drive, even though it wasn't what she was expecting, she rises to meet it without any real surprise.

The car is bursting at the seams: Sheila and the children and Banjo spilling out of the doors, bin liners full of clothes hanging out of the boot. 'You said you'd have us if I need it,' Sheila says, on the doorstep. She has Alanna by the hand and a stuffed holdall on her shoulder. 'Will you?'

'I will, o' course,' Lena says. 'What's happened?'

Banjo is squashing his way past her legs, making for her dogs, but there's no sign of Trey. Lena's heartbeat changes, turning slow and hard. She wouldn't put it past Trey to have told Johnny straight out how she spent the afternoon. After all this time, she still can't predict Trey. She should have found a way to ask Cal. Cal would have known.

'There's a fire in our yard,' Sheila says. She shifts the bag higher on her shoulder, so she can catch Liam's arm and stop him climbing on Lena's geranium planter. 'By the shed. I'd say Johnny threw a smoke that wasn't out.'

'How bad?' Lena asks. She doesn't understand what's going on. She feels like all of this must add up in ways she can't see.

Sheila shrugs. 'Small, only. But everything's dry as a bone. Who knows what it'll do.'

'What fire?' Liam demands, trying to twist away from Sheila's hand. 'There's no fire.'

'It's behind the shed,' Maeve tells him. 'That's why you didn't see it. Shut up.'

'Did you call the fire brigade?' Lena asks. She can't get a grip on Sheila's calm. It's not her usual heavy shield of detachment; this is the vivid, alert coolness of someone expertly managing a complicated situation on the fly. Lena turns to look at the mountain, but her house blocks the view.

'I'll do it now,' Sheila says, fishing in a pocket for her phone. 'I've no reception up there.'

'How do you know?' Alanna asks Maeve.

'Trey said. Shut *up*.'

Alanna thinks this over. 'I saw the fire,' she says.

Lena says, 'Where's Trey?'

Sheila, phone to one ear and a hand over the other, glances at her. 'She's coming,' she says.

'Is she up there? Is Johnny with her?'

'She's coming,' Sheila says again. 'I've no clue where he is,' and she turns away. 'Hello, I've to report a fire.'

———

The door of the shed sways open, showing the tumble of things piled in the wheelbarrow; the smell of petrol curls out like a thick shimmer. Trey picks up the whiskey bottle she left by the door and finds her dad's spare lighter in her pocket. She lights the soaked rag stuffed in the bottle's neck, lobs it into the shed, and is running before she hears the smash of glass.

Behind her the shed goes up with one huge, gentle *whoof*, and a dangerous crackling starts to rise. At the gate, Trey turns to make sure. The shed is a tower of fire, house-high; the flames are already snapping at the spruce branches.

Trey runs. As she jumps for the top of the wall, something sounds in the recesses between the stones, a hollow scrape like bone along rock. Trey, startled off balance, misses her footing. She comes down hard and feels her foot bend inwards underneath her. When she tries to stand up, her ankle won't take her weight.

———

The rhythm of the spade has become part of Cal's mind, something he'll be hearing long after he leaves this place. Johnny sags after every blow. The hole is thigh-deep on him, long and wide enough to fit a small man. Around its edges, dirt is piled high.

The sky has darkened, not only with the coming night: a sullen layer of purple-grey cloud has rolled in from somewhere, on no wind that Cal can feel. It's been so long since he's seen cloud that it looks alien, bringing the sky unnaturally close. The fields have a strange, unfocused luminosity, as if the remaining light is generated from within the air itself.

Johnny stops again, leaning heavily on the spade, his head falling back. 'Hooper,' he says. Cal can hear his breath deep in his chest. 'You're a man of sense. D'you wanta be mixed up in a bad business like this?'

'I'm not mixed up in anything,' Cal says. 'I'm not even here.'

'None of us are,' Sonny says. 'I'm having a few cans in front of the telly, myself.'

'I'm playing cards with these two,' Mart says, indicating PJ and Cal. 'I'm winning, as per usual.'

'Hooper,' Johnny says again, more urgently. His eyes are wild. 'You wouldn't let them leave Theresa without her daddy.'

'You're no kinda father to her,' Cal says. 'And you'll be no loss.' He catches Mart's small grim smile of approval, across the deepening hole.

He still can't tell whether they're just here to run Johnny out of town, or whether the men intend more than that. Johnny, who knows them better than Cal does, believes they mean more.

Cal could try to talk them out of it. He might even succeed; these aren't hardened killers. He doesn't know whether, if it comes to it, he'll try. His personal code doesn't allow for letting a man be beaten to death, even a little shitweasel like Johnny Reddy, but he's gone beyond his code. All he cares about is making sure Trey has what she needs, whether that's an absent father or a dead one.

'Lads,' Johnny says. The stink of sweat and fear comes off him.

'Lads, listen to me. Whatever it is ye want, I'll do it. Just tell me. Sonny, man, I got you outa hot water before . . .'

Cal's phone beeps. It's Lena.

I have Sheila and the children. Trey is at her house. Get her.

Johnny is still talking. As Cal lifts his head from the phone, he smells a faint trace of smoke on the air.

The turn towards the mountain seems to take him forever. High on its dark shoulder is a small, ragged splash of orange. A pillar of smoke rises, glowing, against the sky.

The other men follow his turn. 'That's my place,' Johnny says blankly. The spade drops from his hand. 'That's my house.'

'Call the fire department,' Cal says to Mart. Then he runs, brambles clawing at his legs, for his car.

He's halfway there when he hears the thudding and panting of someone behind him. 'I'm coming with you,' Johnny says, in between raw gasps.

Cal doesn't answer and doesn't slow for him. When he reaches the car, Johnny is still at his shoulder. While he's fumbling his key at the ignition with fingers that feel thick and numbed, Johnny wrenches open the passenger door and throws himself inside.

Trey pulls herself up by the wall, hissing through her teeth to manage the pain, and braces her way along it to the nearest tree. The crackle and flutter of the flames is growing, mixed with strange popping and creaking sounds; when Trey looks over her shoulder, she sees a patch of the spruce grove is made of fire, every needle perfect and blazing against the dusk.

The tree is brittle from the drought, but all the same it takes her four tries to hang her weight from a branch hard enough that it snaps off. The recoil jolts her ankle and for a second she's lightheaded with pain, but she leans over the wall and takes long breaths till her vision comes back.

It's clear to her that she might be going to die, but she doesn't have time to have any feelings about that. She pads the end of the branch with her hoodie and tucks it under her armpit. Then she starts down the path, step and hop, as fast as she can go.

Birds are shooting up from the spruces and the gorse on every side, calling hard and high for danger. The air smells of smoke, and the heat is churning it: small things whirl and eddy in front of Trey's face, flakes of ash, scraps of flame. The path is steeper than she ever realised before. If she speeds up, she'll go sprawling. She can't afford either to lose her crutch, or to get hurt worse than she is.

She keeps her pace steady, and her eyes on the ground for rocks. Behind her, the mutter of the fire is building towards a roar. She doesn't look back.

———

'God almighty,' Johnny says, with an exaggerated puff of air, 'I'm glad to be outa that.'

Cal, flooring it and dodging potholes, barely hears him. The one thing on their side is the windless air. The fire will spread fast enough all by itself, in this bone-dry country, but with no breeze to twist it, it'll lick uphill. Trey will be heading down.

Johnny leans closer. 'They weren't going to kill me or anything mental like that, now. You get that, don't you? Me and the lads, we've known each other all our lives. They'd never hurt me; they're not fuckin' psycho. They just wanted to give me a bit of a fright, like, just to—'

Cal swings the car hard left, up the mountain road. He says, 'Shut your fucking mouth or I'll kill you myself.' What he means is *If anything's happened to the kid I'll kill you myself.* He's not clear on how exactly this is Johnny's doing, but he has no doubt that it is.

Up the road in front of them, too close, is the fire. It backlights the trees with a ruthless, pulsing orange. Cal is wishing for Trey with such ferocity that every time they round a bend he truly expects to see her in the headlights, loping down the path, but there's no sign of any human creature. He drives one-handed to check his phone: nothing from Lena.

At the fork where Rushborough was dumped, Cal hits the brakes. He doesn't dare take the car any farther; they'll need it safe to get them out of here, if they come back. He grabs his water bottle and the raggedy towel he keeps for wiping down his windows, soaks the towel, and tears it in two. 'Here,' he says, tossing half at Johnny. 'You're coming with me. It might take two to get her out. Give me any hassle and I'll throw your ass in there.' He jerks his chin uphill, at the fire.

'Fuck you,' Johnny says. 'You were only a lift. I'd be here with or without you.' He jumps out of the car and starts up the path towards his house, wrapping the towel round his head, without waiting for Cal to catch up.

Cal has never been near a fire before. His old job brought him to the aftermath of a few, soggy black ash and sour reek, sulky threads of smoke curling here and there, but that was no kind of preparation for this. It sounds like a tornado, a vast relentless roar sliced through by crashes, squeals, groans, sounds that gain added terror from their incomprehensibility. Above the treetops, smoke boils in great rolls against the sky.

Johnny can only be a few paces ahead, but the dusk is coming down hard, the air is hazy, and the fluttering glow confuses everything. 'Johnny!' Cal yells. He's afraid Johnny won't hear him, but after a moment there's an answering shout. He heads for it, makes out a shape, and grabs Johnny's arm. 'Stay close,' he yells in Johnny's ear.

They hurry up the path with their elbows clumsily locked together, heads bent, like they're fighting through a blizzard. The heat charges at them like a solid thing trying to wrestle them back. Every instinct in Cal's body is clawing at him to obey; he has to force his muscles to keep moving forward.

He knows Trey could already be long gone, by some hidden back trail, or else trapped behind the flames where he'll never reach her. The air is blurred with smoke and whirling with blazing scraps riding the currents. A hare hurls itself across the path, practically under their feet, without a glance their way.

The crackling roar has grown to something almost too furious to hear. Up ahead, the path disappears into a billowing wall of smoke. They come to a standstill, without meaning to, in the face of its immensity.

The Reddy place is behind that, and everything behind that is gone. Cal twists the wet rag tighter around his head and takes a deep breath. He feels Johnny do the same.

For a splintering second, the thing hobbling out of the smoke looks like no living human. Blackened, lopsided, juddering, it's one of the mountain's hidden dead, woken and animated by the flames. Cal's hair rises. Beside him, a sound comes out of Johnny.

Then Cal blinks and sees Trey, smoke-blotched and limping, one arm spasming from the pressure of her makeshift crutch. Before his mind even figures out whether she's dead or alive, he's running for her.

———————

Trey's senses have split apart. She sees Cal's eyes and for some reason her dad's, she hears their voices saying words, she feels arms across her back and under her thighs, but none of those things connect. Smoke floats between them, keeping them separate. She's nowhere, moving too fast.

'Keep her foot up,' Cal says. There's a hard bump as her arse hits the ground.

It jolts things back into focus. She's sitting on the dirt, with her back up against the tyre of Cal's car. Her dad, bent over with his hands on his thighs, is panting. Thin streams of smoke drift, unhurried, down the path and between the trees. Below them, twilight covers the road and the heather; uphill, the mountain is blazing.

'Kid,' Cal says, close to her face. His head is covered in something red and white; the parts of his face that show are smudged and sweaty. 'Kid, listen to me. Can you breathe OK? Anything hurt?'

Trey's ankle hurts like fuck, but that feels irrelevant. 'Nah,' she says. 'I can breathe.'

'OK,' Cal says. He stands up, pulling the towel off his head, and winces as he rolls one shoulder. 'Let's get you in the car.'

'Not me, man,' Johnny says, lifting his hands, still breathing hard. 'I'm not chancing my arm going back. I was lucky to get outa there alive.'

'Whatever,' Cal says. 'Trey. In the car. Now.'

'Hang on,' Johnny says. He kneels down in the dirt in front of Trey. 'Theresa. We've only a minute. Listen to me.' He takes her by the arms and gives her an urgent little shake, to make her look into his eyes. In the flickering muddle of dusk and firelight his face is ancient and shifting, unfamiliar. 'I know you think I just came back to squeeze a bitta cash outa this place, but that's not true. I wanted to come anyway. I always wanted to. Only I wanted to come in a limousine spilling over with presents for all of ye, fire a cannon fulla sweeties outa the window, diamonds for your mammy. Show 'em all. This isn't the way I meant to come home. I don't know how it all went like this.'

Trey, glancing over his shoulder at the smoke, says nothing. She can't fathom why he's telling her this, when it makes no difference to anything. It strikes her that he just wants to talk – not because he's upset, but because that's how he operates. Without someone to listen and praise or commiserate, he barely exists. If he doesn't tell her, it won't be real.

'Yeah,' Cal says. 'Let's go.'

Johnny ignores him and talks faster. 'Didja ever have them dreams where you're falling off something high, or down a hole? One minute you're grand, the next you're gone? My whole life, I've felt like I was in one of them dreams. Like I'm slipping all the time, digging my nails in but I just keep sliding, and there was never a moment when I could see how to stop.'

Cal says, 'We need to move.'

Johnny takes a breath. 'I never had a chance,' he says. 'That's all I'm telling you. If this fella's giving you a chance, take it.'

He lifts his head, scanning the mountainside. The fire is spreading, but it's mostly spreading upwards. Along the sides, there are still wide stretches of blackness; ways out.

'Here's what happened,' he says. 'Myself and Hooper, we split up when we got here: he took the path, and I cut up through the woods towards the back of the house, in case you were coming that way. When Hooper found you, it was no good him calling me, in all this noise, and the fire was too close for him to go after me. And that's the last anyone saw of me. Have you got that?'

Trey nods. Her dad's skill with stories is, finally, doing something worthwhile. This one is simple enough, and close enough to the truth, that it'll hold while he slips through every noose and away. And, at last, it lets him be a hero.

Johnny is still intent on her, his fingers tight on her arms, like he wants something more from her. There's not one grain of anything that she's willing to give him. 'I get it,' she says, and pulls her arms out of his hands.

'Here,' Cal says. He takes out his wallet and hands Johnny a fold of notes.

Johnny, straightening up, looks at them and laughs. He's got his breath back. With his head raised and the firelight catching in his eyes, he looks younger again, and mischievous. 'Well, God almighty,' he says, 'this fella thinks of everything. I'd say the two of ye will do great together.'

He takes out his phone and tosses it in among the trees, a long hard throw towards the flames. 'Tell your mammy I'm sorry,' he says. 'I'll send ye a postcard someday, from wherever I land.'

He turns and starts running, light as a boy, up the other fork that leads towards Malachy Dwyer's and over to the far side of the mountain. In seconds he's disappeared, into the dusk and the trees and the thin drifts of smoke.

Somewhere far away, under the wordless roar of the fire, Trey hears a rising whine: sirens. 'Let's go,' Cal says.

21

The smoke is thickening. Cal pulls Trey up by her armpits and practically throws her into the car.

'What the almighty *fuck* were you *thinking*,' he says, slamming his door. He feels like he might hit her if he's not careful. 'You could've *died*.'

'I didn't,' Trey points out.

'Jesus *Christ*,' Cal says. 'Put your seat belt on.'

He spins the car, gravel crunching, to face down the mountain. The slow drifts of smoke make the road appear to move under the headlights, shifting and heaving like water. Cal wants to floor it, but he can't afford to hit one of the many potholes and get stuck up here. He keeps it slow and steady, and tries to ignore the fluttering roar swelling behind him. Somewhere there's a crash, immense enough that he feels the car shake, as a tree comes down.

The siren is rising, straight ahead of them and coming fast. '*Fuck*—' Cal says, through his teeth. The road is too narrow for passing, there's nowhere to pull off; the only thing he can do is reverse, straight back into the fire.

'Turn right,' Trey says, leaning forward. 'Now. Go.'

With no idea what he's doing, Cal spins the wheel hard, sees the headlights skid across tree trunks and feels the tyres bump over something, and finds himself on a path: narrow and overgrown enough that he's passed it for two years without ever suspecting its existence, but real. Behind them, on the road, the siren wails by and fades.

'Mind out,' Trey says. ''S twisty.'

'This gonna be wide enough for the car?'

'Yeah. Widens out in a bit.'

Even with the windows rolled up, smoke has seeped into the car, thickening the air and catching at the back of Cal's throat. He forces himself to keep his foot off the accelerator, peering through the windshield for the faint track that weaves erratically between trees, so close that branches scrape the sides of the car. 'Where's this go?'

'Down to the foot of the mountain. Comes out a bit farther from the village. Up by the main road.'

Things dart out of the darkness across the headlight beams, small leaping animals, frantic birds. Cal, his heart jackhammering, slams on the brake every time. Trey hangs on tight against the jolts and the bumpy track. 'Left,' she says, when the headlights come up against what looks like a dead-end cluster of trees, and Cal pulls left. He has no idea where he is, or which way he's facing. 'Left,' Trey says again.

Gradually the trees thin and give way to weeds and gorse. The track widens and becomes defined. They've left the thick of the smoke behind; the small steadfast lights of windows shine out clearly from the fields below, and the western horizon still has the last faint flush of turquoise. The world is still there. Cal starts to get his bearings back.

'Lena brought me into town today,' Trey says, out of nowhere. 'To your man Nealon. I told him I saw no one that night. Just my dad going out.'

'OK,' Cal says, after a second. He manages to find enough spare brain cells to unravel a few of the things that means. 'Did he?'

Trey shrugs.

Cal doesn't have the resources left to put things carefully. 'How come you changed your mind?'

'Just wanted to,' Trey says. She stops, like the words took her by surprise. 'I wanted to,' she says again.

'Just like that,' Cal says. 'Gee, I shoulda guessed. After putting the whole place through all this shit, you woke up this morning and went, "Fuck it, I'm bored, I guess I'll head into town and change my story—"'

Trey asks, 'You pissed off with me?'

Cal can't imagine how to even begin answering that. For a minute he thinks he might start laughing like a loon. 'God, kid,' he says. 'I have no idea.'

Trey gives him a look like he might be losing it. Cal takes a breath and manages to pull himself back together a little bit. 'Mostly,' he says, 'I'm just glad this whole shitstorm looks like it's on its way to over and done with. And that you managed not to get yourself fucking killed up there. Everything else is low on my priority list.'

Trey nods like that makes sense. 'You reckon my dad made it out?' she asks.

'Yeah. It's spreading fast, but the way he headed, nothing's gonna be cut off for a while. He'll be fine. Guys like him always are.' Cal is done with being nice about Johnny Reddy. He feels he's gone above and beyond by resisting the temptation to shove the little shit right into the heart of the fire.

They've reached the bottom of the mountain. Cal turns onto the road towards the village and tries to breathe deeply. His hands have started shaking so hard he can barely hold the steering wheel. He slows down before he sends them into a ditch.

Trey says, 'Where we going?'

'Miss Lena's,' Cal says. 'Your mama and the kids are there already.'

Trey is silent for a second. Then she says, 'Can I go to yours?'

Out of nowhere, Cal feels tears prickle his eyes. 'Sure,' he says, blinking so he can see the road. 'Why not.'

Trey lets out a long sigh. She slouches deeper into her seat, getting comfortable, and turns herself sideways to watch the fire, with the still gaze of a kid on a road trip watching scenery stream by.

Lena makes up the spare bed for Sheila and the little ones, and puts bedding on the sofa for Maeve. She helps Sheila bring in all the bags from the car boot, and dig through them for nightclothes and toothbrushes. She finds milk and mugs and biscuits so everyone can have a snack before bed. She doesn't ring Cal. As soon as he can, he'll ring her. She keeps her phone in her jeans pocket, where she'll feel it vibrate no matter how many people are talking. It must be the only phone in Ardnakelty, apart from Sheila's, that's not ringing. Once she feels it vibrate and drops everything to grab for it, but it's Noreen. Lena lets it go to voicemail.

It's night, but above the mountain, the cloud has a fractious, pulsing orange glow. All the way down here, the air is thick with the insistent smell of burning gorse. Sirens go past, out on the road, and Lena and Sheila pretend not to hear. Lena knows Trey well enough to be certain there must have been a plan. She also knows, from Sheila's thickening silence as time goes on and Trey doesn't come, that this wasn't in it.

Liam is unsettled and bratty, kicking things and climbing on furniture, demanding every ten seconds to know where his daddy is. Neither Lena nor Sheila has attention to spare for him; Sheila has enough to do with Alanna, who refuses to let go of her T-shirt, and Lena, while she empathises fully with Liam's mood, is having difficulty not telling him to shut the fuck up. In the end it's Maeve who takes him in hand, asking Lena for the dogs' brushes and herding him off to groom them. Neither of them has much of a clue what they're at, but the dogs are patient, and gradually Liam settles to the rhythm of the job. Lena, passing with towels, sees him asking Maeve something in an undertone, and Maeve shushing him.

When her phone finally rings, Lena almost knocks over a chair getting out the back door. 'Cal,' she says, shutting the door behind her.

'We're at my place. Me and Trey.'

Lena's knees go loose and she sits down hard on her back step. 'That's great,' she says. Her voice comes out calm and steady. 'Any damage done?'

'She twisted her ankle and picked up a few little burns. Nothing to write home about.'

His voice is carefully steady too. Whatever happened up there, it was bad. 'That'll all heal,' Lena says. 'Is she eating?'

'We just got home this minute. But yeah, she's already bitching about how she's starving. I said I'd fix her something after I called you.'

'Well,' Lena says, 'there you go. As long as she's hungry, I'd say she's grand, give or take.'

She hears Cal draw a long breath. 'She wanted to come here,' he says. 'I'll keep her awhile, if that's all right with Sheila.'

'You'd better,' Lena says. She takes a deep breath of her own and leans back against the wall. 'I've nowhere to put her; she'd be sleeping in the bathtub.'

'Their house is good and gone. I don't know how much besides.'

Lena says, 'Sheila reckons Johnny musta dropped a smoke.'

There's a second of silence. 'Johnny was down at the foot of the mountain,' Cal says. 'When the fire started.'

Lena hears the layers in his voice, and remembers Mart Lavin saying he'd see to Johnny. 'Probably it smouldered away for a while,' she says. 'Before it caught.'

Another second's silence, while Cal takes his turn listening to the unsaid things, and Lena sits in the darkness and the smell of smoke, listening to him listen. 'Probably did,' he says. 'By the time it's out, they're not gonna be able to tell one way or the other.'

'Where's Johnny now?'

'He's skipped town. I gave him a little cash, help him get clear. I can't swear he made it off the mountain, and it'd probably be good if people get the idea he might not have. But from what I could see, he should've been OK.'

Lena finds herself relieved, not for Johnny but for Trey, who won't have to live with the thought that she had a hand in her dad's death. 'About fucking time,' she says.

'Just in time, more like,' Cal says. 'Guy was deep in the shit.'

'I know, yeah.'

'With more shit headed his way. The kid told me you and her went to see Nealon.'

Lena can't tell what he thinks about that. 'I was hoping she'd say it to you,' she says. 'I wasn't sure. She was afraid you'd be pissed off with her.'

'Goddamn teenagers,' Cal says, with feeling. 'I got so many things to be pissed off about, I can't even make a start, or I'll be there all year. What's bothering me is she won't tell me what changed her mind. That's her business, but if anyone gave her any hassle, I'd like to know.'

'No hassle,' Lena says. 'She got sense, is all.'

Cal doesn't ask, which Lena is glad of. The answers could be a burden to him, or a complication, neither of which he needs right now. After a minute he says, 'I don't reckon Johnny killed that guy.'

'Me neither,' Lena says. 'But he might as well come in useful, for once in his life.'

They're looking for each other in the silences, feeling their way. Lena doesn't want Cal in blank air over the phone. She wants him where she can touch him.

'There's that,' Cal says. 'Not my problem, either way. All I give a damn about is that he's gone.'

In her mind Lena sees Nealon, the naked triumph swelling in his face. 'Back when you were a detective,' she says. 'When you knew you were about to get your man. What did it feel like?'

There's a silence. For a minute she thinks Cal's going to ask her where the hell that came from. Instead he says, 'A relief, mostly. Like I got something fixed that was all messed up. When it stopped feeling that way, that's when I quit.'

Lena finds herself smiling. She reckons, although she feels no need to share this, that Cal wouldn't have enjoyed working with Nealon as much as he thinks. 'Good call,' she says. 'Now Rushborough's not your problem.'

'Thank Christ,' Cal says. 'I gotta go feed the kid. I just wanted to check in first.'

'I'll be over to you in a bit,' Lena says. 'I'll see this lot settled in bed and show Sheila where to find everything, and I'll be there.'

'Yeah,' Cal says, on a sudden long breath. 'That'd be great.'

As Lena hangs up, Sheila comes quietly out the door and shuts it behind her. 'Was that Cal?' she asks.

'Yeah,' Lena says. 'Himself and Trey are grand. They're at his place.'

Sheila catches a breath and lets it out again carefully. She sits down on the step next to Lena. 'Well then,' she says. 'That's that sorted.'

There's a silence. Lena knows Sheila is leaving it deliberately, so that she can ask any questions she might have – as a matter of fairness, since she's after taking them in. Lena has no questions, or anyhow none to which she wants the answers.

'Johnny's done a legger,' she says. 'Cal gave him a bitta cash. If he's in luck, everyone'll think he got caught in the fire.'

Sheila nods. 'Then that's that sorted as well,' she says. She smooths her hands down her thighs.

The sky is as dark as the fields, so that they merge into one unbounded expanse. High amid the black hangs a bright, distorted ring of orange. Billows of smoke, strangely lit from below, heave and churn above it.

'Cal says the house is gone,' Lena says.

'I knew that, sure. It'll be ashes. I always hated the place anyway.' Sheila tilts back her head to watch the blaze, without expression. 'We won't be under your feet too long,' she says. 'Coupla weeks, just. If the aul' Murtagh place makes it through, I might ask would they let me have that. Or I might come down offa the mountain, for a change. See if Rory Dunne fancies having us in that cottage, instead of doing the Airbnb. Alanna's starting school next month; I could get a bit of a job for myself.'

'You're welcome here as long as you need it,' Lena says. 'Specially if Maeve and Liam are going to brush those dogs. With the heat this summer, they've been shedding enough to make me fitted carpets.'

Sheila nods. 'I'll go in and tell the kids about their daddy,' she says. 'They're worrying. They'll be upset he's gone, or Maeve and Liam will anyway, but I'll tell them at least he's safe now. They'll be glad of that.'

'Good,' Lena says. 'Someone oughta be.'

Sheila lets out a crack of laughter, and Lena realises how it sounded. 'Ah, stop,' she protests, but she's laughing as well. 'I meant it.'

'I know, yeah, I know you did. And you're right, o' course. It's just the way you said it, like—' They're both laughing much harder than it deserves, so hard that Sheila has her head down on her knees. 'Like it was cleaning a manky toilet, "*Someone* oughta do that—"'

'"—but I'm not touching it—"'

'Oh, God—'

'Mammy?' Alanna says, in the doorway. She's bare-legged, wearing an oversized red T-shirt that Lena's seen on Trey.

'Oh, Jesus,' Sheila says, getting her breath and wiping her eyes with the heel of her hand. 'Come here.' She holds out an arm to Alanna.

Alanna stays where she is, baffled and suspicious. 'What's funny?'

'It's been a long day, is all,' Sheila says. 'A long aul' time. Come here.'

After a moment Alanna curls onto the step, in the crook of Sheila's arm. 'Where's Trey?'

'At Cal's.'

'Is she gonna stay there?'

'I don't know. We've a loada things to decide on. We're only starting out.'

Alanna nods. Her eyes, gazing up at the mountain, are solemn and dreamy.

'Time for bed,' Sheila says. She stands up and, with a grunt of effort, lifts Alanna off the step. Alanna winds her legs around her, still gazing over her shoulder at the fire.

'Come on,' Sheila says, and carries her inside. Lena stays where she is for a while, listening to the sounds of the place full of people getting ready for bed. She has no desire to make the arrangement a long-term one, but just for a few weeks, it feels like a worthwhile thing to have other people in her house again.

———

What with everything that was going on, Trey missed dinner. She's considerably more concerned about this than about her ankle, which is baseball-sized and purple but doesn't appear to be broken, or about the spatter of red patches and blisters on her arms where burning flecks settled. Cal, whose hands are still shaking, doesn't have the wherewithal to cook anything substantial. He straps up the kid's ankle and makes her a sandwich, and then another one, and finally dumps the bread and various fillings on the table and lets her go to town.

He's watching her for any number of things, trying to remember every word Alyssa's said over the years about trauma and delayed reactions and attachment disruption, but for the life of him he can't see anything worth watching. What the kid mainly looks is hungry, with a large side order of dirty. He would give a lot to know what turned out to be more important to her than her revenge, but he has a growing feeling that that might not be something she'll ever be willing to share with him.

Probably he ought to talk to her about – among a whole mess of other things – the fire: the people who could lose everything, the animals whose homes are gone, the firefighters putting themselves in danger. He's not going to do it. For one thing, right now he's too blown apart by relief that she's here, and apparently in one piece, to have any room left for matters of conscience. For another, it would have no impact. If she set her place on fire, Trey was getting rid of evidence. Cal can only see one reason for that, and it's not one against which anything else would hold weight.

'I'm not gonna ask you,' he says suddenly.

Trey looks up at him, chewing.

'About any of it. Anything you feel like telling me, go for it anytime, I want to hear it. But I'm not gonna ask.'

Trey takes a minute to examine this. Then she nods and shoves the last hunk of sandwich in her mouth. 'Can I've a shower?' she asks, through it. "M manky.'

Cal takes himself outside while she does that. He leans on the wall by the road and watches the fire. A few days ago he wouldn't have been easy leaving Trey alone in the house, but any danger to her is gone. He's not sure what complicated weave of allegiances led her to the decisions she made, but that doesn't matter – for now, anyway – as long as those decisions look acceptable from the outside.

He's still out there when Mart comes stumping down the road. Even with the orange glow lighting the sky, it's dark enough that Cal hears the crunch of his feet before his shape separates itself from the hedges. He recognises Mart by his walk. It's jerkier than usual, and Mart is leaning hard on his crook: all that time standing still, watching Johnny dig, has stiffened him up.

'Hey,' Cal says, when he gets close enough.

'Ah,' Mart says, his face cracking into a grin, 'the man himself. That's all I wanted to know: you made it back safe and sound. Now I can head off to my beauty sleep with a clear conscience.'

'Yep,' Cal says. 'Thanks for checking.' His enforced alliance with Mart is over, but something has shifted between them, whether he likes it or not.

Mart sniffs. 'My God,' he tells Cal, 'there's a terrible bang of smoke offa you. You'd want to give yourself a good scrub before your missus calls round, or she won't go near you. Did you get close to the fire?'

'Just for a minute,' Cal says. 'Got Trey in the car and made tracks. She's inside. Sheila and the other kids, they're at Lena's.'

'Ah, that's great,' Mart says, smiling at him. 'I'm delighted they're all safe out of it. What about the bold Johnny, Sunny Jim? Did you push him in the fire, or where is he at all?'

'Johnny thought the kid was still in the house,' Cal says. 'He headed up round the back of it, looking for her. I dunno what happened to him.'

'That's lovely,' Mart says approvingly. 'That'd warm your heart, so it would: the good-for-nothing waster sacrificing himself for his child. I'd say that'll go down a treat; everyone loves a bitta redemption, specially with a comeuppance thrown in. Didja push him in? Just between ourselves, like.'

'Didn't need to,' Cal says. 'He ran off.'

Mart nods, unsurprised. 'That's what he was always best at,' he says. ''Tis great when a man's talents come in handy. Did he mention where he was headed, at all?'

'Nope,' Cal says. 'And I didn't ask, 'cause it doesn't matter. As far as anyone needs to know, he never made it off the mountain.'

Mart looks at him and starts to giggle. 'Well, wouldja look at that,' he says. 'I finally got you settled into this place good and proper. You've got the hang of it now, bucko; there'll be no holding you.'

'Even if Johnny did make it out,' Cal says, 'he's gonna run a long way, and he's not coming back. We're shed of him. And Nealon figures Johnny's his guy, so we're shed of him, too.'

'Well,' Mart says, his eyebrows jumping. 'Isn't that great news? Good riddance to the pair of them.'

'I'll drink to that,' Cal says. Mart isn't asking what changed Nealon's mind. Cal didn't expect him to.

'I'd say you will. D'you know something?' Mart asks meditatively, turning his head to examine the blaze's progress. 'There was a few votes in favour of just setting Johnny's place on fire to begin with, instead of foostering about with spades and what-have-you. 'Tis a mad aul' world, when you think about it. Whatever you do, it all comes to the same in the end.'

'You hear anything about how bad it is?' Cal asks.

'Gimpy Duignan and his missus got told to evacuate, and so did Malachy and Seán Pól and everyone higher up, and a few over the other side as well. The fire lads are hoping they'll have it under control before it gets that far, but it all depends on the wind.' Mart squints up at the sky. 'Not just the wind, maybe. I thought I'd never hear myself say this again, but will I tell you something, Sunny Jim? It looks like rain.'

Cal looks up. The sky is thick and starless; the air has a weight and a restless tingle that have nothing to do with the fire.

'If I'm right about that,' Mart says, 'the damage mightn't be too bad after all. The sheep up there have more sense than most men; they'll have got themselves well clear at the first sniff of smoke. We'll lose a bitta forest and plenty of gorse, but sure, no one minds that; it'll clear the land for grazing, and God knows we could do

403

with any help we can get. As long as no more houses go, this could be a blessing in disguise.' He shoots Cal a sharp sideways glance. 'Would you have any idea how it happened to start?'

'Sheila Reddy reckons Johnny started it,' Cal says. 'By accident. Threw down a smoke that wasn't out.'

Mart considers this, still examining the sky. 'I'd line up behind that,' he agrees. 'I hate to speak ill of the dead, but Johnny was a terrible man for not taking into account the consequences of his own actions. That adds up nicely.'

Cal says, 'Were you guys gonna kill him?'

Mart's face creases into a grin. 'Less of the "you guys" there, bucko.'

'OK,' Cal says. 'Were we gonna kill him?'

'You tell me, Sunny Jim,' Mart says. 'You were there. You tell me.' Struck by a sudden thought, he fishes in the pocket of his trousers. 'Come here, I've something to show you. I was on my way home, and my headlights caught that feckin' zombie yoke of yours. I'm the observant type, and I noticed something different about him. So I pulled over and had a look. And have a guess what that fella was wearing.'

He shakes something out with a triumphant flap and holds it up in front of Cal's face. Cal has to lean close to identify it. It's Mart's orange camouflage bucket hat.

'He didn't like me taking it off him,' Mart says, 'but I fought him off like Rocky Balboa, so I did. No one comes between me and my hat.'

'Well, I'll be damned,' Cal says. While keeping his mouth firmly shut, he always figured Mart was right and Senan was behind the hat's disappearance. 'Senan's an innocent man.'

'Exactly,' Mart says, wagging the hat at Cal. 'I'm not afraid to admit when I've been wrong. Senan was over at the foot of the mountain, with yourself and meself, when this was planted, and I owe the man an apology and a pint. So who was it robbed this on me, hah? Next time you fancy poking about in a mystery, Sunny Jim, you put your detective skills to work on that one.'

He pulls the hat down on his head and gives it a satisfied pat.

'All's well that ends well,' he says. 'That's my motto.' He lifts his crook to Cal and hobbles off up the road into the darkness, whistling a chirpy little tune and trying to favour all his joints at once.

———————

Trey's house has, or had, only one bathroom and never enough hot water, so she takes advantage of Cal's place to have the longest shower of her life with no one banging on the door. She keeps her bad foot propped up on the stool they made, back when she was shorter, so she could get things off high shelves. The hot water stings her burns; there are small, raw bald spots among her hair.

The day flashes disjointed images across her mind: Nealon tilting his chair back, trees made of flame, Lena striding up the path, petrol splashing onto the heaped wheelbarrow, her mam's hands on the table in sunlight. All of them, except the fire, seem like years ago. Sometime she might feel something about them, but for now she doesn't have room; her mind is too crowded with the flashes. The single thing she feels is relief that she's at Cal's.

When she comes out of the shower, Cal is nowhere to be seen, but Rip is peacefully asleep in his corner, so she doesn't worry. She sits on the sofa, re-strapping her ankle and looking around. She likes this room. It has clarity, a place for each and every object. The books are lined up in neat stacks under the windowsill; Cal could do with a bookshelf.

Trey finds herself rejecting the idea. Paying Cal back for taking her in would be stupid, a baby thing to do. She's already, finally, found something worth giving him: her revenge. Her debts to him are cleared, in a way that doesn't allow for going backwards to little-kid shite like ham slices and bookshelves. They're on a different footing now.

She finds Cal out front, leaning on the wall and watching the fire. 'Hey,' he says, turning his head, when he hears her steps on the grass.

'Hey,' Trey says.

'You're not supposed to be walking on that foot. Rest it.'

'Yeah,' Trey says. She leans her folded arms on the wall next to his. She's relying on him not to talk to her, at least not in any way that demands thought. She's had enough talking and enough thinking in the past few weeks to last her the rest of her life.

The fire has burned itself out on the side of the mountain, and risen to run along its crest; the familiar outlines are traced in flame across solid blackness. Trey wonders how many other people in the townland are at their gates or their windows, watching. She hopes every man and woman of them recognises this for what it is: Brendan's funeral bonfire.

'Your mama get any of your clothes out?' Cal asks.

'Yeah. Most of 'em.'

'Good. Miss Lena's calling round here in a while; I'll ask her to bring you a change. Those smell like smoke.'

Trey pulls her T-shirt neck up to her nose and sniffs. The smell is fierce, black and woody. She decides to keep the T-shirt as it is. She can use it to wrap Brendan's watch. 'Ask her can she bring Banjo as well,' she says.

'And tomorrow,' Cal says, 'I'm gonna take you into town and buy you some jeans that cover your damn ankles.'

Trey finds herself grinning. 'So I'll be decent, yeah?'

'Yeah,' Cal says. Trey can hear the unwilling grin rising in his voice, too. 'That's right. You can't go round showing your ankles in front of God and everybody. You'll give some little old lady a heart attack.'

'Don't need new jeans,' Trey says, by reflex. 'These're grand.'

'You give me any shit,' Cal says, 'and I'll stop by the barber while we're there and get this whole beard shaved off, clean as a whistle. You can say hello to my chin warts.'

'Changed my mind,' Trey tells him. 'I wanta meet them. Go for it.'

'Nah,' Cal says. 'No point. The weather's changing. Smell: there's rain coming.'

Trey raises her head. He's right. The sky is too dark to see clouds, but the air is stirring against her cheek, cool and damp in her nose, moss and wet stone underlying the flare of smoke. Something is sweeping in from the west with purpose, gathering overhead.

She asks, 'Will it put out the fire?'

'Probably, between that and the firefighters. Or at least wet things down till it can't keep spreading.'

Trey looks up at the mountainside, where Brendan is lying and where she almost joined him. Her chance of finding him, a slim one from the start, is gone now. The fire will have taken any signs she could have spotted; if his ghost was ever there, now it's a slip of flame, twisting upwards amid smoke and gone into the night sky. She finds, to her surprise, that she's OK with this. She misses Brendan as much as ever, but the jagged need has gone out of it. With him, too, her footing has changed.

Something light as a midge hits against her cheek. When she touches it, she feels a speck of damp.

'Rain,' she says.

'Yep,' Cal says. 'That'll make the farmers easier in their minds. You want to go inside?'

'Nah,' Trey says. She should be wrecked, but she's not. The cool air feels good. She feels like she could stay right here all night, till the fire is out or till the morning comes.

Cal nods and rearranges his arms more comfortably on the wall. He texts Lena about Banjo and the change of clothes, and shows Trey the thumbs-up she sends back. The rooks, alert and edgy in their tree, make hoarse comments on the situation and tell each other to shut up.

The line of flame has stretched wider across the horizon, following the dips and rises of the mountains' crest. The sound of it reaches them very faintly and gentled, like the shell-echo of a far-away ocean. It's late, but far into the distance on every side, the fields are dotted with the tiny yellow lights of houses. Everyone is awake and keeping vigil.

''S beautiful,' Trey says.

'Yeah,' Cal says. 'I guess it is.'

They lean on the wall, watching, as the rain flecks their skin more thickly and the bright outline of the mountains hangs in the night sky.

Acknowledgements

I owe huge thanks to Darley Anderson, the finest ally and champion any writer could have, and to everyone at the agency, especially Mary, Georgia, Rosanna, Rebeka, and Kristina; my wonderful editors, Andrea Schulz and Harriet Bourton, for their near-magical ability to see exactly what this book needed to be and then show me how to get it there; superstar Ben Petrone, Nidhi Pugalia, Bel Banta, Rebecca Marsh, and everyone at Viking US; Olivia Mead, Anna Ridley, Georgia Taylor, Ellie Hudson, Emma Brown, and everyone at Viking UK; Cliona Lewis, Victoria Moynes, and everyone at Penguin Ireland; Susanne Halbleib and everyone at Fischer Verlage; Steve Fisher of APA; Ciara Considine, Clare Ferraro, and Sue Fletcher, who set all this in motion; Aja Pollock, for her eagle-eyed copy edit; Peter Johnson, for rabbit preparation tips; Graham Murphy, for working out what's not on the telly on a Monday in July; Kristina Johansen, Alex French, Susan Collins, Noni Stapleton, Paul and Anna Nugent, Ann-Marie Hardiman, Oonagh Montague, Jessica Ryan, Jenny and Liam Duffy, Kathy and Chad Williams, and Karen Gillece, for laughs, talks, support, creativity, nights out, freezing our feet on a beach in winter, and all the other essentials; my mother, Elena Lombardi; my father, David French; and, more every single time, my husband, Anthony Breatnach.

Discover the first mesmerising Cal Hooper mystery...

THE
SEARCHER

A DISAPPEARANCE. A SMALL TOWN.
A QUESTION THAT NEEDS ANSWERING.

Cal Hooper thought a fixer-upper in a remote Irish village would be the perfect escape. After twenty-five years in the Chicago police force, and a bruising divorce, he just wants to build a new life in a pretty spot with a good pub where nothing much happens.

But then a local kid comes looking for his help. His brother has gone missing, and no one, least of all the police, seems to care. Cal wants nothing to do with any kind of investigation, but somehow he can't make himself walk away.

Soon Cal will discover that even in the most idyllic small town, secrets lie hidden, people aren't always what they seem, and trouble can come calling at his door.

A gripping tale of breath-taking beauty and suspense that asks how we decide what's right and wrong in a world where neither is simple, and what we risk if we fail.

'Terrific – terrifying, amazing' Stephen King

'Completely, indescribably magnificent' Marian Keyes

Order now!